Microwave Man

A New Superhero for the Rogue Male

JONATHAN GORNALL

PENGUIN BOOKS

PENGUIN BOOKS

Published by the Penguin Group
Penguin Books Ltd, 80 Strand, London WC2R ORL, England
Penguin Group (USA) Inc., 375 Hudson Street, New York, New York 10014, USA
Penguin Group (Canada), 90 Eglinton Avenue East, Suite 700, Toronto, Ontario, Canada M4P 2Y3
(a division of Pearson Penguin Canada Inc.)
Penguin Ireland, 25 St Stephen's Green, Dublin 2, Ireland
(a division of Penguin Books Ltd)
Penguin Group (Australia), 250 Camberwell Road,
Camberwell, Victoria 3124, Australia (a division of Pearson Australia Group Pty Ltd)
Penguin Books India Pvt Ltd, 11 Community Centre,
Panchsheel Park, New Delhi – 110 017, India
Penguin Group (NZ), cnr Airborne and Rosedale Roads, Albany,
Auckland 1310, New Zealand (a division of Pearson New Zealand Ltd)
Penguin Books (South Africa) (Pty) Ltd, 24 Sturdee Avenue,
Rosebank, Johannesburg 2196, South Africa

Penguin Books Ltd, Registered Offices: 80 Strand, London WC2R ORL, England

www.penguin.com

First published 2006
1

Set in 11/13pt Monotype Dante
by Palimpsest Book Production Limited, Polmont, Stirlingshire
Printed in England by Clays Ltd, St Ives plc

ISBN-13: 978-0-141-02053-2
ISBN-10: 0-141-02053-9

'Microwave cooking is not natural, nor healthy, and is far more dangerous to the human body than anyone could imagine. Eating microwaved food causes loss of memory, concentration, emotional instability and a decrease of intelligence'

The Hidden Hazards of Microwave Food,
Anthony Wayne and Lawrence Newell

'Anyone who tries to duplicate these demonstrations does so entirely at their own risk. There is a chance that you will damage your microwave oven. There is a chance that you will cause a fire. There is a chance that a heated object will explode. Heated water can unexpectedly burst into violent boiling. Messing with a microwave oven is stupid if you don't know what you're doing'

Warning from *Unwise Microwave Oven Experiments*

'It is ludicrous to read the microwave direction on the boxes of food you buy, as each one will have a disclaimer: "THIS WILL VARY WITH YOUR MICROWAVE." Loosely translated, this means, "You're on your own, Bernice."'

Erma Bombeck (1927–96)

Acknowledgements

To the following (names have been changed to protect me): We'll always have whatever it was we had (wherever it was we had it): Kim, Jane(s), Carole, Carol(s), Laura, Margaret, Vanessa, Alicia, Alejandra, Claudia, Melissa, Mercedes, Rebecca(s), Olivia, Nicky, Nicola, Nic, Virginia, Valerie, Sara, Sarah(s), Sally(s), Elizabeth, Elisabeth, Lizzie, Paloma, Toni, Rachel, Raquel (*no, not that one, sadly*), Eloise, Hilde, Erica, Pauline, Paula, Jo, Joanne, Antonia, Antonio (*it was dark, it was Rio*), Abigail, Esther, Delilah (*why, why, why?*), Eve, Ann, Anne(s), Anna(s), Cressida, Danica, Hannah(s), Whatshername (*I'll never forget whatshername*), Hanna, Linda, Lynda, Lindi, Lourdes (*ain't no cure for love*), Maeve, Maive, Mave, Emma, Madison, Olivia, Abigail(s), Alexis, Ashley, Samantha, Isabella, Grace, Alyssa, Lauren, Kayla, Molly, Caitlin, Amelia, Bethany, Lily, Georgia (*no longer on my mind*), Millie, Eleanor, Jasmine, Daisy, Alice (*who the hell is Alice?*), Courtney, Shannon, Erin, Isabelle(s), Isabella, Abbie, Abbi, Abby (*bit of a habit*), Amber, Freya, Poppy . . . and countless others (*sorry if I've missed you off the list, but you know who you are, even if I've forgotten*).

And to Sandra. And her dad. And to Adam.

But most of all to Emily, with whom very few of the above (and almost none of the below) would have been necessary.[1]

---

[1] Are we buying this?

I

How to Expose Yourself

Dear Microwave Man

   I do enjoy your column, but sometimes I have the guilty feeling that I am laughing at somebody with a disability. You are, after all, forty-nine, and not only have you failed to find lasting love, but you seem unable to form attachments with anyone of anything remotely like your own age. In addition, there is a whiff of paranoia about your words, as though you fear that the modern world is, in some way, out to get you. The other day I was thumbing through one of my poetry books and rediscovered a piece by Stevie Smith. I hope you don't mind my recommending it to you. Perhaps it might serve as a wake-up call – or a lifebelt, as it were. It is called 'Not Waving but Drowning'.

   I only hope this resonates with you.

Mrs R. Coolidge (age 38), Cumbria

Microwave Man (age 47 still, actually) writes: Thank you for your concern. Stop reading poetry. You will only become wan and affected and, in all possibility, dissolute. And I am not drowning, merely microwaving.

Most things begin by mistake and this thing is no exception. I make the mistake of wandering into a features planning meeting at the national newspaper where I have been lying low successfully for about ten years. I know why it's happened, why I've made this stupid, amateurish blunder. It's because I'm distracted. I'm broken-hearted (again, and this time at forty-seven, which, frankly, is a little embarrassing), and I'm not thinking straight.

   I suppose it could have been worse, marginally. I could have stepped off the kerb and into the path of a big truck delivering a consignment of Valentine's Day cards, although that would, at least, have had the advantage of being both comic and ironic.

But instead, I stepped into this bloody meeting.

Being forty-seven, and a man to boot, I have, of course, very little to contribute, but I do have some downtime to kill between arriving late and leaving early for lunch, and it gives me a chance to doodle stuff on an A4 Cambridge notebook (designs for the riverside house I will never build, outline of airport thriller that will sell millions and secure my decidedly insecure future, plans for an even cheaper mass-produceable gun to replace the AK-47 – that sort of thing). I can nod ingratiatingly at everything my attractive, glass-ceiling-shattering boss has to say and generally put in some valuable face time – so much more effective than simply leaving a spare jacket over the back of the chair.

Besides. It keeps me away from the telephone and the temptation to text the Boer.

Actually, I say I'm forty-seven, but really that's forty-seven going on twenty-seven, still convinced I am going to live for ever and addicted to an obsessive, early morning gym habit designed to keep mortality at bay.

Despite a generally unfulfilled yearning for fame and fortune (frustrated, I feel, as much by a tendency to bone idleness as a distinct lack of talent), until just over two months ago my main ambition was to secure an expensive redundancy package. Armed with this, I planned to buy the yacht, sail away to the sun and write the Great British Novel, pausing each day only to make love under the Mediterranean moon to the beautiful Plucky Boer, the tall, blonde, twenty-seven-year-old South African farm girl (going on thirty-seven) with whom I had lived for the past three years (spending all my weekends with her choosing, buying and soiling lingerie instead of writing the Great British Novel).

And then, suddenly, and with no prior warning, she heeded the call of the womb.

Before I could remind myself that this was one of the finest candidates on my shortlist for the vacant position of Love of

Life, I hesitated a fraction of a fraction too long when faced with the stark choice – 'Breed: yes or no?' (I paraphrase.) With the stubbornness bred into her forebears by years of veldt-trekking, wagon-laagering and growing indifferent crops on stony soil, she refused to accept anything other than my first answer, saying, 'If you don't want what I want, then I don't want you.'

Which, surely, was the chorus of an Abba song?

A week later and we're still together and I think I've got away with it. But the day after that she is gone, leaving our home, her job and me – and announcing that she is writing the Great South African Novel. (Set in London.)

With one hand on my broken heart and the index finger of the other on my pulse (can't be *that* broken: resting heart rate still a very satisfying fifty-five beats per minute), I have been trying, and failing, to put her out of my mind. In fact, I have been trying very hard, seeking comfort and affection wherever I can find it.

But one thing I don't have my finger on is the pulse of the conversation into which I have now stumbled.

As far as I can tell, the cool young people are talking about a cool redesign to accommodate the new, cool, in-house cook. She has been contracted at great expense and an entire spread has been conceived to accommodate her column. I didn't even know we *had* a cook, and certainly had no idea the readers were hungry for one, but then again I am forty-seven, and if I really knew anything about newspapers and how to sell them, then I would probably be editing one by now.

But for the record, if I was, I wouldn't be hiring any bloody cooks.

There are five of us in the room struggling with this problem – three more, I register, than it took to split the atom.[2] Cornelia, as elegant as ever, sits behind her desk, more or less listening to her acolytes with one section of her *Cosmo*-defined,

2 And how come Ernest Rutherford was awarded the Nobel prize for *chemistry*, rather than for physics? I mean, it's hardly rocket science.

multitasking perfect-modern-working-mother mind, dashing off emails with another and throwing out bright ideas with a third. Yet another few million spare brain cells allow her to answer the phone, interrupting some poor sap mid-flow ('Yeah, hold on, must get this . . .') to coo briefly to one of her children: 'Really, darling, did you? How clever. You must tell Mummy all about it. Later. Yes, love you too. Kiss kiss.' Click. 'OK, go on . . .', which can be a tad disconcerting, leaving one feeling a little like . . . well, one of her children.

From time to time I've tried to penetrate Cornelia's deceptively limpid eyes with one of my much-practised and generally infallible 'My God, I know I was supposed to have been listening intently to what you were just saying, but I have just been struck by the full force of your beauty' looks, but she appears to be having none of it.

Pity. One of the highlights of my day – any day – is to cravenly amuse her to the point where she tosses back her head, flicks her hair away from her face and gives that shrieky little laugh that grips one in the essentials and, for a split second, gives her the delicious appearance of vulnerability. But only for a split second. And only an appearance.

Luckily, one of the few working parts of my brain – and, being a male brain, it has, obviously, far fewer parts with which to multitask[3] – always steps in at that point to take the other sections in hand, just before they are fatally short-circuited by the flow of rising sap.

If you plant your mouth on hers, says the right prefrontal cortex (or possibly part of the anterior cinguate), wagging its finger admonishingly, *bending her back over the desk with one hand around her shoulders and the other in the small of her back – a course of action I think we all know that you are considering right now – the next time you see her will be at an employment tribunal, at which you will appear with several days' worth of stubble and more than a faint whiff of Pernod about you.*

---

3 As scientists in search of funding and, therefore, headlines, are constantly discovering.

And control, more or less, is restored. Still, Rome not ravaged in a day and all that.

(And talking about brains and love and scientists, hats off to the researchers at University College, London who set out to pinpoint the seat of love in the brain – romantically testing their subjects' true-love claims with a lie detector – and found activity deep in a part of the cortex associated with 'gut feelings'. Tricky for ill-equipped non-medical types to apply this test without causing irreversible brain damage, but anyone can operate a lie detector. The only challenge might be wiring up the love object – preferably *before* lashing out on an engagement ring – without arousing suspicion.)

In front of Cornelia's desk sits Margaret, her able second-in-command and, like the languid one, a former *Daily Mail* hardcase in soft designer clothing. Great legs, great hair and – as is especially apparent on the occasions when she wears one of those frail, diaphanous tops to work – great body.

But, cruel rumour has it, as mad as the Mad Hatter's maddest mad milliner.[4]

Even the other figure-obsessed women in the office allow their perfectly shaped eyebrows to rise (briefly risking frown lines) at the sight of Margaret picking gloomily at her daily bag of bleakly unembellished carrots. And, come to think about it, how does she maintain those breasts? There certainly isn't an ounce of subcutaneous fat anywhere else on her body (unless she has the chubbiest feet in Christendom). Most athletes can measure their body fat in percentages as low as 6 or 7 per cent. Margaret, on the other hand, is probably in negative equity, fatwise.

As a result, she is always cold, even during the long hot summer we have just had, when entering her small, glass-walled office fully clothed was akin to risking a romp through Death Valley dressed like Flanagan (or Allen). Visitors sit there sweating bullets,

4 It was the mercury they used to turn fur into felt that drove hatters mad, although I seem to recognize some of the symptoms – trembling, loss of coordination, slurred speech, loosening of teeth, memory loss, depression, irritability and anxiety – and I've never worn a Homburg in my life.

their minds shrieking, 'Water!' Water!', and conjuring up mirages of palm-fringed oases on the far wall, while she, shivering like a freshly trimmed Chihuahua unleashed in Lapland and pulling her cashmere cardigan ever tighter, notches up the fan heater under the desk with a tap of one expensively shod foot.

Great legs, too. And, from time to time, more than a flicker of something awfully bad and quite possibly spankable in those eyes.

A pity. Posh mad women are usually spectacular in bed – biting, scratching, demanding filthy abuse and swearing pornographically in an accent not so much received as bestowed. But, sadly, sooner or later, they do have to get up and resort to their customary lunacy. Not that such things would put me off. Besides, I suspect her described madness – and, on reflection, it is only men who seem to have formed that view – is more akin to pickiness. I've seen it in her eyes, from time to time. That look which says, 'Not a chance, mate.' So, more maddening, perhaps, than mad. Nothing worse for one's ego than a woman who knows what she wants – when it clearly isn't you.

Thinking of these things helps me to heal my broken heart. Or at least to staunch the worst of the bleeding. It also gives me movement, but I keep my legs crossed.

Next to her sits Bella. Not sure what she does. Tall, thin, blonde, dressed like a Chanel model, beautiful one moment and, like a plastic hologram linked to an appalling hit movie and free with packets of breakfast cereal, gauntly scary like a death's head the next. She has that unnerving habit that some women have of catching a man's eye and smiling in that dangerous way that could mean either, 'I need you inside me, now, like I need blood and oxygen,' or 'Hello. There's nothing much going on inside here, you know.'

I always smile back – you know, just in case – but never apply the full, hooded-eyed wattage because – well, you know, just in case.

Oh, and there's some bloke in the room, too. Steve, I think. Yes, that's it. Steve.

What do you think? says Cornelia, and after a couple of seconds the silence tips me off that she is talking to me.

I think . . . I begin, scanning the earnest young poker faces for clues. *I think that* . . . I think that I have no idea what you are talking about and I know that I am trying far too hard to look like I do. My head (vast sections of which are engaged not in their normal pursuits but in pining pointlessly for the Boer), instead of helping, is singing. It always does that at times like these, and it's never terrifically useful, to be brutally honest. I have been poisoned by years of popular music. My brain is an out-of-control iPod that automatically soundtracks my life, even the misery. Especially the misery. Take now, for instance. Curse you, Russ Ballard.

I am saved by my inquisitor's impatience.

'Come on, we haven't got all day. We need five new daily columns to fill this space next to the new fashion spread and opposite the cook. We have four: "Mrs Scatty", "Poor Bitch", "Home Alone" and "Baby Talk". Number five?'

Oh, God, yes. Aka women on Prozac, women on a budget and women on the shopping channel, or something. And Paul, reluctant token New Man, on the dubious delights of shit-stained nappies, with that old standard of inventive journalism everywhere: 'Journalist is First Person in History of Planet to Have Baby Shock.'

Cornelia cuts in: '"Mrs Scatty", tales of a bright but scatty-brained professional woman . . .'

I smile, 'Super'; I think, *God help us*.

'"Poor Bitch", the struggle of a once-landed and married-into-money professional woman now scraping by on only her own earnings . . .'

I smile, 'How charming'; I think, *Lord save us*.

'Then there's "Home Alone", a kind of domestic goddess about the home, a former professional woman now richly if not happily married and pouring all her creativity into her beautiful home and her lovely children . . .'

Despite myself, my smile fades. *Jesus wept, and so he ought.* This paper is turning into a propaganda sheet for women, whose tough, brilliant, multitasking selves it never tires of celebrating, while simultaneously reminding its female readership that men are poor dumb creatures who can barely pat their tummies at the same time as rubbing their heads. (Or is it the other way around?)

This is 'Oh, gosh, isn't she clever, how does she do it?' journalism gone mad. The endless droning of privileged, professional, middle-class women who think they are some kind of a cross between Joan of Arc, Mother Teresa and Alberta Einstein, saving the world, or at least their share of it (which, despite all the talk of glass ceilings, appears to be most of it. Looking around, within twenty yards or so of the inner sanctum, I can see at least three people without testicles who could sack me).

And how *does* she do it? Well, who gives a toss, actually? But might it have anything to do with the fact that all she does is write a couple of columns a week for an extremely handsome salary, that her husband also earns more than some small nations and that between them they have sufficient staff to handle the little time-consuming chores of life, such as children? I guess it might.

And do you know what the most annoying thing of all is? We've never sold so many copies of the paper. Apparently it is, as journalists are fond of saying, what the readers want. What do I know? As I say, I'm forty-seven, and if I knew anything about running newspapers, I'd be sitting on the other side of the desk.

The only man in the line-up for the new columns so far is Paul, and the only reason *he's* in is because his (bright, talented, multitasking, etc.) wife has just given birth to a new baby. Hence 'Baby Talk'. A serious writer, he's not wild about the brief ('Lots of stuff about how rubbish men are when it comes to raising babies. Or anything else. Especially rubbing their tummies and patting their heads'), but, hey: a column's a column.

Oestrogen central, I sneer inwardly.

Only, it seems I have sneered out loud – gone and done that thing with the mouth before doing that other thing with the brain. This often happens when I'm tired. Or well rested. Oh, come on! I'm only a man, after all . . . pat, rub, rat, pub . . .

Three pairs of shiny, pointy shoes on the end of three sets of even shinier bare legs twitch menacingly.

I know. I'll laugh it off.

'Well, come on! How about something for the guys, for a change? Who knows, we might even pull in a few ads for cars, or tractors. Or radio-controlled stuff . . .'

Nothing. FX: wind whistles through room. Can't stop the mouth, can't stop the mouth . . .

'I don't know: how about a column about a fortysomething rogue male, lovable but ultimately unloved? On the shelf again at a time of his life when other men of his age are worrying about university fees, wistful for the Perfect Relationship he thinks he once had in the way we all look back to a time when everything was slower and calmer and we didn't have to choose between eighteen electricity companies and decide in which of a dozen flesh-eating-narcotizing-fasciitis-raddled NHS hospitals we should have our piles done. But really quite keen on shagging as many women as he can while he can still get it up and at the same time plotting to win back the love of his life with who, he now realizes, he should have bitten the bullet, and married and impregnated – probably on the same day or at least while she was wearing the wedding dress . . .'

Eyes have widened, which isn't necessarily good. I feel like my flies are open. *Maybe they are!* I try to check and succeed only in appearing to rub my crotch.

'Whom,' says a voice from the open doorway.

I look round to see an angel framed against the brilliance of the strip lights behind her, turning her blonde hair into a halo. 'What?' I manage.

'With *whom* he should have bitten the bullet, and married.'

'Right. Yes. With whom. Whomever. Whatever. Anyway . . .'

How long has she been stood there? How long has she been listening? Why do I care so much about how stupid I must have sounded? Never mind the flies: is my mouth really open?

Whoever she is, she puts me out of my misery by saying, 'Cornelia, sorry, I'll come back later, when you've done with,

9

um, this . . .' And she nods at me, spins on her heels – her impressively long heels, it has to be said – and disappears.

Cornelia, incredibly, is barely distracted by the interruption, still listening, waiting for me, and not even looking at her emails but doing that one-handed spinning-round thing she does with the pen, like it's a cheerleader's baton or something, which means I have to go on talking. And so, stupidly (and, secretly, happily, because I do quite like the sound of my own voice), I do, but not before I write in capital letters on my notebook 'WHO WAS THAT??!', tear out the page and place it on Cornelia's desk. She slides it under her keyboard like a riverboat hustler palming a card.

And, 'So,' I continue, 'he loves going to the gym because he's still in good nick and a bit vain, thinks he ought to settle down with a woman more his age but can't seem to break the cycle of twentysomethings who pass through his arms and anyway is quietly convinced that any woman over thirty-five is either married or mad – and, hey: watch out for the ones with cats – and is experienced enough to know that the best possible sex is sex with another man's woman, preferably married, who is bored sick with her so-called love life, very hot to trot, and who will pop round for a screw on stolen afternoons or Saturday mornings, won't want to hang around any more than you *want* her to hang around and will never, *ever*, go on about you missing her birthday because she will be so guilty about spending it with her husband and, besides, what would she do with anything she couldn't either eat or drink there or then or conceal about her person?'

Pause for breath. Appear to be heavy-breathing. Don't touch the crotch, *don't even look down there.*

Does Margaret have cats? I bet she does. Shame. Great legs.

'Does he cook?' asks Cornelia.

'Does he what?'

Who the hell was that woman?

'You know, put raw food in an oven to impress his conquests with fabulous meals *à la* Naked Chef?'

Does he bollocks! 'No. If it doesn't go in the microwave, it doesn't go in her.'

10

Not quite what I meant to say, but at least Cornelia is smiling. Oh-oh. *Cornelia is smiling*. And rocking back in her seat. She has had A Good Idea, of which she is proud, and of which, shortly, we will all be proud.

'*Voilà!* That's it! The fifth columnist!'

Oh, very good, very droll: the fifth columnist, the enemy in the midst, the fox in the chicken run. A guerrilla operating at the fringes, a Falangist sympathizer during the Spanish Civil War of the sexes . . .

I just pity the poor bastard who has to knock that one out every week. It would mean extra money and some exposure for a freelance, but it would be just an unpaid labour of love for any idiot on the staff stupid enough to fall for the glittering lure of a regular byline.

'And that's you! Bridget Jones's elder, sleazier brother!'

Eh?

'Off you go: 750 words every Friday.'

What? Me? *I'm* the idiot stupid enough . . . ?

'So what shall we call it?'

I thought we were calling it 'The Fifth Columnist'? But what do I know? I'm still stunned. And let's not forget heartbroken.

'Er, how about "The Fifth Columnist"?' I say.

Genuinely blank looks. I mean, *really* blank.

'How about "The Bastard"?' snorts Margaret, uncrossing and recrossing those legs. You know, that carrot diet really is very good.

'How about "The *Lucky* Bastard"?' mutters Steve. He's even older than I am. And married and stuff. He must hate this. Ha.

Must think quickly. If I am going to have to make an idiot of myself in print, I don't want to compound the mortification by being lumbered with something dumb, something embarrassing, something like . . .

'"Microwave Man!"' shrieks Cornelia.

. . . like 'Microwave Man'. Exactly. An arse is born. *But who was that woman?*

Back in the Game
Friday 12 September 2003

It was not without affection that I laid a tender hand on my old friend and picked absently at what appeared to be a small piece of fossilized baked cheese on his face – a token of our last time together.

'Well, old pal,' I said, 'it's just you and me again.'

And what a pal. No recriminations for the three years of neglect; just that warm, familiar glow and hum. Lugging the old microwave off the shelf could easily have been one of life's Great Depressing Moments: a sign that, at forty-seven, I was back on the shelf myself, having once again hitched my emotional wagon to a younger filly (twenty-eight, since you ask), only to hesitate fatally when she popped the big question: 'Breed: yes or no?' (*Must learn from this.*)

Sure, the B-word had cropped up in conversation. But in three years she went from not wanting babies ('Good Lord, no!') to unbridled fecundity – needing at least three (all of whose names appear to have been chosen in tribute to characters from the TV cowboy series *Bonanza*).

And so, like one of Hoss's unbroken horses, she bolted.

Still, as one stable door closes, another door opens – in this case that of my trusty 800-watt Panasonic, inviting me to sample once again the profound pleasures I had set aside in exchange for the hollow baubles of love, affection, home cooking and regular sex.

To be honest, I'm just being brave about three of the above. But, home cooking: why does it always have to come to this? When affairs begin, feeding takes place in restaurants. As things heat up, eating becomes little more than refuelling, often conducted *al duvet*. When one does pad into the kitchen to slip something from Tesco's Finest range into the microwave with a flourish, the carefully cultivated culinary ineptitude is deemed charming.

But no woman worth her Maldon sea salt tolerates it for

long. Out goes the unthreatening only-here-for-a-night valise, in come bulging supermarket carrier bags. The neglected oven perks up. Strange stuff appears in cupboard and fridge; boxes of dill; a faintly suggestive vegetable-type thing, pinkish and shaped like a bell; lumps of fresh Parmesan (so it doesn't come only ready-grated?).

And, of course, the bloody sea salt.

If I had to point to one bad thing about the Boer, it would be her cooking. It's not that I didn't like it: I did. It was just that there was too much of it, every night, and, by the time we both got in, too late. The proof that all those puddings are bad for your health came just over a week ago. Having struggled in vain for a year to lose weight after a back operation, I had begun to accept that 14st 4lb was my new fighting weight. Two weeks after she had gone, I thudded on to the scales with my customary resignation and found myself performing several comedy double-takes: 13st 12lb. Yee-ha!

Moral: not only does love hurt, it can actually be bad for your heart.

I spent the rest of the evening in joyful reunion with pair after pair of long-forgotten 34-inch-waist chinos and toasting my miraculous regirth with Stella Artois, Kettle Chips – and a Beef Bourguignon from Safeway's Best range.

Ding! goes the bell, and in four minutes flat both microwave and Microwave Man are back in the game.

2

How to Break a Heart

Dear Microwave Man
    Are you called Microwave Man because you're always done in five minutes?

            Ms TM, Kalbarri, Western Australia

Microwave Man writes: Is that the TM with whom I once spent a passionate six minutes (on account of heating from frozen)? The answer to your question, clearly, is no, and if I am now flooded with contradictory emails from former amours I will, of course, ignore them. Anyone who cares to step forward with an unsolicited testimonial to the longevity of my performance, on the other hand, guarantees themselves a mention in the column PLUS five minutes' worth of Microwave Man Bare Miles™ (conditions apply). (But not many.)

The trouble with things that run on rails (life, love . . . and trains, obviously) is that, when things go wrong, there is only one place for them to go.

    Off.

    I have a confession to make here. I have never, ever, ever, travelled on the railway without a valid ticket. Not even in Bolivia, where the officials, too busy stealing my camera and the bag of food I had brought along for the interminable journey from the coast to La Paz (I can recommend it to anyone heavily into the redistribution of wealth), neglected to check that I had paid. Now, on that occasion, I freely admit, I dearly wished that I *had* cheated the system. In fact, to make up for my loss, I passed on the offence, stealing a goat from the woman in the thoroughly ethnic bowler hat[5] and stripy dress-and-shawl rig with whom I shared twelve inches of bench space for a journey that lasted, oh, I don't know, maybe no more than twenty-six years?

Actually, I didn't steal the whole goat. It was a cooked goat and she was peddling greasy chunks of it around the carriage, her business assured thanks to her light-fingered friends having stolen the supplies brought on board by the stupid tourists. And then she made the classic amateur-greasy-goat-flesh-trader's mistake of leaving the carcass unguarded for a moment, and that's when I struck, sinking my teeth into it like an anaemic vampire.

Yum. The shits for a week. Crime never pays.

In fact, goat meat aside, I have, so far, stolen only one thing in my life: a cardboard-packaged cassette tape of the Beatles' *White Album*. I was young, I was poor, I was in Ipswich. What can I tell you? (Other than that I didn't own a cassette player.) I sold it to another boy and spent the proceeds on a bottle of cream soda and a dollop of ice-cream to float in it.

Yum. Heaven. So perhaps, sometimes, crime *does* pay.[6]

So back to the tracks, off which trains – and lives – so often plough. On 12 October 2001, I was on board the love train (with a valid ticket, naturally), hurtling towards the third biggest emotional derailment of my life. Not that I knew it. Had I done so, I would of course have pulled the emergency communication cord, or at the very least got off at the previous station (look, shall we agree that continuation of this particular metaphor is

5 Bolivia is about the only Spanish-speaking country in South America with a sizeable native population, on account of the Europeans deciding, for some reason or other, not to bump them all off. (And *this* is how they repay us.) Assuming that such benign governance must surely be a product of British intervention, the relieved locals immediately adopted the bowler hat as a token of their gratitude, and wear it to this day. Some historians argue that this gesture is directly linked to the survival (also *to this day*) of the Bedfordshire millinery industry, in turn traceable as the likely cause for Luton Town Football Club's promotion to the then First Division of British football in 1987. It was, of course, then only a matter of time before club manager David Pleat would be apprehended by police in his white Ford Granada, kerb crawling in the town's notorious red light district. Cf: *mad hatters*.

6 Officer, this is a novel, remember?

going to be very tiresome indeed, and discontinue it right now? Good. Done).

When I met her, the Plucky Boer was taciturn, or, if you prefer, emotionally retarded. God knows why I got started with her in the first place. It might possibly have had something to do with her fabulous body, long blonde hair and striking good looks, but it certainly wasn't on account of her emotional expressiveness.

It took her, I swear, six months even to start using my name when she spoke to me. Truly. If we were at opposite ends of an aisle in a supermarket and she wanted to point out the latest heinous marketing departure from the purity of Crunchy Nut Cornflakes, she would walk the length of the displays rather than raise her voice and say, 'Jonathan'. Or 'Jon'. Or 'Jonny'. Or even, 'Hey, you.'

Now, was this weird? I thought so. And yet I persevered with her – slowly, gently, sympathetically easing her out of her shell because I saw the promise of warmth in her frozen heart, a plea for help in her cynical eyes and, frankly, the most magnificent pair of breasts I had ever encountered.

When I did finally manage to persuade her that the use of personal terms of endearment didn't actually signify a catastrophic loss of self-determination, she never quite got the hang of saying 'Babycakes' or 'Sweetiekins'[7] without bracketing the words around with gigantic comedy quote marks.

She voortrekked through life, opening up to no one, giving away nothing emotionally (and, one had the sneaking suspicion, never quite forgiving the British for that business with the Cape Colony, or herself for leaving the new, post-Mandela republic in the lurch, along with all the other 'salt dicks', as South Africans so charmingly describe those with one foot in either country). She was twenty-five, a secretary who'd married young: at

7 These aren't, obviously, the true terms of endearment she learnt to use. Such a detail would, I feel, be a revelation too far, and the release of it into the public domain might do untold damage to her progress, perhaps setting her back years. Why, it took me twenty-four months even to make her cry, and then it was only because I had beaten her at Swingball. And squash. Ha.

nineteen she had been in love with a Cornish surfer/accountant (or, possibly, accountant/surfer) and they'd hung ten down the aisle partly so she could stay in Britain. When they left the church the happy couple passed through a tunnel of raised surfboards, so that was always going to last.

Three years later, she'd trained as a physiotherapist, got bored with that, and retrained as a journalist. Then she got bored with that and, last I heard, was in the throes of recasting herself as a novelist.

And then she got bored with me.

I know. Hard to believe, but true, and just like that. Just like a train wreck. Only, this time, just like a train wreck with unforeseen but ultimately excellent consequences.

But a train wreck nonetheless and, disconcertingly, the third such wreck in a row. Now, what is this? This strange and unnerving ability of a woman to be – or at least to *appear* to be – happy and loving and (more or less) sane and cat-free for 975 days and then, utterly without warning (no talk, no tears, no hints, no scenes, no storming-outs), to be able to pull the plug. On everything. Instantly. Utterly. From 100 mph to dead stop, in no seconds. You'd think that the emotional deceleration alone would kill her, or at least bend her a little out of shape.

And so picture the scene, if you will, at the dawn of Day 976. We have just spent a weekend away, out of town and in a hotel by the seaside, and it's been a good one (lots of food, wine, sex . . . OK, *some* looking at boats, but there's the redundancy to plan for and, besides, at my age you have to pace yourself).

I had climbed out of bed at around 9 a.m. on the Sunday – late for me, extremely early for her – and left her for less than an hour. One hour. Sixty minutes. 3,600 seconds. To go for a run. I run because a) I'm vain, b) it keeps me fit enough to sleep with twentysomethings and c) because I like the feeling of superiority it gives me over mere mortals. Especially those extremely mere mortals who smoke.

Run done, I pace through the hotel lobby, drenched in sweat and still breathing hard, past the reception desk (catching once again the twinkling eye of the dark-haired, purple-uniformed receptionist drumming her chubby, trailer-trash-manicured fingers on the blotter) and quicken my pace down the corridor as that wonderful, warm glow of arousal begins to spread through my thighs. I am going to strip, shower, slide back into bed and wake her up the way she loves to be woken up.

Christ. Was it room 218 or 217?

Look down at the newspapers. *Observer* and *Sunday Times*. That must be us. Pick up the papers. Catch my reflection in the door plate. Smile. Swipe the card. Green light. Push the door.

And that's when it all came off the track. Later, I wondered what signs I'd missed. SPADs. *Signals Passed at Danger.*

She is out of bed, standing, fully dressed, in jeans, her horrendous old black clogs and that chunky red jumper failing to hide her perfect shape. She must have only just pulled it over her head, because the long blonde hair is still tucked down the neck. Something is wrong. Well, obviously. She's been crying, for one thing – still is, actually.

Still the yearning doesn't subside, but the duty officer in my head knows something is up and is desperately hauling on levers and trying to tell the boys down below to throw the groin into reverse.

I step back, lean out of the door and check the number. To her, it probably looks like I'm doing this for comic effect but, actually, I have that very second remembered that our room is definitely 217, because I have this annoying habit of adding such numbers together in my head and I distinctly remember that the room into which we staggered last night – slightly drunk, extremely horny and far too impatient to get as far as the bed – added up to ten. Two plus one plus seven. (I also divide letters on roadside posters, or book covers, or Crunchy Nut Cornflake boxes, or anything, really, into groups of three, searching for hidden omens. Do you think this is a related condition, or something different?)

But now it doesn't add up. Maybe I *have* walked into the wrong room. Walked into someone else's unpleasantness. As I am already halfway out of the door, checking the number, I glance up and down the corridor. Maybe some other sucker is just getting back from a run and I have, somehow, inadvertently stumbled into his Bad Sunday. His Bad Life.

I step back into the room and the heavy, sprung door shuts with a bang behind me.

What's happening? I say, although actually I know exactly what's happening. I know because I have been here before. Twice. Once with Rebecca. Once with Laura. And now with the Boer.

Sob. Sniff. Sob, sob. Snuffle. Christ. I can't bear all that. It makes me want to put my arms around her.

I'm sorry, she says, *but I can't do this any more.*

Funny, that's exactly what Rebecca said, fifteen years ago. And Laura – eight years ago? Let's see: with Rebecca for – what? Four years? Yes, four. Plus eight with Laura, that's a total of twelve, add on the three years vanishing down the toilet right now, that comes to fifteen, one plus five equals six . . . six. Is that a significant figure? At least it's divisible by an even number . . .

For Christ's sake, man. Sudden and traumatic catastrophic emotional loss and I'm doing the maths. Maybe I should be on something. Everyone I know is on something. Why should I miss out?

Funny what runs through your mind in the hour-long seconds of a train crash.

100 mph to nothing, in 3,600 seconds. I can hear the rushing in my ears. It's so loud, in fact, that I absentmindedly touch the side of my face and stare at my fingers, half expecting to see blood, but all I see is sweat. And that my hand is shaking.

Unbidden memory flash from a forgotten western: gunslinger turns to his buddy before the big showdown and holds out a rock-steady hand. *You'll be fine,* says his grizzled compadre. *Yeah,* says the gunslinger, holding out his other, violently trembling hand. *But this is the hand I shoot with.*

What does she mean? Can't do what? It's been three years and every day seemed great. Right up until now.

What do you mean? I say, voice just a little too high. This is the hand I shoot with.

You know, she says.

I don't, but I can see that she thinks I ought to, and so I just slump down on the small leather armchair, afraid to say anything in case it makes things worse. Worse? I become acutely aware of the sweat-wet shorts against the back of my legs. From somewhere I dredge a memory of reading that the mind shuts down most of the nerve endings in the body most of the time. If it didn't, you'd tickle yourself to death just by wearing clothes.

She sits on the edge of the bed, dabbing at her eyes with a tissue. Her jeans are low at the back and I can see her knickers. We bought them yesterday. I stood behind her at the cash register and she pushed back against me, rhythmically, while we waited in line. And she's wearing them now to leave me. Can that be right? I drop the papers in front of her and she looks down at them. She fingers the plastic bag containing the monstrously swollen *Sunday Times*. Get her reading that and we'll be here for hours. Normally I get impatient, try to prise her away from the papers, but right now it seems like a dream scenario and, stupidly, I feel hope stir. Drama isn't really her thing, I tell myself. Perhaps she has had enough of this scene now and just wants to get on with having a normal Sunday.

Or perhaps not.

She has made the bed, I suddenly realize, and that's when I really understand that the game is up. All this trauma and tears and yet *she has found the time and the concentration in that hour I was away to make the fucking bed*. She *never* makes the bed, *especially* in a hotel room. Straightening out and tucking in the sheets, sealing up any possibility, any hope, that I can make this better by taking off her clothes, by taking her back into bed, where all things can be made better. Or at least covered up and, for a while, forgotten.

Although the sheets are quite probably still damp from last night's sex, the bed has, inexplicably, unbelievably, become a body bag containing the already rotting corpse of our love. Or, as perhaps the coroner will find, our 'love'.

I stand up and take off my wet T-shirt. I sweat a lot when I run. To recap: I am fit and I run fast because I am vain and it makes me feel good and look good and, above all, feel superior to ordinary human beings. And a fat lot of good it's doing me now. Perhaps right now, on rooms either side of this one, there are fat blokes untroubled by their imperfections and lying along-side beautiful women who love them for who they are, not for what they are. Perhaps she has found someone else. Perhaps he is as fat as those two imaginary blokes in rooms 216 and 218. Perhaps I should stop thinking, before my whole shallow life-philosophy goes up in cigarette smoke and chip fat. Oh, go on, chuck in a couple of battered saveloy as well.

She looks away from my bare chest, the product of endless lengths of the pool and countless thousands of bench presses. Yesterday she fell asleep with her head upon it, stroking the hair with her fingers, as though she never wanted to rise from it.

I'm just going to have a shower, I say, and drop my shorts and push off my running shoes with my feet. They hit the floor and lie there, awry, stupid dumb symbols of my hubris. And before I can stop it the iPod is whipping one off the mental playlist. Hands up who likes Del Amitri? No one? Yes, funny that. Odd how their concerts are always sold out. And funny how Justine and the lads from the dour Scottish pop combo are singing along inside my head right now: 'What I Think She Sees'. Only, some-thing in the way my iPod's wired allows the triumphant independence of that number to come out as a torch song for the serially rejected.

Maybe it's because it's the only song I know with a line about running shoes in it.

I stand up, kick one of the bloody things across the room – damn, damn! Not cool! – and walk awkwardly towards the bath-room. I am suddenly conscious of my nakedness.

When you've done, she says, *could you give me a lift to the station?*

I stop, turn and just look at her. I forget my nakedness. I struggle to find something to say – something gigantic, some-

thing so right and so big and sensibly magic that it will switch
lights back on inside her head, or in her heart, or in whatever
organ it is that's driving her with the lights off right now, but
I fail to find anything, not even the smallest word, let alone
the right combination of words, to undo this spell, despite the
torrent rushing through my head . . . *that day near the begin-*
ning in the sun by the river near the cottage on the beached boat with
the wine when we sat and watched the shelducks protecting their
chicks and their patch of foreshore and your short skirt rode up high
on your brown legs and we suddenly stopped talking rubbish and you
managed to hold my gaze for just long enough to let me know that
it was the right time to jump the gap between us and set my hand
down gently on your thigh and then kiss you . . . you told your
husband you had an outing with the rest of your course but instead,
heart pounding, you got on the train and came to see me and we
spent the entire day both of us not knowing if the other wanted the
same thing until the very end when I said may I kiss you and you
answered with your mouth and then we were on the floor and in the
dust . . .

But, instead, all I say is . . .

Yes. Of course.

Yes? Of *course?*

I spend a long time in the shower. It gives me time to think
but I don't come up with anything useful. Instead, I think about
running and where it has got me. I remember how I started
running when I was unhappily married – not to get fit, particularly, although God knows I needed to, but just to get out of
the house. About how running ran me, at the end of eight
increasingly pointless but entirely faithful years of marriage,
into the arms of my first affair; about how I started Laura
running, and how I thought she was the love of my life, and
about how, eight years later and months after she'd left me, I'd
visited her new home and saw her new man's new running
shoes in her new wardrobe – *the man she had run away from me*
to be with – and how that was the first time the full weight of
her betrayal hit me. And how even then I knew that Del Amitri

had got it all wrong, but even still it was much better to have an anthem that I could at least *pretend* spoke to my self-esteem.[8]

And about how running then ran me into the arms of the Boer.

I first noticed her in the gym at work. She was pounding away on a treadmill and I was lying on my back at her feet – symbolically, as things turned out – doing crunches. With her hair tied back it took me a while to recognize her as the quiet secretary from the news desk (quiet but beautiful, and that's why I had always gone out of my way not to look at her), but when I saw who she was I threw in an extra fifty or so sit-ups.

Back in the office we exchanged our first emails . . . *God, I'm so embarrassed you saw me drenched in sweat* . . . she wrote. *You looked pretty good to me* . . . I replied and looked round and caught her eye and she smiled. And blushed.

And that was more or less it.

A while later she volunteered for a team I was putting together for a corporate race in Battersea Park. What can I tell you? That there was free drink? That I put the team together only so she could volunteer for it? Maybe. Only, actually, depressingly, it was more about the running.

On a training run along the Thames one day she started to fall back, and I stopped and let the others go on and waited for her. She insisted I didn't stay with her although I wanted to more than anything in the world. She hated weakness in herself and loathed having to stop. She hated the sense that I wanted to protect her – or that I might think that she *needed* protection. I should have called it a day right there and then.

After Battersea Park, we walked together to the Tube. I was heading home to my then girlfriend, an Australian who was flying home for good in a few months and wanted me to go with her. We had been together for almost a year, but I had already decided not to head south for my winter. Firstly, I hated long flights. And secondly, I recognized that if the thought of a

8 Besides, how many other songs can you name with a reference to jogging in them?

long flight was putting me off, then I probably wasn't on the brink of a new life.

I learnt that the Boer was married, to an Englishman. They had been in love, she said, although they probably wouldn't have married if it hadn't been for his passport. But now she was no longer happy. I wondered briefly if he knew that but didn't for a moment care. Instead, on that twenty-five-minute walk I fell in love. Or, at least, I *thought* I had. I thought she had too. Six months later, her husband was gone, the Australian was gone and we were together.

Until a few minutes ago.

And they say running's good for you, I think, as I soap my temporarily redundant cock, distractedly, for the third time, like an obsessive Howard Hughes washing imagined filth from his spotless hands. Only without all those millions to make everything better. Or at least cleaner.

And here's a funny thing. Suddenly, I get movement. That part of me the Boer has christened the Cane Rat perks up. And it worries me at the same time as it excites me because I'm not sure what it says about the way I really feel about anything, but, despite what is happening, despite the sudden, crushing blow that has fallen upon me, I find that a significant part of my brain is thinking about the twinkling eye of the dark-haired, purple-uniformed beauty drumming her chubby fingers on the blotter at reception . . .

Sometimes, I despise myself. But not much, and not for long.

I was too young to care about JFK and too indifferent to recall where I was when John Lennon took his bullet, but I will never forget where I was when I heard the news that Jim Fixx, the running guru, had died.

I had just got home from a run.

This summer it will be twenty years since Fixx, a sixty-miles-a-week man and the author of the bestselling *Complete Book of Running*, which set me and countless millions of others on the road to fitness, popped out from a hotel for his daily jog and keeled over dead from a heart attack, aged fifty-two.

Some guys have all the luck.[9] Now, for most people, the message they take from Fixx's fate is 'Don't run, it could kill you.' But to me it says, 'Run, and keeping running till you drop.'

And ain't that, after all, really what those running shoes are for?

Little Black Book
Friday 19 September 2003

Now I remember why I gave up being single in the first place. Exhaustion. In one week of involuntary freedom, I have fallen asleep at my desk at work (it's OK, nobody noticed); at the wheel (spent an hour kipping on an A12 forecourt; woke, heart pounding, with a brake-pedal-stabbing start, from an 80 mph dream, contact lenses welded to eyeballs); and, God help me, in a woman's arms (luckily, she'd dozed off first. Gee, thanks).

If you are one of those sad, stock-taking individuals driven to compiling Libran lists of pros and cons to help you negotiate life's bumpy road, there are plenty of advantages to jot down under the 'yup' column while trying to convince yourself that being single is A Good Thing.

To take just three of mine (no particular order):

1. Being able to play, *and sing along to*, Wishbone Ash, Doors and Belinda Carlisle CDs in the car.
2. The freedom to say, 'Yes, I'd love to go for a drink/Rollerblading/watch a film/get to know you better after work,' without worrying about whether the Significant Other will find it Entirely Appropriate.
3. To flick through one's 'e' equivalent of the little black book (and who can forget Belinda's 1991 seminal hit of the same name?), fan a few old flames and see what flares up.

---

9 But not Robert Palmer, dead of a heart attack at fifty-four. Never mind running: that's what being addicted to love will do to you, every time.

And what does? Well, let's say it isn't exactly a heartwarming commitment to monogamy. Frankly, I was shocked. Pleased, too, but shocked. According to my statistically irrelevant survey, at least 80 per cent of seemingly lurved-up women in long-term relationships would be more than happy to take a walk on the wild side of memory lane with an ex-squeeze, in pragmatic rejection of the Disney fantasia that one person can give you everything you need, for ever.

And I am pretty sure that a further 10 per cent could be persuaded to dip their toes in the gutter, which leaves just one man in ten who doesn't know just how lucky he is.

As a recently happily cohabited man, I bristle to learn this. As a newly single bloke, I say, *Wah-hoo!*

I have known how it feels to discover that the woman to whom one is prepared to donate at least one kidney has been Seeing Somebody Else. On the other hand, there is something darkly electric about Spending Time with another man's woman (illicit sex really is Euphemism Central, isn't it?).

Plus, she doesn't want to hang around any longer than you want her to, she has no interest in hearing the 'L' word and there is absolutely no question of buying her anything that can't be consumed instantly (champagne, say) or concealed about her person (use your imagination).

Catching up with former girlfriends can be fun and sexy – and here I return to my original point – and extremely enervating. Carousing, cavorting, sliding around in the backs of black cabs. These things demand the kind of endurance many forty-seven-year-olds have long since seen vanishing in the rear-view mirror ('Caution: your youth may be a lot further away than it seems'). Hence the hitting the gym at 7 a.m., and thus the kipping off at random moments.

All of which brought me, yawning, to the weekend, determined to see nobody, to rest and recharge – and, by Saturday evening, sick to death of my own company (not half as fascinating as I had fondly imagined it to be) and longing for the everyday and yet magical familiarity and affection that, until a few weeks ago, was mine.

Never mind Mr 10 Per Cent. The potentially cuckolded nine blokes in ten don't realize how lucky they are either.

3
How to Fix a Heart

Dear Microwave Man

    Can you answer something I have often wondered about? I can see that a forty-seven-year-old man and a twenty-eight-year-old woman might fall in love with each other despite the near twenty-year age difference. But how easy is it for each of them to get on with the other's friends? The whole cultural hinterland is so different.

                                   Ms JL, Oxfordshire

Microwave Man writes: In my experience, it isn't difficult, it's nigh-on impossible. My twenty-eight-year-old was very grown-up (whereas I, obviously, am a tad retarded emotionally). I think the trick is not to try crossing too many boundaries. Let her go to the club with her friends but do not be tempted to act her age and follow suit. Stay at home and take your drugs there. (This is a joke.) As for cultural hinterland, when the twenty-eight-year-old woman comes from South Africa, there's a whole lot more to worry about than mere differences of generation (and didn't England do well on Saturday?).

You will, by now, have gathered that this isn't a cookbook for sad bachelors (or even happy ones), so if you've eased it off the three-for-the-price-of-two shelf where it was mistakenly wedged between *Seductive Flavours of the Levant* and *How to Eat*,[10] licking your lips in anticipation of whipping up a short-order Kibbeh Batata Al-Jabal in double-quick time, *bad news*, my little oven-ready turkey.

    The good news is that lips do get licked in this book, although not because they are smeared with cream or chocolate (well, not

---

10 To save you the expense, the answer is, generally, 'With your mouth.'

always). But not always by the people who are *supposed* to be licking them.

There is, of course, no such thing today as the little black book, but then Belinda was singing about hers in 1987. That was before she had email, and before she had a cell phone – the twin serpents in the modern game of snakes and ladders. I might have trusted Belinda then. I certainly wouldn't now.

Do you trust your partner? I mean, not just assume that they are where they *say* they are, or that they haven't been in touch with that ex they never quite got over, but really *know*, bet your life on it and all that, that they are trustworthy?

And how about you? Just how trustworthy are you? Maybe that's why you never ask them where *they've* been.

Take the mobile phone, Eros's golden gift to adultery. It has launched millions of affairs and assisted in the conduct of countless more, serving as a vital link between two people for whom it is vital that their link remains secret. But look: here's a game you can play with your partner. It's not a nice game, and there will be no winners, but at the end of it at least you will know for certain whether or not they have something to hide.

But a word of warning. Don't play it if you have something of your own to hide. And we both know that you do.

One day, when you know that your partner won't really be needing her mobile phone, pretend yours has broken and ask to borrow hers. That's it. That's the game. I know it's not exactly bridge, or even pétanque (or even Swingball), but after that opening gambit it's about what you make of it.

Funny, eh? Why is she so uncomfortable, making all kinds of lame excuses? Perhaps she isn't 100 per cent confident that Mr X won't call, or that Mr Y won't text. Or perhaps she's 100 per cent certain that they *will*.

And here's a confession. All through my three years with the Boer, although I was, *more or less*,[11] completely faithful, my mobile

11 I know, it isn't possible to be more or less faithful. But you know what I mean, right?

phone was my link to the past and, thus, to a possible alternative future. A parachute. A lifejacket. Just in case.

Anyway, once your partner has, one way or the other, refused to let you take her phone, here's another relationship-wrecking game you can play (if you're still together, which, quite honestly, you really shouldn't be by now). Ask her to scroll through her address book while you watch.

She will almost certainly refuse, 'on principle', although it might not be clear whether this is the Holographic Principle, the Superposition Principle, Le Chatelier's Principle or the Uncertainty Principle. (My money's on the first, which is a modern work-up of Plato's Allegory of the Caves. In this, all these guys chained in a cave can see only the shadows cast by a fire on the walls and this, to them, is reality. When one of them escapes, sees the reality of the real world and comes back to tell them all about it, they assume he's mad. Like them, you might prefer to stay as you are, chained up happy and snug, close to the fire, and watching the shadows.)

If she does refuse, then you have a stand-off and you both lose. If she agrees, ask her to explain who all those men are, and why, if they are all 'just friends' ('Tony? Oh, he's gay'[12]), you have never heard of them or seen them before. In this case, you both lose again, but then you were losing all along and just didn't know it. At least you get to escape from the cave.

All those men are, of course, her ex-lovers. Ex, that is, if you are lucky. Then (if you're still in the same room, and breathing), ask her why she still has their telephone numbers.[13]

I don't believe that we keep our bridges open because we are always looking for greener grass. I think the real reason is a lot sadder than that. I think it's because nobody, in their heart of hearts – and in their right mind – truly believes that anything is going to last for ever. We are all happy to be swept off our feet,

12 User's guide: any man described by a woman to her partner as 'gay' is on call as an emergency sperm donor to the Errol Flynn Home for Wayward Boys and Girls Well Just Girls Actually.
13 Women: you can, of course, play this game as well!

but none of us is prepared to leave the ground without a parachute.

It's all about trust. There is none. (Well, trust, and the invention of the bicycle,[14] which was the beginning of the end of the bliss of ignorance, and the beginning of the tyranny of choice, but don't get me started.)

I would have struggled to play this game with the Boer. Frankly, I didn't delete the names and numbers of past lovers because, under the right circumstances, I would have slept with any one of them at the drop of a hat. And I found myself in those circumstances the moment I dropped the Boer off at the station.

What? I'm supposed to go into mourning or something?

Instead, I go back to the hotel, walk up to reception to get my key and say . . .

I'm thinking of staying another night.

Purple Girl smiles. 'All on your own?'

Yup. Just me.

Hmm. She noticed. Arm out straight, she dangles the key coquettishly between the long, white nails of her finger and thumb. As I lean forward to take it I catch a glimpse of a tattoo peeking out between her skirt and her blouse. *Trés* trailer. Yum. I smile back and say . . .

. . . so what is there to do in this town at night?

. . . even though I know this town like the back of my hand and know full well the answer is . . .

'Not much,' she says, and laughs. I take the key, which she holds on to for a moment longer than necessary, inducing a short little game of tug.

Oh, well, I guess there's always room service, the mini-bar and pay-per-view, I say.

She laughs, and says, 'Sounds like fun.'

And I say, *What time do you finish?* and she doesn't ask why,

14 The parochial Jane Austen, who firmly believed that 'three or four families in a country village is the thing to work on', was artistically destroyed by the invention of the horizon-broadening bicycle, and made her displeasure public by dying the very same year.

just says, 'Nine o'clock,' and I say, *See you later, then,* and she says, 'OK,' and that, I think, is what you really *call* room service.

Sometimes, it's just too easy.

I walk through into the café, order a coffee but get a bloody latte instead and sit down with pen, paper and mobile phone. I am in a funny mood. I am upset, and a bit angry, but I am also needy. And excited. I feel rejected, of course, and stupid for having committed myself to someone who, as it turns out, doesn't want me. At the same time, I am feeling horny and nine o'clock is still hours away.

Something has changed. At moments like this I used to drag myself off like a wounded dog to die in a gathering pool of my own self-pity, weeping and convinced that life was at an end. Those were the days. Now I'm older and, if not wiser, then at least sufficiently experienced to know that there isn't a bad thing that doesn't appear better looking back. Millions of emotional nanotech robots are swarming through my system, cauterizing traumatized feelings and nerve endings and generally doing the job of healing that used to take months, if not years.

And behind the sense of defeat and loss is something else – a sense of horizon and release and opportunity. A sense of adventure.

The prospect of an empty bed hovers before me as both a symbol of loss and of opportunity. Funny. I would have described myself as a bed-half-empty kind of guy, but here I am scrolling through my phone's contacts book and drawing up a list of potential playmates.

You will, indeed, always be in my little black book.

Right here, right now, I don't want solitude, and I don't want the chore of a fresh start with a new relationship. I want revenge: revenge over whoever will soon (might already, for all I know) be sleeping with the Boer.

I am angry and I am sad, and that is a potent and dangerous cocktail because it releases sentimentality and self-pity to prowl together, and under its influence I will not only say tender things to get my way, but I might, at the crucial moment, even believe them.

This is why women will never 'get' men, which in turn is good news for men who want to get women into bed. For some men, sex is so often either first aid or revenge. Somewhere in the background there is *always* a Helen of Troy, and for such men the sex act is aimed not at the woman he consumes but as a brutal thrust through her into the guts of the invisible, unknown man who haunts him. The Boer, searching for a father for her future children, has left me for a man she has yet to meet (perhaps). And that man is me, only me with the sense and the courage and the lack of fear about his age and his death and the time left between the two to make the most of it. And I hate him and fear him.

Luckily, I have my armour and my weapons to hand. *Bring me my arrows of desire, bring me my spears . . . I will not cease from mental fight, nor shall my, ahem, sword sleep in my hand . . .*

What I want, above all, is reassurance and familiarity and, as I scroll through the names of potential familiars (*Yes. No. Yes, yes. No . . .*), memories of mouths and bodies calm and console me. I want beauty and curves and the flattery of passion. I need to pull the warmth of mutual history around me like a blanket. I have been wounded, and the only cure is the grim joy of stealing another man's woman. Or, preferably, other men's women.

Maybe this is how the Vikings got started. Who knows, if I had a boat maybe I'd be on my way up the east coast by now.

It pays to advertise, and pretty soon I have herded them into a caller group. There are four suspects (in chronological order): Rebecca, Laura, Alice and Kelly.

They have all meant something to me at one time or another, but that doesn't stop me wanting to use them now. And who knows? Maybe at the time I overlooked something, maybe one or all of us has changed. It is, I reason, just possible that one of the gang of four could have been The One. Could *still* be The One.

Not, of course, that I believe in such bollocks, any more than I believe in the *Da Vinci Code*, but you have to read *something* on the plane other than the crash instructions.

At this stage (and, please, remember that this is still only hours after being dumped), I set aside any conscious consideration of the reality that, in all but one case, it was these women who had ended the relationship. I couldn't figure out why then, and I'm sure as hell not in the mood to try now. You could call this self-denial. I call it self-serving. All I can see are possibilities: the possibility that I can overcome the past and reinstate my sense of self-worth by reclaiming (if only for a night) what once was mine.

And, if that comes to pass, then just as surely the possibility of reclaiming the Boer enters the frame.

I haven't had contact with most of them for two or three years. I neither know nor care whether they are in relationships, although I hope that they are. I'm not looking for someone with whom to share popcorn at the bloody pictures. All that remains is to compose the text that will signal my availability and my desire. It takes me several attempts to get it right, but eventually it boils down to a few short words – vague, casual and insufficient to convict even before a jury of suspicious husbands and boyfriends and yet, to the right eyes, under ultraviolet light, utterly unambiguous.

This is what I write: *Hi, how are you? Long time no nothing.*

Or, as translated through each woman's personal Enigma machine: *Hi, remember how great the sex was with us? Want more?*

I am Commissioner Gordon, about to unleash the Bat Signal into the night sky of a Gotham City pulsing with a thousand dark possibilities. My finger hovers, for just a moment, in delicious anticipation, over the send key. The Boer is barely gone, still on the train and rolling back to London. Part of me wonders at the numbness that allows me to callously plot her replacement, but it's not a part that I choose to examine too closely right now. Besides. She started it.

I jab at the key and sit back and stare at the phone. Message sent. After a while, I get up and walk to the counter for another coffee. Sorry, latte. I'm in no hurry. I'm relaxed. I don't even experience my usual pang of anger at being in a Starbucks. I even ask for a 'tall' cup instead of 'small', a distinction upon which I usually, and perversely, insist. Even the annoying jazz twittering from the speakers fails to rouse my ire. Well, almost.

I sit down again and doodle on my newspaper. Glasses, moustaches and horns go on world leaders and victims of crime alike. I start to count the letters in headlines, bunching them into groups of three. Doing the maths again. How many years, I wonder, before I start writing to newspapers in words of three colours?

And then, entirely expected but taking me completely by surprise, one of the most annoying yet exciting sounds in the modern world.

Beep, beep.

Ker-*ching*. Result! Time? Six minutes and thirty-five seconds. Surely some kind of record? Only one question remains: who is it? I delay finding out, taunting myself and weighing the phone in my hand, as if somehow I could guess.

It's too much to bear and I stab the key.

Hello, Mr G! I was just thinking about you! What's up?

Translation: *Of course I remember! Let's go!*

So. Kelly. Only she calls me 'Mr G'. I smile. I have known her, on and off, for almost five years. She has been there, simmering in the background, throughout two live-in relationships and, uniquely in the gang of four, we have never slept together. Well, not really. Not as such.[15]

But now that's about to change.

She was in her early twenties when I first met her – in a multistorey car park, where I had seen her every other day for weeks before we finally spoke. The car park was attached to the swimming pool up and down which I ploughed two or three mornings a week, and as I was leaving she was always arriving to go to her job in a nearby office. The very first time she pulled up alongside me she gave me a brilliant smile – the kind of smile that can mean only one thing – but it was weeks before I finally

15 Clinton would know what I mean.

35

wound down my window and said something cheesy like . . .

. . . *If we are going to carry on smiling at each other like this, maybe we should find out each other's name?*

. . . and then we talked a bit and she laughed a lot with that big, generous mouth, and I smiled back and tried to keep my eyes on her face, but somehow they kept slipping down to her jacket, gaping open as she sat in the car and under which she so obviously wore nothing more than a bra, or perhaps a lacy top, and said, *Let's have lunch some time,* which was fine because she said, *Yes, let's, that would be fun,* but then I drove off rather pleased with myself before realizing that I had forgotten to get her number.

Outstanding.

That night, as I made love with the Australian, I couldn't get Kelly's face out of my mind. To be honest, I didn't try very hard. In fact, to be *completely* honest, in my head it was Kelly I was screwing,[16] up against a wall in the deserted car park. In my fantasy it was always her who started it, leading me into the stairwell without a word and then glancing back over her shoulder and pulling up the skirt of her dark business suit and . . .

. . . and then I didn't see her again for weeks, although I looked every time I went swimming. I ended up sitting in the car for ten, fifteen minutes at a time some days, telling myself I was just catching the last bit of the *Today* programme but, actually, hoping she'd appear. I don't know what I was planning to do. Introduce her to John Humphrys, maybe? I was, after all, in a relationship, and one in which I had promised myself I would remain faithful.[17]

But I guess I knew a parachute when I saw one.

Weeks passed and I almost forgot her. Almost. Then, one afternoon I saw her again. I didn't recognize her at first, partly because she materialized out of context – not leaning out of the window of her car but standing in an aisle in a supermarket – and partly

16 User's guide: men do this a lot. It doesn't necessarily mean they don't love you, or don't find you attractive any more. And yes, don't worry, we know you do it too.
17 You're buying this, right?

because something about her had changed. Even from behind, I could tell that she wasn't smiling. Something about her shoulders. As I moved towards her a woman walked past from the other direction and gave her an odd, second look.

Kelly? I said.

It was her. Same shoulder-length dark hair, same heels, same business suit. What wasn't the same was her face, no longer smiling and down which tears were streaming. Without thinking, I put my arms around her and held on tight as she sobbed. It's at moments like this when there really is nothing else to do but fall in love. I'm not sure I like that. I'm not sure this feeling of strength isn't a weakness.

Wait, a small voice said. *Yet another twenty-seven-year-old? Why don't you pick on somebody your own age? Christ. You're turning into a serial father figure.* But who, other than disenfranchised trailer-dwelling mid-Americans with hunting rifles, ever listens to the small voices?

Over several whiskies in a bar, she told me all. I hadn't known it at the time, but when I first met her in the car park she had just bailed out of her marriage. Since I'd last seen her, she and her husband had decided to give it another go. That had been two weeks ago. It was still so fresh that they hadn't told any of their friends and family, but it had been looking good and she was hopeful and excited.

But she wasn't excited or hopeful now. This was Monday. On Friday – just three days ago – it had all ended accidentally when he had ridden his motorbike off the road and into the afterlife. One of life's unfunny little jokes, with extremely bad timing.

For him, anyway.

The following weekend, I took the Sunday papers round to her house for breakfast. When I arrived, she was painting the living room. It was clear that it didn't need painting, but I sort of understood. She was wearing a big, baggy pair of jeans – his, probably – which hung low on her hips, and an old, tight T-shirt, spattered with paint, that left her belly bare. Her dark skin was dappled with pale blue paint and, as she leant back against the ladder in the middle of the room, I kissed her. First on her hair and then on her mouth, holding the small of her back with my right hand.

I was aching to reach down into those jeans. I've thought about that moment many times since and God only knows how I held myself in check.

I want to, believe me, I want to, I heard myself wittering, *but I know it would be the wrong thing for you right now. It's too soon . . .*

Jesus. Was I insane? What was I thinking? Actually, I'm being disingenuous. I know what I was thinking. I was Doing the Right Thing. And do you know what? I regret it until this very day.

Not that she was much help. In a trice we were on the stairs, kissing and kind of shuffling upwards, a step at a time. I felt her paint-wet hands on my back under my shirt. New shirt, ruined. Concentrate on that; there's nothing horny about *that*, right? But of course, there is. Doing the Right Thing just got harder with every stair-rod.

And then, suddenly, a helping hand from beyond the grave.

We are in the bedroom now. She is backed up to the foot of the bed and those jeans have somehow hit the floor in a crumpled pile. Barefoot, she's stepping out of them, and her thumbs are in the elastic of her black knickers – old, shapeless and faded knickers. The sexiest underwear I have ever seen. All I want to do is to help her take them off. With my teeth.

And then I see it and, even before I ask, I know what it is, and suddenly the danger of damnation has passed.

What's that?

'What?'

That urn thing, on the table by your bed?

She turns to look, crouching on all fours on the bed. A moment before, the sight of her like that would have undone my resolve, but I guess there aren't many men who could maintain an erection in the presence of the ashes of a woman's recently deceased husband. I certainly couldn't.

And so here we are, three years down the line, and she has responded to the Bat Signal, and she's put on just the *slightest* bit of weight and it suits her and that big smile is back. She's working in London now and we meet for a drink or two, and after a few she tells me how she always regretted that we didn't become lovers but that almost immediately afterwards she started seeing someone at work who had been kind to her after her husband was killed, and somewhere in my head an alarm bell goes off in the department that monitors stuff that might one day come back to bite me in the arse . . . *Blimey, that was quick: dependency alert.*

But right now I don't care that she can't stand not to have a man in her life, that she is too frail and hurt to face life alone, even if it means living with the wrong man and selling herself short. It doesn't even really sink in when she mentions that the boyfriend has left office life to become a policeman, but it will later.

Right now I am just pleased with the way the conversation is going and the way she has started to touch my arm and sit closer to me. And, of course, there's that protection thing again.

Suddenly, she leans right in and I feel her breath in my ear. *Take me somewhere,* she whispers, and I get up and pay the bill because I know just the place, and there will be no Doing the Right Thing this time because this time it's *me* who is the vulnerable one.

She is wearing the kind of business suit she always wears in my fantasies, although this time it is grey. She is wearing just-sensible heels and carrying a briefcase and a coat, and as we walk through the lobby of the busy hotel we look just like any of the other business people going about the demanding business of squandering shareholders' money.

She hesitates, puzzled, for a moment as I walk straight past check-in, but follows me, silently, into the lift and up to the tenth floor. The carpets up here are thicker and our feet make no sound as I lead her down the corridor towards the service stairs.

The contrast between the cold stairwell and the warm, wood-panelled luxury we leave behind is sudden and brutal. A strip light casts a vivid glow on the concrete steps. Neither of us says anything and then she starts it, dropping her coat and her brief-case in the dust, putting one hand up against the wall, glancing back over her shoulder and pulling up her skirt.

No old, faded knickers this time. No knickers at all, in fact. I do like a happy ending.

Unfortunately, this wasn't it.

Sitting Uncomfortably
Friday 26 September 2003

In my experience (and I am forty-eight next month), furniture, rather like the vicar in all of life's big moments, takes centre stage for all the grand emotional production numbers. Young lovers play havoc with the shuffle-and-shop flow system at Ikea on Saturdays, gambolling playfully over the displays and sizing up the flat-packed furniture not so much for style or ease of assembly but for its potential as props for sex games.

After the first flush fades, furniture returns to its essential 'chairness' (as Sartre would have had it), which is to say, all we do then is sit on it. The next time furniture and furnishings occupy disproportionate prominence in a relationship, they do so as a symptom of a relationship in crisis.

What did my then wife and I do when our marriage came down to earth with all the grace of a freshly refuelled jumbo hitting the runway with its wheels up? Rush to Relate? No. We recarpeted the entire house. Brilliant.

Good news for the next couple (in within three months), and for the carpet salesman at Shags 'R' Us, but retail failed to save the day.

Which brings me to my new sofa and the extremely delicate subject of 'Tom' and 'Kelly' and the cat-and-mouse game she and I, until last weekend, had been playing. With our clothes off, mainly.

We were having a lot of fun researching what could have led to a bestselling *Cheapskate Adulterers' Guide to London's*

Top Fifty Hot Hotels. Each Wednesday, I would visit wotif.com to check room deals, and each Thursday . . .

If you can't wait for the book (and, as I've lost my co-researcher, you may have to), I can reveal that No. 1 would almost certainly have been the Dolphin Square Hotel. Kelly and I spent our last night together there, in a delightful three-room suite, tormenting room service and playing the twelve-hour version of Happy Couples. It dawned on me, lounging on a sofa after breakfast, pretending to watch Dermot and Natasha (on one of the two televisions, mark you), but actually basking in the unfamiliar and thus exotic details of Kelly's morning ritual, that we were actors in a theatre of domesticity: a made-up couple on a set, acting out the upside of a Proper Relationship, with none of the down – the cold, back-to-back nights, hollow rows and slow, draining ebb of desire.

It was in this same uncomplicated and erotically charged mood of *faux ménage* that Kelly chose my new sofa as we gambolled in John Lewis. The moment she threw herself on the leather Monaco I had to have it (£895, including delivery, since you ask) and her.

And then, from daydreaming on the softly furnished set of *Same Time Next Year*, crash – into the jagged plot of a J. G. Ballard novel. After a weekend of ominous silence, I receive a stark text message (for such is the way we live now): 'I'm in hospital, car accident, surgery tomorrow, don't worry . . . X.'

Fear, pain, guilt and morphine: she tells Tom 'everything' (I hardly think so; at least, I *hope* not). He calls me and we have the exact same conversation I had six years before with the man I discovered was sleeping with the 'love of my life'. They are going to make it work, I should crawl back under the stone, etc., etc.

Actually, despite the sudden loss of my sleeping partner, I hope they *do* make it work, but my hunch says, buy shares in Shags 'R' Us.

His agony is that I know more about his relationship than

he does. My agony is that I don't get to eat the patient's grapes, stroke her hair or see her again.

And, yes, I know it serves me right.

As for the Monaco, it feels bigger now I sit on it alone in my otherwise sparsely furnished flat. Or maybe it's just that I feel a little bit smaller.

4
How to Give Advice

Dear Microwave Man

Like you, I find myself suddenly 'single', but with the added complication of children just approaching their teens. I do not feel that I could inflict a succession of 'friends' upon them and I think I would have to be pretty sure about a woman before even introducing her to them. Is this unrealistic? Also, how do you get started on dating again? I am finding it hard to contemplate the idea.

Name and address withheld

Microwave Man writes: I guess a lot depends on the circumstances of your finding yourself single (not many women are drawn to wife-killers, for instance). I don't think it is unrealistic for you to consider your children's feelings, but surely the more of a deal you make of this issue, the more important it will become to them? And would you having a series of 'friends' really be an 'infliction' for them? Maybe you are using them as an excuse to put off action; besides, your happiness is probably more important to your children than you think. And, remember this: the kids will grow up, have lives and ruined relationships of their own and will probably dump you in some lousy home for dribbling old folk the first time you 'have a fall'. Don't think of it as dating so much as self-defence.

There are a lot of very seriously screwed-up people out there. (Actually, there are plenty in here, too, but at least you know where they are during working hours.) I know this because, as soon as my first column appears, they all start writing to me.

Men don't get the joke, and ask me for advice. I mean, isn't it obvious that, if I knew anything about relationships, I'd be in one for longer than a week? And women *do* get the joke, but *still* ask me for advice, as though advice is something they need so desperately, they are prepared to seek it even from an obviously, clearly corrupt and inherently untrustworthy source on the slightest of wholly imagined off chances that, for them, and just this once, all that corruption and lack of trustworthiness might be set aside.

Which is, I suppose, the same thinking that convinces every woman that she is the one who will change that man. The sixth Mrs Henry VIII was like that.

Soon, I am appearing weekly on the newspaper's website, conducting live 'surgeries'. I am the lunatic on the locked ward who has found the psychiatrist's white coat with the name badge still attached:

'All alone with your sofa, your DVDs and your little black book? Microwave Man, guru of the bachelor classes, answers your questions.'

Guru of the sodding bachelor classes? Christ, even the *newspaper* doesn't get the joke. I think I might write a self-help book. Now that *would* be a joke.

God knows, I wish I *was* writing a self-help book: that's where all the money is, coping with 'afluenza', now that none of us really has anything to worry about – you know: starvation, rickets, polio, global warming. Oh, wait, no; that last one's still a bit of a concern, right? But never mind all that: what about *me*?

Just look at the miles of shelf space given over to self-help in any bookshop (although, curiously, I have never seen anyone, except for the occasional plain, thin woman reader, standing and thumbing through books in this section of any bookshop. And I visit a lot of bookshops. Not for the books, obviously, but for the CDs, DVDs, magazines and coffee shops which make them such a great place to while away a slow Saturday afternoon and to pick up plain thin women clearly in need of some kind of help coming from anyone other than themselves).

Do you know, I once stood in a bookshop in Khartoum,[18] the camel-shit-stained capital of Sudan, the largest and one of the poorest countries in Africa, where people starve to death with the seasons, and watched in amazement as poor but proud, rag-wearing locals who had queued through the night at the central Khartoum branch of Barnes & Noble for a signing by the author of *How to Get What You Want and Want What You Have* rioted when they found that what they couldn't get was the book.

It had sold out, and it had sold out because the store had ordered only half as many copies as it had of the new, cartoon-illuminated, Eezee-Read® UN Food Council book, *How to Grow Enough Food to Get You and Your Large Extended Family through the Inevitable Upcoming Drought*,[19] figuring reasonably enough that this was the type of reading that might appeal to a subsistence-level community with one of the highest child mortality rates (and the lowest literacy rates) in the world.[20] Only, it wasn't.

Here's the thing about self-help books: just like Orwell's Ministry of Truth, the entire genre is predicated on precisely the opposite of the declared principle. *Self*-help would entail dealing with a situation by one*self*, or at least by harnessing those resources one was fortunate enough to have around – friends, family, inherited wealth, armed robbery (aka inherited wealth with violence). Buying a book which claims to present a universal solution to precise, unique, genetically fingerprinted psycho-emotional dilemmas is to abrogate responsibility for your own happiness and, as a consequence, to cut yourself off from your own emotional resourcefulness – to deny, in fact, that you even *have* such resources.

It's part of the same instant-gratification, hole-in-the-wall culture that has some of us reaching for a high-powered rifle and heading for a tall building with a good field of fire if one small thing doesn't go our way in an otherwise near-perfect day: 95

18 No, I didn't.
19 I made this one up, too; that's what you can do when you are a novelist.
20 I was going to back this up with statistics here, but why bother?

per cent happiness is no longer good enough. Caught at a red traffic light for longer than thirty seconds? *Jesus fucking Christ, I can't fucking well believe this is happening to me! What have I done to deserve this??? This is so fucked!!*

If you don't believe me, visit a bookshop, find the windswept 'self-help' section, pull up a bushel of tumbleweed and check out some of the titles. I mean, would *you* be seen reading such books on the Tube? How come I've never seen *anybody* reading one in public? Who in their right mind (and with even a scintilla of self-respect) would cast aside all those thousands of years of hunter-gatherer self-reliance in favour of the kind of pseudo-psychological advice packaged cynically into such books as *Anxiety Toolbox* or *Is Your Family Driving You Mad?* or *Why Men Don't Listen and Women Can't Read Maps* or *Women Who Run with the Wolves* or *Women Who Think Too Much* or *Sorghum, Millet and Maize: How to Grow Cereals in Sub-Saharan East Africa?*[21]

Oh, sorry; that last one must have been slipped in there by some kind of satirical social prankster.[22]

Maybe people shop for this stuff in private, secret, after-hours sessions and read it only in private, or under false book-jackets.

The worst thing about this type of book (aside from the offence of the easy solutions it falsely promises to complex problems) is the fact that the advice it peddles boils down to a handful of old saws and clichés of the type you might expect to hear if you poured out your troubles to a barmaid.

So, here: why not save yourself the cost and the embarrassment? Cut out and keep this universal five-point panacea to all

21 Yet another fiction, but I bet there's something like it out there. I just wasn't about to waste time looking it up. Life's too short for facts (especially in sub-Saharan Africa); that's why fiction is so great.
22 The same kind of satirical social prankster who works at Waterstones off Fenchurch Street in the City of London and whose guerrilla shelf-stocking has made it my favourite bookshop, *despite* the absence of a café. This tripping free-thinker on the staff has placed two volumes of Aldous Huxley's *The Doors of Perception* among all the execrable self-help books. How refreshing to find advice there, from the man who dismissed meditation as 'doze's first cousin', that the best self-help that one can administer is four-tenths of a gramme of mescaline. I don't know about that, but have you seen how *fast* that snail is moving?

emotional ills. My gift to you. Who knows? This could even be the chapter that earns me a coveted slot on the self-help shelves.

The next time someone feeds your heart through a meat-grinder, never mind: take a few deep breaths, perhaps count to ten, put on a brave smile, look on the bright side, perhaps even dust yourself down and start all over again, and then cheer yourself up with your favourite adage:

(Start cutting here) ....

1. Never mind, plenty more fish in the sea/pebbles on the beach.
2. Never mind, what doesn't kill you makes you stronger.
3. Never mind, time's a great healer.
4. Never mind, worse things happen at sea.
5. Come on, we all know life has no real meaning, you might be better off dead. I mean, after all, Albert Camus said that deciding to take one's own life was the only real free choice open to mankind. Mind you, that didn't stop him playing football for Algeria, and playing to a pretty high standard, come to that.[23]

(Stop cutting here) ....

The very, very worst sub-genre of this type of book is that which cranks up the expectation levels by promising a miracle cure for the incurable in *extra* quick time. And, rather like those men's magazines that promise on the cover, 'You too can have a body like this in just eight seconds' (by hanging around Soho and picking one up, darling), there is such fierce competition for the sucker buck in this age of instant gratification that publishers and authors are laying claim to ever more amazing and rapid results.

Thus, *Letting Go: A Twelve-Week Personal Action Program to Overcome a Broken Heart* or, for those of you to whom three months seems like an awfully long time, how about *How to Heal*

23 Not all barmaids will say this, obviously. This was from Sally at the Cartesian Dualist's Arms, Croydon (The Fox and Gynaecologist until the hunting laws changed).

a Broken Heart in Thirty Days? If you really are in a hurry to get happy, let me recommend *Change Your Life in Seven Days* (that's easy: move to Sudan with just $5 and try to make it as a subsistence farmer. Or maybe head for Texas, rob a bank and kill a cop. That should change your life fundamentally. And quite possibly shorten it).

Studying medicine and fulfilling a lifelong ambition to help others while improving your own self-esteem will, regretfully, take rather longer. But hey: who the hell is going to buy a book called *Change Your Life in Seven Years. Minimum. Before You Even Get Near Patients with a Scalpel in Your Hand*?

I get a lot of self-help books sent to me. Not because publishers care about my happiness, but because they care about their sales, which is fair enough. I find they come in very useful: one small pile is standing in for the missing leg of my coffee table and another is holding open the fire door to the hallway (which just goes to show how dangerous these things can be). In my experience, this type of book is nearly always written by somebody who is a Top Psychologist. In fact, there are so many Top Psychologists that it's a wonder there is any other kind. But there are, apparently. Ask the British Psychological Society about job opportunities and they'll talk about clinical, educational, forensic and counselling psychology, or health, occupational, teaching and research, neuropsychological and even sport and recreation psychology.

But not top psychology, oddly. Guess all the top jobs are taken.

Then I worked it out. Top Psychology is an accreditation awarded not by some fusty old college after three long years of dull postgraduate research but one conferred instantly by virtue of a single telephone call from a tabloid newspaper or an appearance on a popular breakfast-television show.

This is how it works. I write a column about being broken-hearted, and the very next day a switched-on PR delivers a copy of *How to Mend a Broken Heart*,[24] 'by Top Psychologist Sarah Day'.

24 When the money runs out I'm going to write one about being broke, and sit back and wait for the NatWest bank to send round a sack of used fivers. By Top Royal Mint Printer Stig O'Blomqvist.

I'm about to bin it when something about the author's picture catches my eye.

Hello, I think. I know this woman.

And that's when the training kicks in. That year on the journalism course at Harlow Technical College in 1979 wasn't wasted, I muse, as I make the instant and smooth transition from mild-mannered weekly columnist to Top Investigative Reporter. If I thought it would help, I'd put my underpants on outside my trousers, but it seems unnecessary. Instead, I fire up Factiva.[25]

The first thing I learn is that *How to Mend a Broken Heart* (blinding insight: 'many of us will have our hearts broken several times throughout our lives and between relationships we will be single') is not Sarah's only guidebook for the forlorn. There's also *Get the Happiness Habit: How You Can Choose Your Steps to a Happy Life* and *Get the Self-Esteem Habit* (all three, oddly, published by Hodder & Stoughton's *Religious* Division. Something to do with the subliminal 'habit' references? God only knows. Presumably).

It is only when I visit the desperately depressing website The Continuity Booth,[26] which, entirely without irony and in an atmosphere of apparently genuine reverence, documents and tracks the careers of British television's most minor celebrities – local TV continuity announcers – that I remember where I first saw Sarah: as a co-presenter of East of England regional TV programme *About Anglia* in the late seventies.

That's it! She was the one with the hideous pudding-basin haircut, neck scarf and simpering local-TV manner we used to leer at over tea in our lodgings in Harlow. My God, Sarah: has it come to *this*?

What I didn't know about Sarah was that she had 'started her television career as a lead singer with the Black and White

---

25 A research tool so absolute in its sweep that if you, dear reader, had access to it you wouldn't need the likes of me any more. But keep that under your mercury-contaminated hat.

26 Also known among aficionados, on account of the age of some of the featured stars, as 'The Incontinence Booth'.

Minstrels, where fellow Anglia presenter Pam Rhodes was employed as a dancer'. What I still don't know is what happened to Pam Rhodes, but my guess is that she's now a psychiatrist.

Eventually, Sarah gave up blacking up as a golliwog and, after a punishing few years spent wearing neck scarves and pudding-basin haircuts and telling the east of the nation about a surfboarding chicken in Lowestoft, retrained as a psychotherapist. Well, who could blame her, and who better, after all she'd been through?

Today, our Sarah knows everything and, for a small fee, will lend her knowledge to assist almost any organization with a marketing problem and a cheque book. In 2001, for instance, she leapt selflessly to the aid of the Tea Council which, according to the press release I received, was in turn doing its best to head off a major emotional crisis for the nation's womenfolk, triggered by a flood of weepie films from Hollywood.

'Over 80 per cent of women shed a tear during *Titanic*, and the latest batch of weepies is set to be equally as traumatic,' announced the alarmed Tea Council. I was on the edge of my chair with concern. And there was more. 'Films such as *Captain Corelli's Mandolin* and the summer blockbuster *Pearl Harbor*, with their emotionally charged storylines, could leave film-goers tearful and emotionally unbalanced.'

Nation's womenfolk (So! Emotionally unstable all along, it seems. *Aha!*): 'Good heavens! What is to become of us? What should we do?'

The caring Tea Council: 'Have a nice cup of tea, love!'

Funny, that.

And, 'According to psychotherapist Sarah Day, "The current deluge of emotionally exhausting films will doubtless be very much to the taste of the young British female film-goer, but there's no doubt that she'll spend much of her time watching them in tears."'

Gosh, no doubt at all! So what's the solution, Mammy? I mean, Sarah?

'"I'm issuing a suggestion to all the major cinema chains that they serve the audience tea prior to each performance. If they don't, the nation's fairer sex will have to bring their own 'Rosie Lee' in vacuum flasks!"'

Seriously.

Now, I saw *Captain Corelli's Mandolin*, but I saw women neither crying nor swigging tea from flasks. Certainly, nobody offered *me* any tea to offset my obvious distress. Could it be that nobody was listening to Sarah and the well-meaning Tea Council? Or could it be that the Tea Council was just hoping for a quick plug in the pages of the *Daily Mail*?

In December 2002, Sarah was back, this time on behalf of handbag.com, 'the UK's first and leading site for women'. (Bless. Women must be thrilled.) Anyway, this site's stunt was to have users vote for the UK's Amazing Women. It was a strangely subservient little poll: 'The UK's "Greatest Briton" may be a man,' bleated the release, 'but the UK boasts some Amazing Women who are ready to follow in his footsteps.'

So, behind every great man, there really is a not-so-great woman, then.

Oddly enough, handbag.com hadn't managed to track down Andrea Dworkin for her views on this slightly retrograde development but, luckily, they were able to get in touch with Sarah, who – thankfully for lovers of sound advice everywhere – just happened to be between endorsements.

And here's what she said, in full. Just in case you think I'm making up this stuff.

Psychologist Sarah Day comments on the need for female role models in the twenty-first century: 'In today's uncertain and often bewildering world, we look for guidance from mentors and role models. And these top women certainly fit the bill. Of course, most of us will never meet any of these exceptional females – but we feel that we KNOW them. We certainly know a lot about them. All these women epitomize the best of British characteristics and help us identify our own hopes and ambitions. And, perhaps most interestingly of all, every one of them is entirely individual. There are no clones or poor imitations here! They also have oodles of get up and go and palpable enthusiasm, which is very attractive – and highly inspiring. And above all, we do like to be inspired by our heroines.'

Oodles, eh?

Christmas 2003. While I'm depressed and envying the turkey in the oven at gas mark four, Sarah is taking care of an altogether graver emergency. A press release plops into my in-tray and my eyes light up at the sight of the familiar name. She has been called in by caring drinks giant Diageo to comment on the shock revelation of a survey that 'a staggering 7.3 million Britons could be putting their career on the line at the office Christmas party this year'. The reason? 'Inappropriate behaviour[27] after over-indulging on their drinks.'

This is Diageo, the caring drinks giant responsible for such brands as Smirnoff, Guinness, Baileys and Johnnie Walker and the snappy slogan, 'Every day, everywhere, people enjoy our brands. Together, we celebrate life responsibly.'

Oh, and 'staggering Britons'. I hope you got that, because I'm not sure Diageo's copy-writers did.

Surely, if they were *that* caring, they'd just stop making booze and flogging it to young people? But I expect it isn't booze that gets people pissed: it's people.

As a trained psychologist, former *About Anglia* presenter and erstwhile Black and White Minstrel, Sarah knows all about making a fool of oneself in public and was particularly worried about the young people who might get up and make an exhibition of themselves. Ahem. (Well, at least they would have the excuse of having consumed excessive amounts of alcohol.)

Sarah's clinical insight was, as ever, dazzling in its simplicity: The research reveals definite patterns of behaviour and resulting

27 We are never told the precise nature of this behaviour, but my money's on people getting bladdered out of their tiny skulls on some of Diageo's many alcoholic products, running around like chimps, vomiting on their boss and generally having a good time. But this is only a guess.

scenarios that those drinking to excess can, and regularly do, find themselves in.

No *shit*! Thank *God* for such research.[28]

'There's no doubt that eighteen- to twenty-four-year-olds tend to believe that they have complete control over their actions – irrespective of how much they drink. Unfortunately, research shows that this is not actually the case.' That'll be research carried out by police in Reading town centre every Friday night.

It's almost Valentine's Day before I hear from Sarah again, although she hasn't, sadly, sent me a card. This time she is lending the benefit of her expertise to Mills & Boon, a publisher of romantic fiction for women. (The company boasts that, over the past forty years, its limp characters have 'kissed each other over 20,000 times, shared about 30,000 hugs and headed for the altar at least 7,000 times', but not one of them has, to the best of my knowledge, enjoyed a single shag, which is a bit sad, really.)

In the exhaustive Mills & Boon survey, men came out kind of shamefully on the issue of where, other than on the lips, they best liked to be kissed. According to Mills & Boon, 71 per cent of women would choose to be kissed, if not on the mouth, then on the neck. Forty per cent of men, however, said they would rather be kissed on their knob. Mills & Boon actually said 'an X-rated part of their anatomy', but they meant 'knob'.

So both men and women, in their own way, lied. Speaking for men, at least, you can skip the mouth and head straight for the quivering manhood.[29]

Sarah, however (billed this time as 'Prominent psychologist and relationship expert Sarah Day'), cut directly to the chase with her customary brevity and ice-sharp acuity.

'Kissing,' she revealed, 'is all about romance. Many women tell me that they value kissing more than any other part of romantic contact.[30] Kissing is one of life's greatest pleasures and

28 From the tireless Faculty of the Bleeding Obvious.
29 This means knob as well.
30 'Hi Sarah! How's David? By the way, I meant to say last time I saw you that I value kissing more than any other part of romantic contact. Yup, that's right: even more than full-on oral!'

at its best takes our breath away and makes us swoon with delight. A great kiss doesn't just touch our lips – it's much more than that!'

That's enough from Sarah and the Verbal Incontinence Booth. The point is this: self-help doesn't come out of a book written by a former Black and White Minstrel, or anybody else. *It comes out of yourself.* Or, in the case of my friend Simon, it comes out of a guitar shop. Simon's my age but, almost every Friday and some Saturday nights, he straps on a thirty-year-old Fender Stratocaster, takes to the stage of some smoky, noisy, flock-walled pub and acts like he's eighteen. As a father of two teenagers, with almost twenty-five years of marriage behind him and a large mortgage still firmly ahead of him, some would say he's in denial, but he says he's in De Nile, which is the name of his three-piece band (combined age, 153).

And, as therapies go, it sort of works. Well, that and the Prozac. He's not harming anyone and has probably done more singlehandedly to support the guitar industry than Eric Clapton (who probably doesn't even have to buy his axes). Every time Simon gets depressed and the drugs aren't working – he buys another guitar. He has about twelve, at last count. And countless effects pedals, recording devices and software programs, none of which has been *quite* the right device to help him make the big breakthrough to superstardom. 'Technology has failed me,' he likes to say.

Not that he really cares. On a good night, De Nile rock da house, even if the house comprises three drunks and a bored barmaid at the Fox and Gynaecologist in Bedford. And some nights, he plays that Fender like his soul is on fire. Which, of course, some nights, it is.

Occasionally, I go along to a gig (on these nights, it's three drunks and a Diet Coke-drinker, trying to chat up the bored barmaid). One night, after the drummer and bassist had gone home and I was helping Simon carefully to coil his cables and neatly pack everything away into the trunk of his large family BMW (he is just a *little* anal about stuff such as the way his cables are curled), we were talking about this and that but nothing much, and I had crammed myself into the front passenger seat with two guitar cases wedged between me and the dashboard when, right out of the blue, just as we got to his house, Simon started crying. Just like that. Great, big, gulping, sobbing crying. For a moment I thought he was joking, or maybe overreacting to my having slipped a Del Amitri CD into the player. I mean, OK, they can be a little bit cheesy but they aren't *that* bad.

You know someone for twenty years and then you don't know how to put a hand on their shoulder. I tried and kind of put my wrist there instead, hand and fingers dithering safely out of contact. 'What's the matter?' I asked, and he shook his head and said, 'I . . . *sob* . . . don't . . . *sob* . . . know . . . *sob* . . .'

'How can I help?'

He nodded towards the CD player and said, 'You . . . *sob* . . . can . . . *sob* . . . turn . . . *sob* . . . that crap . . . *sob* . . . off, for a start . . . *sob* . . .' and then sort of laughed and sobbed at the same time and snorted stuff out of his nose. I pulled a tissue out of my pocket and handed it to him. He wiped his face and then banged his head down on the centre of the steering wheel, which made the horn give a little toot.

'Oh, God, it's such a bloody cliché, but I suppose it all boils down to the big question,' he blurted out.

'Which one? What would have happened in the World Cup if Bobby Moore hadn't been arrested for shoplifting at Mexico 1970? If the Samaritans are so bloody good how come they never call you? What were the Beatles *really* saying in the run-off track at the end of *A Day in the Life*?'

'Oh, ha bloody ha. No, you know: "What's It All About, Alfie?"'

'Ah, *that* big question.'

I looked around the big car stuffed with toys – enough amps and guitars and effects boards to make Hendrix look like a part-timer – and through the windscreen at the big, beautiful house, with its perfectly trimmed lawns and gravel drive, and thought about his two children and his small, beautiful wife asleep upstairs in their huge bed. I thought about the day, maybe twenty-five years ago, when Simon and his then band, the Idle Frets, had spent a week visiting every A&R man in London with their demo tape. He still tells the story of how Waterman, of Stock, Aitken and Waterman, had half-listened to the tape while simultaneously yelling to an underling on the phone, and had then slammed down the phone and jabbed at the reject button on the cassette player, spinning the cassette across the room to Simon with a cursory, 'Nah, nothing I haven't heard a thousand times before'. Simon gave up writing songs after that. Waterman went on to make a fortune with Kylie Minogue. Simon should have been so lucky.

'You want my advice?' I asked. He shook his head, but I gave it to him anyway. 'Buy another guitar. Thirteen could be your lucky number. And another thing. You know the third chord in the chorus of "Can't Stop this Thing We Started"? It's wrong.'

He raised his head from the steering wheel and looked at me. His face was wet with tears, but at least the sobbing had stopped. 'Wrong? What do you mean, "wrong"?'

'As in, not right. It struck me tonight. I'm sure it should be some kind of major chord, and you're definitely playing a minor.'

He shaped his left hand around an imaginary guitar neck, muttering his way through the song and changing the chord fingering as he went. 'Oh, yeah, maybe. I see what you mean . . .'

'Got any beers in the fridge?'

'Does the Pope crap in the woods?' Now smiling again, Simon jumped out of the car, 'But first . . .' and starting peeing up against one of the ornamental shrubs that guarded the entrance to the house. He is *so* rock 'n' roll. Then we started unloading the BMW.

Please, Don't Quote Me
Friday 3 October 2003

I don't normally fall back on quotations, but indulge me as I whip out a cracker from the fabled Aesop, who said: 'Never trust the advice of a man in difficulties.'

I mention this only because ever since Microwave Man began answering questions from readers online once a fortnight, I have noticed that while women merely express a certain cynical sorrow/horror at my situation/attitudes, men, rather alarmingly, actually ask my advice about relationships.

I mean, *come on*. Haven't you been paying attention? If I was any good at the relationship thing, do you really think I'd be on my own at (almost) forty-eight, sleeping around and dining out of plastic containers? Besides, as François de La Rochefoucauld once quipped, 'Good advice is something a man gives when he is too old to set a bad example,' and the sun has yet to set on my said setting.

Don't get me wrong. I love that we're bonding – even with you, Adele Briskman, of Melbourne, Australia ('Why are you soooo vain?' Um, because I think this song is about me?), and you, Mick Barfield, of Southend ('Regrets? You seem to have a lot. What's the secret of your lack of success?') – but when you take me too seriously I start to blink rapidly and wonder if it isn't getting just a little too hot in here. I mean, can't we just be friends – maybe see each other once every week or so?

But tough love I can handle, so bring it on, Ms Name-and-address-withheld ('Would you describe yourself as safe in a taxi?'). My Ernie Wise Straightman Award goes to Trevor Holmes, of Southport. His opening salvo, 'Microwave my arse!', has to rank as one of the great smash-me comedy lobs of all time.

So, OK, Trev, will three minutes at full power do it for you?

Trev continues: 'Men can cook for themselves as well as females can, if not better. What's stopping you?'

Ooh, well, let's see now . . . apart from a pathological fear of pinnies, oven gloves and fat-spattered body parts, three things: a) I could slave my (unmicrowaved) arse off all day and still fail to produce anything as tasty as the worst thing from the Tesco's Finest range; b) I have many better ways to spend my time (and can think of several things I'd rather be doing with an electric whisk than whisking eggs); and c) cooking is for fat 'celebrity' chefs and fear-crazed 'new' men who delude themselves into believing that they can earn chocolate brownie points with the Polit-Correct Bureau by assuming a constant state of fricassee frenzy.

Take my tip, Trev: get out of that kitchen and stop rattling those pots and pans. It's not big, it's not clever, Trevor, and (here's the real point) women only *pretend* to like it when men muscle in on the Miele. (Although not Nora Ephron's mother, whose sharp take on cooking was that 'if you worked hard and prospered, someone else would do it for you.')

Talking of microwaving *derrières*, a big *merci* to the anonymous correspondent who introduced me to the fabulous website Unwise Microwave Oven Experiments. Once you wade through more disclaimers than a double-glazing commercial on local radio, you are into a fabulous cornucopia of incendiary insanity.

Although the authors of this site should clearly be locked away for their own protection, there is much real science to be learnt (and dangerous fun to be had) from such experiments as 'Cuppa burning plasma', 'Snifter of neon', 'Fun with grapes' and 'Creating ball lightning'.

In one particularly entertaining section, the site's own resident Microwave Man shows himself, in his replies to readers' queries, to be my kind of guy.

'Doesn't microwave energy lower the food's nutrition?' enquires one sap. 'I don't know,' snaps our hero. 'Who cares?'

Quite.

5
How to be a Bad Father

Dear Microwave Man
Doesn't it make you uncomfortable that some of the women you go out with aren't that much older than your son's girlfriend?
Name and address withheld

Microwave Man writes: No, but it keeps him on his toes.

So far in my life, I have had a total of five Momentous Phone Calls. So far. This, in chronological order, is roughly how they went:

Momentous Call Number 1:
Jonathan, I have just had a visit from your girlfriend's mother. She has found your letters.

Sick, lurching feeling, sitting, aged fifteen, listening to my mother on the phone in the housemaster's study at school and mentally reviewing the catalogue of increasingly depraved letters I have been exchanging with the girl I picked up in the park during the last school holiday. My mother moved home a lot. I'm not sure why – sherry debts, maybe. Whatever the reason, at the end of almost every term I found myself on my own, in a strange place, with no friends.

And, at fifteen, with lots of unemployed erections.

I can't remember the girl's name now, although, oddly, I can see her chubby little face quite clearly. We were sitting on the swings in the park near my mother's rented house in Bromley when she grew suddenly bored of conversation, pulled up her skirt and showed me her knickers. She was older than me and, I think, more experienced.

In the last few days before returning to school we did almost everything except the one thing I really wanted to do but had no clear idea of how to go about doing. Back at school I was counting down the days to the next school holiday, fantasizing about parks and swings and knickers and turning a lot of the excess steam into steamy letters. Chubby Girl had stored them under her bed, where her mother, it seems, had found them. I expect she spotted the steam escaping from the envelopes.

The thought that my mother has read them is almost enough to render me impotent for life. Almost.

Momentous Call Number 2:
Jonny, I have some bad news. I think I might be pregnant.

Me: 'Who is this?'

Sick, lurching feeling, aged twenty-seven, a few days after splitting up with the caller, a casual girlfriend.

Momentous Call Number 3:
Jonny, I'm worried. My period is late.

Sick, lurching, etc., a year or two later. A different caller. The same solution.

Momentous Call Number 4:
Hello, caller, our best information at this moment is that the individual you are calling about is not, repeat not, among the casualties listed in the incident to which you refer.

So my son is alive. Relief of sick, lurching feeling triggered by a stupid, stupid, stupid, insensitive midnight news broadcast at the beginning of the invasion of Iraq: *'It is thought that a member of 539 assault squadron Royal Marines has been killed in action near Basra, but details will not be released until relatives have been informed.'*

Thanks for that, BBC News 24. A very, very, very long night.

And now . . .

Momentous Call Number 5:

Hello, Jonathan?

As surprise telephone calls go, this one was a cracker.

'Yes. Who's that?'

It's Jonathan.

'Jonathan? I'm Jonathan.'

'Me, too.'

And so on. Well, I didn't say it was gripping dialogue, and I'll spare you the full transcript. Suffice to say that, after some confusion on my part, I learn, while sitting at my desk towards the end of a day and thinking about nothing much in particular beyond my plans for the evening with Purple Girl, who is coming down to London for a rematch, that I am not the only Jonathan with those genes. And that the other one is my brother.

Well, half-brother. And there are two, actually. And a demi-sister. And they have living grandparents, which means I do too, and cousins and uncles and aunts and a whole galaxy of blood relatives.

Bloody hell.

I'm forty-seven (still, just) and *now* they tell me. All along I've had the sort of emotional extended family network support system for which anyone in their right mind, *supposedly*, would give their right arm, and I've never known it.

I'd like to say that I sat down with a thump, that I felt numb, or shocked, or emotional, that I wept down the phone or behaved in any way like one of those distressingly sad, stupid individuals conned by graduate researchers for TV shows into making public arses of themselves on programmes such as *Trisha* and *Jerry Springer*. But I didn't. In fact, to be honest, the only thing I remember idly thinking was, 'I wonder if sleeping with a half-sister is incest?'

Which, apparently, it is.

I have never understood those people who bemoan the fact that they have never known their parents, although I can't help noticing that it is, usually, women who get up on those TV programmes or appear in the touchy-feely features sections of newspapers (what we used to call the women's pages) weeping and agonizing over the father/mother/brother/sister/family cat they have never met. Adoption, it seems, is just as bad as abandonment, or maybe worse, but perhaps not quite so bad as being the child of an unknown sperm-donor. But either way, for my money, it boils down to this: if a parent gives up their child, it's because they don't want them. In which case, sod them. Besides, families can be such a collective pain in the arse. When you've escaped all that crap, why go looking for trouble?

I never knew my father, although I did see him once. My mother and I travelled to Preston by coach when I was about six or seven. I had no idea where we were going. I knew only that it was a great adventure that involved getting up before the birds and getting away from the bombsite that was, even as late as the early sixties, Peckham. We stayed with a relative on my father's side and I remember I got into trouble because she kept offering me more buttered fruit loaf and I kept eating it, and later my mother scolded me for being greedy and said, 'They are even poorer than us.' But I wasn't being greedy, I was being hungry, and they can't have been that poor because they had a fire burning in the grate *during the day*.

On the way up the M1 the sun rose as we stopped in a motor-way service station, and I had never seen a sunrise before, and I have had a weakness for such places ever since. And, to a lesser extent, for sunrises. I find it very, very hard to drive past a motor-way service area without stopping. No woman I have ever been with has understood this, or my similarly sourced penchant for Little Chefs.

My father, on the other hand, didn't seem to find it so hard to walk past me as I sat, swinging my legs, on a chair in a wait-ing room outside a solicitor's office in Preston. My mother and I had travelled to the North for her to sign papers relating to their divorce. He just looked at me for a moment and then walked on. I just kept on swinging my legs, which is about all you can do when your feet don't reach the ground, and I never saw him again. I wouldn't know him now if he bit me, although if he did, I would be surprised because – as I now learn from the half-brother I never knew I had – he is dead.

And, until I was the father of my own child, I never thought about him again. Adam was about six or seven and he and I had just spent a few days in the Lake District. The road home took us past Preston, land of my fathers, and before I knew it I was peeling off down the slip road and heading for the village where, thanks to my grandmother's stories, I knew that the family had a pub.

What was I thinking? I suppose I was thinking that maybe, just maybe, my father ought to know he had a grandson. I have no idea why I thought this. Maybe it was the effect of too much fresh air, or of spending time with my son, of whom I had seen precious little since he was three years old and his mother had taken him to live abroad. Perhaps it was just transferred guilt.

Adam was fast asleep in the back when I found the place, and I left him in the car park and ran through the rain and into the bar.

I knew it was a mistake the moment I got through the door. There was a handful of locals, and they all looked at me like I had just walked on to the set of *Deliverance* wearing a party dress and high heels. And they, I swear, all wore those bloody Lowry stickmen flat-hats. Their trousers weren't actually tied off at the ankles with string, but for all I knew their pants were stuffed with tripe and whippets.

Behind the bar I found a man who, it turned out, after some agonizing cross-questioning, was my father's brother-in-law. Out from the back room came a woman who said she was his wife and my father's sister. Or, if you prefer, my aunt.

Well, fancy that, I remember thinking. I have an aunt.

The man was just plain surly, insisting on pronouncing what until then I had always thought of as *my* second name all wrong with his long, dull, flat northern vowels. The woman was, at least, friendly and she took me out the back, made a cup of tea and started to show me photographs. Through the window and the rain streaming down the panes I could see Adam, still fast asleep in the car.

I felt panic rising as 'Auntie' started to itemize the extended family living within a few streets of where we sat. Everyone in this sodding town, it seemed, was a relation. I even had a living grandmother, just a few houses away. Did I want to meet her? No. I didn't. I already have a grandmother, thanks very much, and she is dead. I felt trapped, at the centre of some spider's web of unwanted, claustrophobic intimacy and responsibility, and I just wanted to get the hell out of there.

I mean, can you *imagine* the Christmas card bill?

Before I left, I wrote my name and telephone number on a piece of paper, which she promised to give to my father.

'Funnily enough, love, he'll be home next week for a holiday.'

So he's alive. Check for feelings. Funnily enough, find none.

Daddy, it seems, had enjoyed the Suez crisis so much that, after he left the army, he had moved back to Cairo with his second wife.

'I don't want to cause any problems,' I said. 'I just thought he might like to know that he has a grandson.'

She pulled one of the lace curtains to one side and peered through the rain at the car and Adam, and then said: 'Would you like to see a picture of your father, love?'

I had only ever seen one, which my mother had kept in a silver frame, as if it might have meant something to her, although I couldn't be sure because the only time she ever talked about him was when she was drunk and then she was never really that complimentary. As for Suez, it seems there were really only two things in it for her, and both of them had become lifelong irritants (but not in the good way that leads to pearls in oyster shells) – sand, and me.

There were two men in that photograph, both wearing baggy fifties-vintage trousers and jackets, each standing straight-legged, as men did in those days, one hand in pocket and the other holding a cigarette, and squinting against the sun towards the camera.

In the background was a line of fighter aircraft and, when pressed at school (frequently), I made out my father had been a Spitfire pilot who'd bought it in a dogfight over London during the Battle of Britain. To perpetuate the myth I ended up spending all of my meagre pocket money on Airfix models. By the time I left my prep school I had more Spitfires, trailing plumes of cotton-wool smoke and dangling from the ceiling above my bunk, than Leigh-Mallory had been able to muster for one of his Big Wings[31] in September 1940.

Although in my mind I opted for the taller of the two, I wasn't 100 per cent certain which of the men in the photograph was actually my father, because my mother and I had never, ever talked about anything remotely important at all, other than how badly I was doing at school. I would always promise to try to do better next term, and that was that until the next school report. I always prayed that it would burst into flames or be snatched from my hands by a swooping eagle before she could read it but, oddly, it never was. Things got a bit better when I started to forge exam results for various subjects, but while numbers were one thing, it was difficult to alter the sense of such uncompromising statements as, 'Jonathan is wasting his time and that of other people.'

Besides, I was. Well, who the hell needs a sodding chemistry A level anyway? Apart from chemists, obviously.

And who needs to see a picture of the father he never had? 'No,' I said. 'No thanks, I don't think I do.'

'Auntie' nodded as though this made some kind of sense to her. I never did hear from my father and, quite frankly, I was relieved.

And now here I am sitting outside a riverside pub opposite a bloke, *sporting a ponytail and an earring*, and his not unpleasant wife, listening to a saga of family life which I am struggling to identify as something I give a shit about. Because I don't. Even as he tries to seduce me with pictures of happy families, he

31 The entire flight was destroyed one night by Gibbs Minor, armed, improbably, with a Sopwith Camel and one slipper.

reveals the fissures which run through this one, as they seem to run through all of them. He hasn't, he lets slip, even spoken to his own brother for months for a reason that neither of them can now quite recall.

Now, why, I wonder, would I be reluctant to plunge into that particular gene pool? Well worth spending the odd Christmas alone to be free of all that. Besides: I'd only end up trying to sleep with my half-brother's wife and, while I'm not absolutely certain, I'm fairly sure there's a clause about that somewhere in the Bible. And she really is quite pretty in this half-light.

Dad, it seems, had three children after me, but neglected to mention to any of them that he'd been a father once before. It had all come out, as these things do, at a family wedding, a few years after my father – their father – had died. In a scene that appeared to have all the makings of an episode of *EastEnders*, his wife, perhaps the worse for drink, had announced, 'There's something I think you all should know.'

Classic soap. But not for me, thanks very much.

But now this bloke opposite me, supposedly related by blood and talking and smoking (*smoking!*) and, God help me, from time to time *crying*, is acting like he has found his long-lost elder brother. Well, he has, I suppose, but where exactly does he think we're going to go from here?

He's a computer programmer, or something like that, and lives in Croydon (where, coincidentally and thanks to our mutual father, I was born in shame in a private nursing home), but he's still got the Black Country accent and he wants me to meet his brother, and their sister, who still live up in Lancashire.

I suppress the urge to say no outright or to ask, 'Is she pretty?', and go away promising to call but wondering exactly what it is that these people want.

Later, alone at home, I start to get angry. This lot have had the works: mother, father, siblings and family on a scale to rival the Windsors, and yet they want *more*? What about me? I'm the one who's grown up alone, with only an ailing grandmother, an alcoholic mother and an Action Man platoon for company, and yet they're the ones acting like they've been deprived of something.

Hell! It should be me boo-hooing! I try for a bit, but it doesn't happen.

The more I think about it, the more incensed I become. Finally, half-bro' calls again and I tell him that I don't want to see him, or any of them, again. After that my half-sister calls me a couple of times, half-drunk, late at night. Her children want to see me, she says, but after years of inoculation, I am immune to emotional blackmail from pissed women and, compared with my mother, this one's a shambling amateur. And, actually, she didn't say children, she said 'kiddies'.

I have come through forty-seven years on my own. To embrace a family now would be an admission of failure. Besides, I have a family of my own. Well, part of one.

Talking of failures, after my wife and I tried, half-heartedly, and failed to patch up our differences by recarpeting the house, she took Adam and went to live in Tenerife. He was aged three, and I struggled with two emotions: a kind of anguish that was little more than self-pity, and the joy of liberation. I have just five key memories of the first two and a half years of Adam's life:

1. Leaving the hospital, aged twenty-six, carrying miniature humanoid lifeform. Filled with panic at thought of how utterly dependent it is on me and how utterly ill-equipped I am to be that depended upon. Grapple for a few moments with idea of handing baby to his mother and running off down the street, never to return.
2. The terrible, noxious stench of the average soiled nappy.
3. Endless sleepless nights spent either pacing up and down with Adam, temporarily placated, dribbling over my shoulder, or lying wide awake, praying for sleep but tensed for the inevitable first snuffles from the room next door signalling the next bout of pacing up and down. During one long, dark night of the soul, understand with shocking clarity how easy it is for parents to batter babies. (Especially if they live above a fish shop.)

4. When Adam finally discovers how to sleep, lying awake hoping to hear sounds indicating he is still alive, tiptoeing into his room every half an hour to make sure he is still breathing and thus disturbing him and leading again to cycle outlined in 3, above.
5. Pulling Adam out of his baby seat in the car after a shopping trip one Christmas, seconds before drink-driver mounts pavement and smashes into back of it. Pure chance. Almost left him in there, sleeping, while I took the potatoes indoors instead.

And that's it, really. I don't remember him saying 'Da-da' for the first time, or anything else. I don't remember him starting to walk, using a potty, blowing out candles on a cake, learning to ride a bike or agreeing to eat mushrooms.

Aged twenty-nine and finally off the hook on which I had impaled myself eight years before, I travelled and played and generally enjoyed myself. From time to time I sent stuff to Adam – bows and arrows from the Amazon, a dried piranha fish, shark's teeth from the western beaches of Florida. That sort of stuff.

A couple of times, including one memorable three-month visit when he was five and which covered the high points of fireworks night and Christmas, he came to stay with me in England. Both of us remember that Christmas, and that bonfire party. They mean more, somehow, than if we had repeated the same ritual every year. That, at least, is what I tell myself.

Then, when Adam was seven, I visited him in Tenerife and stayed for a fortnight, playing daddy. I booked an apartment near the beach and Adam stayed with me. Every morning I got up early to drive him to school. Even the morning after the night I traded slugs of Southern Comfort with an Australian barmaid I was trying to seduce, only to discover that she was a lot better at handling her drink than I was.

I woke with a splitting headache. Adam was standing alongside the bed, dressed in his shorts and regulation white shirt and ready for school with his little He Man backpack over his shoulder. Through my agony I could see Loraine, or Sherri, or whatever her name was, lying alongside me. Actually, I smelt her before I saw her: a subtle potpourri of perfume, sweat, chlorine and Southern Comfort. Nice.

'You got her, then,' said Adam, who had witnessed the early stages of my attempted conquest at the pool bar.

'No, I think she got me,' I said, groaning as I sat up.

As I put my feet on the cold tiles, a stab of pain flashed from my right shin. It was covered in blood and had stuck to the sheet, which had now torn off. The wound was bleeding again. I had a vague memory of tripping on the steps on the way up from the pool. I had other vague memories of swimming in the pool, of throwing up on the side of the pool (at least, I hoped it was on the side) and of lying on a sun lounger under Loraine, or Kylie, and the stars, wondering why they were cartwheeling across the night sky so much faster than usual.

What I didn't have, however, was any memory of having sex with the woman now lying alongside me.

Outstanding.

The drive in the rickety old Seat hire car up the mountain to the school that morning, however, was memorable. I have no idea how I negotiated all those hairpin bends, stayed on the right side of the road and failed to drive us over one of the many sheer drops. I'd say it was my innate sense of responsibility for my son, white-knuckling the dashboard alongside me, but I can see how that might not wash.

Christ, I felt rough – and not just because of the alcohol. It was the first time I had ever seen Adam openly disappointed in me. When, somehow, we reached the school in one piece, he jumped out of the car and ran through the white gates before I could get out and embarrass him, but I managed it anyway, falling asleep slumped at the wheel in the hot, bright early-morning sun until a teacher had to ask me to move the car so the school bus could get out and take the children on their outing to the volcano. Even through my sand-blasted eyeballs, I could see that she was quite pretty.

As I looked for Adam's face in the passing bus and saw him staring pointedly in the other direction, I remembered far too late that I had promised to get up early and make him sand-wiches for the trip, to which he had been looking forward all week. He'd even put his He Man bag in the kitchen the evening before. He'd obviously made the sandwiches himself. And ironed his own shirt. Oh, crap.

I tried much harder after that.

By the weekend, at the end of the first week, Adam had forgiven me and invited me to come and see his room. I hadn't been to the house where he lived with his mother and her jeal-ous boyfriend but, as Pedro was away, I drove up into the hills to see the quiet little village my son called home.

It was curious to see my ex-wife again. We didn't meet very often, and so every time we did there had been a gap of months, or even years. She was almost nine years older than me and, out here in the sun, she looked it. I remembered meeting her and marrying her, but I remembered it like I might recall the blurred details of a savage car crash. Looking back now, I haven't the slightest idea what I was thinking when I married her. She was a decent person and pleasant enough, but so different from me in most respects that I can only think, looking back, that I must have been in some kind of shock when I met her. Now, she was living with a Spanish guy called Pedro who obviously had a problem understanding that I no longer had a shred of interest in the woman who had been my wife. My wife. *My wife?* Even as I write those words, I can't believe them, can't believe that they refer to me. Perhaps they don't. Perhaps all that is a figment of somebody else's imagination, and that's a convenient place to hide from that part of my past, which is what I do most of the time. Except, of course, when I think about Adam – bless him – who is the living evidence that proves the past. And certainly the best thing that has accompanied me out of it.

I had met Pedro once before, on a previous visit a couple of years before. I learnt later that he had fretted for days about what to wear. A member of a local football club, he finally opted for full white England soccer strip, the studs of his freshly cleaned football boots clip-clopping as he strode across the flagstones towards me, hand outstretched in sombre greeting.

'Paul Gascoigne,' he said, leaning forward so far to shake my hand that I thought he might topple over. His shirt was so bright I had to pull my sunglasses down.

'Juan Carlos,' I responded, with equal solemnity. I knew little about English football and nothing about Spanish, but I did know who the Spanish king was and even what he looked like in profile. His face was, after all, all over the coins.

Today, Pedro was on Gomera, another island, playing football. I had no idea where Juan Carlos was. Adam showed me around the cool, tiled townhouse he had called home for the past four years. I didn't feel like his father. I felt like a stranger.

I met Adam's half-blind dog and his collection of snakes and lizards and some of his Spanish schoolfriends, and saw the little square where the children kicked footballs and the old men played cards every evening, long into the warm nights. Adam's blond hair stood out vividly among all the other, darker kids, and it was strange to hear him chattering away and shouting in Spanish. He kept bringing kids over to meet me. His obvious pride choked me. It was all I could do not to cry.

He took me on a hike into the hills with two of his little friends, the three of them scrambling like goats along a gully known as the Boca del Inferno – the mouth of hell. Actually, it *was* hot, but not that hot, and it ended in a big pool, fed by a waterfall, where we all swam. It was, Adam said, an adventure. Like the ones I had had in South America.

The kids wanted to know if I had seen any snakes. I had, and I told them all about it as Adam translated. José decided he was going to go to Venezuela when he was older, to find a giant anaconda. *'Me también,'* said Adam. He kept switching back and forth between languages, sometimes forgetting and talking to me in Spanish. Normally, he refused to speak Spanish to me, as if he was ashamed of the language.

He was very excited, and I could see his friends were growing just a *little* tired of having to listen to all the great stuff he was telling them about me. I wanted to say to them, 'Come on, guys, be patient: he's had to be around you and your dads every day for the past few years, he's just thrilled that you can finally see he has one too,' or something like that, but my Spanish was nowhere near good enough.

Come to that, neither was my English.

Back at his mother's house, Adam showed me his room, and that's when I did, finally, cry. Everything I had ever sent him was hung carefully and proudly on the walls. Postcards, model planes, the bows and arrows, the piranha, giant shells, photographs of me . . . me in a canoe, me backpacking across the Gran Savana in Venezuela, me generally having a great deal of fun but not, in any particularly recognizable way, me being anything close to like a good father.

And the worst thing about it – the thing that actually seemed to be literally burning inside me – was that he didn't even seem to have noticed my gigantic failing. He was just pleased to see me.

I looked at his trophy wall and at his beaming, happy face, and knelt down and grabbed him to me, partly to hide my tears, and partly because I guessed it was about time. How to be a good father, I thought. We stayed like that for a few minutes, saying nothing. I could feel the little convulsions that told me that he, too, was silently sobbing. I held on and, over his shoulder, watched yet another lizard – possibly an iguana, basking in the sunlight spilling in through the window and into its glass tank – staring at me. Its beedy, unblinking eyes were fixed on mine, and every few seconds its long tongue darted out.

Personal Admin
Friday 10 October 2003

Now, my son and I share the same shoe size – ten – but somehow the boot has got on the other foot. Six years ago, when my expat ex-wife and I realized that, while charming, the small

Canarian village school that was teaching him such fluent Spanish was teaching him very little else, Adam came to live with his father in Suffolk.

Each week I abandoned him to his own devices in the idyllic cottage we rented on the banks of the Orwell. Every Saturday we went shopping together and stocked the (large) fridge-freezer with all manner of convenience foods. Every Monday I'd disappear down to London, with a cheery reminder to 'Try doing some washing-up this week.'

Every day he'd get the bus home from college, run up a huge sex-education bill with Sky Movies and carefully – and not without artistic merit – stack the sink to the brim and beyond with every plate, cup, glass and piece of cutlery in the place.

And, every Friday evening when I got home, boy, would I nag him.

Looking back, I can see that this might have been his way of punishing me for his relentlessly samey diet of pasta with meatballs or dumplings with stew. Fair enough. But now the punishment continues, and with a bizarre twist.

Recently, Adam and his girlfriend came up to the seaside to spend a week at my flat. Now twenty-two, he has been in the Royal Marines for two years (joining, I now wonder, as a reaction to the sublime lack of discipline at home?). I first notice something odd soon after I pick them up from the station. There is a mild commotion in the back seat and, instead of young folks fumbling, in the mirror I am disturbed to see Adam wielding a plastic carrier bag, tutting theatrically and picking up rubbish.

Of which, it must be said, there is a lot.

Half-drunk bottles of water; empty, crushed cans of Diet Coke (still coming round to the new vanilla flavour) and far too many Ginsters Buffet Bar wrappers (I cannot recommend this delicacy highly enough: available at all good filling stations).

'Personal admin,' he says, tapping me on the back of the head. 'V. important.'

Personal admin? V. important?

Oh, my God. There's a non-commissioned officer from central casting in the car. I try to remember what's in the sink at home.

In the flat, as his girlfriend, Leah, slumps in front of the TV, Adam goes to work, entirely unbidden, like one of those Japanese cleaning robots. I hover, nervously, as he marches from room to room, sniffing towels, scooping up old newspapers and slinging assorted shirts and underwear at me every time he passes: 'Clean or dirty?'

He tackles the alien lifeforms in the sink without a care for his own safety.

Finally, with the washing machine gurgling happily and everything in its place, he says: 'So. What's for dinner?'

I see my chance. It is not without a sense of triumph that I slide past him, into the as-new-again kitchen, and reach for the freezer handle (less sticky than I recall). Our eyes meet in close-up, a spaghetti-western moment. The age-old battle between youth and experience. I'm thinking Cronus *v* Uranus. But with a happier ending for the older guy, obviously.

'Dinner,' I proclaim, whipping open the door and pulling out a Safeway microwave spaghetti bolognese, 'is served!'

But before I can so much as remove the outer packaging and pierce the plastic film in several places, he says, 'I don't think so,' opens his military Bergen and produces the makings of fajitas for three. Which he proceeds to knock up in no time at all.

Where did I go wrong?

6

How to Have It All

Dear Microwave Man

I think my wife might be having an affair. In fact, I think she might be having an affair with you. She snatches the paper from me every Friday morning, reads your column and then spends twice as long as usual in the bathroom. In case you aren't sure, she's the short redhead with a tattoo of an oilcan on her hip. What have you got to say about that?

Mr DH, Westgate-on-Sea, Kent

Microwave Man writes: You'll have to be more specific: right hip or left? But seriously. I love what you've done with the spare room.

And, let me tell you, I have seen more than my share of spare rooms.

And thinking about that got me to thinking about what it takes to be a fully fledged conductor of affairs, an *homme de la nuit* (or, more accurately, an *homme de* midday) or, if you prefer, a complete bastard. Because I accept that there is nothing noble about knobbing somebody else's love interest – especially when one has attachments of one's own. No. Not proud of all that, but *slightly* pleased with the professional way I have always conducted myself in such situations. It's not just a question of dropping one's pants, you know. There's a great deal more art to the whole thing than that. Oh, yes.

But look: here's what I'll do. As a gesture of reconciliation, I'll pass on a few hard-won tips and some advice. My gift to you if you think your wife might be having an affair – or if you're thinking about embarking on one of your own. Or, if you are a woman who would rather like to be having a bit on the side but doesn't quite know how to go about it, how to have one with aplomb. Or with me. (Just kidding, guys.)[32]

And so back to the spare room. This is where married women often take you when they invite you to the marital home. No photographs to hide in drawers (and to remember to restore to their proper position later) and no immediate Code Red forensic concerns (hairs, bodily fluids, etc.). This is where, after a brief but passionate snogging session in the kitchen (or quite possibly the utility room – nothing like a laundry basket full of freshly Bounced knickers to stir the blood), they will lead an illicit lover, strip down to their specially purchased M&S underwear and stretch out languidly in the way they imagine that women having affairs should stretch out.

Now, I like all this because it speaks not of unbridled passion but of carefully thought through and ultimately pragmatic planning, which, counterintuitively, can be as sexy as hell. Rumpling up somebody else's marital bed in a frenzy of unfettered infidelity *sounds* like a great gig, I grant you, and is all very well, but I've been there and, frankly, what it says about the woman of the house somehow takes the edge off it.

What's that? Because of some kind of misguided solidarity with the husband? No. Sod that.[33] It's because, if I am sleeping with a married woman, it isn't because I want her to lose control, confess all to her husband, leave him and drive round to my place with the kids at 3 a.m. (or even at 3 p.m.). It's because I know that, while what she wants is sex of the kind she is no longer getting after fifteen years with the same man (which, although I take it to be a compliment, I recognize could very easily be almost any kind of sex with almost any kind of man), the very last thing she actually wants to do is demolish the family unit.

This works well for me. I even love the barely suppressed panic that sets in the moment the waves of her orgasm begin to

32 Not completely, girls.
33 Hell: it's being married that makes you so irresistible. But it's OK: it's all about the future of the human race. This is genetically moderated immorality.

subside and her temporarily Canuted sense of family comes crashing back in like North Sea breakers in January.

'Christ, Christ, I forgot,' she says, leaping up, grabbing the unfamiliar stockings, knickers and bra from the bed. 'Jack' (youngest boy) 'will be home any minute! He forgot his bloody violin this morning; and Samantha' (daughter, I suppose) 'needs a lift from school to her friend's house. Shit! Is that really the bloody time?'

I suppress a smile as I watch her pulling on her knickers and doing up her bra, and I try to look just ever so faintly hurt. Not *too* hang-dog, mind – she already *has* a husband – but just enough to put my 'hurt' somewhere on the fringes of her radar.

'Oh, pity,' I say. 'I was hoping we could go for a coffee somewhere, or maybe a walk.'

No, of *course*, I wasn't hoping anything of the kind. Be most generous with the gifts you know can never be accepted.

'A walk? Are you mad? The streets around here will be crawling with mothers from Jack's school any minute. Christ! If I'd wanted walkies, I'd have got a dog.'

And I leave, knowing that I'll be back but bemused that anyone can be so stupid as to conduct an affair *in their own house*.

But there again, that smacks of a kind of innocence, which is also as sexy as hell.

What isn't so sexy is when a woman blames everything but her own libido for her infidelity. Actually, I've never met one who does. It seems they only come over all self-deludingly analytical when they get cornered by a pollster carrying out a survey for some magazine. Women really do want it all, it seems. They want to be independent and to be able to have affairs, just like men, but when it suits them they want to be seen as innocent, gullible victims. I know this, because I read it in *Newsweek*, under the curiously seventeenth-century[34] headline, 'The Secret Lives of Wives. Why They Stray.'

And is that really the best service to which women can put a

34 When, as *Newsweek* pointed out, a wife caught with a bit on the side was liable to be hanged – right alongside her lover. Descartes would have seen the reason in that, I'm sure.

century of battling for equality? Shagging around, just like guys?

I don't recall that Emily Davison, just before she flung herself under the king's horse at the 1913 Epsom Derby, shrieked, 'For the right to vote and the right to book hotel rooms on wotif.com for afternoon sex with someone I fancy in the office,' but maybe she did, I wasn't there. Probably only she and the king's jockey know, and they aren't saying, on account of being history.

And here's an interesting, if depressing hoof-note (that's why I haven't put it down there with the footnotes): Davison (whose moment of sacrifice was captured by a *Daily Mail* photographer: even then the paper was in the business of warning women about the perils of straying too far from the hearth) never intended to kill herself. The silly cow had actually planned to step out, stop the king's horse and pin a suffragette rosette to its tackle. She'd practised this in the days beforehand, although presumably with a beach donkey, because the slightest grasp of physics would have told her that she was on a hiding to nothing (1000 lb horse travelling at 40 mph meets 80 lb suffragette equals messy).

Of course, the next edition of the *Suffragette* (no more firmly anchored to reality than the *Daily Mail*) wasn't about to let the facts stand in the way of an excellent opportunity for martyrdom. Presumably unable to afford the *Mail*'s going rate for the exclusive photograph, it fell back on a drawing of Davison materializing as a winged angel on the racecourse, arms aloft, and wearing a fetching halo bearing the words, 'Love that overcometh.' (Overcometh what, they don't say, but maybe it was common sense and an elementary grasp of physics.) Underneath was the stirring legend: 'In honour and loving, reverent memory of Emily Wilding Davison. She died for women.'

Actually, of course, she died for want of a few extra brain cells, and the few she had were kicked out by Anmer, the king's horse.[35] And it's not even as though the king cared. Anmer was

---

35 In this less respectful age, her successfully idiotic self-extinction would have qualified for no more than a mention in the Darwin Awards, which annually recognize those who have selflessly done their bit to clean up the gene pool. My favourite is the washing-machine-repair man who tumble-dried himself to death.

already trailing in third from last. But hey: why spoil a good story?

Men, of course, many of whom already had the vote, were about to indulge in a little bit of sacrificing themselves. Within a year of Emily's exit, millions of them (no doubt chuckling about how much better life was for them than it was for the poor, disenfranchised women forced to sit, warm and safe, by the home fires) were heading off to France to fling themselves under the machine guns of the king's old mate, the Kaiser. Which all told killed 800,000 of them. Funny old game, equality.

And what were the women up to, meanwhile, besides toasting their tootsies by the fire? They were rolling up their sleeves and producing the bullets and shells that were killing German men and, in their spare time, handing out white feathers to any of their countrymen they deemed to be chickens. All this proved a lot more effective than headbutting galloping horses and, in the 1918 General Election, by way of a thank-you from a grateful government, 8.5 million women over thirty were rewarded with the right to vote.

But I digress.

After *Newsweek*'s earth-shattering exposé, 'The Secret Lives of Wives', the British press, in that lazy way we journalists have, piled in and joined the feeding frenzy. And guess what they found out?

Yes! Women *are having affairs* (shock)! and, yes, *it isn't their fault* (less of a shock there)!

'Many,' reveals my very own newspaper, 'don't see it as shameful. Indeed, some see it as their entitlement.'

Their entitlement? What – like maternity leave and the vote?

The mind-bogglingly lame excuses trotted out include: 'I'm taken for granted', 'My husband gives me no attention' and – my personal favourite – 'I work so hard I deserve it.'

Is that a bit like 'My wife doesn't understand me'?

Actually, it's even more brazen than that. Men! Try this one on for size next time you fancy a bit of extracurricular: 'Darling, you know I've been working late the past few nights on that report for Nigel? Well, I'm going to take one of the secretaries out for a drink this evening and then shag her in the car on the way home. Oh, come on; don't be like that, sweetie! I've been working hard . . . *I deserve it.*'

Yup, that'll work.

So, under the latest terms of the ever-shifting definition of the word 'equality', if a married man has an affair, he's just a horny bastard who can't keep his penis in his pants. Fair enough. But, on the other hand, if his partner sleeps with somebody else, not only is it not her fault, but she will have been driven to it – virtually against her will – by her husband's neglect, by the modern-day pressures of holding down a job while raising children, by the evil influence of modern communication systems, such as the internet and mobile phones, and by the (cynical, male) office smoothie who takes advantage of all this by telling her how hard she works, how beautiful she looks and how much she deserves the reward of a drink after work. With him. Followed by a shag in his company Ford.

She will have been driven to it, in fact, by almost anything other than her own sexual appetite.

How convenient to be able to suspend temporarily one's modern, independent, feminist sensibilities in favour of the essentially sexist stance that, if a woman strays sexually, she does so against her will and as a victim – of a man's neglect or bad behaviour.

Without wishing to moralize (which, as anyone who knows me well would agree, would be a bit rich), it all boils down to free will, determinism and (brace yourself: shocking concept follows) *moral responsibility* – as philosophers from Aristotle onwards have been pointing out for . . . well, since Aristotle, I suppose.

If, when you next remove your freshly purchased Agent Provocateur knickers in the Dolphin Square Hotel, you are acting freely (wherein acting freely, as the Stanford *Encyclopaedia of Philosophy* puts it neatly, 'entails the ability to have done otherwise at the time of action'), then you will have nobody to blame for the ensuing adulterous shagfest but yourself. No matter how much football your pot-bellied pig of a husband watches on television.[36]

But it isn't the hypocritical duality of responsibility that surprises me. I'm not *that* naïve. What really uncorks my eyeballs is the feigned surprise at the 'news' that more women than ever before are having (sorry, *are being driven into*) affairs. I've had enough experience over the years (on both sides of the sheets) to conclude that almost anyone – man or woman – is rarely more than one glance, two well-chosen compliments and three glasses of M. Perignon's sweet elixir away from adultery.

As for the suggestion that working life has presented women with more opportunities (sorry: *excuses*), I can say only that I have spent some very pleasant afternoons indeed being entertained in other men's castles[37] by women who have never done a day's work in their life.

Besides, to say that an adulteress isn't really looking for raw sex, passion and mind-blowing orgasms (oh, dear, no: all she really wants is to be 'appreciated', perhaps have a bit of a cuddle) is to subscribe to the myth that a woman's sexuality is just a pale imitation of a man's. I've slept with enough partnered women[38] (and I take full Aristotelian responsibility for that, of course) and what has always impressed me has been the self-honesty and ruthlessness with which they cheated on their husbands. Yes, they wanted to be 'appreciated' (up to three or four times in one session, if possible), but I never once heard a woman whine, 'My husband doesn't understand me.'

The reality – which I thought that all grown-ups had recognized by now – is that women hunger for sex just as much as men do, and that sometimes the excitement of the forbidden proves irresistible.

In fact, while we're lining up the excuses, it seems women

---

36 Have I already mentioned that the Dolphin's superior suites feature two televisions?
37 And, talking of castles, may I note here that, presumably, the chastity belt wasn't introduced during the Crusades solely to make peeing difficult.
38 Although, what is enough, really?

might hunger for sex even *more* than men do. I may have been guilty of a terrible injustice. I had always assumed that Laura (the long-term partner who, overnight, about eight years ago, became my ex) had embarked on what later turned out to have been something of an orgy of faithlessness on account of being, well – a bit of a slapper. But, not so, it seems. Scientists (and, by way of a change, ordinary, homegrown ones and not the usual 'American Scientists') have revealed that, in fact, the poor soul was among the one in five genetically cursed girls who, like Jayne Mansfield, 'just can't help it'.

Professor Tim Spector and colleagues at St Thomas' Hospital, London (which, however good it might be at curing the sick, still hasn't quite got the hang of the possessive), assembled more than 1,600 pairs of female twins and quizzed them about their sex lives. Why? Well, because it was a hell of a lot of fun, obviously, and because they had cunningly set up the Twins Unit – because they could, but also because, by comparing results from identical and non-identical sets of twins, they could work out what impact genetics had on sexual practices.

In this particular study, the competing camps of nurture and nature appear temporarily to have settled their differences: the scientists concede that, although tight jeans (sorry: the *right genes*) might contribute to a propensity in a woman to shag around, the correct environmental conditions must also be met (although this seems to boil down to the conclusion that she must also have both somewhere to do it and someone attractive to do it with. Brilliant, professor! Another triumph for the Faculty of the Bleeding Obvious).

The good news for unfaithful men floundering around for a decent excuse is that the same team will be turning its attention to a similar sample of males and, they say, fully expect to find the same results (which would appear to make the whole exercise, in a very literal sense, purely academic, but hey: funding is funding).

If so, the work will confirm what I have always suspected – that my own innumerable infidelities committed during the same aforementioned relationship weren't my fault: I was driven to it by something in my jeans.

The researchers say that genes can account for infidelity in the same way they can for migraines, so perhaps the one genetic predisposition might cancel out the other ('I'd love to, tall dark stranger with clear potential for improving the gene pool, but I'm afraid I have a headache').

Isn't nature wonderful/perverse?

Depressingly for anyone planning a stroll up the aisle with an identical twin, however (and besides: how would you choose between them?), only 17 per cent of the quizzed women who had had affairs believed infidelity was wrong, which presumably means that 83 per cent took their marriage vows with fingers crossed behind their backs.

On the other hand (the one without the ring, I'm guessing), the discovery means that children may now be tested at birth for the presence of the Slapper Gene and named accordingly as a warning to future prospective partners (steer clear of anyone named Helen or Cressida, for a start).

However, as any fan of Playboy's 'Twins and Sisters' specials will tell you, the study is, of course, statistically flawed. Not only because genetics is a hugely whiffy field (such genetic causality is, says the report, 'not seriously disputed', which we all know – even though they think we don't – is boffin talk for 'our funding rivals at Cambridge think this is a pile of ordure'), but because the scientists have (for a change) overlooked the Bleeding Obvious: that female identical twins are presented with far more opportunities for sex generally, because so many men can't resist exploring the classic male fantasy. (I imagine that the question, 'So, girls, do you do everything together?' was the first on the researchers' clipboard.)

And so evolutionary scientists and faithless spouses alike are vindicated: Aristotle and Co. were wrong about individual responsibility, and Darwin is personally responsible for all unacceptable human behaviour.

Forget all that non-productive and oddly provocative 'Darling, it didn't mean anything, it was just a moment of madness' cobblers. Your cast-iron excuse for shagging around is that it gave you no pleasure whatsoever to have sex with all those women beyond the humbling knowledge that, driven irresistibly by the same urge that inspires the incredibly ugly bottom-feeding grenadier fish to seek out only the most repulsive companions, you had selflessly done your bit for the gene pool.

One thing, however (as journalists like to say when nothing is certain), is certain: with the phone numbers of more than 1,600 pairs of largely immoral twins in his possession, I bet that Professor Spector is invited to an awful lot of parties over Christmas.

As the American playwright and actress Cornelia Otis Skinner said, 'Women's virtue is man's greatest invention.' And she should know, having been something of a goer in her prime – friend to filthmeister Dr Alfred Kinsey (the famous tree-doctor who went from studying woods to studying woodies), her written work included such schoolboy-friendly titles as *The Ape in Me*,[39] *Tiny Garments* and *Nuts in May*. She finally confirmed what everyone had really known all along when she published *Our Hearts were Young and Gay*, which, being a witty lesbian travelogue, was quite probably the first recorded use of the word 'gay' to mean anything other than brightly cheerful.

And she was so right about the virtue thing. So true. And that's life. That's humans. If you don't like it, marry a swan.

But that's enough about alibis. What about not getting caught in the first place? Many people will tell you that having an affair is all about passion and spontaneity. Wrong. Anyone can ruin their life and the lives of those they love with an ill-judged moment of madness. That isn't an affair; it's a cry for help. On the other hand, having a successful affair takes a huge amount of forethought and careful planning – and success, in this instance, is defined simply by not getting caught.

Well, by having lots and lots of illicit sex *and* not getting caught.

---

39 Not half as much monkey-business fun as it sounds, sadly.

These days, we have it easy. In days of old, as recalled in the classic song 'Flash, Bang, Wallop, What a Picture',[40] the lack of easy methods of communication made illicit sexual congress such a drag that it's a wonder that a bloke ever got out of his tights, let alone into anybody else's. Knocking out sonnets was all very well and good, but by the time you'd found a word to rhyme with 'temperate', snapped a quill or two in frustration and splashed ink all over the place (and then waited for hours for it to dry), the object of desire would, in all probability, have either been overcome by the vapours, entered a nunnery or moved on to the contents of a more handily located codpiece.[41]

But it isn't just about technology and texting. The successful affair must be conducted like a military espionage mission. First of all, take nobody into your confidence. Do not be tempted, in a post-coital haze, to tell anybody – barber, boss, pal, colleague – about this wonderful new thing you've found. The secret *will* leak out, at the worst possible moment, because that is what secrets are for. And beware of falling into the familiarity trap. It is not unknown for amateurs engaged in affairs to start mentioning the name of the illicit loved one *to their cuckolded partner* as often as possible: 'Mike says this . . . Mike says that . . . Oh, look at that on the news: "Scientists have discovered that Belgium is twice as interesting as was previously thought." Fancy that. No wonder *Mike* cycled across Belgium last year . . .'

If Mike is mentioned more than twice on the trot, fear the worst (and with somebody who goes cycling in Belgium, for Christ's sake).

Choose your partner in crime carefully. Although a single woman with a handy apartment of her own has some short-

40 Tommy Steele's finest hour, immortalized in the 1967 film *Half a Sixpence*, in which we hear of the tragic plight of Romeo, who, consumed with passion but unable to scale the drainpipe to reach his love, symbolically falls to the ground below with tragic consequences for his rapier. What's a sixpence? Oh, do sod off.
41 I was going to insert a Shakespeare quote here, but when I looked for one I was more taken with the website that came up top of my search. It listed, in this order, 'Love quotes', 'Inspirational quotes', 'Funny quotes' and then 'Chicken recipes'. There were some good ones, too . . .

term advantages, a lover in the same boat as you (that is, married and with plenty to lose) is unlikely to rock that vessel when it hits the rapids.

Hotels will do just fine, but be wary of online booking forms that seek your home address. It might be tough explaining away that 'Congratulations, Mr and Mrs Gault-Dupont![42] As regular customers you have been selected for our Valentine's Day special deals' mailshot.

Travel Inns and Travelodges are the best bets: you can get into the rooms from midday (excellent for lunchtime trysts), they couldn't care less who comes and goes (as it were) and bookings can be cancelled up to 4 p.m. on the day (economical for those last-minute rows/pangs of conscience/forgotten school concerts).

You would think it fairly basic and obvious that no receipts connected with your infidelity should be kept, but time and time again a crumpled Visa slip is found in a coat pocket bound for the dry cleaner, leaving the idiot who left it there gasping like a landed fish as he tries to explain the unmentioned dinner for two at a favourite restaurant at a time when he was, allegedly, working late and alone.[43] What motivates this madness? Is it a self-destructive urge? If it is inspired by meanness – an attempt to claim lust-induced expenses on the firm – then frankly you deserve all the slashed suits, scratched cars and cleared-out bank accounts you will surely get.

Blondes do have more fun – but not on your watch, right? Unless, of course, your wife is also a blonde. The point is that it is insanity to embark on an affair with a long-haired golden girl if your wife's hair is short and dark. Sooner or later – and almost certainly it will be sooner – she will spot the one stray hair that, inevitably, has escaped your attention. It might be on your coat. It could be on the headrest of the passenger seat in your car. She might even find it in your pants, tossed carelessly in the washing basket. (If this sounds far-fetched, take it from me that it is not. And try washing your own clothes, you

42 A tip: no one uses 'Smith' any more.
43 Another tip: stop lying at this point and try for mercy.

caveman.) And if you *must* buy your lover a gift (a slippery slope, this), why not make it a bottle of the same perfume you bought your wife for Christmas, thus preventing her smelling a rat when she smells it on you?

Of course, if your lover ends up looking like your partner, smelling like her and perhaps wearing the same underwear as her, you could say that you might as well have stuck with your partner in the first place – which is, after all, more or less what you kind of agreed to on your wedding day. But where's the fun in that?

And remember, don't try any of this at home. Bringing your lover home for carnal canoodling in the house you share with your partner is unforgivably bad practice. No matter how careful you are, the mere presence of another woman instantly transforms the entire property into a crime scene. Your real partner lives there. Subliminally, she knows every inch of the place – what belongs where, what doesn't. Shift a rug slightly out of place without good cause (and frenzied coupling on the shag does not constitute good cause in this case) and your entire web of lies and deceit begins to unravel.

If your loins leave you with no choice and you simply have to play at home, think damage limitation before the action kicks off. Secure the area to keep the problem from escalating out of control. Be realistic: you could try confining the action – and, thus, the cleaning-up operation – to the hallway, perhaps by feigning unbridled passion that must be sated there and then, in the shadow of the catflap.[44] That's plausible, of course, but it would take a high level of skill/chutzpah to then get away with persuading your lover to leave directly afterwards (taking her long blonde hairs with her).

If she somehow manages to break out of the sterile zone (and most women finding themselves in this situation will be almost pathologically driven to inspect the premises, awarding mental

44 You could try sealing off the rest of the house with police incident-tape, but your lover might ask why, and then what are you going to say? 'Oh, there was a brutal murder here last night'? Bit of a passion-killer, that.

marks for cleanliness and taste. She's not there only for sex. One such post-coital visitor asked me where we had bought the curtains and even started to plump up the cushions on the sofa), make a mental note of where she goes in the house and consider all such areas contaminated. The marital bed, of course, must be avoided at all costs, unless you have sufficient time afterwards to wash and dry the sheets and remake it – but ask yourself (because your wife will surely ask *herself*): is this something you would normally do if you didn't have something to hide?

Women are walking clue-machines, distributing incriminating evidence like a snake sheds scales. And you know what? I think they do it on purpose. An earring, a thread of cotton or a button off a coat, an alien hairclip – perhaps all lying unseen (for now) on the hall carpet.

And there's so much *stuff*. Count it in, and count it out: those earrings, necklaces, rings, watches, hairclips, mobile phones, car keys, knickers . . . a strange lip balm left unnoticed (by you, at any rate) in the bathroom is the bullet that will take you down.

The trick, contrary to all those wild scenes of passion in the movies, is never to lose control of the situation. Crucially, you must never, ever let her brush her hair before she leaves. This is equivalent to a battlefield biological weapon going off. If the damned brush comes out as she passes the hall mirror on the way to the door, try seizing her to you with a cry of 'My God, you're lovely,' planting your lips on hers and then guiding her with a tremendous show of reluctance to the door.

If she *does* make it to the bathroom with her handbag, prepare yourself for a forensic fingertip search of the floor and all other surfaces (although, frankly, you might just as well give up at this point and confess the moment your wife comes home). Here, and on other hard floors, such as in the kitchen, there is no substitute for the dustpan and brush. The Hoover might seem quick and easy, but it *will* betray you. And when you have a pan full of hairs, don't put them in the bin, idiot – flush them down the loo. And don't forget the plughole in the sink: horrify yourself by hauling out those long blonde hairs before somebody else does.

And, while you should prevent your visitor from showering at any cost – consider feigning a heart attack, if necessary, to head off this potential catastrophe – wherever you conduct your affair, if she so much as kisses you (and, if it's to be any kind of an affair, let's hope she does), then make sure you have the time and place to shower and change clothing before seeing your other, other half. Going to the gym is a good trick. Although you might not, in the grip of post-coital ennui, be able to pump much iron, you will be able to sweat off the biological and chemical evidence and shower with somebody else's towels.

Think decontamination chamber. Again, women are harder to clean up after. Whereas the most a man is likely to leave is a whiff of some obnoxious aftershave about the skin and clothes, a woman who has her heart set on seduction will have titivated herself accordingly. This could mean lipstick marks on shirts, foundation smears on your dark suit and, lurking somewhere on your skin, that awful sparkly stuff that seems to infest so much make-up. Like a time bomb waiting to go off, a single, tiny, over-looked particle of glitter will remain invisible until later that same night, or even a week hence, when the glow from the bedside table lamp, switched on by your wife, lights it up like the neon sign outside a cheap motel.

Not that I'd want you to think that I'd thought about this a lot.

The spare room is where I first slept with Alice. The spare room in which her wedding dress, in its transparent plastic bag, hung from the door of the wardrobe.[45]

Now, if there *is* a God who sends people to hell for the bad things they do in their life (and nine out of ten Britons, apparently, believe this, but, luckily, I'm not one of them), then my eternal roost on a hot rock was reserved and guaranteed one sultry summer's day over a decade and a half ago. Alice was a God-fearer then and, aged just twenty-one, was about to get married. I really do think I ought to spare you the sordid details

45 Don't fret; I'm getting there.

of how she filled the time in those last few hectic weeks before the big day, interspersing frantic arrangements for receptions and honeymoons with frantic couplings with a man she had just met (me: do try to keep up).

Let's just say I saw her in her wedding dress before her husband did. And then again afterwards.

The point is, I know what I'm talking about. I have had dozens of sordid affairs and one-night stands. I'm not proud of that. What I am proud of is that I was never found out. Well, until now, obviously.

And just in case you think I'm looking for sympathy over the Boer thing, for the record, here's a confession to save you even bothering. I was screwing Alice before I met Laura, the 'love of my life'; I was screwing her all during the eight years I was with her (on and off, obviously) and I carried on screwing her long after the so-called love of my life had left me for someone else.

In a funny way, I suppose that makes *Alice* the love of my life, whatever the hell *that* is. Or maybe just a girl who can't say no. Who can blame her? It's in my jeans. And judging by the text message she has just sent me, it won't be long before, once again, I will be in hers.

Tea and Crumpet
Friday 31 October 2003

An odd but rather lovely thing happened at the weekend. I was conducting my usual last-minute superficial home detox (from pit to palace in 9.75 minutes) in anticipation of the imminent arrival of Alice. I don't see Alice that often, but I have been seeing her, on and off, for sixteen years, and when we have met it has nearly always been for sex.

Our first meeting, taking place as it did on an escalator in Debenhams, doesn't, I grant you, sound desperately romantic, but it was one of the most intensely passionate moments of my life.

Alice was just twenty-one then and riding down to cosmetics, and I was thirty-one and heading up to home furnishings (God knows why). She stared at me in a way that no woman has looked at me since, with a sexual intensity that I felt sure must have lit me up like neon, and that was her place in my story (and bed) secured.

What I didn't know at the time was that the man standing behind her (faceless then and now) was her husband-to-be and cuckold-in-waiting. I can't remember the exact timing of events but I do recall one afternoon dropping off a still-warm Alice at the hotel where she had final arrangements to make for her impending wedding reception. (And then, later, there was the incident with the wedding dress . . . but another time, maybe.)

Anyway, the point is that that husband, perhaps not surprisingly, is now a memory, while I, perhaps more surprisingly, am not. And I say, 'that husband', because there has been another one since, but not in a way that has had any significant impact on Jonny and Alice.

And so to that odd and lovely thing. Just as I have bundled the last pile of crap into the cupboard by the door, the phone rings. It's Alice, who arrived back in the country at 3 a.m., is shattered and has a window of only two hours. As the drive from the marital home to my place takes almost an hour, that would give us about one minute for torrid goings-on – short, even by my Brief Encounter standards.

So, instead of sex, we meet in a café midway for a nice cup of tea and a teacake. (I wanted hot buttered crumpet, but it was off the menu. No, really.)

We sit there, almost like an old couple, but our passion is set aside not permanently (and not far) but just for now. As I watch her, sleepy-eyed and tousle-haired, talking about her trip, one hand resting on my leg, I realize I have, kind of, been happily in love with her for years, even when I have been more conventionally enamoured of others.

It's not a one-knee, ring, vicar, ever-after kind of love, but

I have a good feeling that it is certainly a till-death-do-us-part number (which is more than can be said of those now vanished others).

How my concept of ideal love has changed. Once upon a time (conscious application there of the fairy-tale prefix), I yearned for the single, eternally bonded love of James Taylor's 'Never Die Young' but now I go easier on myself.

Alice and I will never shop for curtains or vegetables, but neither will we endure those long silences and back-to-back nights. Months often pass without us seeing each other, but when we do she always looks at me with those dark, escalator eyes.

There are no promises made, and so none are broken.

Now, as I grow older, I prefer Charles Kingsley's take on the long game to James Taylor's: 'When all the world is old, lad . . . And all the sport is stale . . . Creep home and take your place there/ The spent and maimed among/ God grant you find one face there/ You loved when all was young.'

I don't know when I'll see Alice again, but I do know that I will.

7

How to Lose it All

Dear Microwave Man
   Given your succession of failed relationships, how hopeful are you
that the perfect woman is just around the corner?

   Name and address withheld

Microwave Man writes: 'Failed' is a touch harsh, surely? Some of them
were pretty successful in the moment and nothing, including life, love
and batteries, lasts for ever, right? As an imperfect man, I'm not sure
if I'm looking for the perfect woman; besides, perfection is overrated,
in my view: the most interesting people tend to be those with interesting flaws (take me, for example). However, I live in constant
expectation of falling hopelessly in love at any moment. It's happened
before, so why not again?

At last. My own stalker. Well, I say my own, but actually it seems
I am sharing her with two of my male colleagues. Still, it's a step
in the right direction. At least I have finally attracted the attentions of a mad *woman*, which definitely represents some kind of
an upgrade from the mad *man* who has been bombarding me
with 7 lb handwritten letters laced with portentous biblical[46]
bollocks ever since I slighted Liverpool.

   Well, not so much Liverpool as John Lennon (although the
one seems to have ended up meaning little more than the other).
And not even Lennon, really, but the gormless statue of Lennon

---

46 Not that I wish to imply that all the words to be found in the Christian Bible are, *per
se*, bollocks – although, of course, as most of us know, they are. It's great living in a
Christian country. Say what you like about the incumbent deity without the slightest
danger of a fatwa. Allah be praised.

they've tucked away (out of sheer embarrassment, presumably) on one of the walkways at John Lennon Airport. I dunno. You slag off every person you've ever slept with – and nothing. But you say *one bad thing* about John Lennon . . .

All of which brings me, curiously and circuitously but pinprick precisely, to Laura.

She had a stalker. Well, that's what I thought at the time. But, actually, her stalker was a lover who'd gone bad. I'd had my suspicions at the time, but I didn't learn the whole story until later. And by then it was just another one in a whole series of whole stories.

I remember the phone call quite clearly. She was at work, I was at home. She sounded worried. More scared, in fact, than I had heard her in six years.

'There's a man downstairs at reception, and I can't leave until he's gone.'

'What?'

'He's asking for me and he's obviously a bit, well, bonkers. Security have called the police.'

'Well, who is he?'

It turned out he was a man who had come to lecture on rainforest destruction during the break year Laura spent doing an MPhil in South American studies at Cambridge. Largely at my expense. It turned out that they had kept in touch. Also largely at my expense. It also turned out that he had completely 'misinterpreted' the many lunches and other trysts they had had since then. All of which came as a surprise to me. As did the two or three visits she had paid to him at his family home in Kent. While his wife and children were away.

Indeed, by such a degree had he 'misinterpreted' those many trysts, it turned out, that he had left his wife and family. Which had come as a surprise to them, too. Laura, it turned out, was pretty good at rainforest destruction.

When I first met Laura I was thirty-two and she was a sweet and charming and flirtatious twenty-four-year-old who had been through university, was aware of her good looks and quite pleased with the way she had deployed them to snare a local car-dealer, who – aside from the Wanking Santa, perhaps – was one of the biggest catches available in Northampton.

Northampton is famous for three things: cobblers and the Wanking Santa. I know that's only two things, but somehow that just doesn't have the same ring to it, and I can't think of a third.

And, of course, both the Wanking Santa and all the cobblers are now gone, redundant, which leaves Northampton with nothing to boast about other than having the largest market square in the Midlands. Hmm. (In 1831 one-third of the men of the town were shoemakers, and that's a load of cobblers. And today, although the town's museum boasts the largest collection of old boots and shoes in the world, can you get a new heel put on anywhere in the shopping centre?)

The Wanking Santa was the fond nickname given by the excitement-deprived locals to the robotic Santa Claus kindly installed every year by the Express Lift Company at the top of the extremely tall and desperately unsightly elevator testing-tower that, to this day, looms priapically over the town. The tower and, over the Christmas period, its lit Santa, were visible for miles around. His giant jolliness, innocently easing himself in and out of the top of the tower – as if it were a chimney, you see – looked for all the world[47] (and certainly to the countryside for miles around) as though he was rubbing himself off against the brickwork. Ho ho ho.

Northampton's big break had come in 1675, when it burnt to the ground. This gave the locals a chance to rebuild, but town planning by disaster is rarely a success.[48] This was before the invention of the horizons-broadening bicycle and, because nobody had ventured further than Kettering (and hadn't liked it much, either), nobody really knew what to do with all that new fire-cleared space.

All they knew was that Kettering had a largish market square, and they would be buggered if the county town was going to

47 But not, it seems, to the company's management.
48 Dresden being a notable exception.

be eased into second place on any front by that dump up the road.

As a result, Northampton is now blessed with one of the largest market squares, not only in the county, not only in the Midlands even, but *in the whole of the country*. It says something about Northampton that the locals are still inordinately proud of this, even though the only things that get brought to market these days are pirated DVDs, cheap and nasty clothes for poor people and the most horrendous examples of arts and crafts to be found anywhere. All the great size of the market square means today is that, once a week, shoppers have to walk slightly further between the tacky stalls than might have been expected.

Today, Santa is no more – rather like the lift company, sold off and closed down with the loss of 500 jobs (501 if you include the Wanking Santa). The wanker, like the tower, seemed to have been around for ever, but in fact he had been rubbing himself off for only twenty years. I say, 'only'. To Santa, at least, the closure must have come as something of a relief.

The tower went up in 1980, was opened by the Queen two years later and closed again before one could say, 'Happy Golden Jubilee, ma'am' (although neither Her Majesty, nor any other member of the Royal Family, showed up for that particular cere-mony). It was, however, immediately listed and protected (unlike the jobs that surrounded it), so now – barring another Great Fire of Northampton – there is no chance of ever knocking it down. It will stand there for eternity (or until the mortar crumbles, whichever is soonest), a giant finger held up to the former employees (many of whom, still wearing their 'Testing Division Engineer' name badges, spend their redundant days haunting the tallest buildings in town, mournfully riding the lifts up and down, up and down, and ticking boxes on faded yellow worksheets attached to rusty-springed clipboards).

I expect that somebody will one day open a restaurant at the top – or, given the limited space up there, perhaps a novelty toilet. And why not? It might be 125 metres high, but with an elevator travelling at 7 metres per second, even the most desperately needy could be settling down to check out the dull vista in a little over seventeen seconds. It could be marketed, perhaps, as 'A Poo with a View'. Although I think the engaged sign should be at the bottom of the tower, to prevent unnecessary and frustrating journeys.

My years with Laura began with the Wanking Santa, which she pointed out to me on our very first date. We could see it from the funfair on the Racecourse,[49] where I had just puked up after stumbling off one of the rides. It didn't seem to put Laura off (my puking, not Santa's wanking) and, in all, we were together from that moment for about a decade. We split up, oddly enough, the very same year that Santa wanked no more, and I've always found that a little touching, somehow.

Like the Santa, and the tower and the shoemakers, we thought we'd be around for ever. Which was, like so much to do with Northampton, cobblers. What we had, or thought we had, was love; we thought we had found 'the one'. We thought we had found a true companion for life – when, in actual fact, what we had was a listed monument to infidelity.

At the time, of course, and right up until the end, I thought it was just me. I was unstoppable. I told Laura I loved her, and I did. I mean, I *meant* it, but I could never quite square my behaviour with my feelings for her.

I remember once telling her that I would give her my kidneys if she ever needed them. (Not for breakfast, obviously; for transplant. Remember: be most generous with the gifts you will never have to give.) She seemed quite grateful but hoped it wouldn't come to that. What I had meant was, that if push came to shove, I would give up my life to preserve hers. I meant this. Or, at least, I believed it. It helped me to settle things in my own mind. It made me feel better about cheating on her, although, to be honest, that was never much of a struggle. It was my equivalent, I suppose, of bringing home cheap flowers from a petrol station, only it was even cheaper than that,

49 Another Northampton anticlimax. It's *called* 'The Racecourse', but it isn't a racecourse.

because the promise would probably never be called in and would thus never cost me anything.

In the end, it helped me to decide that, sure, while sleeping with other women was clearly not the decent thing to do, it didn't mean that I didn't love Laura. Afterwards, when everything (or most of everything) had come out, she agreed. She agreed because she kind of had to, because, although she, too, had been sleeping around prodigiously, it didn't mean that she didn't love me.

Supposedly. Bitch.

It still makes me angry. I know how that sounds, but our two wrongs don't make either of us feel right. How could it? How would you work that? My y number of infidelities against her x? If I have out-shagged her, ten to nine, say, does that mean she has 10 per cent more reason to feel betrayed, hurt, cheated upon?

I didn't think about this much at the time, of course. Barely at all, in fact. I slept with as many women as I could and, to my delight and fleeting shame (depending on which side of the orgasm equation I found myself), I quickly discovered that quite a few women fell into this category. God knows why. I don't know what suddenly changed about me, beyond the adoption of contact lenses and the dropping of the comedy Michael Caine spectacles.

Heck, that could have been it, I suppose. Or perhaps it was the confidence and the leg-up to the old self-esteem bestowed by the love of a beautiful woman. My exhaustive studies over the years have revealed a curious phenomenon: women everywhere are more attracted to a man with a mate – and some of the more spookily attuned can tell this about you even when you are alone. Something about the way one walks, perhaps, swinging the family jewels around with brio.

And why does this draw them, like tiger sharks to a bucket of chum?

Personally, I have no truck with the daft Darwinism which, based on the 1879 sighting of a small female frog eschewing diminutive male members of the same species in favour of a larger model, insists that all human sexual behaviour is similarly inspired, i.e., that the male's aim is to spray his sperm around as many ovaries as possible in the hope of ensuring the genetic continuance of his line, and that the female is on the lookout for the largest pair of bollocks in the hope that she will be banged up just as soon as she is looked at, for the same spurious genetic reason.

Not, I have to say, in my experience. Or perhaps there is a Darwinian explanation for the sensational performance of shares in the pharmaceutical companies that make morning-after pills?

Personally, I put it down to competition that has nothing to do with biology. We're taught – or assume – that only men are competitive, that women are all sisters together, but actually we're all relatively rotten under the skin. Women want what the next woman has just to prove to themselves that they are as good as – or better than – her. Stay sober and take your field glasses to the next party to which you are invited. Observe.

Whatever the cause, the discovery at twenty-nine that the world was full of women who were keen to get to know me better (with their clothes off) was, in the jargon of self-helpism and, for a man who had spent his twenties harnessed to a marriage that had begun as a cry for help, empowering. I'd spent the years when I should have been out sowing trapped in B&Q and Ikea (unable to find anyone who knew where the shelf brackets were) and, by the time freedom arrived at twenty-nine, I was ready to do it for myself.

It was Laura's misfortune that she strayed across my path just as I was getting into my stride (and, frequently, out of my strides). I had dallied awhile with Rebecca (or, rather, she dallied awhile with me) and then, suddenly, bleakly dumped, I looked up and there she was. She began as just another celebration of my new-found confidence and just kind of stayed and got the job: official Love of My Life. But the fact that we started to live together – and planned to do so for ever – didn't curb my activities. I merely shifted the focus of my theatre of operations: among other things Laura brought into my life (including reluctant tolerance of the cello as a house-trained instrument, a loathing for the supposedly endangered rainforest and a lifetime aversion to the Liberal Democrats) was a new circle of female acquaintances, and I busily set about getting to know as many of them as well as I could.

You see, it wasn't just the rainforest that was endangered.

At times it was, frankly, exhausting. Strangers, wives, friends, wives of friends, friends of friends, wives of Laura's friends, Laura's girlfriends, their sisters, her workmates, friends of her brother, women I met at work, in the pool, in the apartment two doors along the corridor.

Hell, I'd have slept with her mother if she hadn't voted Liberal Democrat.[50]

I was prodigious. With each woman I experienced the same bell curve of emotion, starting at lust, rising through excitement, peaking with ecstasy and falling off as rapidly into guilt and contrition. When each act was closed, I couldn't wait to leave the stage and vowed that each such performance would be the last.

But it never was. I became careless and cavalier. I had begun by limiting my escapades to those times when Laura was out of the country – working or visiting her brother abroad (or, perhaps, 'working' or 'visiting her brother abroad') – but I quickly tore up the rule book. While Laura was at work and, quite possibly, liable to come home, I entertained other women in the flat we shared. (I say 'entertained', but there was very little juggling and almost no card tricks.) I had sex in our bed, in and on our car (front seats, back seats and bonnet) and in the dark corners of London streets.[51] In the shower, on the edge of the bath, up against the walls, on the stairs, over the kitchen counter and on the floor. I even had sex on her dead grandmother's sofa (which Laura had had lovingly restored and re-covered).

I was like a man possessed. My finest hour was actually my

50 No I wouldn't. This is nothing more than a cheap joke at the expense of the Liberal Democrats.
51 I could write a guidebook, a kind of *A to Bed*.

finest two minutes, when I had extremely brief and very urgent sex in the kitchen with one of Laura's friends. While Laura was in the loo. We stopped only when we heard her washing her hands. I'm not very proud of that. Well, just a little, maybe.

And yet all through these years I never wanted to lose Laura. On one occasion, one of my lovers asked me if I would leave Laura for her. I remember looking at her incredulously and saying, 'You don't understand.' She didn't, but as the years wore on I began to think that I did. I began to work out for myself, not a moral defence, but at least a reason for my actions. I was, I decided, still smarting from the absence of my mother's love and thus so overwhelmed by the approval of any woman that I had to see through to the bitter-sweet end the slightest display of sexual interest. Well, it sounded pretty convincing to me.

But I learnt something else during this process, and it was something far more depressing than the understanding that – for whatever reason – I was an untrustworthy cad. It was that almost nobody can be trusted. No, scratch that: make that nobody at all. Nearly all those wives and girlfriends and best friends who slept with me were in turn betraying someone else: a husband, a boyfriend (a girlfriend, on one memorable occasion), or Laura. And that, for a man whose favourite song is 'Our House', is a very, very depressing thing to learn. Made better only by plunging into yet more exciting, flattering illicit sex.

I hope you're buying this. Not least because I'm not the only man out there who is like that. Let's just say that if we hired Wembley Arena for an annual dinner, we would need several sittings. And one hell of an after-dinner speaker.

Of course, it all had to end and, one October, it did, on the day before my fortieth birthday. The curious thing is that it didn't end because Laura found out about me. It ended because I found out about her. I think this is what they call dramatic irony.

I can't remember what tipped me off, but the fact that nothing had until then should be a warning to all you cosy couples out there. Right up until the day before the truth dawned I had never doubted – not a single once in all the years – that Laura was as faithful to me as she assumed I was to her. Looking back, the clues were there, of course, but I wasn't looking. Despite the lessons I had been busy learning, I trusted her. Ha.

She was going away for work, again, and while there was nothing unusual in that, there was something about the destination – Bonn – and the fact that she had been there before only very recently, that triggered an alarm.

She was going away on my birthday, so we were planning to spend the night before together drinking wine, snacking on dips, watching *Friends* on TV. But something didn't fit and, at some point during the afternoon, I called her at work. It was a short conversation, with a couple of even shorter pauses.

'Hi, what's up?'

'Hi. Listen, I want to ask you something and I want you to tell me the truth.'

Pause.

'Oh. OK, sure. What?'

My head is whirling. Suddenly, I feel quite sick. I could be on the merry-go-round on the Racecourse. Only, I'm not. Although I have the distinct feeling that I am about to fall off the sodding merry-go-round.

'Are you seeing somebody else?'

Another pause. Not long, barely noticeable to a stranger, but long enough, and uncharacteristic. I know this woman so well that I can make deductions even from the things she *doesn't* say and the way in which she doesn't say them. And, eventually, she says, 'Yes,' in a little, scared voice that makes me want to put my arms around her.

And that's my failing, right there. That protection thing. I didn't realize it back then, but I do now. I need protection, and I seek out someone to protect in the way I want to be protected myself because it's easier as a man to demonstrate what you want rather than to come right out and say it. And I guess that's why men like me never get what they want. We are too busy dishing it out and – slowly, slowly – the resentment at being failed by a woman who has absolutely no chance of not failing you because you give her not a clue about what it is you really need from her builds and builds until, finally, it engulfs what you first mistook for love. When in fact it wasn't love at all: merely your own neediness projected on to someone else. A giant Bat Signal in the night sky. Or a huge Wanking Santa.

Now, are we buying this? Please say yes.

Later, after Laura has cycled home on the sit-up-and-beg bicycle (complete with basket and floral paint job) I bought her two years before (like a lot of things, in a fit of contrition after yet another now-forgotten bout of faithlessness), we sit on her grandmother's sofa. Yes, that's right, the one on which I . . .

She really does look scared, God help me, and she is crying. She tells me that she has been seeing someone but nothing has happened.

Nothing?

Well, they have kissed.

What?

Yes.

Just the once?

Well, more than once, and, yes, she has been visiting him where he lives in Germany. They met when she was writing pieces for an English-language magazine in Munich.

Munich. München. Nazis. Munich air disaster. Steiff bears, even? I don't know it right then, but I am doomed to spend the next few years smarting every time I see the word 'Munich' in the windows of travel agents. And you'd be surprised how many flights go to Munich. And not just from Manchester.

Behind us where we now sit, on her grandmother's re-upholstered sofa, is the desk at which we write. Just a few months before this night, I was sitting at that desk one evening with Laura on my lap. I was helping her to write a piece for that self-same magazine. Helping her, I now understand, to impress the man whose cock had been inside the woman with whom I was fully prepared, eventually, to have children and, quite possibly, maybe, to marry. But certainly to whom I was ready to offer at least one kidney. But probably not both.

Nice, I think.

On the other hand, I also recall sitting at that same desk while one of Laura's friends knelt at my feet and, for a few minutes at least, made me feel very, very good about myself, and her.

Equally nice, I think.

Everything is swirling around in my head. And I do mean everything. Colours that we mixed together to make the bright Brazilian Jubilee yellow that covers the walls that we painted to celebrate our trip to South America and which now stand, dumb and surrounding and never again to cocoon us together against the world. Dull, boring stuff: a tune that keeps on humming in my head.[52] I notice for the first time that the shelves we fitted on the far wall aren't completely straight, I wonder if we are going to be able to catch the episode of Friends *despite all this, and I can't figure out when she could have sneaked home to put all the presents she has bought me on the coffee table in front of us and to lay out all of our favourite snacks . . .*

After disappearing for a week, she finally calls from the Lake District. A week during which I have humiliated myself by calling around her friends to find out where she is. Lucy, one of those friends, comes round to console me, and we do it like animals on Granny's sofa. I don't know what motivates Lucy but I know what's inspiring me. 'I guess it's because you're free now,' she says, which comes as a bit of a surprise to me, although it doesn't seem to occur to her that she isn't. Giles, her husband, is expected later, driving round after work to pick her up. He is early and knocks on the door while Lucy is consoling me for all she is worth, but somehow we get away with it. She straightens her clothes and lets him in while I calm myself in the bathroom. When I come out, they are kissing, leaning against the breakfast bar, and I put the kettle on for coffee.

I can't begin to tell you how savagely addictive and irresistible this stuff is. And that when it is happening how much I feel like I am falling from a tall building, but with no chance of ever hitting the ground.

From time to time I go running with this man, who, despite being a commodities trader (whatever the hell that is), is a really

52 On the in-mind Walkman. This was before the invention of the iPod.

nice bloke. Lucy is in a constant state of guilt, not because of her faithlessness (and I don't kid myself that I'm the only one), but because she comes from a long line of lefties and she has married a capitalist. A very successful capitalist, which does take the edge off her pain, obviously, but a capitalist nevertheless.

So confident is this capitalist in his success and charm and money that he seems incapable of conceiving that anything remotely bad could happen to him. This leads him to trust me absolutely to be left alone with his wife, which is an open invitation for all sorts of far from *remotely* bad things to happen. This is his mistake. There is no exchange rate for fidelity on the money markets. Money does not buy faithfulness – on the contrary, in my experience. Perhaps it has something to do with a woman's deep-seated resentment at being the minority stockholder in a relationship.

Besides, I have known Lucy for years. We've been screwing, on and off, for most of them and have many memories we shouldn't have. My favourite is lying naked with her a week after her return from her honeymoon, the tiny white bikini marks vivid against her otherwise golden body. I can still remember feeling the ring on her third finger against my skin.

My favourite memory up till now, that is. On this terrible day, in this hour of my loss, amidst the genuine agony that grips at me almost constantly and reduces me to self-pitying tears at the drop of a hat, Lucy makes everything so much worse, and yet so much better.

And it gets worse. And better. There's no milk in the flat and Giles volunteers to fetch some from the shop round the corner. This, too, is his mistake. Leaning against the breakfast bar, we can see him through the first-floor window, strolling down the alleyway towards the shop. We know we will see him making his way back long before he gets inside the building.

Lucy turns and smiles and kisses me and lifts her dress and leans forward over the counter and we carry on where we left off.

We finish, more or less together, just as her husband reappears around the corner, swinging a two-litre carton of milk. He can't see me, which is just as well, as I am still bound tightly to his wife, but I can see that he's also bought the papers and some digestive biscuits, which is good, as I am now starting to feel quite hungry.

I think I already mentioned just how savagely addictive and irresistible, etc., this stuff is.

Laura, it turns out, wasn't in the Lake District. At least, not the *English* Lake District, where we had often played together. Not that I learnt that from her. I heard it from Lucy, in whom she had confided. She'd been in the lake district of southern Germany. With the English guy she had been seeing. With the guy she had now left me for.

Later, as the months and then the years went past, Laura and I played the occasional game of revelations tennis. Sometimes I would learn something new about her, but more often it was her who learnt something fresh about me. I lost a lot of points, and I lost a lot of friends. Or, rather, I lost a lot of male acquaintances whose partners had slept with me. Oddly, given my loathing for the way he made his money (and, it has to be said, he did make rather a lot), I was really upset only about Giles. I really did like him. But revelations tennis took no prisoners and that smash serve was heading his way. One day Laura rang me out of the blue, talked about this and that and then, quite suddenly, said: 'Just tell me one thing. Did you ever sleep with Lucy?'

And then it was my turn to hesitate fatally.

When the shit had started hitting the fan, Lucy and I had agreed that neither of us would ever tell anyone. She didn't want to lose Giles any more than I wanted to lose Laura. Then Lucy found out that I had also slept with her elder sister, and she went crazy-bat ape-shit bonkers and all bets, I deduced, were off. She told Laura, she told Giles, she told almost everyone in the world other than three Icelandic fishermen who had been out of radio contact for the critical two-day period during which her storm raged. By the time it had abated a few more relationships lay in smouldering ruin (although the fishermen were none the wiser).

A few months later, Giles and I met up for a pizza. This, I thought, was very grown-up. Frankly, although I like pizza, I was nervous. He would have been within his rights (and well within his physical capabilities) to beat me to a pulp, but instead he was unbearably decent, which somehow hurt even more than a good pasting might have. It turned out that the heat was off me because, in the meantime, he had discovered that Lucy had also been seeing some other guy. It never rains, and all that. He'd kicked her out that very morning. She'd thrown a few knickers and tops in a bag and, for all he knew, she had gone round to this other bloke's house.

Seeing some other guy? Cow! Oddly, I found myself consoling him. Even odder, I found myself choking back emotions. Not on his account, you understand. I was, as usual, feeling sorry for myself.

'Listen,' I said, as he ignored his pizza but kept knocking back the Peroni beers. 'Exactly what do you want from all this?'

It seemed pretty clear to me. He could play games now, punish her like I'd punished Laura and risk losing her. Or he could cut out all that crap and fast-forward to the place where he wanted to be. If the place where he wanted to be was with her.

'I know you're angry now. I don't blame you,' I said, generously. Well, I hardly could, could I? 'But it boils down to this: do you want Lucy in your life? Don't think about anything else right now. Just focus on that. Do you want her? Yes or no?'

He dropped his loosely held fork on the floor. The pretty waitress came right over, bobbed down and picked it up. I tried really hard not to take my eyes off Giles. Almost succeeded. She really was very pretty.

He nodded, slowly.

'That's it then. Cut out all the crap, call her now, and start again from that point. Here. Use my phone.'

It was only as I pushed it towards him that I remembered that his wife was listed in my mobile's memory not as Lucy, but as Juicy. But I needn't have worried. 'It's OK,' he said, ever so *slightly* pointedly. 'I do have her number.' Well, of course; he would have. Oops.

I spent the rest of the evening telling him how, sure, something had to be missing in his relationship with Lucy for her to have done what she had done but that, at heart, she wanted him as badly as he wanted her and was just as willing to figure things out. As I got bolder, I got into my stride and told him that the affair she had had with me had been entirely my fault. I had sensed that she was vulnerable and needy and had played on it, flattering her, seducing her, leading her astray. Yes. It was entirely my fault. She was all but innocent. I had virtually bullied her into screwing me. Countless times. For years and years. Oh, come on . . .

But he was buying it, because he *wanted* to buy it. No doubt this other bastard was doing just the same thing, I said. He was taking advantage. *I bet he was*. She didn't want him any more than she wanted me. *She'd better not*. All this was a cry for help, and she needed him, Giles, to answer it.

All of which was, of course, bollocks. The truth was that she was an exceptionally randy little minx who loved sex – and *especially* dangerous sex – went out of her way to get it and would not take no for an answer. Even, I recalled, suppressing a fond smile, standing at the sink, washing up, with a gaggle of post-dinner-party guests chatting away in the next room. God, that was a night . . . And, actually, it was worse than that. More than once Lucy had asked me to run away with her. Including the time when I was giving her a lift home and she tried to persuade me to get my passport and drive instead to the airport. I damn near did: it's hard to resist that kind of passionate insanity. I didn't tell Giles any of that. I couldn't see how it would be particularly helpful at this point.

I had no idea if they would work it out, but at least it felt good to be doing something approximating The Right Thing for a change. And, besides, Lucy being with Giles was one thing. I mean, he was *married* to her, after all, and I was used to that. But I'd be buggered if I was going to stand by and let some other twat shag her.

Giles did call Lucy and, as far as I know, they are still busy living happy ever after. That was maybe seven years ago now, and I don't hear from either of them these days. They stayed together, moved to the country and had kids. Three, at the last count. I do like a happy ending.

How did they manage that? I mean, how did they overcome all that betrayal and pain? I have no idea. Laura and I never could. Later, she told me that on the night it had all fallen apart she had come home to face the music convinced that I would go berserk and hit her. I'm not sure what she based this on. Probably just the scale of her guilt. As it was, she found my stunned apathy even more distressing. Hitting her had never occurred to me. I had just felt desperately sad. And, in a clear, cold corner of my mind, rather pleased that it had been her and not me who had been found out. Besides, as I quickly realized, I was a bed-half-full kind of guy.

We missed *Friends* that night, the bottle of wine popped its cork in the freezer, and by the morning the guacamole had healed over in its opened pot. The night before, it turned out, was the last time we slept together in that bed. Or, for the next eight years, in any bed. I can't remember the last time, but I can remember the first time. Why is it always like that?

She packed and left, and I didn't try to stop her. I just lay on her grandmother's sofa and stared at the ceiling, listening to the sounds of her leaving. It didn't take her long. For years afterwards, I wished that I had tried, wished the advice I had so glibly handed to Giles had occurred to me then. I used to torment myself by imagining how different things might have been had I got off that sofa when I heard her crying in the bedroom, or when I heard her open the front door and leave. Even then, I could have run down the corridor after her.

If only I'd been man enough to say, 'Actually, I have something to tell you, too,' but at the time I was just relieved to be having a lucky escape. Besides, the breeze on the moral high ground was bracing, and by the time it had turned just plain chilly, she was long gone.

I have never forgiven her for what she did and she has never forgiven me for what I did. From time to time we see each other. Sometimes we fight like it was yesterday and sometimes we don't, but I think we realize that we have both come so far now that there is no going back. At least I still have both my kidneys.

Birthday Blues
Friday 17 October 2003

Until my son, Adam, was born, twenty-two years ago this month, I remembered only two birthdays: my own, and that of the son of God (and His only because of the months of annual worldwide pre-publicity).

This year, however, I forgot even my own birthday. The telephone call that reminded me of my impending forty-eighth year on earth came from Laura, the woman with whom I spent the best part of a decade (and, so far, at least, some of the best days of my life) and for whom 364 days a year of love and affection never quite compensated for an annual failure to recall one simple date (her birthday).

In my head, life divides into the pre- and post-Laura eras, a glorious reign that ended abruptly in 1995, on the eve of my fortieth birthday. Despite the Vesuvian eruption which blew us apart, we have kept in touch over the years. Or perhaps it would be more accurate to say that we have been unable to cut the link between us – a tie sometimes golden thread, sometimes bloodied barbed wire.

Over the eight wonderful, volatile, love-of-our-life years we were together, we both, from time to time, betrayed the other, although at the time neither of us knew about the other's 'indiscretions'. I think it fair to say that, while she was bad, I was very (or quite possibly very, very) bad, but hey: who's counting?

And so, last week, the phone call: 'What are you doing on Thursday?' she asks.

'Er, what's Thursday?'

That old, familiar sigh. 'Your birthday.'

To Carluccio's in Smithfield for a strangely poignant little birthday dinner, at moments as if nothing had changed – her finishing my sentences, me finishing her food.

This is the first birthday I have spent with Laura since the nightmare night, seven years back, when I came home from work to find an assortment of surprises. I recall three, only two of which were wrapped: a Wallace and Gromit novelty radio, an over-large lilac shirt (Lilac? Clearly, I remember thinking, bought with another man in mind) and the news that Laura was Seeing Somebody Else. Happy birthday.

That was the last night we spent together. She left, coming back later, but only for Wallace and Gromit. Then, for the best part of two years, we played shocking and wearing revelations tennis: the messy dissection of a love gone bad, but never, it seems, quite gone for good.

These days, the one thing guaranteed to unite us is quiet scorn for cocksure couples who, having heard the admittedly grim stories of betrayal, primly declare: 'Well, you can't possibly have loved each other.' What, we tell each other, do they know?

This week I took a walk past the flat in which it all fell apart. As though abandoned in the wake of some natural disaster, it is the same, only faded: the deckchair on the balcony, its colour bleached; the Brazilian Jubilee yellow dulled but still on the walls (along with the blood). The unknown lovers who sleep in our airy bedroom overlooking the Thames do so, unknowingly, above a love letter Laura and I wrote and placed under the wooden floor I laid (despite a deep loathing of DIY) in a Desmond Morris spasm of nest-building.

The spell we wove still holds us both, although not in a way we anticipated. We have never been together since – like the couple in a weather-house clock, when one of us is out in the cold, the other is snug indoors – and may never be again, but so what?

Perhaps love, as Sarah says to Bendrix in *The End of the*

Affair, doesn't end. In the same way that people love God all their lives, without ever seeing Him.

Is love more true because it's written annually on a Hallmark birthday card and then forgotten in some drawer, or less true because it's scrawled on a scrap of paper and buried, along with the bodies, beneath the floorboards?

8

How to Help Yourself

Dear Microwave Man

   Doesn't the secret of success with younger women as a middle-aged bachelor depend on good looks and money? Bet you wouldn't be so cheerful if you'd fallen out of the ugly tree and hit every branch on the way down.

                                        Mr JD, Glasgow, Scotland

Microwave Man writes: You've hit the nail on the head, JD – perhaps while falling out of that tree? Although, frankly, when you look as good as I do, the money is less important. But it sure helps! As does the enormous penis. But seriously. One does see some very beautiful young women out and about with very fat, ugly older men (especially in Glasgow). Are you telling me that all they are interested in is their wallets? Gee, that would be pretty cynical, don't you think?

One of the drawbacks of being a journalist is that, sooner or later, one has to interface with members of the public – and, indeed, members of your own profession. You can leave as many jackets on the backs of as many chairs as you like, but sooner or later someone above you in the extremely long and thickly populated food chain is going to remember that you exist and that you haven't written anything since 1823 (but what a fine critique of Ferdinand VII's restoration of absolute monarchy in Spain that was).

Now, many members of the public are just like you and me – pretty weird, on the whole – but some lurk on what can be described only as the lunatic fringe.

Like anyone whose name and face appears in print, I attract

my share of these, from the stalker I share with two other male writers ('Was that you I saw waving frantically from the back of a donkey-drawn dustcart in Bangkok last week? Sorry if I ignored you, Jonathan, but I get pestered these days by so many people in the media, even when I am on a well-deserved pilgrimage. PS: still no home, hope or hair.') to the anonymous, lunatic correspondent who, like all anonymous, lunatic correspondents, feels compelled to write in green ink or, even, when the subject is particularly important to them (brainwashing by mobile-phone waves, the plot to poison poor people's fish and chips with the ink off the newspapers in which they are wrapped, the Royal Family are all alien reptiles, etc.[53]), in ink of three or more different colours.

Other than deep-brain thrombosis, self-obsession and caffeine poisoning, there are few perils attached to sitting in front of a laptop posing as a journalist, but they do include the ever-present risk of exposure to wild and crazy ideas from the fringe. Dealing with commissioning editors, of course, comes with the territory. Occasionally, however, one is privileged to receive from a reader a communication so inexpressibly bonkers that it at once reinforces one's belief in gated communities and serves as a reminder that care in the community is a concept that really does need a bit of a rethink.

I get all my shit-hits-the-fan mail forwarded by the office. Not that they sniff it for anthrax or scan it for wires or anything. Once a month, they just bung everything into one large brown envelope and fire it off in my direction. Inside these undiplomatic bags there are frequently strange, lumpy packages which could, quite easily, contain a small but effective amount of, say, Semtex (but which so far, I have to say, have contained nothing more explosive than the occasional butt plug or anal dildo. Microwave Man attracts a lot of that sort of thing).

So receiving (thoughtfully forwarded from the office) twenty

---

53 Some of these theories have more credibility than others, obviously. Clearly, if the ink used by the *Financial Times* really was poisonous, the printers would have to wear gloves and, as far as I know, that isn't the case. But we all know about the Royal Family.

sheets of plain white A4 perforated for filing (should I care to) and covered with what, at first glance, appeared to be a wild and random jumble of numbers, words and newspaper cuttings made a nice change.[54] That's the way it looked at second glance, too. This was plainly the work of what my friend Merv would refer to (with the necessary, carapace-hardening callousness of his profession) as a window-licker.

I had written about John Lennon Airport in Liverpool, and this, clearly, had got my correspondent's satanic goat. Under the heading, '666 airport', he (or, I suppose, to be fair, she: why, in the face of all personal evidence to the contrary, I continue to assume that all nutters are men, I have no idea) proceeds to apply mad maths to a series of dates, names and places. And he always shows his working-out – a retired maths teacher, perhaps, driven insane by the demise of the slide rule? For instance, '8 December 1980' (the date of Lennon's death) is boiled down (torturously) to 666, The Number of the Beast (as is every such extrapolation over the following nineteen pages. Except one, where, despite much frenzied working-out, back-tracking and recalculation, the best he can come up with – and I guess that's slide rules for you – is 668. The Neighbour of the Beast, presumably).

By now, of course, I was hooked, and the rest of my day went to hell as I tried foolishly to decipher my correspondent's multi-coloured ramblings (why do these people use at least three coloured inks?).

Occasionally, by way of a change of pace, he offers some music criticism: (red ink) 'Lennon trivial ringmaster' (blue), 'purveyor of the' (green) 'rotten noise' (red again), 'and gross' (back to blue) 'blasphemer'. He even comes up with a half-decent idea for a feature (obviously not a commissioning editor after

54 A nice change from bullying letters from Oxfam. I find I can salve my social conscience nicely with a simple, modest, monthly direct debit. Now the buggers keep writing to say, 'Hey, know anyone else you can rope in?' or 'How about giving just a little bit more?' Well, how about remembering that now I've got internet banking I can delete that direct debit with a single keystroke? Now sod off and dig those bloody wells I've paid for. Jesus. It's not easy, caring.

all, then): 'Fast for a week, do a diary in *the paper*, no guts, eh? Cowardy custard not up to it, just like I thought.'

Generally accurate factual references to incidents at Dungeness, Windscale, Chernobyl and Sizewell B ('0.0378 of an inch from meltdown', apparently. Well, we'd all guessed as much, I suppose) blend seamlessly with allusions to Jonathan Miller, Stephen Hawking, George Gallup and Richard Dawkings (so at least I won't be short of decent conversation on Judgement Day).

Writing, don't forget, is nine-tenths displacement activity, so this was a godsend. Literally. The biblical references flew thick and fast, and it became clear that my man knew his way around the arcane cracks running through the Old and New Testaments: his references come from not only the common biblical canon but also the Apocrypha, that body of early Christian writing that has found itself either deleted from or never included in most versions of the Bible.

And with good reason, doctor.

All very *Exorcist*, and all appearing to boil down to the single message: 'God is not mocked.' I, on the other hand, *am* mocked, as my correspondent takes a break from doom-saying to offer a spot of constructive literary criticism: 'Grow up, stop gribbling, stop being mawkish, read Derrida – it will cure you.'

Gribbling?

To be fair, he has a point about the mawkishness. Jacques Derrida, on the other hand (who died, spookily, on 9 October – the date of the birthday I share with Lennon), is no help in deconstructing the obscure ramblings of my new tricoloured-pen friend.

So who is the author of this mad missive? All I know is that it was posted in Wales, a comforting distance from London (I wasted some time searching for a village called Talwyd Y Post DG before discovering that this was Welsh – yawn – for 'Postage paid UK'). So, a retired religious maths teacher from a small former mining village just across the valley from Llareggub, perhaps?

Should my correspondent be reading this and care to get in

touch again (perhaps, who knows, confining himself to one side of A4 and plain language?), there is just one thing that intrigues me. What the bloody hell are you banging on about? Because, if the end of the world truly is nigh, I'd quite like to know. In words of one colour.

Can you imagine the solitary celebrations in bed-sitting-rooms up and down the land the day they invented that three-in-one pen – the one with three different colours available with a simple thumb click?[55] Although, if I were that way inclined, I think I would save up for the Magico Merlin 600, featuring as it does not only *four* different-coloured styluses and a light 'to enable you to carry on writing in the dark' (presumably when the meter runs out, or perhaps for when you don't want Them to see what you are writing), but also a small but potentially deadly knife. It's the kind of pen that means that you really can be a danger not only to yourself but to other people as well.

And talking of dangers to other people, I find myself, once again, sitting opposite Cornelia. She's not in a good mood, and I wonder if she is about to can the column – which, frankly, would come as something of a relief. Writing about my life is starting to get me into trouble. Especially with the people in my life I sleep with and then write about.

But no such luck.

I can't help noticing that a trend has emerged since I began writing Microwave Man – a tendency to typecast me. As a result, I get to write about the things that really matter in life: if there's a piece to be done about adultery, I'm their man. Ditto pornography, ditto older guys going out with younger women, ditto men generally behaving badly: I'm their man – their Microwave Man. Until, one wonderful day, I was asked to write 2,000 words on the impact of the Franco-German EU *alliance secrète* on the English national identity.

No, *of course*, I wasn't.

Not that I really care. I never really understand actors who

---

55 The Parker Nutter, I believe it was called.

complain about typecasting. Don't like being typecast as an employed loser? Try being typecast as an *unemployed* loser. No sirree, that's not for me. It gives me a curious pride to recognize that, in the eyes of my editor and my colleagues, I am a fully employed *professional* loser.

Cornelia is telling me that Rick Raddice ('Is that pronounced Raddicé, with an acute accent, Rick?' 'No, mate: Raddice, like radish'. Well, OK, then), an Australian psychotherapist (they *have* psychotherapists?), is in town to promote his latest book, *Manpower*.

Just what the world needs, I say. *Another contribution to the groaning self-help shelving. I bet it's printed in at least three different colours.*

'Well, I thought you'd say that,' says Cornelia, flicking through the pages. On the cover I can see a loathsome picture of some reasonably butch but obviously sensitive new man, stripped to his bathers and standing knee-deep in the sea on some beach with two boys – presumably meant to be his kids. He's gripping their hands just a *little too tightly*, and it's *just* possible but sadly not very likely that he is getting ready to drown the scary, alien-looking little bastards who, like him, are quite clearly from Planet Touchy-Feely.[56]

In other words, this is hate-on-sight material. And I hate it on sight.

'That's why I want you to interview him,' says Cornelia. 'He says here . . .' *flick, flick, flick,* 'he says here that "philandering men who boast of their independence are fooling themselves and living hollow, artificial lives". Who better,' she says, looking up and smiling, 'than our own Microwave Man to challenge his theories?'

Oh, who indeed? Buggeration.

'Treat it as a counselling session: talk to him about yourself and your life and see if he has any suggestions.'

'You mean, go for counselling and then write about it?'

'Something like that.'

---

56 With any luck, while he's splashing around knee-deep in self-approval, his wife is off shagging someone else. His publisher, perhaps.

'What about patient confidentiality? I could sue the paper.'

'Or, you could do as you are told and carry on drawing your fabulous pay cheque.'

She really is very attractive when she's on the cusp of losing her patience. Obviously, the trick would be to keep her constantly oscillating between this and the girlish head-and-hair-tossing laughter, although I suppose that could get a little wearing.

'Cornelia,' I say, reaching over and taking the book from her hands, 'how come you never take me to lunch?' I give her both barrels of what I fondly imagine to be my most penetrating, smouldering stare, but she appears to be wearing bullet-proof glasses.

'What are you talking about?'

'Well, I can't help noticing that over the past year or so you've fed almost everyone in the department. I'm sure I even saw you in a taxi last week with that bloke who always turns up to clean the photocopiers just at the moment we need them most. When's it my turn?'

'What, to clean the photocopiers? Could be sooner than you think.'

I stare at her, as straight-faced as I can manage. Not only does she blush – just a little, but, hey – I absolutely swear that I see a brief sparkle in her eyes of something, if not outright naughty, then certainly a shade east of appropriate.

'And if you can't manage a lunch,' I continue, pressing my luck, 'how about dinner one evening? I could slip something in the microwave . . .'

The giggle. The shriek. The head-thrown-back thing. Result! Her secretary, eyebrows raised, turns to look disapprovingly through the glass wall. Maybe she's just seen my expenses.

'Microwave Man,' says Cornelia, regaining her composure, 'I am a married woman! If you think I'm going to be seen getting into the back of a cab with the likes of you, then you are sadly mistaken. Now sod off and do some work.'

So, no lunch, then. I grab the book and get up to leave, but just as I reach the doorway, remember something I have been meaning to ask her.

'Cornelia, who was that woman? The one who stuck her head around the door when you were dreaming up Microwave Man?'

'Ah, I wondered when you'd get round to asking,' she said, leaning back in her chair. 'You can forget that one, MM, far too good for you.'

'Oh, come on! Name?'

'Do your own dirty work! Better still, read the bloody section and you'll see her byline picture. Here's a tip: fashion.'

'I don't know anything about fashion.'

'Obviously, darling.'

Later, she forwards me the email correspondence that has passed between one of her commissioning editors and The Radish's publisher, explaining my candidature for the interview-cum-therapy session. It leaves me in little doubt as to what they really think of me around here.

'Jonathan,' it says, 'has a column in which he recounts his struggles with love, commitment, etc. He is forty-nine, divorced, with a son in his early twenties, and I'm sure he wouldn't mind me saying that, in a lot of people's eyes, he might seem quite screwed up.'

Gee. Thanks. Only *quite* screwed up? And it's forty-eight, actually. No wonder The Radish looks a little tense when we are left alone in a small office at his publisher's, with me sat between him and the only way out. His PR minder hangs around for a few minutes, looking anxious as I plug the microphone into my iPod, until I ask her if she'd mind leaving.

'Rick and I have issues to discuss. Male issues,' I say, as seriously as I can manage. The Radish blanches visibly.

'No, no, not at all,' she says, smiling and jumping up, a bit embarrassed. She edges towards the door, glances at Rick and, pointing through the glass wall, adds reassuringly, 'I'll be right out there, Rick . . .' . . . *in case he goes mad and tries to kill you.*

As she walks towards the door she brushes past me and shoots me a smile, and she is, I notice for the first time, quite pretty, in a librarian-chic kind of way. Now I wish I hadn't asked her to leave. Women *do* respond to sob stories.

Alone at last. The Radish is not quite what I was expecting, which was a cross between Iron John and a gourd-touting new-age sandalista just a tad too firmly in touch with his feminine side. Despite the stockman's hat,[57] he does wear his manhood lightly, but I soon learn that the softly spoken thing is slightly misleading. The Radish wields an iron fist in his ethnically sourced fair-trade velvet glove.

I had arrived bristling indignantly over his book, which begins with a series of generalizations about modern man which appear to be part of that long, sad train of modern male apologies for manhood hitched abjectly and cravenly to the post-feminist band-wagon. The Radish is, without doubt, another Auntie Tom.

'Most men don't live,' is the book's gut-chucking opening salvo, 'they just act,' and this sets the tone for a book through which the phrase 'most men' runs like a mantra.

The Radish, craven bum-licker that he is, admires women (naturally) for the way 'they protect and nurture one another', while decrying 'most men' for keeping up a pretence of happiness. 'Most women' (naturally) 'are superior emotional animals . . . increasingly, women transcend the everyday, transported on feelings and spiritual sensibilities . . . living in a fifth-dimensional commune of mutual love and support . . .'

Blah de blah de blah blah.

'Most men,' on the other hand, 'are killed by loneliness.' *Oh! And not, as we thought, then, by heart disease, cancer or working till they drop because, let's face it, no other bugger's going to?*

Nope. And most men, he says, 'breathe their last with a look of fear and failure', which, I get the impression, he thinks kind of serves them right. In an all-encompassing tour of male failings that whips breathtakingly in and out of 'the clearly implied incest between sons and mothers', as if that goes without saying, we learn that the 'dramas' that guys like me 'create with affairs

57 Free of corks, to be fair.

121

and endless conquests lose some of their appeal when one real-izes that all they are doing is trying to sleep with their mothers'.

Blimey. And I thought I was just shagging around.

The Radish is no less dogmatic in person; a tad more likeable than I would have liked, but not *so* likeable that I can completely shake off an almost overwhelming urge to knock that stupid bloody hat off his pointy head. Then, perhaps sensing my hostility and, rather like an end-of-pier psychic[58] who comes out with all the stuff you want to hear, he says: 'You strike me as a tender-hearted person.'

God, yes, Rick. I am.

'You're not cold or putting up walls like a lot of English guys do, so it's like your heart is out there to be in loving relation-ships with people.'

Rick, that is so me it's scary. *All I really want is to be loved, mate.*

'Not everyone is cut out for intimate long-term relationships, but my gut feeling is that you are.'

Absolutely. And maybe that explains why I have had so many of them? Often simultaneously.

But that hand-embroidered, fingerless velvet tribal glove doesn't stay on for long. In The Radish's world there are basically two types of guy: 'One view of a man is that he stands alone on the mountaintop through his own strength and power – the John Wayne thing.'

Yup, I think, *that's the one for me.*

But not for Rickie boy. Live like that, he says, and you are a loser. He should know. He was, he says, that fool on the hill before the epiphanic episode sixteen years ago that rocked the world he shared with his wife. That, he says, and the radical Radish way in which he pulled his crashing plane out of its death dive, prompted him to write this stupid book.[59]

'There are,' he says, in a voice even quieter and more sensi-tive than usual (and, let me tell you, that is *really* quiet and sensitive), 'seven years between our two children . . . and that's

58 And I don't mean to imply here that there is any such thing as a *genuine* psychic.
59 No, not *this* stupid book, stupid; *his* stupid book.

because there was going to be one in the middle. And that,' deep breath, 'that was the *miscarriage*.'

He pauses, glances down at the desk that separates us, draws a picture in the imaginary dust. It's hard to say, looking at it upside-down, but I think it's meant to be a house.

'It really tilted us off balance and in different directions. I was no use to Deirdre, and she was no use to me. What should have happened in a sane society was that I would have landed with male support and been propped up and put back together, but there wasn't any. I had admirers, but I didn't have friends, and I decided my life was just an act.'

He starts fiddling with the brim of his bloody hat. I'm still trying, reluctantly, to tune out Crosby, Stills and Nash singing 'Our House', and waiting to hear about the real problem that evolved from this common enough mishap, and then it dawns on me: that's it. Up to a quarter of all pregnancies end in miscarriage, but that's the biggest excuse for a life-shattering moment that this cat in a hat can come up with? No affairs, no alcoholism, no suicide attempts, no cross-dressing, necrophilia, no drugs/porn/corpses found under the eldest kid's bed? *Christ, he doesn't know he's born, yet he takes it on himself to preach to me and the rest of his sex, handing down his judgemental saccharine-coated tablets of disapproval.*

I wonder if he knows Sarah Day?

He sniffs and recovers his composure, and it's the sniff that pulls my gaze back from the glass wall, through which I have been trying to establish eye contact with the now less-anxious press minder. She's sitting at a desk, checking her emails. She gives me a smile. I smile back. She really is *very* pretty.

The Radish coughs. 'Post-miscarriage', plucky Rick then set out to 'put myself back together as a man' and to 'work at building the support systems I needed'.

'Yes, yes,' I say, pretending I not only understand but empathize whereas, in fact, I have absolutely no idea what he is going on about, although I do instinctively mistrust and despise his construction metaphors, the smug misappropriation of the images of labour and toil, the suggestion of hard graft, of manual labour and brick-laying.

He tells me how he upped and moved the family from the glamorous isolation of a big, successful-person's house in the wilds to a modest five-bedder in the parochial but supportively communal world of suburbia, plugging into every brother-in-law he could find and 'engaging with the community' for the express purpose of making friends. He even went to church, even though he doesn't believe in God and it was 'a bit crap', because 'that was the indigenous faith' of the place where he had chosen to live. I bet the vicar was thrilled. And he tells me all of this in the tone of someone who clearly thinks he has done a great, brave, generous, epic thing.

'We downsized everything,' he says. 'Even got rid of two of the cars.'

Got rid of *two* of them, you say? Well, hell, Rick, that *is* tough.

'Life is not,' he says, droning on, quietly, 'to do with financial or material success.' *Christ, we used to talk like this in the fifth form.* 'It's about who would come to your funeral.'

Really? Who would actually give a shit, I think, even if it was just them and Father McKenzie, wiping the dirt from his hands as he walked from the grave?

'Not *because* of the funeral, but because of the quality it builds into the second half of your life, when you mean a lot to a lot of people.'

But to go back to the funeral for a moment there, Rick: I was rather hoping that mine would be attended by lots of women wearing black veils. Who knows: maybe they would all get talking, go down to the pub, have a few G&Ts, realize that they all had quite a lot in common and end up the best of friends.

What the hell is he talking about? Suppose he gets lost at sea and doesn't *get* a funeral? He might as well have stayed in the four-star mountain des res. In fact, if he *had*, and hadn't moved to the coast, then maybe he wouldn't have got lost at sea.

The thing is that, like all converts, Rick zealously wants us all to see the same light that's mesmerizing him, and that's the problem with being sucked into the world of self-help: if you don't buy into the magic solution on offer 100 per cent, you are left feeling that there must, therefore, be something wrong with you. And that's just plain nasty.

What we are reading in *Manpower* is actually Rick's own story, an account of his journey from the lonely, windswept summit of the mountain of manly self-isolation to the lush, sun-kissed valleys of family life and community love. And now that he has successfully reconnected with his dad (and you have to feel sorry for the old boy, driven at one point to a remote beach by the issues-laden Radish, who refuses to take him home again until they have talked – 'He came through very well.' I bet he did. Anything to escape the relentless incoming tide of bullshit), he thinks we should all know about it. At £14.99 a pop.

There is, he says, something wrong with men who, like me, are either literally fatherless or 'desperately under-fathered'.

Better than being desperately under-shagged, I mutter.

'What's that?'

'Nothing. Please, do go on.'

He does. And on. And on. Missing the vital 'Factor F' and denied a mentor to help our growth 'into real men', we blokes stagger to our lonely graves 'lost, depressed and empty, unable to relate properly to women, children or each other, and so unable to build happy families or communities'.[60]

All of which presupposes that this is the recipe for happiness, which is no less fascistic than a doctrine that says any woman who fails to have children is unfulfilled. I mean, supposing I don't *want* all that community crap, surrounded by dozens of odious cousins twice removed and forced to get up early every Sunday to fake orgasmic connection with a religion I don't believe in just to guarantee a final full house? Maybe I *want* to remain aloof on my mountaintop, quite happy to end up alone in a home, dribbling in a comfy chair, sucking up thin soup through a straw, watching the History Channel's six-programme loop, smelling

60 What about the bunch of ageing broads swilling gin down at the Old Dog and Gusset after my funeral? That's a kind of community, isn't it?

slightly of wee and comforted by thoughts of passions past. I mean, Christ, it's a *plan*, at least, isn't it?

Rick's clearly been shown my column and gets stuck into my much-valued independence and serial philandering, which is, he says – forcing me to suppress a schoolboy smirk – 'a booby prize'. Like an antipodean ghost of Christmas future, he conjures a bleak winter of discontent: 'When other people have got adoring children at their knee and real, staunch equality with a woman who is worthy of them . . . when you are sixty, seventy, the lifestyle you have now just gets sadder and sadder if you continue with it.'

Rick, I know you are doing your best, mate, but you are failing to depress me.

'You've done the hardest bit, which is to make it in the world without emotional support, so you might as well enjoy the benefits of the second part, which is to get nicely mingled with some of the human race.'

Not just the twenty-six-year-old blondes? Apparently not: 'It's a safe bet they would be a lot less challenging and easier to contain and manage compared with someone on an equal footing.' *What about the brunettes?* I think, trading a brief smile with the one on the other side of the glass wall.

In the book, he condemns men who yield to 'the temptation to exercise power over women rather than meet them as equals'. Once I am proud of my gender, he says, I won't be afraid of risking rejection. The right woman, he says, will come along, and all I have to do is 'define what you are looking for. I'm not generally guilty of being cosmic or new age, but in this regard I am: when you are ready, the right people show up. In the same way that you have manifested young women who have been willing to go out with an old codger like you.'

Old codger? Steady on. Besides, it's the ones who are willing to *stay in* with an old codger like me that I'm interested in. Which brings me to my plans for a precautionary vasectomy. Getting the wrong person – or maybe even the right person – pregnant now, I begin weakly, would be the end of life as I know it.

'I mean, I'm fifty next year and . . .'

The Radish becomes agitated and shifts around in his seat. He looks at me as if I've just declined single-handedly to re-seed an otherwise doomed human race and comes over all evangelical. 'Look. You've *done* that life,' he says. *People pay money to hear this?* I think. 'You can just continue it or have another one. Yes, it's scary, but, look . . . look . . . Jesus, I have photos of my kids here that I could show you . . .'

Oh, God, please don't . . .

'The point is, it's treasure, unbelievable treasure, and it just grows by the month and the year. It might be you'll find a woman in her forties who has some kids, and you could be part of rearing them. It will be difficult, but it is the biggest trip there is. The price of it is your life, take it or leave it . . .'

Um . . .

It is, he says, a 'baby's world view that you can have everything. The first sign of a mature adult is when they realize that everything has a cost, and the choices you make mean not being able to go the other way.'

And then, right on cue, in comes the pretty press officer to signal game over. The Radish slides his business card across the table, to give me his email address, 'Just in case, mate,' with a nod and a wink. I guess that this is my chance to start my emotional networking, tapping into the 'invaluable maleness of older, wiser men', without which, says The Radish, a man is like 'a TV without a socket'.

Well, maybe. I am, for instance, quite attracted to some of the bullet points in his final chapter, a kind of manifesto for tomorrow's man, even though Ricky seems to be pushing another little agenda on the side that seems to have more to do with establishing a new world order than with my personal happiness. I'm buying in big-time, for instance, to the work less, play more thing. I'm having a *little* bit more trouble with becoming 'committed to, almost religious about, ecological activism'. Ordering us to 'choose world music' is, frankly, stretching it a bit – and as for dressing 'in more colours' and wearing 'handmade and decorative clothes and jewellery', forget it.

Frankly, it's not his email address I'm after. It's Susan's. It's going-home time for the pretty PR and she picks up her coat and walks me to the lifts and, without a shadow of a doubt, she has sprayed on some perfume in the loo. It's making my eyes water.

How did it go, then? she says, as we ride down to the lobby. Up close, she looks even younger than I thought. Twenty-five or -six, tops. Oh, dear. Rick would be so disappointed in me.

Fine, I say. *Not bad.*

There's a pause, and then she says, 'I always look forward to your column,' as if she is confessing to masturbating in the loos. I didn't expect this when I took it on, but my weekly confessional, far from purging sins, is spawning far more. Curiously, although many of my female colleagues in the office appear to disapprove heartily, in Readerland, Microwave Man seems to attract more women than he repels, although they do fall into two camps: those who despise me because of it but want to sleep with me anyway and those who don't despise me but still want to sleep with me.

I've thought about this, and this is all I can come up with: it's not about fame, because the column is low-key; it's not about looks, because even if I was the best-looking bloke ever to write 750 words of bollocks every week (and I'm not, obviously, saying that I'm not), my face doesn't appear with the words. It's about self-delusion and wish-fulfilment. Women want a man who appears at once tough and capable of picking them up and tossing them on to the bed and fighting off the imagined advances of other men, but at the same time they want a man who has feelings and frailties and isn't afraid to show them. Or to write about them, at any rate.

A hard-boiled sweetie with a soft centre. A caveman who moisturizes. A Lothario who screws a single mum and then offers to babysit her kids. But without Rick's dresscode of handmade and decorative clothes and jewellery.

Not that I mind. It works for me. I get sentimental, like anyone else, and I can very, very easily feel sorry for myself, and if you want to mistake that for vulnerability, be my guest. Always available for mothering. And you would be surprised how many times I have heard a woman utter the words: 'I want to take care of you.'

'Don't you dare put this in your column,' is another line I almost always hear at some point in the proceedings. Sometimes, curiously, the look in their eyes says, 'Please write about this,' but while Susan might be in PR, publicity is the last thing she's looking for tonight. That's OK. I'm quite happy to sleep with her in my spare time, with no prospect of expenses.

I hold her gaze and her face starts to flush. The autopilot kicks in, and I let it run because I can, and because it's easier than thinking about The Radish's words, and because it promises something a lot more pleasant than going home alone and listening wistfully to Crosby, Stills and Nash singing 'Our House'.

I smile at her and say, *You know, it really was quite distracting having you sat out there in view the whole time. I barely heard a word he said . . .*

She laughs and blushes as the lift reaches ground level. We walk towards the revolving door and I *almost* can't be bothered but, after listening to The Radish banging on about what I really need, what I *really* really need is a drink. And then sex. Funny how they always go together, like drinks and nibbles[61] at a bar.

So how about a drink?

'Sure! But don't think I'm interested in becoming just another column.'

Ker-*ching*! A couple of hours and more than a couple of drinks later, we are in her small flat off Tottenham Court Road, doing our best to shake her Habitat bed back to its original, flat-packed state. Like a good boy, I'm not taking notes. Somewhere in the background, almost submerged in the noises we are making,

61 Although, strictly speaking, one should never nibble nibbles from a bowl at the bar. Think of all the blokes who go to the loo, don't wash their hands and then come back and rummage around in the nuts.

the muffled throb of the traffic and the sound of the rain drumming on the double-glazing, I think I hear the message tone on my phone, dropped with my jacket in her hallway. It doesn't distract me from the job at hand, but I can't help wondering who it might be.

Sod The Radish. Having sex is almost always much better than thinking. In fact, it's almost always much better than anything else.

Right here, right now, with this twenty-five-year-old (as she has turned out to be) riding me eagerly, her dress bunched up around her waist and her sweat-damp hair matted across her face, I can barely remember what The Radish looks like (except for that stupid bloody hat, of course), let alone what he had to say. And as for all that bollocks about families and friends and funerals, I bet he'd risk it all to swap places with me right now.

Cobblers to him, and his stupid family, inherited masculinity and network of mates in their stupid bloody hats wearing their appalling handmade and decorative but distinctly masculine clothes and artefacts. Right now, for one night only, this woman is my family. These breasts are my friends. This penis my distinctly masculine artefact. I'd give *everything* to be right here, right now.

Which, of course, I pretty much have done.

An hour later, having ridden the rollercoaster up and now down, I'd give anything to be somewhere else. Preferably, back in the arms of the Boer. Outside, it's still raining, and there's not a taxi in sight, but at least the streets are shining with Christmas lights. Ho ho ho. And why not? It is, after all, the middle of sodding *November*. Bloody hell.

Just as I am about to disappear into the Underground, I remember the phone and read the message, and my mood lightens and suddenly I don't seem to be missing the Boer quite so badly. Hey ho.

Wotcha, gorgeous, I read, and smile. Despite the intervening years, I can almost hear that slightly vacuous, privately schooled but barely educated voice. *Long time indeedy. Call me! But not before ten and not after six (or at all at weekends yikes!!!)*

Well, she took her time getting back. I'd written her off. Rebecca. Sweet, innocent Rebecca. Not quite so happily married after all, then. Nor so sweet and innocent any more, either, it seems. I perk up considerably and set my phone alarm for ten in the morning.

Meet the Twins
Friday 28 November 2003

Is it only me, or does everyone struggle to remember the last time they made love with an ex but have a crystal-clear memory of the first time?

One evening last week, as I headed for a rendezvous of uncertain outcome with a former lover, I whiled away the journey thinking back nearly twenty years to our first time. Such had been the size of Rebecca's dark, nineteen-year-old eyes and the brightness of the innocence that shone from them that I didn't know whether to make love to her or to call Disney and tell them that one of their Bambis was missing.

For a moment, in a curious and subsequently never repeated clash of primal instincts, my first urge was to defend her from men like me. But only for a moment. I had, after all, in a paroxysm of romantic preparation (and, I might add, years before Sam Mendes stole my idea), strewn the bed with rose petals. Quite frankly, there's no going back after an effort like that.

And so here I am back in the now, parking, as instructed, out of sight of the nosy neighbours, and there she is, standing by her gate, those eyes glinting in the streetlight.

We sit on her sofa, drinking wine and driving side by side down memory lane – for her, a fifteen-year journey over smooth and bumpy roads, via several unsuitable relationships, one currently shaky marriage and two children. Two children, I twig with a slight jolt of excitement, not around tonight.

Suddenly we are petal pals again, hands and mouths recalling long-dormant routines. In some bureaucratic department of my mind, a clerk ticks boxes: yes, she still keeps her eyes open when she kisses; still uses her tongue lightly; still . . . but something isn't quite the same.

The clerk and I confer but can't put our fingers on what has changed: sure, this is not *quite* the face of the nineteen-year-old, but it is still luminous and, at thirty-eight, very little about that beautiful body seems to have gone west. It is only as my hands and eyes wander, reliving memories of their own, that the brain finds out what the fingers already know. Far from heading south, two points in particular, despite the rigours of child-rearing, seem if anything to have migrated farther north.

'So what do you think?' she asks delightedly, suddenly popping out someone else's breasts and cupping them proudly in her hands. '£3,500 the pair.'

And despite myself, and a vague disquiet about cosmetic surgery in general and preternaturally enhanced breasts in particular, I think: *Blimey! A bargain. I'll take them!*

Rebecca had felt so uncomfortable about her post-rearing breasts (and her husband had felt sufficiently comfortable about parting with the sterling) that she had had them enhanced. That had made her happy, and that made me happy: not because they were big, or small, or anything else, but because her rebuilt confidence had made her sexy again.

Us chaps aren't, despite the stereotyping (and chicken-lovers aside), 'breast men' or 'leg men'; it isn't about whether boobs sag or resemble twin pointers sniffing the autumn air for trace of grouse. And it's not about pert versus cushion-sized bottoms or fat lips *v* thin. What men love above all else is a woman who loves herself. Don't say: 'Do I look fat in these?' Do say: 'Don't I look great in these?'

Before I saw Rebecca's twin secrets (a first for me, incidentally. For the record, slightly harder to the touch than the real thing, defiantly anti-gravity and, well, in your face) I was sniffy about the whole idea of cosmetic surgery (not that it's my place to approve or otherwise). But after hands-on experience, I can now see the point. It's not that I find her new breasts sexy *per se*; it's the fact that she does and that her confidence is now a size 32D.

'I think I'm sexy, therefore I am,' as Descartes might have said, had he been smarter.

9

How to be a Bad Friend

Dear Microwave Man
  Do you have any male friends?
  Name and address withheld

Microwave Man writes: What for, exactly?

Actually, of course, even making allowances for his time, Descartes wasn't really very smart at all, despite spending eight years having the classics, logic and traditional Aristotelian philosophy (among other things) rammed into him by the Jesuits. By rights he should have been the early seventeenth century's Man with a Silly Haircut[62] Most Likely to Succeed, but Descartes was a bit simple, really, and a bit of a conman. Not to mention a lazy bugger. And I can empathize with all of that.

His big thing was mathematics, which, he felt, explained all other big things. I wonder if he added up stuff obsessively like I do? Probably not. But maybe he should have. Scientists today realize that he pretty much made up everything he espoused. To be fair, in a world where a sizeable majority believed that the Earth was flat or, at best, a globe supported by a tower of precariously balanced turtles, there wasn't a great deal of incentive for rigorous scientific procedure.

Most of Descartes' work is now recognized to have been . . . well, I was going to say 'flawed', but a fairer description might

62 Not unlike the 'mullet', a style favoured by a number of British footballers in the seventies and by some trailer-dwelling inhabitants of America's deep south to this very day. Signs outside barber shops in the panhandle proclaiming, 'A Descartes for a dollar,' are not uncommon.

be 'rubbish'. For instance: a vacuum, he said, was impossible. He abhorred the very idea. The idea of gravity pulled no weight with him, and he wrote an entire treatise on why water that has been boiled freezes faster. Which, of course, it doesn't.

Funny who goes down in history, and what for. Descartes' fellow geniuses were inventing for all they were worth – Hans Lippersley (the refracting telescope), William Outred (the slide rule) and Jean-Baptiste Denys (blood transfusions), but who the hell's heard of any of them?[63] Or the inventors of the barometer, micrometer, air pumps, pendulum clocks or pocket watches, come to that?

And so who do we honour in perpetuity from the seventeenth century for his contribution to civilization? Not Lippersley, Outred or Denys. No. Instead the names on everyone's lips 350 years later are Dom Perignon, for a fizzy drink that makes girls giggle, and some old lunatic whose greatest gift to the students of the future was the slogan that so many wear on their T-shirts to assist them in their studies to this very day: *I drink, therefore I am.*

Oh, well done. But hey. A slogan's a slogan.

Maths finally did for Descartes – he died of pneumonia after repeatedly getting up at 5 a.m. in freezing weather to explain tangents to Swedish royalty – but it did all right by me. Unlike René, I was so bad at it at school that I was finally expelled from mathematics, which was the best thing that had happened to me since I was expelled from chemistry. As the lessons usually ran back to back, I ended up with several double free periods a week, which I spent hanging around the language labs, supposedly in an attempt to brush up my German but actually in a bid to brush up against the German master's golden daughter.

In fact, other than the occasional phrase, which has rarely come in handy, I remember little from studying German at school. I can, however, still recall the thrill of thumbing through the extremely well-thumbed copies of *Stern* magazine as I lurked, waiting for the strapping Marlies to show. Turning page after

---

63 Although they do know all about the slide rule in Talwyd Y Post DG.

glossy page of dreary, serious articles on *Politik, Wirtschaft, Wissenschaft und Kultur*, never quite knowing when I would stumble upon an unrelated photograph of some flaxen-haired Rhinemaiden with her breasts out, I learnt a lot about the value of sexual anticipation (and, I suppose, about German sauna culture). How, I wondered, did these people ever lose the war?

'*Gott im Himmel. Hände hoch. Mein Wecker ist kaput,*' (I told you it rarely came in handy) I would mutter when, in a reversal of the anticlimactic moment when a *Playboy* reader happens upon an article about trains, I finally came across the oddly unexplained snaps of Frieda and her friends. Eventually, my persistence paid off and, finally, I came across Marlies. A little too quickly for her liking, actually, but I was only sixteen and had spent months building up a head of steam staring at pictures of bare-breasted fräuleins in her father's magazines. As I said, I never did learn much German, but I did develop a lifetime weakness for big women with hairy armpits.

Hairy men, however, I have never really liked (apart from myself, obviously), thanks to having spent eleven years at boarding school with hundreds of the dull buggers, listening to them farting, burping and masturbating their way through adolescence. Small wonder that I prefer the company of women and can count my close male friends on one aching hand.

One of them, of course, is Simon of De Nile. What I both like and envy most about him (other than his collection of guitars) is the solidity of his existence: married childhood sweetheart, produced two lovely children, climbed sure-footedly up the housing ladder and joined the golf club. So far from my world that it is almost exotic, and a great place to check my normality bearings. Or so I thought.

And then, shortly after the Boer buggered off, it all started to go slightly odd. Or maybe I'd just been too busy before to notice. Like many men of a certain age, Simon fell into a slough of despond. The first clue had been the post-gig sob in the BMW. Next came the earring, which appeared just after he turned forty. Soon it was joined by a chunky necklace and alarmingly louche shirts. I decided to approach the tricky subject sensitively. 'Hello,' I said, 'why are you dressing like a girl?'

His response was to throw his arms around me in what could have been a manly hug – the type of physical contact from which I have shied ever since being in the school 2nd XV pack.

I gritted my teeth and muttered: 'Nothing wrong with men embracing, I suppose.'

'What's that?' he said. 'Men in braces?' and released his grip quite suddenly.

The impaired hearing was a product of his disturbing return to the golden age of his youth, during which he had become something of a big noise (or, at least, a loud one) on the local music scene. A few years back he started reading *Q* magazine again, dug up a former bass player and drummer and resurrected a three-man band with the combined age – but none, tragically, of the royalties – of Led Zeppelin. The hair grew longer, wavier and – suspiciously – darker.

Meeting Simon in public had become a question of embarrassment limitation. Not only was he certain to fling his arms around one and say loudly, 'I love you, man,' but the possibility of a bristly peck on the cheek just couldn't be ruled out. A sports car joined the BMW on the gravel drive and Simon joined the gym.

Not that he actually went much.

Like Kevin Spacey in *American Beauty*, he took to drink, Prozac and pornography (a self-help cocktail of inebriation, medication and masturbation). Next up was a large spa bath in the garden, in which Simon and Sally entertained friends on even the chilliest of evenings, swigging wine and basking in each other's oily sludge in scenes straight out of *Suburban Secrets*.

Then it all fell into place. One evening Sally was working, and Simon and I were returning from our customary outing to Pizza Express. 'How about a dip in the spa?' he chirped as we arrived home. 'Or is that a little too gay?'

'Perhaps a little,' I demurred.

Either, I reasoned, he was having an affair, or he had discovered his true sexuality. I didn't mind which (although, if the former, God only knew where I would go for my Happy Families fix), but if I was going to be hugged by a bloke, I felt I deserved to know why.

I was half right. Simon *was* having an affair. With a married woman. His wife.

Oh, for God's sake.

Despite (or because of) the depression and the drugs, at the point where most men seek reassurance in the arms of another (always younger) woman, Simon has blundered into a passionate extramarital affair with the one he married twenty years ago.

Sally comes in from work, tired. Her arm goes straight around Simon, and he gives her a squeeze. I can see that she isn't about to catch up on lost sleep. Later, lying alone in the spare room, failing to block out the sounds of porn-fuelled passion, I wonder at the ability of human love to endure and evolve and ponder the possibility that not all relationships are doomed to end in betrayal.

And, if happiness for all is the result, surely the odd earring and same-sex hug is a price worth paying?

'Yes! Oh, God, *yes!*' shouts Sally through the wall.

Fair enough. Perhaps now he'll tell her about that £1,800 acoustic twelve-string he's been hiding in the office for six months.

I'm not sure why I have never tried to sleep with Sally, because I do find her very attractive in a house-proud, cake-baking, knitted-loo-roll-cover kind of way. I'd like to say that the reason I've never reached over playfully to pat the flour off the back of her skirt is because I respect Simon and value our friendship far too much, but of course we both know that would be a load of bollocks. (As I have been known to say to Simon from time to time – you know, just in *case* – 'A mate's a mate, but a shag's a shag.') I think it's more that the open amusement and contempt she displays for me and what she clearly considers to be my feckless and worthless life makes it pretty clear that not only is she not on the market but is several miles, two awkward bus journeys and a yomp over rutted fields away from the town where the market is held.

Yes, I know. Hard to believe, but true.

I've thought about it, obviously. But although I have kept an eye on her, in that way that men like me do – looking for cracks in the armour, a glimmer of suggestiveness – I have never caught so much as a whiff of promise. And, trust me, this is unusual.

It was different with my mate Merv. I *did* try to sleep with the woman who became his first wife, but, being young and inexperienced, I failed, so that was OK. Besides, I knew her before he did, when she and I were both junior reporters on a local paper, and I always felt that gave me a kind of *droit du seigneur*. And in the end she left him for another woman, at which point she didn't want to sleep with *either* of us, so I was off the hook and stopped beating myself up (but not off) over her.

I hated Merv before I met him. In fact, I still hated him *after* I met him, because he was King of the World, or at least the bit that I inhabited. That was twenty-eight years ago. He was depressed then, like he is now, but then it was a fun kind of depression. No drugs, just a length of hosepipe he used to carry around in the boot of his company Ford Sierra and a constantly altering plan to gas himself – in this wood, or that lay-by – which he used to discuss with infectious enthusiasm.

Because I had a car (but no hosepipe), I used to pick up Valerie every day on the way to work, and she would almost always be crying. She was crying because her parents hated Merv because before he had started sleeping with her he had been sleeping with her elder sister (with whom, years and years later, I also slept, but only the once. Why only once? Three words: 'Jane', 'Austen', 'cats').

I could see their point, but I didn't hate him because she was crying, but because I wanted to sleep with her and she was too busy being dramatic about him to think about me.

In fact, the crying thing I quite liked. It meant that every time she climbed into my car she would throw herself across the bench seat (I loved that Morris Oxford) and into my arms for comfort. OK, so I often arrived at work with a very wet shoulder, but the upside was that, throughout that long, hot summer, for the whole ten-minute drive, as her chest rose and fell with all that sobbing, I got to feel her small, pert right breast rucking up and down against my chest.

I was twenty-one. These things meant a lot to me then. And now, actually.

And guess what? She knew all about it. Once, still sobbing gently, she reached into my lap, closed her fingers around my erection and squeezed it firmly. Twice. As if to say, 'There, there.' This is still right up there among my Top Ten Erotic Moments.

I first met Merv at a party. Lots of junior reporters getting pissed out of their tiny minds on cheap wine. He was the grown-up, at least four years older than the eldest of us, lounging on the only sofa and clearly despising all around him.

It was cheap wine because Home Counties Group was a cheap employer. Home Cunties, we called it, wittily. The company collapsed years ago, shortly after the death of its chairman, Cecil Gibbs, and the simultaneous disappearance of his secretary, Vera Golightly, and all of that month's pay packets.

One day, Cecil – a fat Caesar schlepping with ill grace to the furthest outpost of his fish-and-chip-wrapper empire – had visited the Milton Keynes office. He had come, it seemed, to deliver a lecture about the moral turpitude that was, he had decided, gripping the company's lowliest serfs. (And serfs we truly were, indentured to the company for three years.)

When you are invited to lunch by a public relations firm, he began, sweeping the room with his bushy-hooded eyes, *or perhaps offered a weekend away – or even a week's holiday – ask yourself this.* And he pronounced his question as three separate words, as though he were addressing half-wits: *Who. Really. Gains?*

The serfs, among the lowest-paid people in the country, if not the whole of Europe (including the local council's toilet cleaners. True: we checked), looked around at one another. They might have been cheap, but they weren't entirely stupid. Who really gains? Well, we do, obviously. You. Fat. Git.

One young chap – I forget his name now: he disappeared pretty shortly after this – piped up, ill-advisedly.

Mr Gibbs?

The big man looked startled. These people *speak?*

Mr Gibbs, about the only freebie I have enjoyed since I began working here a year ago was the gift of two tickets to see an excellent, if over-long, production of Uncle Vanya, *staged in the Bletchley Leisure Centre by the Bletchco Players. Believe me, I didn't want to go, and if I could have refused I would have, but the newsdesk was adamant that it wanted a review. Was I wrong to go? Perhaps I should have bought my own ticket and claimed the cost back on expenses? What do you think?*

This was a tricky one for Cecil. If there was one thing he loathed more than moral turpitude, it was paying journalists' expenses. Playing for time, he reached into a pocket of his curiously decorative waistcoat, and took out and glanced at his hunter. He probably had a free lunch to get to. But before he could reply, the talking dead man continued.

So I was just thinking: if you paid us a bit more money, perhaps we wouldn't be quite so tempted by all those free lunches and stuff . . .

The dead man sat down, but then stood up again, briefly, spurred by an intriguing afterthought: *For tea last night I had sardines on toast, by the way.*

Sardines? I got his desk, which was the farthest away from the news desk, which was by far the best place to be. I didn't, however, get Valerie, but I did, somehow, get Merv as a friend. Despite our first meeting.

Who's that twat sprawled all over the sofa? I asked Valerie.

That's Merv, she said, punching me on the arm.

Why did girls of my age always go for older men? Just like at college. God, how I lusted after Tina,[64] princess of our year at Harlow Technical College, but she was always far more interested in the older (working and paid) boys on the block-release courses or, failing them, one or two of the younger lecturers.

64 And we'll get there too. Just as I did, eventually.

Or, failing them, the older ones. It works for me, now, aged forty-eight, but back then all it meant was far too much self-dating and not enough shagging.

Merv didn't get up, just carried on sprawling in his brown, wide-lapelled and flared-trousered grown-up's suit, resting his head on one hand and fondling Valerie's bum with the other. She was smiling like a sexually deviant Cheshire Cat.

So, sneered Merv. *What's the front-page exclusive tomorrow then, eh, Jimmy Olsen?*

Bloody hell. He's Welsh, as well as everything else! Not a strong accent, mind, but a coal-caked boyo from the valleys nevertheless. Working-class lad made good. Very chapel, too, I shouldn't wonder, despite the louche veneer. That would explain the Aberfan-sized chip on the shoulder. I had to come back with something good. My mind, dulled by plonk, whirred into life, slowly beginning to spin some absurdist insult involving sheep rustlers and Welsh philosophy students and Wellington boots and . . . but before it could do its stuff my mouth got bored and fired off a holding shot.

Oh, fuck off, you twat. Then adding, brilliantly, as the intellect caught up, *Welsh twat.*

Over the years, the Welsh twat has turned out to be a good friend, which is why, a couple of months ago, having dropped the Boer at the station, I gave him a call.

Merv, the perpetual philosophy student, is, as you might expect, always philosophical about life. By the time he emerged from university (and a brief fact-finding incarceration in a locked ward), he bore a striking resemblance to Franz Kafka – partly on account of his severe haircut, prominent nose and big ears, and partly because of a philosophy for life which can be summed up in one sentence: *One door closes, another one shuts.*

Let nobody say that an expensive university education is wasted.

Merv even shares my disdain for Descartes (something for which he is far more qualified than I) and even seems to have shared the same maths teacher – although I suspect all maths teachers from the Rhondda valley are called Taff Evans.

And the funny thing about Merv is that he has always been there when I've needed him, no matter how long has passed since I last spoke to him, or that we fell out the week before he emigrated to Australia for three years ('Rex and Courtney: the lost years', as he likes to call it) and didn't speak again until, two kids heavier and bored with endless sunshine and funnel-web spiders, he returned to England, picked up the phone and carried on a conversation we'd been having thirty-six months before as though nothing had happened. I hadn't the slightest idea what he was talking about.

And all of this despite one of his favourite sayings (quite possibly stolen from the now-dead British comedian Tommy Cooper): 'A friend in need is a bloody nuisance – get rid of him.'

Luckily, I wasn't dumped by anyone while Merv was in Australia. But he was there for me before he went (Rebecca) and after he came back (Laura). And again now.

Now I was presenting to him the dossier on my latest disaster, a moment he always relished, confirming as it did his and Franz's firmly held belief that man's lot is to live out his years in fear, isolation and bewilderment – a prisoner in a nightmarish, de-humanized world. In a funny way, he and The Radish might have got on.

Excellent, he said. *So what the fuck did you expect? She's twenty-five, you're forty-seven, the novelty's worn off, now she needs to move on and play the field for a while before she breeds.*

Ah yes. The breeding thing. I did recall a brief conversation about that. The Boer and I were walking along the Thames at Richmond on a beautiful summer's day, talking about my son, Adam. She asked me – casually, I thought – *Do you think you would ever have another child?* I replied – casually, I thought – *No chance. Not for all the tea in Rwanda.*[65]

The sun beat down, but the river instantly froze over. I didn't

---

65 They actually have more tea in Rwanda than in China.

even realize I was skating on thin ice, but within a month I was single again.

Merv and I meet in a pub near the Angel. He's in London for a few days. 'I reckon,' he says, sipping his pint of lager, 'I reckon there's more to the Boer thing than meets the eye.'

I know what's coming and smile indulgently.

'I reckon,' he says, 'that she bats for the other side, and maybe she just doesn't know it yet.'

This is very nice of him to say, kind of, but this is always Merv's diagnosis in these situations, which probably means he wouldn't make a very good psychiatrist. Or relationship counsellor. Besides, I know he is, more or less, joking. Although you can hardly blame him: he did lose his wife to 'the other side'.

'No, I think it's something else,' I say. 'A couple of times she hinted to me darkly that if I knew what was going on inside her head I would be horrified.' And, as it turned out, I think the secret lay in the subject matter of the novel she had been banging out during our last six months together.

During the three years that Karen and I spent together, she slept with Henry Miller almost as much as she slept with me. One or other of the steaming Tropics from the freeloading feelthmeister always lay festering by the bed, like a Gideons Bible in a cheap hotel. But where Gideons is intended to lead one down the path of righteousness, Cancer and Capricorn appear to have served as street signs directing the Plucky Boer down the sleazier back alleys of the mind.

I knew she was writing a book, but then a lot of people are 'writing a book' (in the same way that I am, one day, going to study medieval stonemasonry in Bruges or strangle with his own braces the next City boy who lights up a turd-sized cigar in my presence). Dreams, after all, are sometimes best left as dreams; velvet ropes on which to pull ourselves through our safe but dreary lives.

But then, out of the blue, I receive an email from her. Well, to be precise, I and everyone else she has ever met or slept with receives an email from her. It's the first I've heard from her since she walked out of my life and it's a round-robin. Nice. Not only has she written her book, it reveals, but the first 10,000 words have earned her one of the five places in the final of Lit. Idol, a competition that comes to a head at the London Book Fair.

While I was with her, Karen never quite summoned the courage to let me read what she had written but hinted darkly that I might not like her much if I knew what seethed inside her head (which, it transpires, includes penises crushed under stiletto heels and sex with double-amputees, among other things. No wonder she moved on from me. I had two legs to stand on).

This reluctance to expose herself to even friendly criticism was a by-product of an almost crippling competitive streak that rendered her unable to take advice. One of our most spectacular rows took place in the shallow end of a pool, as I tried to teach her how to breathe and swim without drowning. By the end, I could have cheerfully drowned her myself.

Despite the endless nights I had spent lying awake, willingly enough, listening to her tapping out her secret words, I had had no more of a preview of the finished product than anyone else in her email address book. Now she was directing all and sundry to the website where they could read 10,000 of her innermost thoughts. My jaw hit the floor when I received the round-robin. Among the other recipients, I spotted at least three other lovers, including the one she had taken up with after we split (at least, I *think* it was after) and the husband she had left before taking up with me (at least, he *thought* it was before).

The words 'crass' and 'insensitive' sprang to mind, but hey: that's artists for you. Henry and Anaïs would have loved it.

On the competition website to which I am directed, a lousy picture of a woman I know to be beautiful, and a few words by the author herself about her hopes of producing a book that is 'amusing, gritty and reflects the sordid, frantic and anonymous London I know and love'. She dreams, she writes, of being a female Miller – that is, when she is not indulging her 'weaknesses for peanut butter, rare steaks and Agent Provocateur underwear'.

Or, what we used to call our perfect weekend.

Then I make the mistake of reading those 10,000 words. *Dirty Women* is no *Sexus* but a kind of clit-lit: the story of two women, a high-class French tart with a heart (what other kind is there in literature? No abused, drug-addled victims here, oh no) and a penniless waitress who . . . well, you know the rest. Plenty of filth, anyway. I guess the Plucky Boer has become the Mucky Boer. I can't tell if it's any good: the glimmering shards of the bits of our life I recognize stand out too sharply from the fiction (or what I take to be fiction). Everywhere there are bits of me and her (and, presumably, Fergus, Julian and Ben, and who the hell knows who else), embedded in the woodwork like shrapnel from an explosion. No copyright on feelings.

'You're well off out of it,' says Merv, reading the printout of the email I've given him and shaking his head. 'That's pretty bloody callous.'

'Yes,' I agree. 'I am. It is. To be honest, I had harboured thoughts of getting back together with her – maybe even re-opening negotiations on the baby front . . .'

Merv's eyes widen, and he puts the back of his right hand against my forehead. 'Bloody hell! Quick, nurse! The screens!'

'. . . but not now,' I add quickly. 'Not after this. I needed this. A shot of reality, a bit of common sense. What a cow! If I could be arsed, I'd call her and tell her just what I think of her. But I don't want her to know I'm thinking about her.'

'Absolutely right. Move on; she always was a bit weird. I never did understand what you saw in her.'

'Apart from the body?'

'Yes, apart from the body, obviously. And those legs. And that mouth. Oh, yes, God: that wonderful mouth . . .'

'I say, steady on!'

'Sorry. But come on: you'll have no trouble finding short-term replacements. Get out there and enjoy yourself.'

'I already am, actually. Oh, thanks for Rebecca's number, by the way.'

The eyes widen again, and he gives me an old-fashioned look.

Do you know, after all these years, I still think he still harbours a little grudge there. Ha!

'Rebecca? Don't tell me you've gone and shagged her? My God, it must be twenty years! How is she, anyway?'

'Bigger,' I say.

Later that evening – a bottle of wine later, in fact – the phone in the pocket over my heart vibrates. I check the message and find a name I'm not expecting to see.

'Who is it?' asks Merv.

'The Mouth.'

And as terse as ever. The message kicks off with the same old four words she always uses to start almost any conversation, in any medium. But four words aimed this time, at least, just at me, not half the population of South London and South Africa: 'Hi, how's it going?' But followed by three more that I really didn't see coming: 'Fancy a coffee?'

Well, well. Her very own Bat Signal.

Merv snorts. 'Probably a round-robin inviting all her ex-boyfriends to the screening of her first porn video. Tell her to fuck off.'

I start to tap out a reply. 'I will,' I say. 'Absolutely. Bloody bitch . . .'

But I'm writing, 'Sure, why not. Thursday?' and enjoy the thump I get in the heart-shaped place as I hit send.

Cold Turkey
Friday 5 December 2003

My first (and, with luck, last) Christmas card. 'A Happy Christmas to all our Customers,' chirrups the portly and oddly orange gas-company robin. Inside, the subtext: a 'Seasonal Reminder' that, if I haven't had my boiler serviced, then I had better prepare to be gassed to death in my sleep. (Perhaps that's why the robin is orange: one too many whiffs of carbon monoxide?)

Thinly veiled threats from the gas-board usurpers aside (and *do not* start me on privatization), Operation Lonely this Christmas has been going rather well: at work I have secured 'on call' status for the twenty-fifth (in case, I suppose, a reader rendered off-guard by a surfeit of eggnog chokes on a particularly indigestible piece of prose).

But then another little cracker arrives – a request for a reference from a charity on behalf of my most immediate ex, the Mucky – *née* Plucky – Boer, who, it seems, is flinging herself into charitable work with the unloved elderly over Christmas.

Hello, I think. Some irony there.

Do-gooding after a bout of do-badding is a self-cleansing syndrome I recognize from eight years back, when I fled the scene of an earlier emotional pile-up and spent Christmas nobly bringing succour and cold turkey to lonely old folk.

This is Foreign Legion Lite for crushed lovers who can't face the sand and all those German corporals. I spent the day in a grotty ancient building near Victoria (not the Palace), listening to a broken, unshaven old man in a shabby overcoat (hang on, maybe it *was* the Palace) telling me that he had Been Someone in the medical profession until, fifteen years ago, his 'darling, darling wife' had died and he had lost the will to shave, practise medicine or do anything else except mourn. (And wet himself, it has to be said.)

And, tight in my own cocoon of self-pity, all I could think was: 'Lucky sod. At least she wasn't shagging around.'

Unlike the Boer. Recently we have started to see something of each other again, and at these meetings (regular emotional enemas to prove how grown-up we are) she regales me with 'amusing' tales of her sexual exploits. First, we get the formalities out of the way: I, tongue in cheek (mine, not hers, sadly), propose yet again. She, whimsically, rejects me.

Ha ha.

I drop, amusingly, to one knee for a spot of comical case-pleading. She, wittily, dismisses my assurance that I now realize

I was hasty in spitting out my soup when she first mentioned babies.

Ho ho.

All these sessions are, in fact, *desperately* humorous affairs. On Monday she tells me in comic detail about the young Bens, Julians and Ferguses she has been 'seeing', and oh, how we laugh.

As Microwave Man, I am the recipient/butt in the office of such free gifts as the boxes of Durex condoms now being offered alongside the Saturday-night action pants in branches of Topman. I have brought a box along. Ha ha, I say, I imagine you could use these. Ho ho, she says.

And slips them into her bag.

As she does, I notice that the photograph of us in love in Edinburgh is still in her wallet. Only, turned face down. I can see my own handwriting on the back. Funny, that.

Having both rejected 'orphan' invitations, we will, separately, be alone on the twenty-fifth – me braced to respond to any syntactical emergency at the paper, her serving up for (and maybe mopping up after) old folk in central London. Why not, I say, spend the evening together? Pull an ironic wishbone, yank on a dud cracker, exchange unwanted gifts . . . Sniffing a whiff of interest, I press on: 'Nobody should eat Christmas pudding alone. Even if it is microwaved.'

'Hmm,' she says. 'Sounds like a slippery slope to me . . .'

But the possibility hangs in the air like breath on a cold, still December morning. If that slope is slippery, we will slide down it thanks not to Jack Frost, but to Robert. You know: that one about when was it ever less than treason to yield to reason and accept the end of a love or a season? (And just how many more lines might he have got out of that rhyme if he'd persevered? Trees with leaves on, dogs with fleas on, darlin' stop your teasin', Jesus, ain't it freezin'? . . .)

Quite. It ain't over till the fat bird's been gassed.

How to be the Other Woman

Dear Microwave Man
    You pour scorn on faithful couples who don't understand how repeated infidelity can be part of a loving relationship – 'What do they know?' Perhaps you could explain how it works?
                                                    Diana M., Hertfordshire

Microwave Man writes: I could give you a demonstration – say, Tuesday around 2 p.m.? Your place? But seriously . . . I'm not sure repeated infidelity can be part of a loving relationship. What I would say, though, is that the fact it happens doesn't necessarily mean that the people involved don't love each other, and that somebody outside that relationship has no corner on the morals market when it comes to judging who loves whom. So how would Wednesday be for you, then?

Try as I might, I can't winkle The Radish's snidy little barb out of my head, where it has lodged like an annoying and increasingly painful splinter. Am I really a victim of the temptation to choose power over women rather than meet them as equals? And, if I am, would 'victim' really be the right word?

It's true that I always seem to end up with women much younger than me, but I'm pretty sure that I don't set out to hunt them down. Laura, if not my age, was at least within what appears to be the 'acceptable' age range: eight years younger. The problem was that, by the time we split up, I was forty and there was no one of my age group still on the market. Or, to put it another way, women of my age are either married or mad.

Now, if they are married, you can sleep with them with impunity and little fear of fallout, but if they are mad . . . well, if they are mad, you can *still* sleep with them, but then the odds of escaping with all parts of your anatomy attached (in all the right places) start to dwindle.

So what drives them mad? What comes first? The bleak aura of bitter martyrdom? Or the bleak odour of cats?

The chances are that if a reasonably attractive woman is single by her late thirties/early forties, then it is because at some point in the past she has hitched herself to a married man. It is quite amazing just how many otherwise sane, intelligent and self-aware women fall into this trap. What's even more amazing is that they are then capable of maintaining the most extreme self-deception for years and years on end. (Of course, once you have the cats, you really are in trouble, caught in a kind of Cat 22 situation. You can't get rid of them just because your love life picks up, but your love life is never going to pick up if you smell of cat wee. And, trust me, you *will* smell of cat wee.)

Women who go through this process are ruined. No other man will want them because it will have reduced them to pitiful, bitter, angry, depressed, shrunken versions of the women they once were and could still have been. Besides, they won't *want* other men: some part of them never quite lets go of the hope – the belief – that, one day, he will come back to her (and stay longer than one night and some of the next morning).

The fact that this happens to so many women surely gives the lie to all that bullshit about women being the superior, smarter, multitasking version of men. And the smarter the woman, the more likely she is to fall into the trap. It's not just women's sensitivity and innate romantic inclination which is their undoing (although this certainly doesn't help). The woman believes in herself so firmly that she finds it impossible to see how any man in his right mind couldn't fall for her.

And it's about competition. Women, by and large, don't have football, or darts, or video games to help them blow off steam. As a result, they can't just shag somebody else's husband; they have to try to take him away from her. How many men do you know who have put their lives on hold in the hope that a married woman they are shagging will give up her hearth and home to be with them? That's right, none. Because men, generally, have PlayStations.

Men will never do this. They don't have the patience, or the attention span (except for video games). A woman, on the other hand, is prepared to wait it out, to lay siege. She knows it won't happen overnight, so she gets in emotional supplies, a pile of weepy movies and microwave popcorn (and perhaps a self-help book or two by a former Black and White Minstrel) and digs in on the perimeter of the chosen man's life. She has her friends to support her, but pretty soon they get put off by the whiff of self-pity and the endless self-deception – not to mention the tedious, one-track conversations.

Sooner or later, in the face of endless forensic analysis of the man's motives and true feelings, even the bestest best friend will crack and shout, 'For Christ's sake, woman, he is simply using you: move on, forget it, get a life!'

And then, pretty soon, she doesn't even have her friends. And that's when the cats see their opportunity.

The man's not actually innocent, of course. He leads her on; throws her scraps to feed the fantasy. Well, of *course* he does: he likes having sex on tap, likes having somewhere he can go and exercise his sexual self with someone who anticipates his arrival as keenly as children await Santa Claus and who expects nothing from him except hurried, urgent, sorry-got-to-dash-now sex but washes and preens and dresses herself for his use as though his pleasure is the only thing that matters in her world.

Yup, funnily enough, he likes that.

He also likes that, when he turns up, she is never up to her elbows in dirty dishes, never exhausted after a hard day and half asleep on the sofa, never in the middle of changing the bag in the Hoover or helping one of the kids with their bloody home-work and never handing him the dog's lead as he walks in and asking him to take Bobo out for ten minutes *seeing as how you still have your coat on, darling*. He likes that he can walk in and, if he feels like it (and he almost always *does* feel like it, because, let's face it, that's why he is there in the first place), lift her dress (and she always, always wears a dress), pull her sexy panties to one side (and she always, always wears sexy panties) and do it hard and fast right there in the hallway, up against the wall, without any libido-sapping bikes or school bags or bloody dogs in his line of sight to put him off his stroke and then, if he wants to rush away immediately afterwards, leaving her flushed and panting (and he nearly always does want to rush away immediately afterwards), that he can run back, racked by guilt and self-loathing, to his wife and family.

And she, refusing to understand or recognize the guilt and self-loathing which rises in him even faster than the sap he has just expended, likes it too, because this is what she insists – to her own ruin – on mistakenly identifying as his unrestrainedly animal passion *for her*. As opposed to *it*.

And if you are one of these women, here's a flash that (who knows?) might even be vivid enough to shock you out of your sleepwalking state. Are you ready? Are you sitting down? Got enough biscuits? OK, here it is:

Providing you aren't too hairy[66] or too smelly or too obviously, clearly bonkers, he will happily screw you, *but that doesn't necessarily mean that he even likes you very much.*

Physically, he probably doesn't even find you that attractive (this won't stop him 'fancying' you – that is, wanting to shag you). He might even be embarrassed to be seen in public with you.

Mentally, ditto.

Personality, likewise.

Well, I'm sorry, but I thought it best that you knew.

For such a man, almost the worst aspect of his fear of being found out is the moment his wife claps eyes on her non-rival – and the extreme, weird depth of his perverse extramarital excur-

---

66 While some men – more than women think – are actually drawn to hairy armpits and verdant bush, not one can stomach hairy legs, upper lips or chins. Or that solitary nipple hair which, even on the most beautiful of women, appears as a glimpse of some horrendous genetic transgender aberration. I'm sorry, but it's true. Pluck it, for God's sake!

sion is exposed in all its plain-Jane entirety. Most women would breathe a sigh of relief if they could see their 'competitors' and realize they are no more a rival than a blow-up doll would be. Perhaps less. (Some of today's modern dolls can be very convincing and are seldom hairy.)

But, actually, they wouldn't. Like the women who are being screwed and who convince themselves that they are irresistible, the cheated-upon wives insist, perversely, on being convinced that there must be *something* about the other woman that sets her above them, something that she has or does that makes her more attractive to their man than they are.

There isn't. If there was, he would leave his wife for her. All the other woman has that the wife can never have is that she isn't his wife, his symbol of containment and of a closed-off, finished life. The other woman is, simply and crudely, a door left ajar, through which he almost certainly has no intention of passing. She is somebody different to shag, where the need to do so is driven not – as Hollywood husbands caught out and obliged to undergo sex counselling would maintain – by an uncontrollably rampant libido, but by a deeply located fear that This Is All There Is, the end of the line, and that the next stop can be only death.

Look at it this way. A woman has childbirth to sustain her. This, or even the notion of this, links her, mentally and physically, to the future. The child in her mind, in her womb, at her breast, at her feet, blocks the very possibility of the one question that sets men and women apart: what's it all for?

For a man committed emotionally and intellectually to one woman, that single question starts to bang away like a drum – softly at first (certainly on his wedding day), but gradually louder and louder. Sex with other women, he comes to feel, is all that stands between him and the grave and the general and widely ignored futility of the human condition. Men see this futility more clearly than women because their lives are more obviously futile. That's why so many of them top themselves, for no apparent reason. For a man, an affair is, almost always, nothing to do with the woman involved. It's not really anything to do with sex either. It's about life and death. And that's it, nothing more or less.

I do hope we're buying this.

It's regarded as a terribly empty and insulting platitude, but when a man utters the cliché, 'It meant nothing to me,' he means it, completely. Except that, in a different way – a way that doesn't involve the other woman at all – it means everything to him. Women refuse to accept this, perhaps because they can't imagine being in that situation themselves without some form of emotional attachment, but a man is more than capable of having repeated, regular illicit sex – risking losing the woman he loves and the family they have spawned – with someone he can, quite possibly, barely even stand to be around.

And there you are, sitting at home waiting for the call, keeping your weekends free in case he manages to escape one Saturday like he always promises he will but never quite manages to. I mean, would *you* treat a friend the way he's treated you?

What turns him on is the power he has over you, the illicit nature of the relationship and the way it has of stopping him thinking about tomorrow. What sustains you through all those long, lonely, anxious, jealousy-riddled nights is the thought of the future you might, one day, have together. But can't you see now how that's never going to work? That's it. If he really cared about you, do you think he could bear to see you suffer? That's why he always goes back to his wife. He loves her, and he couldn't bear to see her suffer. You suffering, however – no problem. That, he can bear.

He doesn't set out to be cruel, but sooner or later he will tell you he loves you (because, after a while, it just gets embarrassing if he doesn't) and, once you start putting on the pressure, he will say almost anything to forestall the dawning of reality. It began purely as a physical thing, a mutual arrangement, but, somehow, somewhere along the line, the agreement was changed, rewritten and re-contracted, without anyone consulting him. He is torn because, although he can see that he is becoming everything to you (and he, of course, has absolutely no intention of leaving his wife and family), part of him – a big part, the longer he goes without it – part of him has become addicted to the snatched, sordid, heavy-breathing sex and the endless filthy emails and text messages that bring him to the boil when he is sat at his desk and should be concentrating on whatever it is someone is paying him to concentrate on.

And he is attracted to the danger because – in a way that shopping and taking the kids to the park and family holidays and having safe and secure and frankly not very interesting sex with the same woman for twenty years do not – it makes him feel alive.

He sees that, under his cruel Frankenstein manipulation, his other woman is slowly but surely evolving into a monster who might one day rear up, howling with rage and pain, and destroy the life he has and has never had any intention of abandoning for her, but he is addicted to the gamble that he can play it out a little longer. That he can put his fingers further and further into the fire. He likes being able to tell his mates about it in great detail, joking about bunny-boilers and Glenn Close, *even though his children actually keep rabbits in a cage in the garden, and sometimes, just sometimes, he wonders about that possibility and has even sneaked out on the odd night to check on the hutch.* He knows the guys will be discreet. He knows they have to be, partly because he knows things about them, but mainly because to guard such secrets is to reinforce the male hegemony from which they all benefit, and to betray them would be to undo the false, shaky structure of group self-esteem that helps them to endure their otherwise pointless, powerless, unfulfilled lives. Or something like that, eh, Rick?

And so, despite the dangers, he wields his sword of a cock because he has no other weapon left in this world and he needs a victim, needs a subordinate in life's pecking order, needs power and control and to be worshipped, and the other woman, believing what she sees and hears to be true, falls willingly on the sword and guts herself and sacrifices her own miserable life to feed his. She believes what she wants to believe, including, *of course*, that he is going to leave his wife. Only, he isn't. He never does, and never will, and why the hell does nobody in a dress ever learn this simple truth?

The other woman is, of course, always a willing co-conspirator in her own downfall. Perhaps tough, grown-up, educated, discerning and smart in every other area of her life, she becomes a helpless, malleable, gullible dunderhead who will believe any transparent lie rather than accept that the world view she has constructed is nothing more than a fake, and that she, to her married man, is nothing more than a fantasy.

And so on and on she drones to her friends . . .

. . . *Toby says he can't leave her now because she would fall apart what with the breast-cancer treatment and the boys being only ten and twelve but just as soon as she gets the all-clear or at least there's some sign of remission he will be out of there like a shot, well, the moment the kids have got through their first year at uni, obviously, he'll have to pay for them until they're through which means he wouldn't really be able to afford to move out and get a place with me until they are working and of course he can hardly deny them a gap year each and then there's her mother who must be eighty now and more doddery every day and clearly the best thing would be to move her into the flat over the garage because what with all the soiling and the wandering off without shoes on she needs a close eye on her and Toby would never ever contemplate packing her off to one of those awful places where they leave them to dribble over daytime TV and abuse them systematically because he's far too decent for that, that's why he'd never really hurt his wife because despite everything she is the mother of his children and once upon a time he did really love her and it's hard to forget that sort of thing isn't it, really? Well, of course, I respect him for that: he really is a decent man, I wouldn't be interested if he wasn't . . .*

How do I know all this? How do you think? And let me take this opportunity right now to say . . . sorry, but what the hell did you expect?

Men know women like this on sight. They can recognize them. At work, in bars, passing on the street, reading self-help books on the Tube and hanging around wistfully in the tumbleweed-blown sections of bookshops everywhere. The bitter aura of their disappointment clings to them like a noxious gas; the underlying fairy tale that, despite all she has suffered *and should have learnt from*, there will be a happy ending, clanks at her feet like a rusty ball and chain. Men can smell it and hear it, and they avoid them like the walking dead, because there is nothing less attractive than a woman who has so utterly and obsessively surrendered herself. To another man, that is.

Of course, they'd always shag her, but I think that's where we came in.

The Other Man
Friday 12 December 2003

What a sad sight is the other woman. There she sits, watching the silent phone, alone with the novelty fluffy slippers he bought her for Christmas and the box of chocolates and petrol-station flowers with which he remembered to insult her on her birthday, wondering why he hasn't turned up for their Tuesday-night tryst (he'd forgotten it was the school play).

At times (usually the times when she's hit the Pernod and cranked up the Dido), it seems that her only friend is the cat – and in her heart of hearts she knows that even old Tiddles is hanging around only for the moment when he can chow down on her unloved and unnoticed remains, trapped where she fell, in a drunken stupor, between the overflowing bath and the under-used bidet.

And then, just the other day, as I glanced in irritation at my mobile phone and the text message telling me that my expected Saturday-morning dalliance was off, it suddenly occurred to me.

I *am* the other woman.

Well, the other man, obviously. But it got me thinking. What is the difference between me and the popular stereotype above, and should I start reading self-help books with such titles as

Why All Women are Bastards – and How to Get One of Your Own?

The first thing, I suppose, is a question of quantity over quality. I have had one or two (OK, four or five) relationships with happily married/boyfriended women (occasionally, more or less simultaneously), and I suppose the effect of this has been to dilute my emotional and/or physical reliance on any one of them.

And then, I haven't exactly been moping around, polishing my nails and preening my bikini line, waiting for any of them to leave their partners. Having said that, I did come close with one once, but her indecision was paralysing and, within a very short time, a bit dull.

'Well, what do you want?' I would ask, caringly.

'I don't know,' she would answer, to virtually every enquiry, solicitous or otherwise.

Come on, come on, me or him? I mean, it's hardly rocket science, is it? Try this one: 'What is the capital of Burkina Faso?'

'I don't know.'

OK. Try this: 'What is the thrust, or force, of a rocket expressed as an equation, taking into account air-pressure variables?'

'I don't know. No! Wait. Is it $F=m^*$ Ve+Ae (Pe–Pa)?'

Well, yes, it is, actually. Now that *is* rocket science.

One of the drawbacks of being the male equivalent of the other woman is that one doesn't get showered with chocolates, jewellery, flowers and (thank God for this one, at least) novelty slippers.

On the other hand, there are no empty promises sought, or given, about her leaving him once the kids are grown up. (And a heads-up for the sisters here: it should be a red light with klaxons, bells and slaps around the face for any woman whose lover claims to be staying with his wife solely for the kids. It is almost certainly rubbish, and you are, as the rest of us already know, merely a bit on the side. And if it *is* true, then he's not right in the head. Anyone *that* dependent on his children for his own happiness is heading for disillusion. Don't go there with him.)

Being The Other Man with Realistic, Nay, No Expectations Whatsoever has its attractions. Fluttering indecision is an aphrodisiac; sudden commitment to an insane course of madly passionate action, partnered as it can be by the threat of all kinds of grown-up consequences, is a major rush.

As the great and tragically underrated psychosexual philosopher and poet-balladeer Belinda Carlisle once observed, 'Love is a Big Scary Animal'. How very true. And it's a big scary animal that requires constant feeding. Rather like Tiddles. If you insist on climbing into the cage with the beast, be prepared to feed it often, or it will start feeding on you.

And if love doesn't get you, Tiddles surely will. Lose the cat. And the wee-soaked litter tray.

11

How to be a Bad Mother

Dear Microwave Man

How is a single man at forty-seven viewed by society? Is he a sad, lonely figure, or is he the guy you can always set up on a date with one of your single female friends? Or maybe your mother?

Joe Cornish, Nottingham

Microwave Man writes: I've had your mother and, to be honest, she wasn't all that. Well, sometimes I FEEL sad and lonely (it's not a pretty sight: the bottle, the maudlin CDs, the endless rounds of toast. Seriously. Why should Bridget Jones have all the fun?), because I didn't actually set out to be a singleton at this age. Then at other times I feel liberated, as it were, by the liberty to take liberties with whomsoever I please. I feel most exposed in a supermarket and have been known to buy two of everything to avoid being taken for a sad bastard rather than one half of a couple on my way home for a candlelit meal for two. Although I have never gone so far as to buy candles. But it's a thought.

Here it is: that depressing, tedious chapter without which no book is complete and which features one of two generally dull themes, either, 1. 'My simply dreadful childhood, the grim details of which clearly justify my every subsequent action as an adult' or 2. 'My simply joyous childhood, which, nonetheless, has blighted my adulthood because no woman can possibly match up to my darling mummy.'

But I promise I'll keep it mercifully short, if not sweet.

Now, I don't know about you, but theme 2 strikes me as a little odd, not to say sick and wrong, but there you go. (And isn't it funny how no one puts pen to paper to say: 'Childhood: it was all right. Not great, but not bad either. Just middling, really. Rarely think about it.')

Theme 1 isn't much better. 'Pity me,' it says. (Oh, and by the way, what the hell do people mean when they say, 'I don't want your pity'? What's *wrong* with a bit of pity? 'Sympathy or sorrow felt for the sufferings of others,' it says right here in my Collins dictionary. We all like to be pitied. I know I do.)

So, for pity's sake, here we go (and, to be fair, I should warn you that there aren't that many laughs in this chapter. Well, one or two, obviously, but no real danger of snorting your cereal down your nose for the next few pages. A good chapter for the Tube, maybe – although if you are eating cereal on the Underground then you probably have bigger problems to contend with[67].

It could have been worse, of course. I could have been John Lennon. In fact, I nearly was, bar a decade or so. Well, it was a very close-run thing, with a number of frankly spooky similarities and coincidences. The name, for one thing (John, not Lennon, obviously). We share the same birthday (well, we used to: the dead have no birthdays, of course, just anniversaries), and while John Lennon grew up in Liverpool, my father came from Preston . . . *barely 30 miles away along the motorway.*

Not so sceptical *now* then, are we?

Oh, and both Lennon and I played guitar (and, although he did so with a little more commercial success than me, I like to think I have the edge over him when it comes to self-expression, having designed and made my own electric guitar in woodwork classes at school[68]).

Phew, I say. Setting aside the vast fortune, the worldwide

67 On a scale with those pillocks who insist on carrying hot coffee on to crowded Tube trains. 'Oh, look at me, everyone; I'm so busy and thrusting I don't have time to sit down and drink a coffee, so I'm going to spill it all over you while I pretend to work but in fact play games on my Blackberry. Whatever that is.'

68 Although, to be fair, it didn't work very well. The frets weren't quite in the right place and so tuning wasn't really an option. A few years later and I could have been the first punk and been applauded (but actually secretly despised) by Julie Burchill.

adulation and that eighteen-month-long 'Lost Weekend' spent shagging the delightful May Pang, think of the disadvantages that being Lennon would have brought to my life – having to wear trademark National Health glasses, dress as an Eggman, fight off the advances (physical, not cash) of Brian Epstein and spend hundreds of thousands of dollars simply housing my vast collection of frankly poovy furs. Even worse would have been struggling for the rest of my life to write a single decent song (other than 'How Do you Sleep') after I made the mistake of falling out with the only half of my songwriting duo (thus inspiring the song 'How Do you Sleep') who could actually write songs, living down my reputation as the man who married the woman who broke up the Beatles and then trying to keep pace intellectually (that is, trying not to giggle) with every new piece of 'art' churned out by 'one of the most daring, innovative and eccentric artist-performers of her time'.[69]

Personally, I think Lennon did well to get out when he did. Imagine life with Ono. It's easy if you try. Especially if you read the following from a leading New York art commentator.[70]

In the sixties Ono took the common housefly as an alter ego. Clearly, the artist, mocked and maligned long before she began attracting the misguided ire of rock fans, regards the fly as an embodiment of her public persona – its apparent insignificance counterbalanced by its outsize ability to annoy. But even more important to Ono's associative thinking is the fly's constant, nervous 'performing' and its elusively melodious buzz. Ono has elevated the insubstantial to monumental status, allowing us to contemplate the magic of the ordinary, as well as to comprehend the ordinariness of the seemingly profound.

She was, in other words, 'aving a larf – *but taking it seriously*. Brilliant.

Of course, almost the very worst thing about me being Lennon would have been that I was dead now. But only almost.

69 Peter Frank. No, I've never heard of him either.
70 Frank again. Still haven't heard of him.

163

God knows what Yoko Ono, one of the world's most contro-versial conceptual artists, was thinking privately when in 2002 she flew to Liverpool – now, in honour of the dead one, JLA – to unveil a local artist's horrendously figurative statue of Lennon which, publicly at least, she declared to be 'brilliant'. And come to that, what was she thinking when she responded to a commis-sion by Liverpool Biennial by producing just two photographs – one of a tit, the other a close-up of some girlie bits? Together, they constituted the work of art she entitled 'My Mummy was Beautiful'.

Now, don't get me wrong. As breasts go, this one was fine. Average. OK. Normal-looking. Just like the bush. Just right. Not too hairy, not too trim. But it didn't end there. In an extension of the project as Scousely saccharine as the sickly statue, Tate Liverpool opened a wall where visitors could record their thoughts of their own mothers. Now what, I wondered, would Lennon – like me, very much a victim of the 'f*ck you up' rather than the 't*ck you up' school of parenting – have thought about all this? His father walked out when he was very young, followed shortly by his mother, Julia, who couldn't be bothered to bring him up alone and handed him over to his aunt Mimi. Not such a beautiful thing to do.

His thoughts about his mother were recorded on his debut solo album in 1970, in the cunningly titled track, 'Mother'.

Lennon and I share not only a birthday[71] but also a less than positive experience of motherhood. My father, like Lennon's, buggered off as soon as he could (which was immediately), and my mother handed me over to the care of my grandmother and a series of boarding schools. So I was interested to see if any of the writing on the wall bucked the schmaltzy 'My mummy was beautiful' crap and reflected a broader experience of mother-hood: that not all mothers are saints and that quite a few are, in fact, out-and-out, burn-in-Hell sinners.

But no such luck. This was High Hallmark Country. Only two

[71] 9 October since you ask, but please, don't go mad: book tokens will do.

contributions scratched the veneer and hinted at something darker, jerking the viewer's chain in a way that real art is supposed to – by making them think. Or, failing that, making them laugh. Two of the children railroaded down to the Tate on a school trip had written, 'I haven't seen my mummy for ages' and (my personal favourite) 'My mummy used to jump out at me all the time and frighten me. Is this normal?'

Well, for some of us it is. My mummy used to 'jump out at me' all the time, blaming me for having ruined her life, which inspired me to pen an epitaph for the Tate's wall, but I couldn't decide between my own, *The day my mummy died was the happiest day of my life,* or a quote from Lennon's dirge about all the inexplicable pain he felt the day his mummy died. The pain he'd had to hide all the time she'd been alive.

Carry that weight, as McCartney would have said. And a long time, too, in my case – since 1955.

The words 'Suez' and 'crisis' have a particular meaning for many people. For Anthony Eden, the British Prime Minister who plotted with the Israelis and the French to occupy the canal zone, it was the end of an otherwise brilliant career. For the nation, it was the moment the curtain fell and the days of British supremacy on the world stage were over. For Gamal Abdel Nasser, it was the moment his British military training paid off and he got to dress in gold-braided fancy dress for the rest of his life. For the Americans, it was the moment they realized that they were now the kick-ass kings of the world.

And for my mother, banged up by a uniformed smoothie in the shadow of the Sphinx, it was the moment that her until then rather glamorous life had come to a decidedly unglamorous end. Let's hope it was a seriously excellent shag, eh?

The poppy seeds of my mother's bitterness, which were to flower into full-scale narcotic martyrdom with my birth in 1955, were sown a little over a decade earlier, during the Second World War. Like a lot of young Londoners during the days of rationing, the Blitz and the Glenn Miller Band (fun days when even bankrobbers had to carefully draw stocking-seams on their faces), my mother thought the war was the best time of her life. OK, she lost at least three boyfriends – young navy lieutenants drowned at sea or blown up with their flimsy wooden minesweepers – but hey: there were plenty more young officers on the beach.

Like our own dear Queen-to-be, she volunteered to drive ambulances and spent 1942 touring the streets of the shattered capital in search of the wounded and corpses after raids. She didn't have to look very hard and became something of an expert in what she once described to me as the curious effects of blast. A single high-explosive bomb might, for instance, completely dismember and decapitate one victim but leave another nearby utterly intact (although dead by virtue of having had all the air pressed out of his lungs).

I was about twelve when she mentioned this one day, quite out of the blue. It sticks in my mind partly because, as a rule, my mother hardly ever spoke to me. She worked all the time, during the day and during the evening, and I was never quite sure if it was because we badly needed the money or if it was to keep her away from me. In the event, it was my grandmother who raised me until I was sent away to school at the age of seven.

One day, during a school holiday, my mother, who was working at the time in the typing pool at Shell, came home from the office and, before going off to her evening job as a barmaid, sat down at the kitchen table and had a cup of tea. There was the usual silence until she said, 'You know, I think I'm going to write a book.'

Although we were alone, I wasn't sure she was talking to me, because, as I say, she very rarely did. She was gazing out of the window and down to the wall at the end of the small, neat garden.

'I'm going to call it *The Curious Effects of Blast*,' she said. But, as far as I know, she never did write a book. Instead, she drank lots and lots of sherry (most of which I fetched for her from the corner shop, where they had plastic containers from which you filled your own bottles. And although we didn't have much money, we did have lots of bottles).

The wall at the end of the garden, which seemed to hold such a fascination for my mother, was covered with ivy and bulged precariously, as though the motion of its collapsing had been frozen in time. It had been like that since a bomb had fallen on the house behind ours in 1942. My granny had told me about it. She was very proud of the path which ran around the small garden, which had been laid by her husband, Bert, and was made of LBC bricks he'd salvaged from the bomb-blasted house behind.

'Irene and her daughter, Kitty, and her baby were all killed,' Gran had said one afternoon while we were in the garden – me exercising Terry, the imaginatively named terrapin, on the handkerchief-sized lawn and her pushing nails into the soil to rust beneath her small rhododendron bush. She swore it gave the lilac leaves a vivid streak of . . . well, rust colour. (Terry, incidentally, escaped, developed a soft shell over three days of cold, damp freedom and died. It was, he discovered too late, a jungle out there.)

The Anderson air-raid shelter still stood at the end of the garden, under the shadow of the bulging wall. It looked like a low hill, covered in grass and weeds. My Action Men used to storm it regularly, with horrendous casualties, but there were always fresh recruits, eagerly provided by my mother's endless parade of toadying boyfriends. Or, as I used to think of them, the recruiting sergeants.

'I came out of the shelter once the rubble stopped flying to see if the house was still standing, and the first thing I saw in the light of the flames was Kitty's baby, propped up against our back wall, where she'd landed,' said Gran. 'She looked just like a doll. There wasn't a mark on her, but the poor little mite was dead.'

Irene was dug out of the rubble a few hours later. Bert helped them to dig her out from under the bricks he later liberated for his path. She was alive but died in the ambulance. My mum wasn't the driver. She'd been on leave, visiting a friend in Devon who was in the Land Army. Kitty seemed to have disappeared, which wasn't unusual, but over the next few years she gradually reappeared, bit by bit. Even by the late fifties Gran was still digging up the odd shard of human bone in the garden. One day, a few years after I had heard the story of the bomb, when I was about seven – which would have made it around 1962, I suppose – I was digging a hole to bury yet another dead pet rabbit[72] when my trowel hit something hard and white.

I pulled the bone out of the ground, and for a while it just kept coming. It was much too long to belong to any rabbits, or cats or dogs. I turned to show it to my mother and Gran, who were stood behind me for the ceremony. Gran's hands shot up to her mouth. My mother reached down and took the bone from me.

'We used to have a donkey that died just before the war,' she said quietly, walking towards the dustbin. It was a Tuesday and the dustmen had just been, so when she dropped the bone into the empty bin it made a dull, metallic thud. 'My dad buried it in the garden.'

Gran walked quickly back to the house. 'Oh, Kitty,' I heard her whisper as she passed the bin. I shovelled the soil back into the hole, on top of the imaginatively named Bunny.

Other curious effects of blast were felt in Clayton Road, Peckham. My mother had a childhood bear which during the war was twice blown out of her bedroom and into the branches of the solitary tree outside her window. The bear was given to me when I was born, and I remember, at some stage, being frightened of this big, ugly, battered creature slumped on the chair in the corner of my room.

It certainly looked as though it had been in the wars. One leg was hanging by a thread, and its left eye was missing, the stitching that had once held it in place resembling a livid scar. Worst of all, despite the fact that much of its stuffing had been lost or

72 I had a shocking record with pets. Mind you, I think my mother disposed of my hamsters on the first day of every school term. Each school holiday, Hammy (the imaginatively named hamster) was slightly bigger, or smaller, or darker, or lighter, than I remembered. No wonder we were poor.

replaced with newspaper, its mechanical voice-box still worked. Only, instead of the original growl when you inverted it, the bear gave out a hideous groan, like a soul in torment.

The bear was a Steiff, made in Giengen, southern Germany, and I wondered if it had felt a little bitter at having been blown up, not once, but twice, by its countrymen. Still, like Germany, the bear survived, and so did Steiff, the cuteness and collectibility of its bears unaffected to this day by the nearby operation of several of the other kind of factories for which Germany became so famous during the war. Despite the war, Steiff managed to churn out its bears until 1943 (when it switched over to producing ammunition), and was back in the business of being furry and cuddly again by 1947.

I supposed my mother had loved her bear as a child, but I wondered how she had felt about it after the German bombs started to rain down, and after her elder brother, Ronnie, joined the British Army, was wounded in France – who knows, but quite possibly by a Steiff bullet – and died in a convalescence home in Kent. There was a large pond in the grounds where the recovering men were in the habit of swimming. Ronnie was still weak and, one day, his war, and his life, ended when he dived into the pool and was held fast and drowned by thick weeds on the bottom.

Whatever she thought of the Steiff, my mother worshipped her brother. I learnt to steer clear of her on Armistice Day. Once, after Gran had died and we had moved to a high-rise hellhole called Thamesmead (an estate from the windows of which television sets and the occasional person rained down with tedious regularity), I found her drunk and weeping and surrounded by photographs of all the dead men in her life. She was watching the Cenotaph ceremony on the black-and-white TV.

A picture of the blond, Aryan Ronnie in a solid silver frame was clutched to her chest. Failing quite to focus on me, she nevertheless made a fist of shaking her eyeballs in my general direction and slurred, 'You'll never be half the man he was.'

If she had been a stranger, someone in a book or a TV programme, perhaps, I would have felt sorry for her and her lost life. But The Radish had it all wrong. I didn't want to screw my mother. I wanted to kill her.

It was a couple of years before this that my grandmother had died. She had been ill, and when the doctor could find nothing wrong, she got herself up from her bed and went and sat in front of the coal fire in her scullery. In the days before we had a bathroom installed at the rear of the house, this was the same fire in front of which I had had all my childhood baths, sitting in a zinc tub and watching the sparks gather like stars on the night-sky of soot in the chimney. A chimney that ran up the same wall the other side of which Kitty's baby had fetched up. I always dreaded going out at night to use the outside toilet in the dark.

The sickbed Gran had left for her old armchair was the same one in which she had slept alone during the long years of the First World War while her young husband fought in France, and the same bed in which he had died just after the end of the Second World War. Like the bloody bear, he had survived both wars and the bombing on the constantly raided London docks where he worked throughout the Blitz. What finally claimed him was the flu he contracted in the mud and blood of France, which he had entered as a fourteen-year-old conscript (told by the recruiting sergeant to walk around the block, sonny, and come back a year older), and which, along with a gassing, had fatally ruined his lungs. Thirty years later, his lungs ruined, he became the 421,301st British victim of the Somme.

'He just sat up suddenly in the middle of the night,' Gran had told me, on more than one occasion. She still had his pictures on the wall, and his medals and postcards from France in a drawer. She never went with another man after he died. Just got on with her job as a cleaner and, after I was born, with looking after me. 'He hadn't been well – he'd not been right ever since the trenches – and I thought he was being sick again, so I grabbed the bowl from the side of the bed. "Bert," I said, "Bert?" But he was gone. Just like that. Gone.'

When she wasn't cleaning shops or pottering in her garden or carefully brushing leaves off the bricks her Bert had laid from the remains of the wall toppled by the Luftwaffe, or thinking about the fine young son of her own she'd had and lost, Gran spent a lot of time staring into the fire, watching it like she might have watched a television, if we'd had one. Now, old and sick and unhappy, and bemused because my mother had been impatient with her for days, she sat in her old armchair and stared at the flickering pictures only she could see. I didn't know why my mother had been impatient. I was only young, perhaps eight, but I knew she resented her small life in the small house in Peckham. Perhaps in some way it was my gran's fault, in the same way that my mother's ruined life seemed to be mine.

My mother and I had the top floor of the two-up, two-down house, one of only five in the street to have survived the Blitz. That day I went downstairs carrying the meal my mother had cooked and set it on the table alongside Granny's chair. Gran was just staring at the sparks flying up the chimney. She suddenly took my arm in her bony hand and said, 'What have I done to upset your mother?' I said, 'I don't know, Gran. Nothing. You're just imagining it.'

But she wasn't. My mother resented her in the same way that she resented me, in the same way that she resented having been transported from her glamorous life of officers' mess balls and bombs and bullets in Egypt, not to her next planned posting, in Japan, but back to Peckham, the two-up, two-down world of loss and death she thought she had left behind.

I could see her point. Clayton Road was little more than a bombsite, with rubble and splinters and, if you were a kid with no friends who had the time to kill to look hard enough, shrapnel still everywhere. Our side of the street had been cleared and the gaps filled with prefabs – one-storey homes for heroes, made in America and highly prized because each house came complete with a fridge, an unheard-of modern luxury. (They also came complete with asbestos, then an unheard-of modern hazard, but

I think bombed-out Londoners would still have taken their chances just to get hold of a fridge.)

But she acted as though it was our fault, and it wasn't; it was hers. Even I knew that: I was young, but I wasn't stupid. I knew that all along. I knew it then and I knew it later, when I was a few years older, and each time I was called into the embarrassed housemaster's study and told that I had to go home for a couple of days because my mother was, um, not well (as one tends not to be when one swallows a handful of sleeping pills). I knew that it was her fault because she had had sex and become pregnant. It was her fault because she had chosen not to have an abortion. It was her fault because she had decided to have the baby, not because she wanted it, but because it enabled her to spend the rest of her life in a sacred state of martyrdom.[73]

'I'll never iron another man's shirts.'

That was my mother's battle cry and, like so much else she said and did (and didn't say and didn't do), it still echoes in my psyche. Men's shirts seem to occupy a totemic place in a woman's emotional wardrobe. Or maybe that's just the way I see it. A chap knows he has woken up on the far side of the Rubicon the first time he sees her wandering around the morning after, searching in vain for fresh coffee and clean cups and wearing nought but one's baggy, crumpled Oxford from the night before.

'I can smell you,' she purrs (although she's more likely to be experiencing the twenty-four-hour power of Right Guard Sport), which is all very sweet and sexy. But she just can't let the shirt thing go at that. Later that same relationship: 'I got bored while you were out, so I ironed a couple of your shirts . . .'

I twitch, à la Herbert Lom faced with the unexpected return of Inspector Clouseau. Two points: 1. We both know this is merely a Desmond Morris courtship-dance thing. You are a modern woman who, once in a proper relationship, would no sooner iron my shirts than have my dinner served up on your

---

73 Not that that cut any ice with the local church, who after just two weeks asked her to take me away from Sunday School as her single-mother status was upsetting the other mothers. Never mind. I expect they're in Hell now.

oiled and naked body every night at six; 2. Call that ironed? There are creases in the cuffs, for Christ's sake!

Don't blame me. Blame Mother. And Matron. The former sent me, aged seven, to a less-than-minor prep school run by a retired (and quite possibly cashiered) former cavalry officer, straight out of the box, complete with brush moustache, pipe, plus-fours and a fondness for the type of corporal discipline that had clearly done him all kinds of harm.

One of his small, select staff of perverts, psychopaths and what we would now call paedophiles was Matron, by reputation a disgraced policewoman, by inclination a photographer of small boys at bathtime and by profession a damned fine presser of small boys' white shirts. She taught me all she knew about the art. (She also showed me and 'Pissy' Pulfer a few tricks with a soapy loofah. At the time this seemed like good, clean fun; I actually quite looked forward to bathtimes and, Lord knows, Pissy needed them: he was the only boy in the school with a first name and had earned the honour by wetting himself whenever fear crossed his path – which, at our school, was often.)

And then there was Mother. Apart from committing me to the care of the galloping-mad major and his entourage, her other gift to my evolving psyche was bestowed one evening in the holidays when, having crept out of bed to listen through the banisters, I heard her ejecting the latest in a series of cowering and clearly inadequate (yet car-owning and thus passingly useful) suitors with the immortal and sternly bellowed words: *'I'll never iron another man's shirts.'*

I was too young to know what a euphemism was, so I took her point literally, and it has stuck ever since. She might have fallen into single motherhood from the grace of her privileged 'barbed wire and ball gowns' lifestyle in Suez (getting into a mess with an officer, if not a gentleman), but she was damned if she was going to wait hand and foot on any man by way of penance. As she saw it.

Matron taught me the sensuality of a properly ironed shirt;

Mother taught me how to iron out life's creases for oneself. Result? Emasculation if a woman so much as reaches for my Morphy Richards.

I freed my arm from my gran's grasp. This was the woman who had raised me, shown me affection, let me play among the magical department-store mannequins after hours in Jones and Higgins, where she cleaned, and taken me in the middle of the night to watch the soldiers march – *crunch, crunch, crunch* – around the Bank of England, where she also wielded her mop. I spent hours sitting with her, listening to television programmes without the pictures on her rented Redifusion radio. TV was never the same once it came with pictures.

I hated the sense of having my loyalties torn and walked back upstairs feeling confused and miserable. An hour later, I was sent back down to collect the plate and, as I turned at the bottom of the narrow stairs and started to walk towards the open door that led to Gran's scullery, I knew instantly that she was dead. The plate lay, untouched, where I had left it, and her right hand hung, motionless, by her side. I could see her grey hair over the back of the chair. As I drew nearer – walking slowly, fearfully – I saw that the skin on her face was translucent, drawn and stretched like parchment. Green stuff had appeared at the edges of her mouth, and her eyes, unevenly hooded, were milky and staring not at the sparks in the grate but at nothing. I had no idea what I was doing, but I tried to feel a pulse at her wrist, but all I felt was that she was cold and, already, quite stiff.

We had no telephone. My mother became hysterical, so I went next door to ask if they would call for an ambulance. This was the fifties, and we knew our neighbours, and I knew that of the five remaining households in our shortened little terrace, only the Murphys had a phone.

'Excuse me, Mr Murphy, but could you call an ambulance? I don't think my gran is very well.'

The ambulance took ages to come. I stood by the gate, listening for the bell. Like the police, they had bells in those days, not sirens. I remember it was a beautiful, sunny day, and I stood leaning against Gran's carefully trimmed privet hedge, straining to see down the street. I could hear my mother inside, wailing. Mrs Murphy was making tea in Gran's kitchen. Mr Murphy shuffled around for a bit and then clumsily put his arms around me. I had never been touched by a man before and I wriggled free, but the unexpected hug made me cry.

The worst moment came when the ambulancemen arrived. They didn't seem to be in a hurry. The first thing they did was open the window in the scullery. I hadn't noticed the smell before, but Gran must have voided her bowels when she died. I *wanted* them to be in a hurry – to at least *pretend* that she might be alive – but they took their time carrying her out and into the ambulance, and there were no bells as they drove her away.

I did warn you that there wouldn't be many laughs in this chapter.

On the other hand, the day my mother died, perhaps twenty years later, was the happiest day of my life, and the constant search for the approval of women engendered by her permanent disapproval has meant that, over the years, I have had an awful lot of sex.

Now, reading that back, does that sound as weird to you as it does to me? Quite. As you can see, nothing is my fault. I am the entirely blameless product of my environment, driven constantly to seek the approval of women, who are drawn to me because I, in turn, am driven to seek mothering, and that happens to be where most twentysomethings – hormonally midway across the bridge between ponies and babies – are at. Clear as a bell, open and shut, no further questions, m'lud, I rest my case and move for acquittal.

I've still got the bear. I've always been too scared to throw the bloody thing away. And it still gives out a hideous groan when you invert it. But then, don't we all?

And, by the way, I know that wasn't exactly mercifully short, as advertised, but if I'd have said so at the outset, would you have read on? Well, exactly.

A Mother's Love
Friday 19 December 2003

Nothing in art is quite what it seems (least of all attributions: you get home from the shops with your Correggio only for some smart-arse professor of art history to claim it's actually by some bloke the master had in on Fridays to sweep the floor and daub the tricky bits. Such as hands).

Take the Madonna – one end of a spectrum of male-produced images within which, arguably, real women are stereotyped as either virtuous mother figures or easy slappers. But does the Madonna really tell us anything more about real women than the Athena poster of the tennis player scratching her bum? (Filippo Lippi's 1465 Madonna, for example, turned out to be a beautiful nun with whom Friar Lippi was constantly on his knees. And not in prayer.)

After my own dismal experience of a childhood spent as one half of a dark-hued Single Mother with Child, I latched on to the first motherly type I could find, married her and spent the rest of my twenties ruing the wedding day. Since then, I have steered well clear of the mother figure.

Until last week, when I met a woman who made me look closer at the stereotype.

On the few occasions in the past when I have been drawn to single women with young children, it has been despite the offspring. Now, for a reason I don't quite understand, I am attracted to a woman as much for her status as modern Madonna as for her ability to kiss like an angel and to make me laugh (not at the same time).

Sitting in her kitchen, amid the drawings of 'Mummy' and the times tables stuck on the fridge, and listening to her upstairs, running through the cosy bedtime rituals with her son, I am deeply moved by the love in which this little boy is so obviously swaddled. Where was this woman when I was her son's age? (Six years away from being born, since you ask.)

This Madonna has packed her infant off to bed, and the

well-rehearsed arrangements for keeping him there (a combination of tough-love rules and the white-noise overlapping of stereo and TV to drown out the sound of a strange man about the house) are somehow a part of our evening rather than a distraction from it.

And later, whatever it is I find in her bed (beside the cuddly toys), it isn't simply sex, and it's a great deal more than the mothering it seems that, even at forty-eight, a part of me still craves. And, whatever it is, it is an extremely potent mix.

In the pre-dawn morning our sleepily entwined reverie is shattered by the sound of a small and not-too-distant voice: 'Mummy, can I come into your bed now?' In the nick of time, I am bundled down the stairs, clothes in hand, hopping to my car with my shoes unlaced. And in the rear-view mirror I catch the broad smile on my face.

The classical Madonna certainly gets around: we find her posing in the meadow, on the rocks (later an exciting cocktail) and on thrones, and hanging out with angels, assorted saints and (perhaps far too often for decency) John the Baptist. Rarely is she snapped in the act of actually working for a living, although in Leonardo's £60 million *Madonna of the Yarnwinder* (pinched last year from Drumlanrig Castle in Scotland), there is a suggestion of sweatshop child-labour.

My Madonna hasn't much time for sitting around and looking like an oil painting (although, with little more than a toss of her long dark hair, she does). She works hard, as a teacher, and the piles of marking alongside the heaps of ironing add another quality to the impressive mix.

Right now there is a great deal of controversy about the National Gallery's battle to save for the nation Raphael's £35 million *Madonna of the Pinks*. Until last week, I might have wondered just how many Madonnas one nation needed – the National Gallery alone has forty-one, for God's sake.

But now, hey: what price a mother's love? The more the merrier, I say.

12

How to Stuff a Turkey

Dear Microwave Man

    Since my office is completely empty and I have nothing to do, I'd like to take this chance to comment on how much I enjoy 'Microwave Man'. It is masculine, honest, stylish and amusing writing, which stands out in the paper as a whole and especially from the other dreary and self-absorbed 'slice of life' columns. I hope you are not to be sacked in the current scaling-down of operations in Wapping. Happy Christmas.

Duncan Smith, Purley

Microwave Man writes: Well, there's 'sacked' and then there's 'redundant', one of which leads to Dickensian penury (admittedly more appropriate at this time of year) and the other to yacht ownership. Which do you mean? What have you heard? Besides, I'd have thought a man happy to put his name to the statement, 'My office is completely empty and I have nothing to do,' might be a little more concerned about his own prospects for the new year. But try to have a Happy Christmas, Duncan.

I have a problem with Christmas. Like most misanthropes, I hate the whole thing (except for the way it begins in September, which clearly makes a great deal of commercial sense and brings much-needed jobs to the hard-pressed tinsel-farmers of Guatemala), but I do like Christmas pudding. OK, it's not a tremendously tricky dilemma, but I thought I should mention it. Actually, it's not half the dilemma it used to be; not now that you can buy those little puddings for the microwave. None of that stirring and mixing for four years in advance. Out of the packaging, prick the plastic and wallop: napalm-hot joy in three minutes.[74]

I'm not sure what first hooked me on Christmas puddings, but it might have had something to do with Matron, breasts and prep school (looking back, many things do, it seems. All those things I thought were normal turned out not to be. What I didn't know at the time was that I was at a school for emotionally disturbed teachers).

Back then – and we're talking *circa* 1962 here, remember – there was this wonderful tradition of Stirring the Pudding, which, in retrospect, sounds like a euphemism for something quite fun. But wasn't.

Anyway, the entire school lined up to have a go, killing time by staring at Matron's *enormous* breasts, pale white and visible between the straining buttons of her even whiter tunic, and by coming up with a wish to be made as one struggled to drive the big wooden spoon through a full circle in the thick goo.

I think none of us was old enough to wish for anything to do with Matron's breasts (not even the more matronly experienced Pissy and me, although some of the younger boys, not that long torn from the breast, probably yearned subconsciously for a quick suckle), although I do recall an odd, mysterious stirring down below related in some then unfathomable way to the energetic way they swelled and joggled beneath the starched white severity of her uniform with each hearty stroke of the wooden spoon.

Unfortunately, there was no tradition of licking the bowl, but there you go: you can't have everything. This was the sixties, after all.[75]

But it was the other tradition that caught my imagination:

74 Times may vary from machine to machine. You are, remember, on your own, Bernice.
75 And sadly, although I would dearly love to report otherwise, there was no tradition of licking Matron. Although I do recall being photographed by her on occasions when she asked myself and Pissy to splash around together in the bath, supposedly to 'save water'. Do you suppose these images can be found today on the internet? If they weren't all dead by now, I could, perhaps, sue. Although, to be honest, I quite liked splashing around in the bath to the sound of Matron's motor drive on three frames a second.

the one about choking to death on a threepenny bit.[76] For many kids at my school, this was seen as an opportunity to boost meagre pocket-money funds. This was, after all, a fourth- or fifth-rank private boarding school, and no one who sent their kids there was well off. If you were the one lucky enough to get the threepenny bit, well, super: another Airfix Spitfire trailing cotton-wool smoke to paint and hang with the three million others dangling from the common-room ceiling. But I saw the coin lottery less as a charming old tradition and more as an attempt on my life or, at best, a chance to be choked to death by George VI (or, at least, by a bizarre, dodecagonal brass coin bearing a profile of his head).

When the time came in late December to sit down and 'enjoy' the pudding, I hunched in misery over my bowl. Would this be the year that my young life was finally cut short by a dead king? Obviously not, or I wouldn't be writing this, but I didn't know that at the time and virtually the entire school year for four whole years was overshadowed for me by the impending seasonal tussle with fate. I blame this for my failure to come to terms with maths. And Latin. And everything else.

There were near-misses, mind. One Christmas, the kid next to me bit so hard on the bloody coin that he broke a tooth. This raised a question of practical economics, even among the seven- and eight-year-olds present. They knew full well that the tooth fairy would exchange a tooth left under the pillow for sixpence, so there was some attraction in risking choking and enduring shattered gnashers for a possible total of ninepence.

The next year, somebody actually did swallow it (not that he got to keep it: Matron waited for nature to take its course and nicked it. The things people did in the sixties for threepence). Finally, disaster struck. A new boy choked to death, despite Matron's best efforts to prise the offending coin from his windpipe with a fork. Nobody liked him, and he was an orphan anyway, so no one kicked up a fuss, and in those days the only

76 What's a threepenny bit? Oh, do eff off.

role of school inspectors was to make sure that no boys under eight were being disposed of in satanic rituals (Christian rituals, of course, were just fine). But that wasn't the point. It just didn't seem right.

Actually, nobody died, but they might have. I just wanted you to understand that it wasn't all milk bars, Beatles and swinging in the sixties. We had it tough. There was no such thing as health and safety at work, or school, or in the home, or anywhere else, come to that. Colour hadn't yet made it across the Atlantic from America (most people's lives in Britain then were still lived in black and white), and the wireless, still at an early stage of development and packed with dangerous glass valves, was as liable to explode with the force of a hand grenade as it was to emit the crackly sounds of Joe 'Dead' Loss and His Orchestra, Live from the London Palladium[77] (although, it must be said, most people were divided over which was the worse of the two fates).

On the plus side, although everything on the television was complete rubbish (even if it was presented by blokes in dinner jackets who spoke like minor royalty), it was still so new that viewers weren't yet exposed to endless repeats. (The BBC had yet to work out that it could show programmes more than once.) The first TV programme I ever saw, along with all the other small boys parcelled out by our headmaster to nearby homes, was the funeral of Winston Churchill. It was very long, and it wasn't very good and, as far as I know, it was never repeated.

And why do I share all this with you? Because next to me in the car, as I drive tentatively through the streets of south London towards Christmas with the Boer, sit two top-of-the-range Christmas puddings from M&S, and all this comes flooding back.

I hadn't been expecting to hear from the Boer. I'd have put it down to a momentary weakness – only, she wasn't prone to weaknesses, momentary or otherwise – but the moment she

---

77 The Palladium was for years London's only venue, of any kind. With the invention of the television and the Royal Variety performance, Britons became increasingly bitter, in retrospect, about the Luftwaffe's wartime failure to demolish the building.

agreed to spend Christmas together I was convinced she had realized that she couldn't live without me.

Ha.

We were, as she said, both yuletide orphans. Adam, with his unfailing, heat-seeking attraction to family life, had secured a berth with his girlfriend's large and conventional family. The Boer's parents were in South Africa, and most of her friends had flown south for the holidays.

It made sense to be together.

At first, it all seems to be on track. She is looking after a friend's house (and the attached cat) near Richmond Park, and on Christmas Eve we take ourselves off for a long walk (minus the cat, obviously), ending up in a café in town. A couple of times, we hold hands, just like old times. Once, we kiss, not *quite* like old times, but it's a start, and I'm pretty sure she started it. Then I drive her into town for her shift at the Christmas feast for the unloved elderly, where she has volunteered to serve dinners.

Back in the empty house, I find myself whistling as I wander around, thinking about what the evening and her return might bring. I am nice to the cat, remembering to feed it, watch a bit of television, flick through a book I am supposed to be reading and start strumming a classical guitar I find in the spare room where I am, supposedly, spending the night.

I try to remember the song I sang to Karen, sitting on the edge of the bed after the first time we made love. I know that sounds cheesy, but you had to be there. Actually, it *was* cheesy, but at moments like that you can get away with that kind of stuff. (Look, I don't get many chances to sing one of the twelve songs I committed to memory in my twenties: I take every chance of an audience I can get. In my experience, three songs is the absolute top number you can hope to get away with.)

And, after a while, it comes back to me. 'Love Hurts'. It certainly does. And wounds, and mars, and scars. But possibly not in that order. G, E minor, C, D . . .

Almost every song I know has that chord sequence. I think it must have something to do with the self-pitying misery invoked by that minor chord. The potency of cheap music, indeed. I stop and stand up. I'll take the guitar downstairs, practise the number and give her a rendition when I've collected her from the centre. Smooth, I think you'll agree.

As I start down the stairs, I pass the door to the Boer's room. The cat, which is now my best friend and has followed me, squeezes past my legs and into the room, and I push the door wide open. The bedside light is on, and I can't resist a peek at the bed in which, I am now more or less confident, we will be reunited later. At this moment, that business about cats and curiosity completely deserts me.

It's unmade – the way she always leaves a bed – the duvet thrown back and the impression of her head still in the pillow. The familiarity of the scene makes me smile. Some of her clothes lie around on the floor, as they always did, and I recognize some of them, especially the underwear, most of which we bought together. I put the guitar down, kneel by the bed and push my face against the pillow. I can smell her, and suddenly everything I have missed about her rushes back.

With my face pressed into the pillow, I can see some of her long blonde hairs, close to my face. I remember how they felt, brushing my face, my chest, my belly, when we made love. I don't know whether to laugh or to cry. Or to masturbate. Better not, I suppose. Save your energy. And then, still kneeling by the bed, I catch sight of a carrier bag under the table in the corner. It seems to be full of Christmas presents – I can see the wrapping paper. I'm not sure why, but my heart gives a thump. Not a good thump but a kind of warning lurch. I can hear the cat, now sprawled out on the bed, purring.

Have a look. Who knows? They might be for you.

Maybe I should. Just take a peek. Needn't even take them out. Can probably see the labels if I just move the bag slightly.

Yes, go on. Bet they're for you.

Another, quieter, voice knows better and sounds an alarm, but no one is listening.

OK, this is what you do: you touch nothing, leave everything as you've found it, go straight downstairs, have a drink – just one, you're driving, remember – watch some TV, and then go and pick her up. Oh, and one other thing. That Christmas present you've brought for her?

Yes?

Leave it in the car.

Why?

Just trust me on this. You know I'm always right. We'll talk about it later, if you like, but for now, just forget the present. You'll see. It's for the best.

Somewhere, I can hear a locomotive. In fact, through the half-open curtains, I can just see the flash of electricity, arcing between track and train. Now I'm listening carefully I can hear all kinds of noises out there. I can hear voices; it sounds like a party, maybe a few doors down. A dog barking. A plane flying overhead; we're not far from Heathrow. I start to wonder about all those people hanging there in the night sky, flying home for Christmas, perhaps. And cars on the high street. People in transit, heading home, or out to spend the evening with friends.

But in here, the loudest sound is the sound of the carrier bag rustling in my hands, and it sounds like thunder.

The carrier bag. Now I'm looking inside it. Without touching anything, I can see that at least one gift has been opened, the paper torn just enough so the contents can be seen. It's lingerie, from Agent Provocateur.

Classy, I say out loud, startling the cat, who sits up, looking indignant. Dark reds and black and lace. I smile. I feel slightly nauseous. The cat jumps off the bed and pads down the stairs. There's the label. It's face up, silver, stars. Across the room, lying where they have been discarded on a chair, is a pair of knickers I recognize. They have a tartan pattern, and we bought them together in Edinburgh.

Don't turn it over. Just don't.

But of course I do. Another train rattles past. Two flashes.

'Have a lovely Christmas Day, babe. Can't wait to play with you in these on Boxing Day. Love, Ben.'

That is *so* typical. She was supposed to wait until Christmas Day to open it but had to know what it was. I could *never* keep a secret gift secret from her: she would nag and nag until she found out what it was.

And, *babe?*

I realize I am smiling. I know I am because my hand goes up to my face and feels the lines around my mouth. *You're* smiling? *What the bloody hell is wrong with you?*

There are other, unopened gifts in the bag. I look at the first label I see. It's from someone called Julian. She hasn't bothered to open that, so I don't bother to read the sentiment. If I were Julian, that would worry me. Phew. Lucky break. Glad I'm not Julian! Poor sap.

I drive to pick her up. No music. Just the sound of the engine. The streets are pretty quiet, and I arrive early outside the factory units on an industrial estate off the Old Kent Road where Christmas dinner is being served to all the lonely old people. These aren't people who, by rights, I should be envying. It starts to rain and, through the intermittent wipers, I watch them coming and going, in and out of the darkness, and then it is her, running towards the car, her golden hair, tied back in a ponytail and swinging and backlit by headlights approaching down the street.

On the way back to the house and the cat and the guitar and the lingerie old and new, we don't talk much, but I sense that she senses that I have sensed . . .

Indoors, she goes upstairs to change. The cat follows her, purring like a road drill. I look at the guitar, leaning against the wall where I left it. If it was mine, I'd stamp it into matchwood, but even at moments like this I can respect other people's property. I feel very, very stupid. I can hear the sound of her voice. She's talking, not clear enough for me to hear individual words – and I'll be buggered if I'm creeping up the stairs to eavesdrop – but I can tell she's on the phone. Every now and then I hear her laugh, that familiar laugh she used to laugh when I said something funny, or stupid, or endearing.

And now she is laughing and it has absolutely bloody nothing to do with me. Or, worse, maybe it does.

She comes downstairs, sits in the armchair opposite me instead of alongside me on the large sofa. The cushions are soft, and I sink in deep and, with my knees almost higher than my mouth, I feel absurd, laughable. We start to talk, and it quickly becomes a row which catches fire and roams and flickers over everything combustible that has lain between us since that day in the hotel.

I just can't do it any more.

She still can't, it seems, and she still can't explain what that means, but she doesn't have to now because she is seeing someone else.

Ben.

'Yes. How did you know?'

Was that him you were just talking to?

She laughs the short, nervous laugh she laughs when things aren't funny but she is . . . well, nervous.

I looked at the presents in your room. She laughs again, looking down at the cat and shaking her head slowly.

I am about to make up some excuse – *I was chasing the cat, he knocked over the bag, they fell out, there was the label* – but, actually, I just can't be bothered. I have nothing to lose. It's lost already.

I can't remember exactly what she says, but it is something about how she really had thought that there was a chance for us when she first agreed to spend Christmas together, but that was three weeks ago, and since then something has changed in the way she feels about Ben.

What? That whereas before you felt that he was a bit of an arsehole, now you feel that he's a complete arsehole, right?

That's it, laugh it off. Don't show the pain.

Three weeks. At moments like this there is nothing the withdrawing party can say that won't strike the withdrawee like a spear – and not just any spear: one of those ones with the barbed tip that makes it so difficult to pull out without dragging with it half of your insides. And with the tips dipped in horse dung or Amazon frog-vomit or something so the infection will get you even if the disembowelling doesn't.

Just three weeks?

After three years?

Do *not* show the pain.

We spend the night in separate beds and she closes the door to her room, but for some reason I sleep really well. The next morning, I drive her back into town, through teeming rain and empty streets dressed absurdly in the suddenly redundant Christmas decorations.

Plenty of music this time, played loud, but a bit of a cock-up over the selection.

'Mr Blue Skies'. Despite myself, it's all I can do not to laugh.

'. . . Hey hey hey.'

And I'm singing along, even. Can't help myself. Never could. Besides, nothing to say.

I pull up outside the house she has been sharing with two nurses since we split up. I wonder if it is like the house she was sharing with two other nurses when we first started seeing each other, three years ago. I wonder if she is depressed that she is back where she started. Or thrilled to be starting out again.

I try not to feel protective towards her and, right now, to be honest, it isn't that hard.

But I remember her coming to the door the first time I ventured down into south London to see her. She opened it wearing a simple, white nightie and kissed me, softly, briefly, on the mouth. She had had a hot bath that had made her pale skin glow pink and had brushed and brushed her long blonde hair until it crackled with static. She led me to her tiny bedroom, and we sat on her bed and talked and then kissed and then made love, and for about three years after that life seemed just about perfect.

In a frame on the wall at the foot of the bed was a collage of photographs of her and her equally young husband. I think she was still in a kind of shock, still couldn't quite cut the withered cord. As she sat astride me, head back and eyes closed, rocking slowly, I peered past her gently moving hips and studied the pictures. The two of them at some black-tie dinner, the Boer, looking nervous but beautiful, turning to look over her shoulder and up at the camera. The two of them, travelling in South Africa, him with his shirt off and his bulky surfer's chest glistening with sweat. The two of them walking out of the small Cornish church, laughing and ducking under an arch of surfboards.

An arch of surfboards? Like I said: that was always going to last.

I remember her suddenly coming. I was so intent on the pictures that it took me by surprise. I remember we ended up having a row. I said it was weird to keep the pictures on the wall. She said they had had many happy times together and she wasn't just going to forget them or pretend that they hadn't happened.

I said something crap like, *Pictures are nothing more than evidence that proves the past.* I never kept pictures of my exes, I said. I was lying, but I was trying to make her feel like the odd one out. The next time I came to the house, the pictures were gone. I noticed the frame had been tucked in behind the chest of drawers. It should have pleased me, but it made me feel like the worst kind of bully, and whatever drug or chemical or hormone or Cupid's arrow it is that gives you that unfathomable, ecstatic rush right where cartoonists fancy the heart is was released in overdose. There and then I decided I would love her, cure her of her stubbornness and distrust and emotional isolation and look after her and be with her for the rest of my life. Like it was up to me.

Ha.

And now I am outside another anonymous, temporary waystation of a south London house, like so many throughout this city, full of people waiting for something better to come along, only this time I won't be going in. This time, I'm not the something better that's come along. I wonder if she has hung pictures of me and her on the wall. I wonder if Ben, or Julian, or Tom, Dick or Harry will gaze at them. I wonder if everyone's life, from time to time, founders in this terrible, circular whirlpool of cyclical pointlessness. The rain streams down. She opens the car door, and I think she will simply run to the house and that will be that, but she turns and leans back in the car. She is getting wet. Her hair is tied back, and raindrops run down her face. At least, I think it's raindrops.

'What about my Christmas present?' she asks, trying to smile. The rain has turned to hail and drums on the car like so much spent shrapnel rattling on the tin roof of an Anderson bomb shelter. The badly wrapped present lurks on the back seat.

'I don't want you to have it now.' *Good*, says the voice. *Good*.

She looks at the parcel, which sits on the seat contriving to look faintly embarrassed. I know it's only a parcel, but, I swear, it looks embarrassed. She looks at it as if it might contain something mystical; a plan, a route, a way from here to happiness, via a thorough and liberating exculpation of guilt and blame. For a moment I actually think she might be preparing to make a grab for it, but she doesn't. Instead, she says, 'Fair enough.'

She has one hand on the roof of the car and she is looking straight at me. Now *she* looks embarrassed, more than anything. Or maybe upset. Who knows? Perhaps Ben knows. I never really could work her out. Her right hand is still in the car, resting on the green crushed velour of the passenger seat. Her thumb gently brushes the material, and I find myself staring intently at the nails on her fingers. Nails which, from time to time, I have painted.

And I want to say . . .

Do you remember when I bought this car, three years ago, you were still with your husband but we were drawing ever closer to each other, and the day I went to buy it I sent you a text asking what colour you liked and what kind of material you wanted on the seats because pretty soon you'd be lying back on them as I kissed you, and you said green crushed velour partly because you thought the words sounded so funny and English, and within a few weeks you were in that passenger seat and driving with me up to the cottage, and do you remember that winter night when the stars were so vivid as we pulled up alongside the river

and it was so cold but we made love on the bonnet, still warm from
the engine, and your heels scratched the paintwork, and the marks are
still there. To this day, they are still there and, God help me, as if the
Electric Light Orchestra wasn't enough, here comes bloody Leonard
Cohen droning on about distances and sorrow and how, in his opin-
ion, that is not a great way to say goodbye . . .

. . . but, actually, it's as good as any. And, besides, all I can
manage is . . .

'Goodbye.'

Stuff the Turkey
Friday 2 January 2004

Pride cometh, it seems, not merely before a fall, but as a prelude
to a damn' good kicking.

Regular readers of this column (and a happy new year to
Doreen and Edgar Maldetete, of Walton-on-the-Naze) will
recall my recent evocation of the poet Robert Frost (some
cobblers about not yielding with grace to reason and accepting the end of a love or season, blah blah blah) as I laid plans
to spend Christmas with the estranged Boer. Well, Bob, thanks
for nothing. We did the Christmas thing, but it turned out more
like the Easter thing.

At some point over Christmas I watched David Lean's *Great
Expectations*, without an inkling that my own were about to
be crushed with Dickensian savagery. Two weeks back, the
Boer had begun to go on about some bloke called Ben – just
one of a handful she was seeing, and nothing, it seemed, to
write home about. By the time I turned up on Christmas Eve,
clutching my M&S microwavable puddings and, as it was about
to turn out, hugely inappropriate and soon-to-be-binned gift,
he had somehow achieved Basildon Bond status.

Feeling a little like Pip, who rushes home just too late to
marry his heart's desire, I pondered my next move while the
Boer trotted off upstairs to whisper sweet nothings into her

mobile. I suppose I could have stuck with what is generally regarded as a pretty fine plot and sat it out for a few years.

Pip does, after all, and is rewarded when he learns that his lost love, Estella, who chose some oafish young man (also, curiously, going by the name of Ben), is alone again, and that her coldness and cruelty have been mutated by experience into kindness.

Cue: happy ending.

But you know what? Sod it. Life, unlike *Great Expectations*, is too short. I know it is possible to fall in love virtually on sight: I did, three years ago, with the Boer. Now, after forty-eight hours of cruel and unusual torment, I discover to my relief that it is possible to fall out again with equal rapidity. A silent drive back into town on Boxing Day, and there was only one thing left to say: 'Goodbye.'

And now, to say goodbye to 2003 and all that, I bring you what is almost certainly the last quiz of the year, designed, without a trace of bitterness or cynicism, to determine whether, two days into 2004, you agree that love is *so* last year. (Candidates should write on at least one side of the paper. Score 1 for a, 2 for b, 3 for c. Easy, really.)

1. All things being unequal, would you rather have a) love in a cold climate, b) love in the time of cholera or c) love in an elevator?

2. 'Love is a many splendoured thing.' Does this a) bring to mind the velvet vocal powers of Nat King Cole, b) evoke the on-screen chemistry between William Holden's American war reporter and Jennifer Jones's sultry doctor in Korean-war-era Hong Kong or c) make you snort your Crunchy Nut Cornflakes back out through your nose?

3. In 1850, at the height of his Hallmark years, the beaten poet Alf Tennyson, while attempting to rhyme 'lost' with 'most', knocked out the belting lines: ''Tis better to have loved and lost, Than never to have loved at all.' Do you consider him to have been a) quite right, b) quite romantic or c) quite mad?

4. In a similarly bloody vein, Emily Dickinson penned the less memorable lines: 'To lose thee, sweeter than to gain/All other hearts I knew. 'Tis true the drought is destitute, But then, I had the dew!' If you met Ms Dickinson in a pub, would you a) buy her a glass of water, b) buy her a proper drink or c) give her dew and ask if she would like ice and lemon with it?

5. Microwave Man recently revealed his realization that he had made a grave error of judgement in surrendering the love of the Mucky, *née* Plucky, Boer, and his intention to win her back. Given the events of the Christmas just (thankfully) past, how stupid does he now feel, on a scale of one to ten? Is it a) between 0 and 3, b) from 4 to 10 or c) quite frankly off the scale?

Results: 5–10, you are the Boer, or possibly Ben; 10–15, you are Emily Dickinson, or perhaps her effete brother, Emile; 15 plus, you are me.

Bummer. Happy new year.

13
How to Keep it Up

Dear Microwave Man

I appreciate that you are trying to be funny, but I just had to write to say, please be more sensitive when it comes to cats. Hundreds suffer every year because they are abandoned or mistreated, and it isn't helpful when journalists such as yourself talk about drowning them in canals.

Mr Giles Campion, National Cats League

Microwave Man writes: You are so right. Our canals are clogged up with enough stuff as it is. In future I will recommend ponds and reservoirs.

Picking up the phone – even your own phone – in a newspaper office is seldom to be recommended. It could be (in ascending order of bad news): 1. a member of the public with a complaint about something you have written (*why* the bastards on switchboard put them through, God only knows: they manage to cut *me* off efficiently enough whenever I try to call in from outside); 2. the accounts department with an unanswerable query about your fabricated expenses; 3. some bright-spark commissioning editor with an 'idea' (unwelcome work, in other words).

Almost the very worst thing, of course, is to find the Editor's secretary at the other end of the line, because, as a rule, editors never, ever ring up for a chat, or simply to say, 'Hey: that piece you wrote about anal sex last week? Loved it. Ciao . . .'

Almost the worst thing. Even worse is to find the proprietor on the phone. Legend has it that one sub-editor on late duty one night committed the cardinal sin of answering the phone as he strolled past the news desk on his way to the canteen. He found himself listening to what he thought at first was an irate reader, banging on objectionably about the front-page story in that night's first edition. The sub, increasingly hungry and in no mood to justify somebody else's work to what appeared to be some drunken bum who had stumbled upon the night desk's number, advised the caller, pleasantly enough, to eff off and buy another newspaper if he didn't like it.

After a short, menacing silence, preceded by a sharp intake of breath, a suddenly faintly familiar voice said quietly: 'Do you know who I am?'

'No. Who are you?'

'I am the proprietor.'

A pause. 'Shit,' said our hero. 'Do you know who I am?'

'No.'

Our hero (slamming down the phone and continuing on his way to the canteen): 'Thank Christ for that.'

And now here's my phone, buzzing and lighting up with the ominous legend, 'Editor's office'. I am pretty sure the Editor doesn't know who I am, and I am reluctant to let him put a face to the name. Actually, I am pretty sure he has never read the column. He's new to the paper and, with a reputation as something of a financial guru and an intellectual heavyweight, I can't see him livening up his Crunchy Nuts once a week with a quick whizz through 'Microwave Man'. And if he ever did read it, I fully expected him to pull the plug and release me from my torment.

So maybe this is 'Adios, amigo,' and please take with you as you leave the building this fabulously large cheque in recognition of all the damage you've done over the years. I perk up and run a hand over the cover of that month's Yachting Monthly, a hopeful talisman lying, as ever, amid the chaos of my desk.

Upstairs on the Editor's floor, which he shares with a handful of chosen executives, everything is different. There are proper carpets, for one thing, instead of grotty, coffee-stained carpet tiles, and pleasant reproduction paintings on the walls. There is, of course, an Executive Toilet (which is, obviously, where all the big knobs hang out), water fountains that work and twice-daily visits of the Trolley.

The Trolley. An institution which has endured countless catering cuts and outsourcing programmes and even an assassination attempt on Teresa, the charming, feckless Irishwoman who, after her fashion, runs it. Teresa – slight, aged perhaps anywhere between thirty and fifty – without fail announces the arrival of the trolley on the news floor with one of the traditional cries of Olde London – 'Ter-*rolley*!!' – upon which countless captive news slaves, affecting Teresa's high-pitched, dramatic delivery, chorus, 'Ter-*rolley*!!', before abandoning their screens to swarm around and stock up with dry doughnuts, slightly stale sandwiches, cans of Coke (canned, oddly, in Belgium) and cups of a brand of tea so strong that it threatens to corrode its way out of the ancient urn (at the bottom of which, rumour has it, lies a soggy packet of cigarettes).

Teresa never looks anyone in the eye as she sways around from foot to foot, dropping money into one of the countless pockets in her pinafore and pulling the wrong change out of extraordinary places. There is *some* perceivable method. Five-pound notes, rolled up like fags, are lodged precariously behind her left ear, tenners behind the right. She drops them everywhere, and hopeful, hard-up subs with dodgy habits and countless children to support follow the trolley like seagulls follow a trawler.

She delivers a running commentary on her transactions in her lilting Cork brogue. 'Ah, yes, sunshine, a bar of KitKat, excellent choice, excellent, I'm almost of a mind to have one meself, but not quite, you see, watching the old weight, fighting the flab, Terry Wogan, that'll be 30p, love, but call it 20 for going. Did ye see the match on Sunday? Terrible, terrible, shouldn't be allowed, but I'll tell you what I'll do, I'll chuck in a napkin and we'll call it a oncer . . .'

Teresa is peddling her blarney as I step out of the lift and bounce on the deep carpet along the corridor towards the Editor's outer office. It's so thick that Teresa has her work cut out dragging her trolley over it. Another effect of walking on it after the carpet tiles of the shop floor is to make you think that you have suddenly gone deaf. But not so deaf that I don't recognize the bright Sloaney voice I hear coming out of the office, trading repartee with Teresa.

Cat Woman. Christ! What's she doing up here?

Then I turn the corner and see her. She sees me, and her beautiful, smiling face turns instantly to stone. It doesn't stop her looking beautiful. Over her shoulder, I can see the Editor, sat at his desk behind the glass wall of his inner sanctum. His face doesn't *have* to turn to stone. That's its normal state. And a series of blood-curdling thoughts fly into my mind and assemble themselves in a monstrous montage of possibilities.

Cat Woman is one of a team of senior advertising managers whose job, among other things, is to find out what subjects writers and columnists are planning to tackle so they can persuade advertisers to share the page. Every week for several months she had emailed me: 'So what's the column about this week?'; and every week I had replied, 'Shagging,' which seemed more or less to sum things up.

This went on for some time until, one afternoon, all the columnists were called to a meeting up here on the executive floor with CW and two of her likewise Chanel-suited cronies. I looked around the room at my fellow opiners. Christ, what a miserable, dodgy-looking bunch. If a policeman saw us hanging around in a bus station he'd move us on. CW and her pals did their best to conceal their disdain behind their professional smiles and to dazzle us with their Nobo whiteboards.

After the lecture, as the journalists were shuffling out (pausing only to stuff paper napkins with the tiny, crust-trimmed executive sandwiches that had been provided), CW caught my eye. 'So,' she said, smiling. 'What's the column about this week?' I knew it was a mistake, but I couldn't help myself. Leaning in towards her ear, lightly touching her forearm with my fingertips and feeling the goosebumps jump to the surface, I whispered, 'Anal sex. What do you think?'

She did blush, but, to her credit, held her composure, arched her eyebrows and said: 'Well, try anything once, hey?' And after that it was just kind of inevitable.

Not that I have ever written about anal sex. I tried to, mind, because I wanted to point out that while it is men who get the bum rap for being filthy cat-flap burglars, it is normally women who instigate the old rear entry, but Cornelia was having none of it.

'What's the column about this week?' she asked one day.

'Anal sex,' I said.

'No, it isn't,' she replied. 'You must be bloody joking. I do have to draw the line somewhere.'

'Oh, go on, please,' I mock-begged. 'You'll like it if you just give it a try. I was going to allude to E. M. Forster and call it "A Back Passage to India". Besides: Matthew Parris wrote about it in the paper. Don't you remember? He said it hurt.'

'That's different,' she said. 'That was about a rite of passage. You just want to write about back passages. Forget it. No way. There's filthy and there's dirty, but that's just plain filthy dirty.'

I gave her one of my best smiles. I don't know why I bothered. I know she's impervious, but a chap *has* to try. 'Cornelia, I do like it when you talk dirty.'

'Well, try this: fuck off. And no anal on my pages. That's final. Stick to the front bottom, Microwave Man.' Now that's what you *call* a commission.

'Righto,' I said, but vowed quietly to slip it in behind her back. When she wasn't looking.

'By the way,' I added as I got up to leave, 'I know who she is now.'

'Who?'

'You know: the one you said was far too good for the likes of me?'

'You'll have to narrow it down more than that.'

'Ha ha. Come on – the backlit Angel in the Doorway. She's Amelie, or Amelia something or other like that – your new freelance fashion-writer.'

'Well done. I wondered how long it would take you to work it out. And how exactly did you sleuth her out in the end?'

'I saw her picture in the paper.'

'Ah, yes, that's right. On the spread where she has been appearing opposite you for the past five months. A brilliant piece of investigative journalism. Well done. Do you ever read *anything* in this paper?'

I did now. Everything Amelia wrote, for a start. The horrifying thing was that Amelia probably read everything I wrote, too, on account of her words sharing the same spread as mine, so that made any chance of progress with her a non-starter. Oh, well. Can't win them all.

Funnily enough, it was that very night that CW and I went for our first drink. And then the next night, followed by sex at her place. It went well for a few days, maybe even a week, but then things suddenly took a turn for the worse. I kind of knew they would. For starters, I was breaking two of my own rules: 1. No shagging anyone at work, even from Advertising; 2. No cats. And CW had two. On the other hand, she was tall, thin and attractive in a Home Counties, naked-without-a-Barbour sort of way, and available. And there was another mistake. She was single.

In many ways, she ought to have been ideal for me. For one thing, she was, at almost forty, more or less in my age range and, as a keen horsewoman, very slim and fit and of course I don't have to bore you with all that Jilly Cooper stuff about riding boots and crops, right? If only she had been married. It would have gone so much more smoothly.

I won't say I embarked on an affair with CW as an experiment, but I wanted to find out the answer to the question which many people had, since the advent of the column, started to ask me: 'Why don't you pick on women your own age?' 'Married or mad,' was good enough for public consumption, but for myself I needed something better. Single women of CW's age are few and far between, and it would have been churlish to pass up such a golden opportunity to study scientifically a number of key questions that clearly needed answering:

1. Are *all* single women over thirty-five inevitably bitter and twisted?
2. Are thirty-five-year-old bodies as soft and beautiful as those of twenty-five-year-olds?
3. If not, does it really matter, you body fascist?
4. Is it inevitable that the pattern will run thus?

Date 1: Meet for a drink.
Date 2: Another drink, followed by sex at her place (but not before I have been taken surprise by a sudden and libido-crippling *recherché du temps perdu avec la Boer*).
Date 3: Stay-the-night sex at her place.
Date 4: Stay-the-night sex at my place.
Date 5: Cinema, followed by row and no sex.
Date 6: Sex at her place followed by discussion about the future and children.
Date 7: There is no Date 7.

The experiment went well,[78] inasmuch as it answered most of my questions, but the brief but fabulously torrid affair had ended, not well, about a week before I found myself back up on the executive floor, enjoying the bouquet of that day's freshly installed Executive Toilet rim block.

We had advanced as far as Date 5, and I knew right from the outset that the choice of film (hers) had been a mistake. You don't go to the pictures to see *Love, Actually*, with someone with whom you know, in your heart of hearts, actually, that you will never fall hopelessly in love. In this appalling, cynical, emotional job-lot of a film, there are several touchy-feely tearjerker love-cures-all moments (bollocks, obviously), and in one of them CW reaches out in the darkness *and tenderly squeezes my hand*.

It was a kind of instinctive and brutal honesty, I suppose, that

78 And not least because of the near ceiling-to-floor wall mirror she had inherited from her grandmother and the superb sinewy anatomy enjoyed by most gals who spend every minute of their spare time perfecting their rising trot while subsisting on a diet of radishes, rocket, toffee vodka and organic tofu.

made me whip my hand away as though it had just been stung by a scorpion, but it didn't half piss her off. Nobody, you see, ever wants honesty. *Tell me lies.* But, actually, at my age, sometimes I just can't be arsed. (And, of course, when I *can* be arsed I am usually very good at it, so you really can't win.)

There were no tricks with mirrors that night, just that silence in the car you get when someone's anger is swelling up like a balloon, growing bigger and bigger until you find the right words to prick it and have it burst, messily, all over you. I don't think I've ever escaped a situation like that without having the balloon burst all over me. Nobody ever does. The pregnant silence is not to signal a lack of desire for communication. It's to intimidate and threaten you with the fear of what's to come.

And so you might as well wade right in there and take it on the chin.

'Well, I think that was the worst film I've ever seen,' I say, breezily. 'So completely cynical.'

She snorts, but says nothing.

'I mean, "Oooh, it's Christmas, peace and love to all mankind, there's a someone out there for everyone, 'tis the season to be saccharine, everybody, deck your bowels with sprigs of holly" and all that other commercial crap.'

Another snort. More silence. Nearly at her flat. I put on the radio, tuned, as always, to Magic FM. You can't beat the old songs. Except those by 10cc. 'I'm Not in Love'. Oh, well done, lads. Just the thing. Perfect timing. I turn it up slightly, even though the song annoys the hell out of me (not least because it just isn't right to sing about stains 'lying there'. Nothing *lies* on a wall. It might lie on the floor but not the wall. God, I can be pedantic.) My mind is wandering and I'm quite happy. I sense I'm not going to have sex tonight and, actually, it doesn't worry me that much. It hasn't quite dawned on me why yet, but I'm not *that* committed to sex with this woman.

But this is why. It's because she is single. That should make her safe, remove the danger factor of an angry boyfriend or husband but, actually, it is these complications that make it exciting. And it is precisely her single status that, for me, makes her unsafe. And there's more. It dawns on me just as I pull over outside her building. Right now, sex can be completely happy and abandoned and uncomplicated only if I know there is no chance of involvement. Because – in my head, at any rate, and quite despite my better judgement – I am still involved. With the bloody, Plucky, Mucky Boer.

And there's yet something else. CW is in her late thirties, and there is a sense of urgency about her. She has two cats and she is almost out of time. She has little patience left and even fewer eggs and is simply not prepared to waste time shagging around simply for shagging around's sake. Which is a pity. And the irony is that she might have got a lot further, a lot faster, with me if she had been a whole lot less pushy. Passion wilts in the face of a deadline, but you'd be surprised if you knew just how frequently women make this mistake. Unless you are a man, of course.

Just the weekend before this, when CW and I were still paddling in relatively clear waters, I had called in on a female friend and found myself inadvertently gate-crashing a 'girls' night in' (sadly, there was no nudity or sex-toy salesperson dressed in a maid's outfit). To ensure that the chatter flowed without inhibition, I was declared to be an honorary girl and, during a long and increasingly alcoholic evening, learnt one or two things.

And one was this: that while they might be the multitasking, home-job-and-leisure-juggling, 24/7 queens of the universe, when it comes to understanding men, women are even more hopelessly off the mark than I ever thought possible.

It's not just the married guys they don't get; they're equally mystified by the motives of the single ones as well. Even though they all have the same one. One motive fits all. I will probably be struck off for telling you this, but what the heck. You bought the book, here's your pay-off.

No man *wants* to fall in love with you. He wants to fall into bed with you. Whatever happens after that cannot be – should not be – overtly controlled by you. Enjoy the moment. Enjoy the next moment, too. And then the one after that. Go with the flow. See where it takes you. It might wash you out to sea; it might wash you up the aisle. But whatever you do, do nothing, and demand even less. Be less available, not more. That way he might just start to think about what life would be like without you, and he might just begin to think that life with you is the better option.

On no account (unless, of course, you've had enough and wish to move on) ever say, 'Darling, where are we going?' because your answer will be a clean pair of heels disappearing into a cloud of freshly kicked-up dust.

There. Don't say I didn't warn you. Although I know you'll go and screw it up anyway. This seems to be the basic, programmed difference between men and women: women are constantly searching for a partner, men are constantly on the lookout for a shag.[79] This was true for Raquel Welch two million years ago; it's true for the most modern career woman today. And that's why safe, married women are so appealing to men. They already have the partner, and that frees them to go looking for the shag.

One of the women at the party – 'Sally', attractive, clever TV producer, in her thirties, irritatingly loud laugh – was regaling the company with the story of a man she had met, who, over the course of a fortnight, had slept with her a few times (and seemed to have done a reasonable job of it. Well done, that chap).

This man, she said, seemed to like her and laughed at her jokes (I didn't, but then, I didn't want to sleep with her. Would have, if not for that braying laugh. Funny what puts one off), but after a while the lewd text messages and flirty emails had just fizzled out.

My oh my. You should have heard the self-delusional bullshit this provoked.

Of course he likes you, darling, what man wouldn't? He's just a bit overwhelmed by you, can't handle a successful woman, he's a

79 Except for birdwatchers, who will usually settle for a cormorant. I thank you.

commitment-phobe, closet homosexual . . . an alien, a reincarnated
Buddhist glow-worm, a transvestite vampire afraid of tights . . . blah,
blah, blah . . .

I try to contain myself but in the end can bear no more and
have to put her out of her misery.

'Sally,' I say, as kindly as I can, 'he just wanted to shag you.'

Oh-oh. Forgot I was an honorary girl. It's like I have broken
wind in the whispering gallery at St Paul's on a particularly quiet
day.

'Well, come on, it's obvious, surely?'

Shocked looks. I guess not. Press on.

'Look: he likes you enough to *sleep* with you, but that means
almost nothing. He might even be embarrassed to be seen with
you. You could call him now, and if he was alone he would
probably say, "Come on round." But that *still* doesn't mean he
wants anything from you other than sex. Oh, and by the way:
there is no such thing as a man who can't commit. Just a man
who doesn't want to commit to *you* . . .'

I stopped at about that point. Sally seemed to have something
in her eye. In both of her eyes, in fact (and something big: two
of the others had to go to the bathroom with her to help her
to fish it out).

The next day, having secured Sally's email address from a
mutual friend, I tried to make amends by sending her an ebook
version of *He's Just Not That into You* – the American 'publishing
sensation of the millennium' by two of the now redundant
writers from *Sex and the City* (or, if you prefer, yet another of
those bloody annoying self-help books aimed at self-obsessed
saddos who can't score).

If I hadn't had three women on the go already, I might have
taken the opportunity to console Sally, grating laugh or no grating laugh, but at forty-eight I have to pace myself, so the book
would have to do. I thought she'd take it as a joke. But no. No
wonder that guy stopped calling.

But although the book *is* a joke, it galls me to admit that it
does have a point (the one in the title, so no need to read any

more of it). It just surprises me that it's a point that women, despite several thousand years of first-hand experience, somehow seem to have missed: that if a man doesn't call you, it isn't because he is too busy at work, too scared of commitment, battling with sexual-identity issues, burying his grandmother, overawed by you or stuck in a tunnel without a signal. For two weeks.

It's because he can take you and/or leave you.

If you are a woman and you don't get this (and can bear the painfully, seriously unfunny, finger-clicking, unwise-cracking, God-we're-so-goddamned-funny-we're-New-Yorkers-for-chrissakes hokey tone, combined with infantile presentation in the style of a primary-school coursebook), then go ahead, read the book. Or, rather, just lurk in the self-help aisles and read the first chapter, because the rest of it just goes on making the same point over and over again (guess those Manhattan *Sex and the City*-style broads must be really dumb), and who knows: maybe I'll see you there. It could be the start of a beautiful shagship.

If you do buy it, then you can stick it up there on the groaning bookshelves alongside your red-wine-stained copies of *Don't Call That Man*, *Men are Like Fish*, *Why Men won't Commit* and *If All Else Fails Why Not Consider Plucking Those Nipple Hairs, Madam?* (reader: only one of these titles is made up. You'd be surprised at what can put a chap off).

Alternatively, save yourself £6.99 and email me at microwaveman@hotmail.co.uk. I'm good at this consoling lark. (Please enclose recent picture.)

The car door slams and fetches me back in time to hear 10cc sing, *I'd like to see you, but then again, that doesn't mean you mean that much to me . . .* and, watching CW walk away from the car and up the steps to her house, I realize that I am not yet finished with the Boer and that, until I am, making love to anyone else – let alone planning a future with them – will be a struggle. Not impossible, you understand, but a struggle. Having *sex*, no problem. But not making love. Which, in CW's case, is a bit of a pity, because she really is very funny and very beautiful.

This is exactly as it was with Laura: when I was busy betraying her it was never because I wanted *to be* with anyone else. I was attracted only to people who had no plans for me beyond sex.

It really did mean nothing to me, darling.

I follow CW into the hallway.

This really does mean nothing to me, darling.

And now, as she stamps up the stairs and into the kitchen, where her cats stretch and rub against her legs, she hates me.

'I'm sorry, but I'm just not prepared to go on having casual sex with someone without some kind of future in sight,' she says, putting the finishing touches to her own grave. I almost feel sorry for her and angry at the girlfriends who have told her not to take any shit and to tell it exactly as it is: 'If he wants you, he'll respect what you're saying. If not, then you are better off without him.'

Idiots. Where have they all been? Have they learnt nothing? Life isn't *Love, Actually*.

And just because I call you up, don't get me wrong, don't think you've got it made . . .

Future? I don't want to be herded into the future. I want to drift along as I see fit – to go with the flow and see where it takes me.

'Yes, future. You know: where are we going? Will we be going skiing together?'

Skiing!?

'Where will we be this time next year?'

Next year? Jesus Christ!

I say, 'Don't you think you might be rushing things a bit? I mean, how long have we been sh . . . seeing each other? A few weeks?'

'A few months, actually. I don't have time to waste. If I'm ever going to have children . . .'

Ah . . .

'. . . I'm going to have to settle on a father pretty soon.'

Bloody Nora.

. . . Oooh, you'll wait a long time for me . . .

Actually, I was wrong. I did have sex that night. Eventually. It was touch and go for a while, but it turned out that she *was* prepared to go on having casual sex with someone without some kind of future in sight, for at least one more time.

And it was touch and go because, as I was increasingly finding out, sex at forty-eight is not like sex at eighteen, or even twenty-eight. At forty-eight you really have to *want* it. All the components have to be in place. At twenty-eight the only component you need is an attractive woman. Well, any woman, to be honest. At eighteen all you need is a *photograph* of a woman, or her breasts, torn from the pages of *Stern* magazine. But these days, the Cane Rat has feelings.

And all of this floods through my mind as I see CW glaring as I bounce over the carpet towards the Editor's office. I suppose I have been a bit lax. It's the first time I've seen her since that night, but I thought it best to lie low for a while, and somehow 'a while' just turned into a few weeks and then into permanently. She obviously thought so too, but the vibe I'm getting is that the fact we haven't spoken or seen each other since that night is, somehow, entirely my fault.

Funny how modern women come over all old-fashioned when it suits them.

'Hi, how are you?' I try, smiling.

'Oh, you know, not bad for someone who drinks *toffee vodka*.'

I must look genuinely blank, because she leans in to within an inch of my face and hisses, *'Toffee vodka!'* again, directly into my left ear. 'Thanks for mentioning that,' she says. 'Now *everyone* knows we slept together. Thanks a lot. I mean, really. That was a pretty shitty thing to do.'

Ah. Yes. Last week's column. I wrote about CW. Well, to be precise, it was more about the difficulties of my getting it up. How was I to know that she was known for her toffee vodka? Christ, I'd never even heard of the stuff before I saw it in her kitchen. And besides, she'd read the columns, she knew what to expect. You sleep with me, I write about it. That absolves me, right? Right?

But now I'm worried. Is this what the boss wants to see me about? Is he about to sack me for shagging one of his advertising liaison executives? Can he do that? I mean, Christ, he's got several more, almost as sexy! And then I see the bottle on his desk. Toffee vodka. Surely bloody not? Stay calm. There's a label around the neck. A late Christmas present, perhaps. Just a coincidence.

He's tapping away on his keyboard but looks up for just long enough to say, 'Yeah, come in, come in, have a seat, won't be a mo'.'

I don't know what it is, but there's something about the new guy that doesn't quite fit. Maybe it's the American accent, maybe it's the odd dress sense – high-heeled boots and bootlace ties. Or the way he's covered the walls with all the old paintings of proprietors and editors past. It makes him look like a tourist. Christ, that's it. I'm about to be sacked by a tourist.

He stops typing and reaches out a hand: 'Jonathan, Jonathan, sorry we haven't met before.'

Actually, we have, at the party you threw when you first arrived, but I had been banking on making no impression, and it looks like I was 100 per cent successful.

His handshake is ridiculously firm for such a skinny bloke. Why do men do that? I always make a point of shaking hands as limply as possible. Why do I do that?

'Now then, Jonathan – or, should I say, Microwave Man?'

Pleased with himself for that. I smile, trying not to fawn but failing by a few degrees. I still don't know if he's about to pull the lever to the trapdoor that will send me tumbling down into the obscure purgatory of Special Reports.[80] Bloody inscrutable, these Texans.

If he does, I'm ready for him. I'll go down fighting: tell him what I really think about the changes he's made in the few short months he's been sat in that seat: what a mess he's made of the news pages with his radical redesign, how he's launched a series of frankly dodgy supplements, and how size IS everything and the new tabloid format – sorry, compact, or broadloid, or

80 Also known as The Departure Lounge.

whatever the hell it is that he insists on calling it – means the paper is half the organ it was before. Frankly, it's a mystery to me how the paper's piled on so many new readers, but then if I knew what I was talking about, presumably I'd be sitting on the other side of the desk right now and saying . . .

'I just want to say that I love the column. First thing I read every Wednesday,' he says.

Do what? And it's every Friday, but hey.

'Really?'

'Yeah, great stuff. Love the tone of the dispossessed old fart . . .'

Fart? Old? Steady on . . .

'. . . trying to make his way through the maze of modernity, still trying to make it with chicks half his age. Bathos, pathos . . . great stuff.'

I'm grinning. I can feel it. Grinning like a baboon. Now I'm going to roll over and show him my big red bum.

'Well, thanks very much. And I'd like to say how impressed I am by some of the changes you've made around here. Especially the redesign. Love it.' I know. Pathetic. Outstanding.

Then I notice the photocopy of one of my columns lying on his desk. It's the one about Rebecca and her new breasts. He sees me looking and slides it across towards me. Rolling his chair closer to the desk, he puts his hands either side of the paper and leans forward.

'There's just something I want to know. Something I think you should have added to this piece. Something to think about in future.'

He looks serious. I try to look helpful. 'Sure, fire away. What is it?'

He taps the picture at the top of the column, which is a photo of a large pair of breasts barely contained by a straining bra.

'What were they like?'

Eh?

'What did they feel like?'

Pardon?

'Falsies. Fake titties. Jerry-built jugs. I wanted to know what it felt like when you got your hands on them. Because I think the readers would have wanted to know, too. Needn't go mad: we don't necessarily want pornographic descriptions of a feel-up – not yet, at any rate! – but just a sense of what we're getting here for our £5,000 a pair.'

'£3,500.'

'Whatever. You know – are they hard? Soft? Do they move around much when you jiggle them? Nipples like bullets? That kind of thing. I'm telling everyone this: think consumer-friendly when you do pieces like this. Fill us in. But tastefully, in your case, obviously.'

Through the glass wall I can see CW, still talking to Teresa and trying to look like she isn't hearing every word. As I walk past her on my way out, she avoids my eyes, but I can see she is close to tears. I stop to say something – quite what hasn't occurred to me yet – 'How are the cats?' maybe – but before I can open my mouth, she whispers: 'I gave everyone toffee vodka for Christmas. The Editor hasn't even bothered to take his home.'

He probably knows how disgusting it is, I think, but say, *'You didn't give* me *any,'* and she says, 'No, I gave you something else, if you remember,' and then she really does start to cry, big tears running down her cheeks.

Jesus, why is there so much crying going on all over the bloody place? I'm about to reach out to touch her (stroke her hair, maybe? Or pat her on the head?) when the Editor's deep, southern drawl booms out from the inner sanctum.

'Go on, buddy, and don't forget. In future, tell it like it is: firm or soft. And have a squeeze or two for me! Yee-ha!'

Yee-ha? 'Wretched' is a good word for the way I feel as I slink back to my desk. Wretched and relieved. And rather smug, to be honest. Until I see the beautiful Amelia. She's come in to write something, and she's sitting at a desk about twenty feet away from mine. I think I know what she must think of me and I do my best not to compound it by avoiding eye contact all afternoon. Which is tough when there's a golden halo glowing on the periphery of your vision. I wonder how old she is?

Of Rats and Men
Friday 9 January 2004

Erectile dysfunction.

There. I've said it. Not mine, you understand. Good Lord no.

Nor Pele's, apparently: nice of him to volunteer to become the acceptable face of male impotence, but he spoiled the effect a bit by stressing in every subsequent interview that he, naturally, had never personally failed to score.

Men never, ever, discuss this with each other: 'Have a good time with that Julia Roberts last night?' 'Nah, couldn't get it up,' is a conversation you will never overhear at the water-cooler, or anywhere else.

On the other hand, there isn't a man alive who hasn't, at some point, failed to rise to the occasion. Too much/not enough alcohol, blind terror, going through the motions despite sheer bloody indifference . . . and, um, then there's The Voice in the Trousers.

Men are frequently accused of having their brains in their pants, but an Unpleasant Incident in West London last week reminded me that, while my brain resides in the penthouse north of my shoulders, the beast in the panthouse does have a mind of its own.

I am not a natural anthropomorphizer of body parts. It started innocently enough a few years back: a long, lazy, summer Sunday, with the 'sshhhh' sound of the sea caressing the shore outside the window. The sunbaked floor is covered with news-papers, through which I have ploughed carelessly and from which the Boer is reluctant to be distracted.

I'm bored. I want to play. In a moment of desperate artifice, playing on her known weakness for small furry animals (she has few weaknesses, so a chap has to hit them when he can), I liken my neglected manhood to a sleepy fieldmouse, slowly coming to in the afternoon sun (bear with me: fight the nausea).

She looks up derisively and snorts: 'Mouse? Bloody cane rat, more like.'

Now, I've never seen a cane rat, but an unshakeable image jumps into my head: a cross between an evil dustbin-scavenger and some kind of Gremlin lounge lizard, martini in hand, await-ing opportunities for mischief. (Not invited to board the Ark, it would have swarmed up the mooring lines anyway.) Since he now has a face, he also has a voice, and now I have no choice but to listen to him. And, damn his eye, he does, occasionally, know better than me (he may not, in short, be particularly big, but he certainly is clever).

As a young man, when even a bumpy bus ride could prove too exciting, there was never a doubt that my trouser-dwelling pal would be keen to come out to play. At forty-eight, however, there's no point in getting into a pants-down situation with a new squeeze without the full cooperation of the far-from-silent sleeping partner, but for some weeks Ratty had been strangely compliant. Until Cat Woman popped up on the radar.

Me (invited in for toffee vodka and very keen to impress. Toffee vodka? I know, I know, but she is quite lovely): 'So, Cane Rat, what do you think?'

CR (stretching languidly, enjoying his absolute authority a *little* too much): 'No chance.'

Leaving me to play-act some rubbish about still struggling to get over the Plucky Boer. Or is it rubbish? The problem is, the rat sometimes misses her as much as I do; it's just that he's not so good at hiding it.

But as Cat Woman and I lie there (her pretending to be sleepy, me silently threatening to take the treacherous bastard into the loo for a stiff talking-to), the heavenly one suddenly turns off the bedroom lights, unleashing a firmament of luminous stars on the ceiling, and turns on the CD player, filling the room with the recorded sounds of the seashore.

The beast is instantly placated and the cane rat mutiny is over. Not only does he have a mind of his own, it seems, but he has a sensitive side, too. He and I are never happier than by the sea (even if it is in W12) and under a wide, starlit sky. Embarrassment of the Pele 'he doesn't shoot, he doesn't score' variety is averted, and the three of us have a night to remember.

Listen to your heart by all means. But if you want the real dope, listen to your rat.

14
How to Get Mad

Dear Microwave Man
   Don't you ever wonder what your mother thinks about the things you write? Isn't she ashamed of you?

                                                    Mrs E. Simmons, Kent

Microwave Man writes: I don't see why not – she always was when she was alive.

Ever since I had to visit my mother in one, I haven't been a big fan of locked wards. Don't get me wrong: it's not that I don't think they're a good idea. Especially for those of us on the outside. I don't *want* to have to sit next to mad people on the Tube just because the Conservatives once thought they could disguise cutbacks as compassion. Care in the community, *my arse*.

After I moved to a new town in the Midlands for a job on the local paper, began my search for a mother figure[81] and got married before I was twenty-two (God help me), I found my problematic *real* mother a flat with the council and even a job with a local solicitor. I did all this despite the fact that she had turned up for my admittedly misguided register-office marriage only at the last minute (having announced, in defiance of a complete absence of religion in her life up to that point, that she was going to spend the day praying in a church – a plan she abandoned I suspect on account of having no idea what a church looked like), and then stood around for the pictures

81 And found one, in record time. And that was always going to last, wasn't it?

looking like a condemned prisoner who had been offered a last meal of stale sandwiches because the venison was off.

If only.

One day, about a year after the wedding, a call to the office and a brief interview with my editor, shifting uncomfortably in his over-large chair. Fond memories of schooldays. Half an hour later and I'm sitting at another desk in another, smaller office in the local hospital, across from what appears to be a schoolgirl pretending to be a psychiatrist. Finally, it seems, somebody in a white coat, even if she is only twelve, has taken my mother's half-hearted suicide attempts seriously.

She lectures me sternly on my responsibilities towards my mother, tapping her clipboard with a pen for emphasis. I say nothing until she has finished, when I say, 'Have you finished?'

She looks startled, thrown off-script.

'Er, yes, I think so.'

'Then I'll begin.'

I lecture her back, filling her in on every little horror I can recall from my childhood. We are there for some time. She stops tapping her clipboard, and her shoulders sort of cave in, forwards. I can see from her eyes that she has no idea that this sort of life is out there. She looks like someone who wishes she hadn't started something.

'And so,' I conclude, standing up, 'you will understand why I really don't appreciate being lectured on my responsibilities by someone who has absolutely no bloody idea what they are talking about. Shall we go?'

On the ward, we make our way through the shuffling inmates, or patients, or customers, or clients, or whatever the hell it was they were calling them in 1976. Frauds, in my mother's case. She is sitting on the edge of a bed at the very far end of the ward, physically shrinking from the genuine and quite impressive madness all around her, a swirling potpourri of psychosis, paranoia, psychopathy and general personality disorders parading for all the world like a call-up of coarse actors from Central Casting. One woman nearby is calmly trying to throw a chair through a window, but, with a dull thud, it just keeps bouncing off the strengthened glass. Undeterred, she keeps trying. The madness of persistence.

Two women approach us. One, by far the shorter of the two, seizes the embryonic doctor by the left arm, stands on bare tiptoe and stares intently into her ear. 'All there, dear,' she says, 'all there.' The other, also barefoot but unusually tall, plants herself square in front of me. She is, I guess, about forty-five and, apart from the gown and the slightly dishevelled greying hair, quite normal in appearance. Give her a chain and a perm and she could be the mayor of Stratford-upon-Avon. She stands *just a little* too close, and her breath wafts over me in not unpleasant, pepper-mint waves.

'Are you Alice's son?' she asks, pointing, without taking her eyes off mine, at the woman lobbing the chair.

'No,' I say, and nearly add, 'Thank Christ,' but then find myself thinking that, well, hang on, perhaps it would be better to have a genuinely barking parent than one who simply *pretended* to be unhinged. At least you'd know where you were. And where *she* was, more to the point.

'Well, you're a very, very bad boy,' she continues, 'and the King will be having words with you. You can be sure of that.'

Oh, great. Another sodding lecture. And quite obviously not from the mayor of Stratford-upon-Avon. I look around the ward. The (rather pretty, I notice for the first time) doctor and I are the youngest people here. The place looks like it's populated by mothers who have been catastrophically disappointed by their sons. Apart from the one chucking the chair. She just looks disappointed by the strength of the glass in the ward windows. We slip past the pair and reach my mother's bed. She's sitting on the edge of it, wearing a long, pink cotton gown and holding her hands together tightly in her lap. She looks genuinely scared and hisses at me through gritted teeth: 'Get me out of here now: these people are all fucking bonkers.'

I look at the doctor. 'Would you agree with that diagnosis, Doctor?'

Despite herself, the doctor laughs. As I'm leaving, I ask her if she wants to go for a drink. This proves to be a milestone in two not desperately compatible ways. 1. It will be the first time I have been unfaithful. 2. It will be the first time I have failed to achieve an erection on demand, which, at twenty-three, comes as something of a shock.

We've spent two hours in a pub, and I'm driving her back to her car, which is parked in the hospital grounds. We start to kiss, and then it turns into something more urgent. Well, for her it does. Over her shoulder, off which the unbuttoned white coat has already started to come, I can clearly see the windows of the first-floor locked ward. I can't help looking for my mother, who has been told she is going to be held for two or three days for observation. I can't see her but, at regular intervals, I do see a chair bouncing off the glass of the third window from the left. From here, with the car windows partly open to prevent tell-tale misting, and despite my new friend's quick breathing, urgent kisses and whispered requests, I can just hear the faintest of thuds.

And, although I am only twenty-three and really, really want one, I can't get a stiffy. Christ. Here I am starring in my own *Playboy* short story, with a pretty, white-coated psychiatrist, her white coat open to her pink bra and knickers, kissing me violently and struggling to undo my belt, and . . . nothing. Now she has opened my shirt, and against my skin I can feel the row of pens in the pocket stretched taut across her left breast as it brushes hard against me. But still nothing . . .

Thud, goes the chair.

Thud.

Don't worry, I think, as she walks awkwardly towards her car, running one hand through her dishevelled hair and buttoning her white coat with the other. *You'll look back on this and laugh.*

But actually, I don't. I'm forty-eight now, and I'm still struggling to see the funny side.

And now I'm outside another locked ward, peering through the thick glass window in the door. I jump back as it is suddenly filled with a wild-eyed, madly leering face. Merv. I have come to spend the evening with him, and we're meeting at his work. He's not a psychiatrist, but I have a sneaking suspicion that he might, from time to time, when nobody's looking, pretend to be one. Ever so slightly.

With supreme irony, Merv is now working as a recruitment consultant for an NHS psychiatric trust. There is a severe shortage of psychiatrists in the NHS, and it is his job to headhunt as many head doctors as he can, from other trusts, from Wales, from Scotland, France, Australia, Canada, Austria (especially Austria: Merv speaks German and, rather like any fan of Wittgenstein, waltzes and *Wiener schnitzel*, needs no excuse to visit Vienna) – from anywhere, in fact, where he can find psychiatrists with a minimum grasp of English up to and including the phrase, 'So, how long have you felt this way about your mother?'

The irony is that Merv spent some time on locked wards in his youth as a customer. A student of both German and philosophy (now believed to be a fatally depressing combination and widely banned), it wasn't long before he had read himself into a depression far deeper than the normal student low.

One day, shortly after yet another girlfriend had left him on account of his erratic behaviour, he was sitting at his desk in his fifth-floor room on campus, reading Nietzsche's *The Antichrist*,[82] when he looked up just in time to see a body plummet past.

A first-year physics student (provoked, perhaps, by his recent study of terminal velocity) had killed himself by leaping from the roof, from which he soon accelerated to his maximum velocity of 250 feet per second. His fall had been broken, but not in a helpful way, by Merv's bicycle, which, like the physics student, was damaged beyond repair. Merv had just been starting to tackle the paranoid concept of *Tücke des Objektes* – the malevolence of objects, the surely crackpot notion that objects are engaged in a conspiracy to trip up the human race.

---

82 To this day he insists he had just read the passage: 'I do not point to the evil and pain of existence with the finger of reproach, but rather entertain the hope that life may one day become more evil and more full of suffering than it has ever been.'

The notion, in other words, that bicycles, among other things, are out to get us.

About a week later, Merv, slightly fuzzy around the edges thanks to the pills the doctor had given him to help him to sleep, was back studying at his desk, this time reading Kant's *Critique of Pure Reason*, when he glanced up in happy contemplation of paralogisms and antinomies just in time to see another body plummet past his window.

This time it was the physics student's girlfriend (a second-year geography student), who had decided that life without that particular physics student was a life not worth living and so had stepped off the same roof, without a moment's consideration for her friends or family or – and probably least of all – for the fact that Merv's brand-new replacement bicycle was chained to the same railings below.

And, again, no real help in breaking her fall.

This time, however, while the bike was almost completely unharmed (although it did need a new bell and front light), it was Merv who was damaged, although thankfully not beyond repair. For one thing, he found it quite difficult to sit on a saddle that had been liberally smeared with second-year geography student's brain. He did try, but whenever he mounted up to pedal down into town for a quarter of aniseed twists and a bottle of fizzy pop, he found that his struggle to come to terms with Feyerabend's thesis of incommensurability was jostled out of his mind by unbidden thoughts of precipitation cycles, podzolic soils, population pyramids and plate tectonics.

At one point, he seriously considered switching courses.

It was only when he re-read an essay he had written on Kant's classification of moral duties and discovered that he had jumped tracks halfway through one sentence ('. . . and, while in *Groundwork*, Kant suggests that ethical duties to oneself include the prohibition of injury to the physical and mental bases of one's free agency, as by suicide or drunkenness, census-based analysis of cropping patterns in the Canadian Prairies from the early sixties shows that "increases in special crops, especially pulse crops, canola and durum wheat, have offset a substantial decline in spring wheat in the Dark Brown soil zone".'[83]) that he checked himself into the local bin.

Now he's back, in a more or less professional capacity, and he's in heaven.

He opens the door with his swipe card and comes out into the reception area. 'Sorry, can't let you in,' he says with his trademark manic smile, on-guard in cod karate pose until the sprung door clicks shut behind him. 'Never know what the window-lickers might try! Isn't it marvellous? Now I spend all my time on locked wards listening to psychiatrists telling me *their* problems.'

We go for a coffee in the staff canteen.

'Good morning, Doctor,' says the woman behind the till.

'Morning,' booms Merv, affecting a voice close to that of fearsome consultant Sir Lancelot Spratt in the 1954 film *Doctor in the House*. There are several white-coated medicos in the canteen, each sitting alone and staring moodily into black coffees. One even wears a bow tie. Merv flicks a wave at one who looks up (and just as quickly looks away) and we find a spare table.

'All mad,' he stage-whispers, conspiratorially. 'Every one of them. They have to be. In fact, this Trust prefers it if their shrinks have been on the receiving end at some point in their lives. It's regarded as a qualification.'

'So you *do* have to be mad to work here?'

'Exactly!' he says, slapping the table top with both palms. Everyone jumps.

Merv slurps his coffee in that rapid manner he applies to everything he does – as if there is a train he has to rush to catch, or something even more important waiting to be done. When he entertains at home, he lays the table in the same way – clatteringly dealing out the plates like playing cards – and does the shopping with similar haste. He's always the first one at the local Sainsbury's when it opens at 7.30 every Saturday morning. He arrives at 7.29. And he always buys exactly the same twenty-seven

83 W. J. Carlyle, *Geographical Journal*.

items. 'They say, "Good morning, Merv" when I appear,' he says, proudly. 'They know me.' Merv likes to belong, even though he doesn't.

'Why did that woman call you doctor?' I ask.

He unclips his name badge and pushes it across the table towards me. Alongside a startling photograph of a particularly mad-looking Merv gawping like a surprised version of Kafka, it says, in large, blue letters:

PSYCHIATRIC
RECRUITMENT
CONSULTANT

He laughs, in that ever so slightly maniacal way that can upset people who don't know him well. And some of us who do.

'People don't see "Recruitment",' he says. 'All they see are the magic words "Psychiatric" and "Consultant"!'

He likes this and is very excited by it. He looks conspiratorially over each shoulder, leans forward and whispers: 'To be honest, I have thought about taping over the middle word and seeing how far I can get.'

Luckily for our crowded prisons, however, Merv has his philosophy to play with. He would make a lousy psychiatrist, not just because he desperately wants to be properly mad himself (he keeps a copy of the World Health Organization's IC-10 clinical definitions book on his desk and in quiet moments thumbs through it like a bestseller, excitedly pointing at symptoms and saying, 'That's me! I do that!'), but because he is a big fan of Kant's *Critique of Pure Reason* he subscribes (through functional necessity, I suspect) to the view that there is no such thing as madness: we all receive the same information about the world, but each brain simply processes it differently.

'And who,' Merv likes to ask, 'is to say which interpretation can be described as sane?'

Well, presumably we can start by ruling out the blokes dressed as Napoleon?

But apparently not. 'They could be the sanest of all!'

Later, and not for the first time, I wonder why I'm sitting in the passenger seat of a fast car being driven close to its maximum speed down winding country lanes by a man who, to the best of my knowledge, still carries a length of hosepipe in his boot, just like he has since I have known him.

You know – just in case.

In the way that some sensible motorists prepare for all foreseeable emergencies (perhaps by carrying a hazard triangle, spade, blankets, drinking water, insulated blow-up doll and snow chains), Merv has for years prepared for the possibility that he might one day need to take his own life[84] at short notice. He also carries with him in his briefcase a faded yellow scrapbook containing cuttings of unusual suicides he has culled from newspapers over the years. His personal favourite is the story of the man who built a homemade guillotine to do away with himself. At about three in the morning, his father, in another room, was half woken by a *whoosh-clonk* sound but fell back to sleep. In the morning he discovered the bloody scene and the imaginative lengths to which his son had gone to off himself. A piece of string ran from the pin that had held the blade in place to the key of a clockwork alarm clock clamped to the bedside table. With the bell hammer removed, when the appointed hour came and the bell tolled for him, it did so silently, and his head and his body were parted, with little more than a *whoosh* and a *clonk*, as he slept.

'Not a bad way to go, and with extra points for woodworking skills, dramatic flair and production values,' Merv felt. 'Although, personally, I don't really approve of showboating.'

I don't think Merv ever will off himself. He likes thinking about it too much. He thinks, therefore he is unlikely to. The hosepipe is there just to give an edge of reality to the possibility. Philosophy may have driven him to the edge, but it is the same philosophy that he finds so fascinating and that keeps him permanently teetering on that edge.

84 I blame this on Albert Camus.

Merv has never let philosophy go, worrying at it like a dog with an old slipper. The malevolence of objects, touched on during his traumatic days at university, is his latest favourite topic. 'And I have developed the theory further,' he says as he gives a sharp toot-toot on his horn and swerves punitively close to two side-by-side cyclists.

'When you hammer your thumb, you think it is an accident, or that you are to blame, but it could be the hammer. And things don't get lost. Perhaps they aren't *allowing* themselves to be found.'

Well, perhaps, I say. I knew I'd missed out by not going to university. We all get madder as we get older. Or perhaps we get wiser, and it just seems like madness to the young, who know no better. And now we are on our way to the small Wiltshire market town of Trowbridge and Merv's latest project: a philosophy discussion group. He knows that, post-Boer, I am feeling a little down and so has invited me to spend an evening with some friends of his, to cheer me up. (Although his precise words were, 'If you think *you've* got problems, come and look at this lot. Now that's what you *call* problems.')

When we reach Trowbridge, I find the spirit of Sartre and Wittgenstein alive in the garden at the rear of the closed Berkeleys Café, where philosophy is on the menu once a week with none of the ennui of a Left Bank café in thirties Paris.

The subject on the table tonight, here on the right bank of the River Biss (along with the bottles of wine and the candles) is 'precognition', the latest in a series of fortnightly philosophy discussions organized by Merv's group, which glories in the collective name, Nail Soup. The name refers to a Swedish parable in which a passing tramp demonstrates to a poor woman that, given a rusty nail, a little imagination and some thought, the makings of a filling and nutritious meal can be found in the barest of cupboards. The moral – that, if one makes proper use of one's inner resources, meaning can be found where apparently there is none – is clearly bollocks, but hey: I've got wine and I've got crisps and so I'm happy.

Merv parks the car and briefly comes over all gloomy, slumping back in his seat. 'I don't know why I'm bothering, really. The original intention was to set up a philosophy group and have academic discussions along the lines of seminars at university. This lot just want to have a laugh and a few drinks.'

'Sounds all right to me.'

'You'll see.'

His group certainly is an eclectic bunch: an American children's author, a company director, two software designers, a former vicar, a counsellor-hypnotherapist, a physicist and a university professor. Their host, the owner of the café, is also a member. Despite Merv's weekly opening recitation of Bertrand Russell's maxim that 'when you sit down to philosophize, you must set aside everything you know to be the case, and everything you would like to be the case, and focus on what may be the case based on the evidence in front of you', according to Merv, 'All they want to do is bring up personal experiences. And some of them are bloody hard to shut up.'

Tonight, Merv is planning to re-seize the initiative from his troublesome group of 'civilian' thinkers by thumping on the table what he firmly believes to be a solidly academic topic – one that even the most determined amateur would struggle to hijack.

'But, of course,' he says with a sigh, as his eyes fall on the happily chattering Nail Soupers, 'it will degenerate as usual.'

As the group members, sipping cheap red wine from plastic cups, settle down in the conservatory at the rear of the café, he announces with a flourish: 'I have found an old exam question from university to kick off tonight's topic, which is . . .' he pauses for dramatic effect and gives a little flourish with both hands '. . . precognition.' To his credit, his enthusiastic smile barely flickers as Geoff, the former vicar, says, to sniggers all round, 'I knew you were going to say that.' More than one face around the table – mine among them – betrays wonder that they are in the presence of a person who has kept exam papers dating back twenty-five years.

Undeterred, Merv ploughs on. 'Are you ready? OK, this is the question: "The oracle foretold that Oedipus would kill his father and sleep with his mother. Could the oracle have known this? Was there anything Oedipus could have done to avoid his fate?"'

He looks around, expectant. No one says anything.

'So. What do we make of that, then?'

'Sorry, could you say that again?' says one of the software designers, to titters. 'I was just turning off my mobile.'

Merv repeats the question and then says, 'The question throws up four philosophical problems: precognition, freewill and determinism, causality, and epistemology – what does it mean to say, "I *know* something"?' He slumps back, takes a big swig of wine and waits for precognition to catch fire. He is wearing his favourite Franz Kafka T-shirt, and the famous face stares out at the group with a look not unlike disdain.

Somebody pours wine, somebody else rustles around in a packet of crisps and a few starlings fly past the window, squawking noisily. Finally, after a pause, somebody asks quietly, 'Do you mean premonition?'

Merv sits up straight. 'No. No, I don't.' Kafka twitches.

But too bad. They are off, precognition pushed to one side in an interesting but somewhat off-the-point ramble about premonition. Julie tells an interesting story about being saved from bombing as a child during the war by a neighbour's premonition. Had he been there, Bertrand Russell might have shifted in his seat ('A belief for which no reason can be given is an unreasonable belief'), but the others seem to be enjoying themselves.

Merv, in the manner of a kindly but ever so slightly exasperated professor running an unruly seminar group, gently tries to steer them back on track but is obliged to sit tight-lipped and restless through a discussion of the merits of the Nostradamus predictions. He attempts to blindside them with a keen reference to logical positivism, urging adherence to only the facts – 'For something to be a fact, it has to be verifiable, not just a belief . . .' – but the group clearly believes that premonition and anecdotes about bombings and lottery numbers are a whole lot more interesting than boring old precognition. Whatever *that* is.

At one point, after Simon declares that his life was saved when he was young, and 'I believe I was supposed to live, I'm just not sure why,' Merv's face says, 'Neither am I, Simon,' but he caves in and pours himself another glass of wine. 'All right, all right; premonition, then; precognition is a *bit* hard to get, I suppose . . .'

Simon is running with the ball now and espousing his own theory that the rough framework of life – 'the coarse grain, as it were' – is preordained, but that we can change the finer details through prayer. Ken, an American children's writer, is equally sure that he is in sole charge of his own destiny, and Merv spots an opening and is back in business: 'This brings us to Nietzsche and his concept of eternal concurrence! That there is a limited amount of energy, and therefore a limited number of events and facts.'

An argument ensues over whether Donald's date of birth is a fact. Taken aback, he concedes that all he can really say for sure is that there is a piece of paper with a date on. Allan, on the other hand, knows full well that he was married to Sally on 26 March 1983.

'No,' says Merv. 'You believe it to be the case. It is not a fact.'

'Well, that's a great excuse if I forget our anniversary,' says Simon. He looks at his eight laughing friends and adds, 'What am I doing here with all these crazy people?'

Tom, the owner of the café, says he knows with certainty that there will be cheesecake for sale in the morning, at which Simon, a regular customer, perks up.

Merv's face, by now lit by only candlelight, is a Gothic picture as Julie suddenly interrupts to ask if they would all mind changing the phasing of their two-weekly cycle as it clashes with her wine-tasting group. He rounds on her in mock fury: 'No! I think you are going to have to leave the group. Meddling with calendars? The Romans tried that. It ends in tears.'

Then they are off on a discussion about wine and the possibility of combining the interests of the two clubs. Merv, slumping back with Kafka in resignation, watches as Nail Soup metamorphoses temporarily into a branch of the Bradford-on-Avon Wine Appreciation Society. 'I always thought you were from a parallel dimension,' he mutters, gazing across at Julie.

All that remains is to set the topic for two weeks hence. 'I want to do suicide,' Merv enthuses. 'That's my favourite.'

The others look at him. 'Well, when you study philosophy properly,' he says, pointedly emphasizing 'properly', 'you come to realize that there are very few absolute truths in the world and that most people's lives are based on very flimsy foundations. I lost friends at uni,' he says, proudly. 'I used to go round saying, "You do know life's pointless, don't you?"'

I wonder if he used to say this to students he saw making their way to the roof.

At the end of the evening, I'm not sure if any of us is any the wiser (nor, given the passing debate about the possibly circular nature of time, any older), but most of us are, temporarily, perhaps a little happier. Well, most of us, but probably not Merv. Philosophy, eh? It makes you think.

'Life,' says Merv, banging both hands on the roof of his car before we drive home. 'Over-rated, I'd say.'

'Still got the hosepipe, then?'

He pops open the boot, and there it is, green and coiled, like a waiting snake. Alongside the spade, blankets and snow chain.

Back in the company car, Merv drives home in his usual fashion – like a wanted man with the police hard on his heels. He doesn't need a hosepipe. He just needs to drive more often.[85] There may have been times when I have felt that life wasn't worth living, but all it takes is a couple of minutes in Merv's passenger seat to realize just how badly I want to hang on to my so-called life.

Somehow, we get home. His wife, Helen, has gone to bed, and so Merv and I sit around with two glasses of whiskey and talk about the old times, which is, in itself, just like the old times.

85 And ETA should have given up bombing Spanish holiday resorts. In their most successful year they'd have killed more tourists by opening a series of jet-ski franchises.

Merv is coming down, like a performer who has left the stage and is missing the buzz. He fetches some cheese and biscuits, and then it really is the old times.

My wife and I split up at about the same time as Valerie left Merv for another woman and so Merv and I lived together for a while in his former marital home. I was twenty-nine, he was a couple of years older, and we trawled the bars of Milton Keynes like teenagers. For a while I was seeing an American woman who worked at the nearby top-secret airbase. I knew it was top secret because she told me all about it. I had started to see her at the tail end of my marriage. She was my first affair and drove a left-hooker MGB, had a thing for crystals and unicorns, sang in a country and western band and pretty much taught me all I knew.

About sex, that is, not country and western.

Although, for a while, I even started listening to Linda Ronstadt. In fact, even now, when that big old harvest moon is kissing the sierras and those doggies are fixing to retire and I gaze into the lonesome flame of the dying fire, I sometimes catch myself singing 'Love Has No Pride'. And why not? Because, really, it hasn't.

In fact, if you were the end-it-all sort, this is the kind of song you'd want bleeding out of your iPod as you cut that wrist/popped those pills/stepped off that roof/sucked in those fumes. Because if you were worried about changing your mind halfway down, this song is guaranteed to keep you falling, packed as it is with bad dreams, fine times, sad homes, crap friends, plenty of E minor chords and the basic message that, when all's said and done, the singer would give anything to see the singee again. Anything.

Not that life with Marla around was anything but fun. Too much fun, really, for an Englishman with, as she was fond of remarking, a rod stuck up his 'ass'. At the height of the affair I would leave home for work early almost every morning and call at her house. Sleepy-eyed and wearing a nightie, she would open the door and take me back to bed with her. I would arrive late for work almost every morning. In fact, she was such a good teacher that, fairly often, I would call in again on my way home as well. If only my piano teacher had been so inspirational when I was twelve. I'd be playing the Albert Hall now.

Then, one night in a packed pub with Merv, everything changed when I was bitten on that ass (you remember: the one with the rod up it). I looked round in some surprise to see the culprit: a fat girl on all fours, now barking and growling.

'Pleased to meet you,' I said, reaching down to pat her on the head. 'Have you lost your owner? Would you like a bowl of water? Biscuit?'

This, it turned out, was Sue, who, it turned out, was Rebecca's fun fat friend. Rebecca was the one standing behind her, flushing with embarrassment. She had what novelists used to call porcelain skin, dark hair cascading on to what novelists used to call her bare shoulders and big, big eyes (similar to what novelists used to call limpid pools). Best of all was the pretty, slightly swollen mouth that looked as though it had been painted on. She was breathtaking in a doll-like way but neither Merv nor I paused for breath before deciding that she was the one for us. She told us a funny story about how her father had given up being a lawyer to restore antique dolls, and I'm not sure if I gained or lost points by saying, 'Quick, give me his number: I must call to tell him one has escaped.'

It was touch and go for a while, but I gained the lead when the pub closed and we all went back to Merv's house and I got to travel with Rebecca in her Mini. Her driving was, if possible, worse than Merv's. I was only twenty-nine then and had absolutely no thoughts about suicide, but I confronted death at least twice that night on the dark country lanes. By the time I reached Merv's house with Rebecca I felt like I had passed some kind of test and had earned her.

It turned out that when we had met them in the pub, she and her friends had thought Merv and I were gay. We certainly made an odd couple. For a while we used to meet for breakfast every Saturday in Milton Keynes shopping centre, to catch up on the week's developments. On one occasion, in a café where we were well known, Merv was standing in the busy queue three places behind me and suddenly announced, in a loud voice: 'I have something to tell you.' My ears started burning because I just knew this was going to be unpleasant. And it was. 'After last night, I've been thinking, and I've come to the conclusion that it's all over between us.' It very nearly was.

When we had lured the girls back to his place that night, it didn't help to convince them of our rampant heterosexuality when Merv slipped into his customary silk dressing-gown, sat down at the piano and played Hoagy Carmichael songs for an hour. Actually, it did help me. I used the time to gain ground, and by the time he wound up with a spirited rendition of 'Georgia on My Mind', all the cheese and biscuits were gone, the fat friend had fallen asleep, and Rebecca, aged nineteen, dental nurse and daddy's precious little doll, was mine all mine. And that's the way it remained for four years.

Fast-forward those four years. I'm standing in a bus station in central Milton Keynes. I'm wet and miserable and I have nowhere to go and no one to be there with. Don't get me wrong about Milton Keynes. I love what we used to call 'The new city'. As a junior reporter on the local paper, I watched it grow. I didn't see a concrete jungle populated by concrete cows, the butt of annoying jokes from the even more annoying Radio One deejay Noel Edmunds. I saw a city designed from fields by men and women with imagination and daring, and I watched it blossom around me.

But I didn't love it that day.

It was raining, for one thing, and for another I had just arrived back in England after a dreary coach ride across Europe from Spain. Rebecca and I had returned from South America and spent three more months bumming around, until the money ran out. At the end, in fact, we had enough money for only one of us to fly back, so I volunteered to take the coach. The only thing that had cheered me up during the interminable journey was the sight of the oilseed rape fields as the coach passed through northern France (which, as every schoolboy of my generation knows, belongs to England anyway).

The fields were brilliant – I mean, absolutely alive, the vivid, golden yellow everywhere and almost too much to look at. It must have been April, because I remember thinking, 'This is a month earlier than in England,' and for some reason I started to cry. In my wallet I had a picture of Rebecca, taken two years before, standing in a sea of that same yellow, only taken in Bedfordshire. She was holding her nose with the finger and thumb of one hand and fanning furiously with the other – so much so that that hand was a blur.

It's true, oilseed rape does look very beautiful, but it smells very, very bad. A lot of things are like that, I find.

I took out the picture and held it up at the window and compared and contrasted those nice bright colours, and those greens and blues and human hues of summer. It was enough to make you think the whole world was enjoying a sunny day. Oh yeah. Good old Kodachrome.

But all the colour had drained out of my world by the time I got to Milton Keynes. I found a phonebox and called Rebecca, who had been staying with her fat friend for the week while she waited for me to come home. The fat friend answered the phone. She was crying, which made a change from biting arses, I thought.

'Hi, Sue. Is Rebecca there?'

'She doesn't want to talk to you.'

'What? Yes, she does. Don't be dim. Put her on!'

'No, she doesn't . . .'

It went on like this for a bit, so I'll spare you the blow-by-blow. In the end, she did put Rebecca on, and it turned out that the fat friend was right. She *didn't* want to speak to me, although, between great big, hearty sobs, she spoke to me just long enough to say that she couldn't do it any more.

'I can't do this any more,' was exactly what she said.

Do what? I felt that I should ask, 'Do what?' but it was bad enough hearing it; I was too scared to dig deeper. Besides, I could hear the heartache in her voice, and in my heart I knew what the problem was, and it made me want to put my arms around her. Except, of course, that was no longer my job.

A few days before we had left Spain, we had had one of those conversations that starts casually enough but then trades up into a roaring fire that flickers hungrily over every available stick of highly flammable emotional kindling. I don't remember ever buying Rebecca a ring – it's not my style – but I do remember her pulling one off her hand and flinging it at me during the row. It missed and bounced out into the garden of the rented villa. We never found it. I hope somebody did. This is the only line I remember from that row: *You had a baby with her, why couldn't you have one with me?*

I have no recollection of what I might have said, but by the time I kissed her goodbye at the airport a week later, I thought everything was fine again. She had tears in her eyes as she turned to walk through to Departures, but then, so did I, and she looked back and smiled and nodded when I called out, 'See you in a week!'

As it turned out, what I should have said was, 'See you in eighteen years!'

And then I'm standing in the bus station in Milton Keynes. When I put the phone down I call Merv, which is what I always do at times like this. By now he is living with Helen, and the two of them take me in, look after me and introduce me to one or two inappropriate female friends, with whom I have some appropriate fun. Before I know it, it's Christmas and I'm puking alongside a merry-go-round in Northampton. It must be food poisoning. I feel light-headed and faintly delirious. I'm seeing things. In the distance an enormous, brightly lit chimney towers over the town. At the top is a giant Santa, who appears to be rubbing himself, in a distinctly lascivious manner, against the brickwork.

Bedtime Story
Friday 16 January 2004

I went through a phase, a few years ago, when it seemed that my physical self was made up of more than the normal percentage of water, and that my body was doing its best to expel the excess, through my tear ducts, at every possible opportunity.

I think I was just feeling sorry for myself, but I entertained a number of other explanations, including the alarming notion of having suddenly and rather inconveniently connected with my feminine side (exhibit A: one VHS copy of *Brief Encounter*).

Then, just as suddenly, the taps were turned off again. Until two weeks ago, sitting opposite Rebecca in the High Street Kensington branch of Wagamama.

I like Wagamama. Despite the decidedly non-indigenous nature of the food, the school-refectory ambience ensures a thoroughly English experience: the chance to sit alongside strangers in intimate proximity and ignore them completely.

But it is hard to ignore your neighbour when tears are running from his eyes and down into his moyashi soba – a soup-like dish which is, frankly, watery enough.

The couple sharing what was about to become our extremely personal space were drifting through a less than engrossing '*en attendant*' conversation, of which Sam Beckett would have approved: 'Would she mind?' 'Mind what?' 'Mind if we did?' 'I don't know,' and so on. Even in my advanced stage of distress I wanted to shout, 'For God's sake! What? What might, or might she not, mind?' As for them, instant relief from their own tedium: grown man weeping! Excellent.

I had been moved to tears not by the dull play to my left but by an incident that I thought had lost all its sharp edges years before. Holding both my hands in hers across the table, Rebecca was now wishing she hadn't just produced the photograph of her six-year-old daughter, the product, along with a son, aged eight, of a marriage that was in the throes of drying up. The little girl looked just like her mother.

I met Rebecca when I was twenty-nine, at the end of my own marriage, and when she was nineteen, and here we were, fifteen years later, visiting the darkest reaches of the extended family.

The very first night we met I asked her if she wanted to come with me to South America. She said yes, but first we embarked on a less ambitious expedition, to Ipswich (even then I knew how to show a girl a good time).

There, behind the Gothic façade of the Crown and Anchor Hotel (now a branch of W. H. Smith), Rebecca and I suffered a contraceptive accident that failed to blight our weekend but overshadowed the rest of our lives.

And they sell children's books now in the area by the window where our lovers' bed once stood.

South America was calling. We had no idea that we would stay together for over three years. She had an abortion. Years later, I learnt that she had finally settled down, married and had the two children she had always said she wanted. Phew.

But, mid-flow in an account of her chaotic life, Rebecca looks at me with the big, dark eyes into which I fell two decades before and says: 'Not a week goes by when I don't think, "I should be the mother of a nineteen-year-old now."'

And the dam that, it seems, I have been quietly shoring up since 1984 finally gives way.

In my heart I knew at the time that an abortion was the wrong thing for her, and I assumed it was the right thing for me. Now, although I may never have been much in touch with my feminine side, I am, finally – and far, far too late – in touch with hers.

15

How to Get Even

Dear Microwave Man

  *We have, despite ourselves, been reading your column for months
now. I'm not sure why, because one of us always ends up throwing
the paper across the room. At least we always resist the temptation to
rise to the bait and write to tell you what we think of you. Until
now, so here goes. You are a sad, self-centred, obnoxious, old-style,
so-called man who mistakes cheap jokes for charm and clearly thinks
that women are fit for only one thing and belong in the bedroom,
not the boardroom, and that their lives are incomplete without a
chauvinist old pig like you around to patronize them. Have you
never heard of Andrea Dworkin?*

  Ms J. Smith and Ms F. Sondheim, Spitalfields, London

Microwave Man writes: Sure. Wasn't she that fat old lesbian who had no
respect for men who, happily, but through no fault of their own,
happened to get the penis when God was handing out the naughty
bits? In her book (in all her books, actually), this made all men war-
mongering invaders and rapists. She saw no contradiction in railing
against the objectification and dehumanization of women while making
a career out of objectifying and dehumanizing men as one-dimensional
objects who despised and oppressed women. (She was also very keen
on the death penalty, incidentally, provided it was for men.) Personally,
I think she just needed a good seeing-to. How about you?

I'm sorry about the suffragette gags earlier. I didn't mean to upset
anybody. It's just that, well, you know . . . it isn't easy being a
man these days. In fact, it never was, but somehow women have
got it into their heads (Tsk! Very nearly wrote 'pretty little heads'!)

that men have had it their way for centuries and that guys are fair game for a sharp kick from any passing Jimmy Choo.

To be honest, it never really was that great being a man. You want the lifetime sentence of work with no chance of parole, the heart attacks, the wars? Be my guest. You're welcome to it. I mean, who was it who first decided that it would be cave *men*, rather than women, who would be the ones who had to go and do the hunting rather than the gathering? Was it Raquel Welch? I mean, who in their right mind would rather hunt than gather?

In exchange for a bit of hair-pulling and the occasional clubbing over the head (although I'm fairly certain the anthropological veracity of this behaviour has never been properly scrutinized outside of a *Flintstones* cartoon and the dubiously researched *One Million Years BC*), women spent centuries dossing around in caves, suckling young, nattering about the price of dinosaur eggs and bemoaning the lack of labour-saving devices in the Mesozoic period, while occasionally popping out to pluck a few berries from a nearby bush. Idyllic.

(It was surely no accident that human life really got going in the fertile Rift Valley: it was scorching hot year-round and most caves came with a sea view – no wonder that early woman quickly developed the slinky, bias-cut chamois-leather bikini, as modelled by Raquel Welch. She had to do *something* with her time.)

Meanwhile, a few miles away, Mr Cro-Magnon, armed with nothing more than a pointy stick and a piece of flint, was doing his best to bring home the bacon but finding that the bacon (in this case a gigantic and fairly pissed-off mastodon) was liking it just fine where it was and showing absolutely no interest in coming home with him for dinner. Although he was, by now, *homo erectus* (although where he found the energy for that kind of thing after a hard day's hunting on the plains, God only knows), he still wasn't that bright: he knew that he didn't really enjoy his short, brutish, dangerous life, but he couldn't really find the words to express his sense of what his descendants, living in café societies on the left bank of the Seine, would eventually learn to call existential angst.

How do we know all this? It's in the fossil record, stupid.

Besides, ancient man didn't have time to think, let alone think smart. It was a hominid-eat-hominid world out there and, as far as today's paleoecologists[86] can tell, almost certainly a jungle. It didn't even occur to him to wonder why the female of the species seemed to be at home all day. He was just pleased to find a pile of berries waiting for him every night. Besides, his brain was so small he kind of forgot everything from the day before, so each evening's pleasures came as a fresh surprise. And even if he had developed a longer-term memory, the language centres of his brain weren't up to much. You can't get far with 'Ugg. Ugg ugg?' You can intonate as much as you like, but it's going to be tough to say even, 'How was your day, darling?' let alone make sense of the reply.

The fossil record, luckily, does show, however, that one of the first sentences the female human constructed was something along the lines of, 'Christ, you think *you've* had a hard day . . .' And that, give or take the development of the odd tool, frontal lobe and service stations selling cheap bunches of flowers, is pretty much how it's been ever since.

When I was still quite young, it struck me that ahead, barring the unexpected appearance of riches beyond my wildest dreams, stretched a lifetime of certain work. Sure, I might love it, but what if I didn't? One of the fundamental differences between men and women in the developed world is that a woman can, if she so chooses (and millions do so choose), work until she is fed up with it and then retire to the cave to raise children, pick berries and bemoan the lack of labour-saving devices in her weekend cave.

Who can blame her? Society has given her a parachute, and she would be crazy not to use it. I mean, why go down with the burning plane if you don't have to? Men, on the other hand, generally have to: that's one of the less-publicized benefits of being, supposedly, at the controls.

---

86 And today's pale ecologists are even less certain.

As a junior reporter on the *Milton Keynes Gazette,* I sat through countless inquests. Those of the usual untimely crop of men, women and children lost to drownings, car crashes, drug over-doses and fires were at least explainable, but I will never forget the faces of the women who had come to the court of the North Bucks coroner to try to learn why their husbands had, one day, and without explanation, left home and killed themselves.

They were men in their forties, seemingly happy and married with children, often accomplished in their chosen profession. They rarely left notes. I think I'd leave a note. In fact, the way I'm feeling right now (I'm fifty next year, you know), this could *be* my note.

Dr Rodney Corner, a sensitive, sympathetic coroner, could often offer no more than a legal shrug in answer to the question which would hang over the widow for the rest of her life: Why? As a twenty-year-old reporter, I too had no idea what torment might drive a man to seek salvation via a length of hosepipe attached to the exhaust of his company Ford Granada. But by the time I had turned forty, I had a better idea: it has something to do with the disappointment of so-called 'success' (well, that, and the length of time it takes for cash to come out of a cash machine).

As I said, it's never been easy being a man.

Now, women have equality, mostly, and boy, are they welcome to it. Really. Thank God. What a relief. I think I can speak for a lot of other men when I say we would be quite happy to give up the vote, too, if it would help. And the uniforms and all those noisy gun things. A kind of voluntary disenfranchisement to show how serious we are about making up for all those centuries where we supposedly had everything our way.

OK! See you! Have fun at the controls!

If only it were that easy. But even if men *could* hand over the control that most of us never wanted in the first damn place (along with the pointy sticks and the working until death with no biologically linked chance of remission), would women be grateful? Are they gracious in victory? Are they bollocks! Not only have they mugged us, now they want to give us a sound kicking while we're down.

And men, so horsewhipped into feeling that each one of us should take personal responsibility for the result of the 1913 Epsom Derby,[87] just roll over and take it.

Take Father's Day. Or, if the majority of cards that plop on to mats nationwide are to be taken at face value, 'Farter's Day'. Brace yourself (you fat, lazy, balding, impotent, beer-fuelled, TV-golf-and-footie-fixated buffoon with the dress sense of a clown, chronic flatulence and absolutely no value beyond your wallet) for the usual torrent of 'amusing' abuse, for such is the composite picture of the modern father afforded by a greetings-card industry locked dull-wittedly into a sub-Glen Baxter cheap-laughs school of humour.

Exhibit 1:   picture of a man wearing an all-over chemical protection suit, above the caption, 'Stanley brought his kids up to be responsible. Whenever he farted, he made out that they were responsible!'

Exhibit 2:   a bald, pot-bellied fool gawps at footie on the telly, watched by a woman who is saying, 'You've taped over *EastEnders*.' Caption: 'Dad proved that even at his age he could still drive the women wild.'

Men, eh? Well, you've got to laugh, haven't you?

Apart from a handful of cards celebrating fathers caught in a bizarre fifties-knitting-pattern timewarp setting out for their single, hard-earned day of freedom behind the wheel of a Triumph TR4A (a car famed, incidentally, for its innovatory use of independent rear suspension: I owned one once, for a week. It was sold to me by a man famed, I later learnt, for his innovatory use of balls of newspaper to plug potentially lethal chassis rust-holes), most Father's Day cards are little more than an excuse to mock the begetter-in-chief.

87 The result, incidentally, was that favourite Craganour became the only Derby winner to be disqualified for an incident in the race, and the prize was given to Aboyeur.

An odd little tradition, this, especially if contrasted with the sickly chocolates-and-roses gush dished out to all those Best Mums in the Whole Wide World every March. No doting for Dad. Instead, 'I want to be like you when I grow up, Dad – only with hair.' Search in vain for a Mother's Day card with the sentiment: 'I want to be like you when I grow up, Mum – only thinner, not so wrinkled and without tits like roof-tilers' nail bags.'

I mean, what are we? Baby-eating monsters or something? Small wonder that Cronus was always biting the kids' heads off. Maybe this is why women outlive men? They get love and respect on their special day; we get abuse and derision. Surely it's enough that we live shorter lives, work for longer and top ourselves in droves before we reach retirement? Is a little saccharine sentimentality once a year too much to ask?

As you can probably guess, Father's Day was conceived in America, where, before Prohibition, they all drank far too much and so frequently succumbed to bouts of odious sentimentality, leading first, in 1890, to Mother's Day (God bless her!) and then, in 1909 (in Spokane, a hotbed of emotional effluence), Father's Day (Boo! Hiss!).

Not that dads were supposed to put their feet up, telegram in sick and listen to the baseball on the crystal set even then, oh, heck, no. When President Coolidge finally made the third Sunday in June a national event in 1924, he stressed that it was 'to impress upon fathers the full measure of their obligations' (leading directly to the official definition of a father as a man whose wallet contains photographs where his money used to be). No mention there of the best dad in the world.

Cheers, Calvin.

I am indeed fortunate to be blessed with a son who steadfastly refuses to be drawn into the tacky and insincere commerciality of greetings cards (or gifts, phone calls, letters, emails . . .), and my father, who now art in Heaven (or Hell, if you accept my mother's version of events), never had to endure this kind of institutionalized abuse from me because he had legged it long before I was capable of drawing kisses on a card. Dad took Hemingway's advice ("To be a successful father . . . there's one absolute rule: when you have a kid, don't look at it for the first two years') a step further, substituting 'ever' for the last five words. Think of the money I've saved on crappy cards.

And, without a male influence in my life, think of the money I've saved on tickets to football games and replica Manchester United shirts. Not all men, you might be surprised to learn, give a toss about football, despite what you might take from TV commercials (and birthday, Christmas and, of course, Farter's Day cards). That doesn't stop public relations firms treating all men like idiots. Or like drivers of transit vans.

Talking of transits – and indulging my fondness for curious if seemingly meaningless links – it was a Lancashire man who lived not far from where my father was born who, in 1639, made the first observation of the transit of the planet Venus across the face of the sun. It wasn't Descartes, you will note, who was far too busy dreaming up wacky science and devising a catchy sound-bite that would ensure his utterly unwarranted immortality (and if he *had* thought to look up at the sun, I expect all it would have led to was another popular T-shirt slogan. 'I blink, therefore I am,' perhaps). Who, on the other hand (aside from a few astrophysicists, obviously), has heard of Jeremiah Horrocks? And I ask you: is that right?

Horrocks, despite being only twenty-two when he died, wasn't interested in the slightest in football or student slogans. He did, however, figure out that the orbit of the moon was an ellipse and inspired Newton to quit heading apples and to get back indoors and do some real work.

On 8 June 2004 I was up before the crack of dawn, partly in hope of witnessing only the fourth transit since the one spotted by Horrocks (as a 'guy', I am, of course, always keen to check out a new commercial vehicle), but also because I had been invited to Soho Square to meet some of the 250 busty beauties being sent by *Zoo* magazine to Portugal, where, by flaunting their breasts, they planned to soothe the savage beast of football hooliganism.

Yes, I thought. That'll work.

In the event, it was such a nice day that I went for a swim instead. Heck, there'll be another transit along in a few years (6 June 2012: don't miss it. It'll be the last one in your lifetime) and, besides: once you've seen one insulting sexist stunt kitted out in hotpants and soaking-wet T-shirts . . . well, you've seen them both.

Feminism has come a fair way since Andrea Dworkin insisted that any sex with a man was rape and chicks wore badges declaring, 'I AM NOT A CHICK', on T-shirts proclaiming, 'A woman without a man is like a fish without a bicycle' (not that you'd have known it in Soho, where dumb-named glamouristas such as Sammi, 21, from Manchester, struggled to contain their enthusiasm for law and order in flimsy T-shirts bearing the *Carry On* slogan, 'NO MORE BUST-UPS').

The Dworkian excesses, if annoying, were necessary: one extremist position will yield only to another. As with radical feminism, so with the 'loony Left': the loopiness of the eighties was the bedrock of a gradual acceptance that racism at any level was unacceptable. Banning 'Baa Baa Black Sheep' in playgroups may have been madness, but it was necessary madness. (Exhibit A: such sixties/seventies shit-coms as *Love Thy Neighbour* and *Till Death Us Do Part*, two planks of a genre predicated, as the astonished young American Bill Bryson observed, upon the hilarious proposition, 'My neighbour is a darkie.')

If you doubt how far attitudes to women have come, watch Hitchcock's 1972 film, *Frenzy*. Two lawyers are discussing another victim of the necktie strangler when one, without a trace of directorial irony, perks up on consideration of what he (and, by inference, the audience) sees as a silver lining for the victim: 'Still, at least she was raped first!'

Buy it, watch it, burn it.

And so to Sammi, *Zoo*, 'witty' advertising firms and everyone else who thinks that, having all finally agreed that women are sensible and useful human beings who deserve respect, it is still just fine to portray men as dim-witted, redundant, malleable consumers of beer, cars, birds and footie (never happier than when hanging out of a Venus transit in our England shirt and exhorting you chicks to show us your tits).

And that, I have to say, doesn't half get on mine. Especially when I read rubbish like this, from *Zoo*: 'Top psychotherapist Sarah Day' – *Hey! It's that Black and White Minstrel again!* – has compiled a detailed report which has confirmed that the animalistic instincts of men cause them to react in a more subdued way around women they find attractive.'

Animalistic instincts? Can she *say* that? Apparently. And more besides.

'When a guy's testosterone is occupied with his sex drive, his aggression is defused. Watch a couple of guys have a heated conversation in the pub. As soon as an attractive woman walks by, their heads swivel to watch her and their minds wander below their belts.'

Us 'guys', eh?

Now, I know it's a bit po-faced to take *Zoo* and its unreconstructed rent-an-expert too seriously (this is a magazine, after all, responsibly addressing the nation's obesity epidemic with a search to find its fattest reader. Prize? '£1,000 and your weight in pies'), but then, Alf Garnett was just *'avin' a larf*, right? I don't care about football, and when it comes to hooliganism, give me a good old-fashioned tear-gassing and mounted baton-charge any day. But I am sorely tempted to drive to Portugal in my Venus Transit, pull on an England shirt bearing the slogan, 'I AM NOT A PRICK' and lean out of the cab to invite Sammi and her pals to cover up, grow up and bugger off.

I'm bored with Sarah now. Besides, there are more insidious forces out there, undermining the very point of men. An alien visiting the earth for the first time and reading the papers might be forgiven for thinking that men are all rats, and who needs 'em? Well, not mice, for starters. In a major breakthrough for Minnie (at the expense, naturally, of Mickey), Japanese and

Korean scientists last year produced the world's first mammal offspring with two mothers and no father.

Can that be right?

This latest attempt to marginalize men as mere optional extras reinforces a suspicion I have had for a long time – that women want us for only one thing. In fact, not even for that, if a survey that plops on to Microwave Man's desk from More.co.uk is to be believed. Of more than 1,500 women with an average age of twenty-two, more than 20 per cent rated their love life as disappointing or non-existent. Of those who were seeing action, 21 per cent said that their man satisfied them either not often or never – and a depressing 46 per cent admitted faking their orgasms.

No surprise, then, that there was a lot of reliance on battery-driven friends, with 70 per cent deriving great satisfaction from vibrators.

Meanwhile, back in the lab, the white-coat-and-Bunsen brigade continues what appears to be a gleeful campaign to prove that men are basically a knuckle-dragging subspecies surplus to reproductory requirements. The April 2004 edition of *Nature Neuroscience* (I read it all the time: it does my head in) reported a US study that claimed to have found, in the emotion-control centre of the brain, 'significantly higher levels of activation in males viewing sexual visual stimuli than females viewing the same image'.

In other words, show us guys a smutty photo, or a copy of *Stern*, and we're up for the cup.

Modern women, however – as everyone from advertising agencies to male and female columnists in national newspapers never tires of telling us – are smart, sassy and yet sensitive souls. Joy all round, then, when Pfizer, the company that created Viagra, announced that it had abandoned attempts to create an equivalent pill for women. Why? Well, because while awakening a man's slumbering libido is merely a question of turning on a blood-flow tap, turning on a woman is, of course, a *much* more cerebral affair. (One newspaper went to great lengths to find, curiously,

'a specialist nurse in sexual medicine in North Wales' to specu-
late that 'in women, arousal may come from something in the
ether'.)

Only, balls to that.

I'm not sure if my lifetime of research qualifies as statistically
relevant, but in my experience women can be as instantly and
superficially turned on as any man. And, bearing in mind the
More.co.uk study, it might not surprise you to learn that it has
been the women in my life who have pushed back the boundaries of sexual experimentation (you know who you are).
Pornography, bondage, correction, chickens . . . frankly, I can
take it or leave it (I made up the chickens[88]), but rare is the bird
who wants only to lie back and be plucked.

And I'd get into anal sex at this point, but Cornelia wouldn't
like it. So she says.

Conversely, you might be surprised by what can dampen a
man's allegedly unthinking randiness. For me, it can be a worry
about a work problem, a phone call or an email earlier in the
day from a past love, a concern about poultry husbandry or
merely an indefinable something (in the ether, perhaps) that can
suddenly turn lust to dust. And perhaps you would also be
surprised by how common it is for a woman to take such a reversal as a personal slight. Out goes all that sensitive *Cosmo*
understanding, and in comes incredulity that the human vibra-
tor has, for once, let her down.

What modern man – rightly – would dare to do other than
comfort and understand a partner who complained that she
didn't feel like sex tonight? A chap, on the other hand, can expect
no such mercy. Set off fireworks six days a week, design, build
and swing from chandeliers, move the earth, plumb the depths
and pluck those Rhode Island Reds. But you have one 'Not
tonight, Josephine' moment . . .

A chap, it seems, is only as good as his next shag. It's enough
to give one a headache.

88 Kind of.

And talking of Black and White Minstrels, men's biggest headache today comes not from the sniping of vengeful women, keen to punish for centuries of suppression, but from the constant self-flagellation of over-contrite Auntie Tom men. Such as The Radish. And Professor Stephen Whitehead. The Prof and I have a lot in common. We are both male, both pushing fifty (him from the wrong side) and both need spectacles (too muc h self-dating?). In our own ways (although in my case without any kind of grant or the long holidays), we have both diligently carried out research into 'relationships in the postmodern age' – Stephen, a senior lecturer at Keele University, drawing 'primarily on (pro)feminist poststructuralist theories in order critically to explore men and masculinities, identity, gender and management'.

And me, well, by shagging around.

So why do I want to punch him on the nose? Really hard?

Take a look (but please don't buy it: support your local library) at his latest book, *The Many Faeces of Men* (oops: that crazy spellchecker: that should be *Faces*), in which he posits the facile (dammit: *fascinating*) theory that there are twenty-seven types of men. And to think I thought there were only twenty-three! What a fool I've been.

I'm not sure what I loathe more. Yet another self-appointed relationship expert churning out a potboiler – or the acres of uncritical news coverage that follow as sure as flies on a hippo's hindquarters. Still, any excuse to use (another) picture of Carrie and Mr Big (who, we learn, is 'a Backpacker: sexy but dangerous; a relationship daytripper' become 'Chameleman: adaptable, smooth, urbane and attractive – but never the man you think he is').

The Prof, who naturally rated himself a bit of a Backpacker (sexy, dangerous, etc.) in his wilder days, has now, unsurprisingly, evolved into a Libman ('pro-feminist male, politically correct, very well read'. Well, he would be, wouldn't he, what with all those long holidays).

His headline-grabbing notion (because theory is too good a word, babe) is that men's identity is suffering what he calls 'male crises'. Not that Steve suffers any kind of crisis, ooh no. Not with his Auntie Tom, female-favour-currying, plastic-coated new-manliness, nor his ability to disseminate his, er, thoughts: 'I found,' he says, with an admirable lack of false modesty, 'that I had a knack of putting quite complex ideas down in a simplistic way.' (Sorry, sorry! *Simple!* Curse you, Bill Gates!)

Now, if his wisdom sounds like the type of shallow, plati-tudinous ullage that pours freely out of a bored barman's beerhole ('each type has strengths and weaknesses . . . positive and negative characteristics . . . everything is in the eye of the beholder . . . blah de blah de blah . . .'), then it should come as no surprise to learn that the Prof began his working life as . . . yes! A barman.

Barmen, TV presenters, dancers. Black and White Minstrels. Journalists. Come on, pile in: all advice welcome. And why not?

Today, post-MA, post-PhD and thoroughly postmodern, Stevie is an academic and a 'relationship coach'. But who needs touch-line relationship advice from a man who a) has been married three times and b) met his Thai wife on the internet, for crissakes, while researching his previous book, *Men, Women, Love and Romance* (in which he introduces the breakthrough concept of 'democratic love, where both parties share every aspect of their union'. Or, 'marriage', as I believe vicars still call it).

The good news for lovers of purely academic exercises is that Steve is now working on the follow-up, about – yup – the different types of women. Gosh. I wonder how many there are and what they will be called? Glass-Ceiling Breaker? Brilliant Life-Juggler? Perfect Mother? Psychopathic Bunny-Boiler (irony – don't write in)?

He won't, he says, know just how many there are until he starts researching. Well, Stevie, let me save you the trouble. There are (and please forgive the unfashionable concept of universal individuality, which rejects as patronizing and harmful the pigeonholing of men *or* women) some 3,137,441,032.

And, while we're at it, there aren't twenty-seven types of men – there are at least twenty-eight, if you include The Bullshitter.

Or, perhaps (if you include the type who would use the unfair advantage of a column in a national newspaper to get even with the woman to whom he once offered a kidney but who bloody well had it coming despite the eight-year time lapse and the countless times he has seriously considered trying to make it work with her despite everything including his own infidelities and the fact that her very last gift to him – so clearly an attempt to change him into somebody else – was a bloody oversized lilac shirt), twenty-nine.

Lilac, for Christ's sake!

A Dish Goes Cold
Friday 23 January 2004

Sleeping with an ex is all too easy and nearly always a mistake. Well, not that easy, because in this case it took me more than seven years. But you know what I mean.

Since we split up in acrimonious circumstances (polite-speak for 'both shagging around like biblical begetters given a leaked advance copy of the Ten Commandments'), we have, over the years, been in fairly constant contact. Occasionally, we have been all grown-up and civil and, more often, all furious and spitting feathers over some further outrage that has come to light only lately. (When a love ship like ours founders, it can lie on the seabed leaking the crude oil of revelation for decades.)

When we hit the rocks (upon my discovery, on my birthday, that The One had, in fact, been The Other One for another bloke for over a year), I managed to keep my fury penned inside my head, but in there it rampaged about, doing untold damage to my peace of mind.

For more than a year I honed a production-number revenge fantasy: winning her back, luring her up the aisle and, in front of all her friends and family (and both of mine), delivering a response to the 'Do you, Jonathan . . . ?' question so fiendishly vicious and coruscating that even the vicar burst into spontaneous applause.

In pursuit of the most satisfyingly devastating denouement,

I spent months writing and rewriting the script, dabbling with a dozen different endings, including one involving a male-voice choir and another hinging on what I now recognize to be an entirely unhinged and shameful plan to seduce her mother.

All of this passed through my mind the other night as I found myself sitting on a sofa alongside the object of all this wasted time and effort for the first time in – oh, seven years?

I should have guessed something was up when she suggested coming round to my place. I still didn't twig when she started knocking back the Pinot Grigio and bemoaning the dullness of her current relationship. I did find my internal Leslie Phillips muttering, 'Well, *hello* . . .' when she asked if she could stay the night, but it wasn't until she added, 'in your bed,' that the light finally went on.

Revenge was about to be handed to me on a plate. Great. Only, I suddenly realized, I didn't want it any more.

Of course, I took it anyway, moving seamlessly through the mutually self-deceiving, 'Do you have a large T-shirt I could sleep in?' phase to, well, shagging like the aforementioned begetters. Only, without any of the old urgency. It was OK. Not unlike, I imagine, it would have been if we had stayed together for all those years.

It was curiously sad, yet settling, to discover that the flame of which I had been the keeper for so long had guttered out, unnoticed. Later, as I lay there staring at the ceiling, I deleted one more name from the list in my head headed, 'Is she the one?'

There was (and *Carry On* fans will be ahead of me here) stiff competition, missus, for my year's supply of 366 Trojan condoms (twice on New Year's Eve, perhaps?). I feel I must single out Ms X of Manchester who, tragically, suggests thirty seconds as the average time from penetration to ejaculation. Unless, Ms X, you have been in a series of ill-advised relationships with orang-utans, it seems likely that your lover might be suffering from premature ejaculation.

Don't despair. There is a solution you can work towards together as a caring, loving couple. Dump the loser.

Cheeringly, not one answer was 100 per cent correct, although six entrants did come second (as it were) with ballpark figures. Stand up, then, and receive your sheaths of honour, Ashley Coidan, Chris Purcell, Meg Walster, Monica Patel, Martin Denny and Elizabeth Knight. A second year's supply, first aid and counselling awaits the first of you to use all 366.

16
How to Play Consequences

Dear Microwave Man
   Do you ever consider the consequences of your actions?
                                    Mrs SW, Windsor

Microwave Man writes: Only afterwards. We all learn geology the morning after the earthquake.[89]

You know, given that so many well-intentioned actions result in personal disasters for entirely innocent and unrelated bystanders (the invention of the car, while handy for those little trips to the shops, has killed many, many more people than, say, Saddam Hussein – terrible driver though he was. Even the police in Britain, chasing baddies, manage to knock off thirty innocents a year), maybe doing the right thing isn't always, well, the right thing to do.

Does that make Henry Ford a psychotic mass-murderer?[90] Well, yes, probably, in an Aristotelian, moral sense. But hey. A small price to pay for personal mobility, right?

So I'm not so sure that having good intentions is necessarily a good thing. And it's a short hop from that proposition to the corollary that (as it must, logically, also be possible that thoughtless, careless, selfish actions might have unforeseen beneficial results) having bad intentions is not necessarily a bad thing.

In other words, if I sleep with your wife, I might be doing us all a big favour. Her, obviously. But you as well, maybe. Somehow.

Are we buying this?

89 Ralph Waldo Emerson, author of *Self Reliance*: the only self-help advice a man needs.
90 Any colour you want, so long as it's red.

Well, take the First World War, for example. A Bad Thing, most would agree. A Good Thing, though, surely, that America joined in and sent its brave boys across the pond to save Europe from the Hun? Well, yes and no, depending on how you approach the sums.

Britain lost nearly a million men during the war but close to a quarter of a million more to the flu epidemic that broke out just as peace was declared. (Among the victims, a few years down the line, was Adam's great-grandfather; my gran's husband.) The flu that carried on killing after the generals went home, known as Spanish Flu to the British Tommy and French Flu to the Spanish, should actually have been called Kansas Flu, because that, experts now believe, is where it came from, with a group of infected American soldiers.

I think this is definitely what we can call irony: they came to save the old world from itself and, as an unintended by-product of American foreign policy,[91] inadvertently unleashed one of the world's worst biological weapons of mass destruction, snuffing out 70 million people worldwide. More people died of the flu in India alone than were killed throughout the entire world by four years of global warfare.

Oops! Now that's what you *call* friendly fire. But at least they *meant* well.

On the other hand, I don't think Maurice Saatchi meant well. I think he meant to make a lot of money. Stick with me on this. I think it might possibly be important. It's about consequences and connections and it goes like this.

It's London, 1973, and a black Rolls-Royce pulls up outside an art gallery. Out steps a man in tennis shorts. The gallery owner is about to shut up shop and, a little later, is glad that he didn't. By the time the Rolls departs, the embryonic Saatchi collection is four paintings larger. That same year, a riverside school in Suffolk: a motley collection of boys are variously playing rugby, learning to sail and, when they err (which, being

91 Why does that phrase have a familiarly grim ring to it?

working-class, inner-city types, is often), enduring the tail-end of legal corporal punishment.

One eighteen-year-old is walking down the driveway, looking back over his shoulder for the last time at the beautiful Palladian Woolverstone Hall, built in 1766 for the Berners family on the south bank of the River Orwell.

That eighteen-year-old? That's me, folks!

Woolverstone has been his home for the past seven years. It isn't a private school, and he and his schoolmates aren't privileged children, but they, and 360 like them each year since 1954, have had the privilege of a first-class education. Except when it comes to maths and chemistry, but hey.

But within sixteen years, the gates of Woolverstone will be closed for ever to the have-nots. Woolverstone's remit, as an experimental boarding school for disadvantaged Londoners, leavened with a sprinkling of military brats, was to discover potential within inner-city children and develop it to the advantage of the child and society as a whole.

I was born in 1955, a year after the experiment began, to my single mother in Peckham, then still little more than a bombsite. My escape from the rubble of my mother's life began with an aptitude test at County Hall, home of the Inner London Education Authority. Every term began with a coach ride from outside the building, with a short stop somewhere around Chelmsford for lots of travel-sick little boys to throw up by the roadside, and ended seventy miles away in Suffolk, in a leafy lane leading to the school's Lutyens-designed Corners House.

For me, and for thousands of wide-eyed children before and after me, stepping into County Hall was stepping through the wardrobe into my own Narnia. Until 1989, when that magic doorway was closed for ever. Now, where young lives were once given a second chance, fish swim in an aquarium and Saatchi's dead cows and sharks decompose. The only coaches here now are full of weary tourists, ignorant of the Utopia they have displaced. Can you see how this might bug me?

Saatchi, on the other hand, didn't require rescuing from

deprivation. Born in Baghdad, he was four when his father, a textile merchant, emigrated to Britain. The family continued to prosper in their adopted country. Charles drifted into advertising, found that he had a talent for copywriting and, with his brother Maurice, built an aggressive, edgy agency that bestrode the 1970s.

Oh, well done.

In 1978 Saatchi & Saatchi bagged an entire political party as a client and moved seamlessly from selling products to selling policies, persuading consumers – sorry, voters – that Labour wasn't working. The result was the ascent of Thatcherism and the slow, brutal strangulation of the Greater London Council and its attendant bodies. Starved of money, the Ilea tree began to wither and, in 1989, one of the last branches to fall dead was Woolverstone Hall.

Now, in place of the rugby posts stand the hockey goals of a private school for girls.

Is Saatchi morally responsible for the countless lives blighted by the absence of that educational Narnia? I'm not sure, although greater minds (such as Hobbes, Hume and Mill, more capable of pressing the case for the consequentialist conception of moral responsibility) might say so. Descartes is still thinking about it, but don't wait up.

I'm not sure of the worth or otherwise of the art that Saatchi has hoarded and vaingloriously housed in a temple dedicated to himself – a temple whose original, noble purpose he helped to sabotage. What I know is that the Saatchi Gallery, standing as it does as a celebration of Saatchi's personal success, stands also in sickening mockery of all those lost lives.

And talking about lost lives and the consequentialist conception of moral responsibility, follow me now to the bridge – the Orwell Bridge, to be precise. This concrete monster stretches across the river that ran through my adolescence in Suffolk. It was built ten years after I left Woolverstone (you know: the school the Saatchi boys single-handedly razed to the ground) on the banks of the Orwell, and everyone hated it because it ruined the view looking upstream. They liked it in the end, of course, because it meant an end to what the local paper liked to call Gridlock Ipswich, a new, fast route through to the coast and great footage for local TV crews when lorries and caravans got blown on to their sides by high North Sea winds that funnelled in from the east coast and up the river during the winter months.

I never hated the bridge. I have always been awed by it and drawn to it. At times, when the winds and the tides have been in the right direction, I have sailed upriver in my old wooden Enterprise just to pass under it and gaze up in awe at the gigantic span hundreds of feet above my head. It bestrides the river like a gigantic, concrete dinosaur. You can't see the traffic but you can hear the background roar of an unseen but unpredictable and insufficiently distant beast. It makes my heart beat faster and my pelvic floor muscles start doing press-ups. At least, I think it's my pelvic floor muscles. Do men *have* pelvic floor muscles?

It's funny how, when you look back, you see that your life has ebbed and flowed around a single reference point – a house, a forest, a thought, a decision, a mistake, a person. Or the stanchion of a bridge. As a clumsy, fumbling schoolboy, I once lay with a girl in the grass-covered dunes where one of the monster's giant feet is now embedded in the earth. When Laura and I split up and I returned to the Orwell as an adult, a man without a home town looking for a sense of belonging, my long runs often took me along the banks of the river and under the bridge, or over it, crossing its tall arch.

Later, when Adam came to live with me, his daily bus into town and on to college passed under the bridge. He'd been in the country less than two months when a man jumped from the bridge and landed on the road right alongside the bus. The driver stopped, and all the college kids sat and looked and tried to make out which parts of the oddly marionetted but still possibly human shape on the floor were which, and to figure out which of the strange, whitish lumps of matter were brain, and which skull fragments.

Adam brushed it off when he told me about it later that night, when I finally got home from London.

'Jesus! Are you sure you're OK?' I asked him.

'Yeah, sure. Fine.'

A week later I spoke to his mother in Tenerife, and she said he'd been on the phone to her every night that week for hours. I felt sick.

'I suppose he didn't want to let you down, to seem weak,' she said.

Jesus. How to be a bad father. It's so hard to be true to yourself and to be true to somebody else. It's so much easier to be selfish.

After that, I began to look at the bridge from a different angle. It was a thing of beauty to me. To others, it was an ugly monstrosity but a functional necessity that made daily life just that bit easier. To yet others it loomed large on the skyline as . . . the answer to everything. There's a phenomenon attached to tall constructions that psychologists, depending on the mood they're in and the caseload with which they're struggling, call suicide by design, or manslaughter by design, or (on really shitty, end-it-all Mondays) murder by design. (Architects, naturally, don't much go along with this. Buildings, like guns, and drink, and cars, don't kill people: *people* kill people.)

But the fact remains that, when you go to the trouble to give people something to jump off, they don't let you down: they respond, and the local suicide rate rises as they start falling. Tall buildings talk to people who might otherwise not have resorted to killing themselves. It is as if the structure calls out to the psychologically frail: 'Hey, you! Yeah, that's right, you, you loser! Feeling down and worthless again? And why not? It is, after all, looking pretty hopeless. Well, look, here's a quick, permanent solution to your temporary problem . . .'

Jumping isn't for everyone, of course. Only the committed (or, perhaps, those who might have *been* committed if the Conservatives hadn't so caringly introduced Care in the Community)[92] take the high road to eternity. Of the average

---

92 Which, as one tumbles to one's certain death from a great height, briefly becomes, I suppose, Care in the Air.

6,000 suicides in Britain every year only a hardcore of 5 per cent are jumpers, and these guys *mean* it. This is no cry for help. They aren't coming back. They are more than tourists out to take a peek at the white light and be home in time for supper. They won't get stitched up, or have their stomachs pumped, or come to in their car with a fireman slapping their face, a gigantic headache and a fresh enthusiasm for tomorrow. They'll just get shovelled up off the floor and dropped into a zinc-lined, leak-proof box, like so much mechanically recovered meat slurry.

Let's look at the maths. Two in every one hundred male deaths are suicides. The figure is one in every hundred for women. (Ergo, it really is a man's world of pain.) For men or women, by far and away the exit of choice is self-poisoning. Given that this is a far from guaranteed ticket to oblivion (100,000 a year try but fail to end it all), one can't help thinking that a few of the 24 per cent who *do* manage to slip off into an analgesic or psychotropic fog didn't actually *mean* to go all the way to the other side. The same probably applies to some of the 20 per cent who, like Merv, carry around garden hoses in their cars and choose carbon monoxide. (As for the 2 per cent who burn themselves to death, well, frankly, good luck to them: they've earned a way out.)

But jumpers. They're the ones who get my vote.

Ipswich was a low-rise town until the bridge went up and over the river (even the multistorey car park was subterranean), and when it opened in 1982 the town suddenly found itself cursed not only by a football club that seemed doomed for ever to languish in the lower reaches of football,[93] but by the twin magical lures of gravity and terminal velocity. Since then, roughly one person a year has taken advantage of the bridge's impressively fatal 41-metre height.

And so the well-intentioned construction of the bridge – which has brought happiness to holidaymakers who can now reach the beach much more quickly, and to me because I can sail under it

93 Although what, I have to ask, does one expect (other than provincialism and a flair for ploughing up the pitch) from a club nicknamed The Tractor Boys?

and shout 'Whaaa!', and to commuters who don't have to crawl in their cars through the uninspiring, recession-swathed back streets of a dull town in order to get home in time for their favourite soap – has also brought death to more than twenty people and untold misery to the families they leave behind.

Oh, well. A small price to pay for personal mobility, right?

And it could have been much worse. In six decades, more than 1,200 people have jumped to their deaths from San Francisco's Golden Gate Bridge, and the Jacques-Cartier bridge in Montreal, Canada (the world's second most popular jumping-off spot), despatches at least one a month.

Would-be Orwell Bridge suicides, however, have the advantage of being confronted at either end of the span by a notice placed there by the Samaritans,[94] along with a telephone. But not everyone picks up that telephone.

Whatever drives people to kill themselves, one thing (as journalists, remember, do like to say when nothing is certain) is certain: when somebody swallows too many pills, slashes open an artery or tries to gas themselves in a car (even if they have carried around a hose in the boot for twenty years), it's not hard to put it down as a cry for help, even if that cry gets strangled and they end up meeting their maker. Under no circumstances, however, can jumping off a tall building be described as a cry for help. To step out into space, one has to be thoroughly ready to slip the surly bonds of earth and dance the skies, overcoming a natural fear that is even greater than the fear of death itself.

If you are, by society's current standards, not insane, chemically fucked up or otherwise loopy, something pretty bloody ghastly must have happened to you to drive you to that bridge.

And to drive you to drive yourself and your two eldest children to that bridge in your wife's brand-new company Volvo.

I read the story in the newspapers, but I didn't find out the truth about it until, a week or so later, I received a text message on my phone. 'Hello, Mr G . . .'. Kelly. She has promised never

94 And if the Samaritans are so bloody good, how come *they* never phone *you*?

to speak to me again, but she wants to talk – needs to talk – to close the chapter in her life. I drive her down to London and on the way, when I stop for petrol, she shows me the long, livid scar the car crash has left on her leg. I can't quite understand why she is here, sitting in my car, after all that has happened, but here she is – despite the horrendous discovery by her boyfriend of her infidelity as she lay in her hospital bed. Despite, incredibly, the story she is now telling me. And as she tells it, I realize that this is why she is here: I'm the only person she could possibly tell who could begin to understand what it means.

The story I'd read in the papers said that this man had taken two of his three young children, driven to the bridge, parked in the lay-by alongside one of the Samaritans' signs and, one at a time, and in front of the eyes of horrified passers-by, had thrown the brothers, aged five and seven, to their deaths. And then jumped after them. He left the engine running, but no note.

I'd thought about that scene, about those moments, a lot. The view from that bridge. Best to be the first child? Best to be the second? How would it have felt to be the first? Worse than being the second?

Puzzled. What is Daddy doing? Oh . . .

Worse to be the second?

What is Daddy doing? That? Oh. Now it is my turn. But still hope. Hope that he might come to his senses and change his mind. But then, hope is cruelly crushed. Arms that recently – perhaps only yesterday or this morning – had held me tenderly, protectively, now lifting me, struggling and crying, from the car, and now throwing me over the edge. Over the edge of the bridge that leads us to the beach, or to Grandma's. But not today. Not ever again.

Would the second child to go have caught sight of his father falling just behind him? Would he have heard his scream, or his own (because a witness did say that the man screamed as he fell)? Or would he have heard only the white noise of approaching oblivion as the entire planet rushed up to meet him at 250 feet per second?

I can't remember what this man and his wife did for a living, but they worked at the same company and, it was suggested in the papers, because she was doing so more successfully than him he was shamed not to be the main breadwinner and had killed himself. And two of their children.

But not quite so, it seems. I never really had bought that explanation.

Kelly knew differently, and how she knew differently made my scalp tingle. What she knew was that the husband had discovered that his beautiful, successful wife was having an affair with a man she had met at work. A man younger and much more successful than her husband. It had been this which had driven him to drive the Volvo to his children's school, pick them up and then drive them to their deaths.

Kelly knew this because her boyfriend – the one who had fallen in love with her when she had lost her husband, who had been there for her when I was never going to be and who had given up office work to become a policeman because he wanted to put something back into the community, and who had then found out that the guy his girlfriend had met in a car park years ago had been putting something back into her – because her boyfriend was one of the two young policemen who had been sent to investigate the reports that someone had thrown themselves off the bridge.

I thought about her boyfriend and how he might react to this scene, this car journey, and what he would hate most about it. He wouldn't see it as a final act of closure, but as a betrayal. I thought about Laura and the lover she had been screwing for months while we were still together. And I thought about the running shoes he had left in her new flat. I thought about Wallace and Gromit and the stupid bloody novelty clock which had finally ended up alongside her bed. *Their* bed. It had been my birthday present but she had kept it. Did he know that? Would he have cared? Would it have put him off his stroke had he known – because surely he would have wondered what it really meant to her?

And as we drove on I thought about Alice and her husband,

and something she had told me just two or three days before, but it wasn't something I could share, right now, with Kelly, not least because it was something Alice had told me as we lay in bed after sex. The route from Alice's marital home to my flat took her over the bridge, and this time she had almost an hour to spare and so, instead of tea, we had sex, and after we had sex we lay there and talked about the three deaths.

Although, as it turned out, it had been four deaths.

'Do you remember my friend Angela?' she said. 'You met her that time you came to the beach.'

'Oh, yes.' No, I didn't, but still.

'She lives next door to that family. When the police came round, they found the wife lying in the hallway, stabbed to death, but the youngest child was upstairs and alive. They asked Angela if she would look after it until social services could get there. The young copper holding the baby was as white as a sheet.'

I bet he was.

Six degrees of Kevin Bacon, and all that. And none of us more than a few stiff drinks and a flirty exchange away from an affair, or a calamitous, life-changing decision, a vicious pile-up and, if we are very, very lucky, nothing more than a scar to remember it by. Kelly, me, Alice, Saatchi, President Woodrow Wilson, some soldiers who sneezed, the bloke who designed the Orwell Bridge and the woman whose infidelity drove her husband mad enough to throw himself and their children from it. I'm not sure I want to play consequences any more. I'm not sure I'm up to it.

Kelly hovers in limbo for a few more weeks, unable quite to cut free. There's no more sex, partly because I sense she is closed to all that now and partly because the sight of the long, livid scar which runs from near her right knee and up inside her thigh shrivels my desire. It says far too much. J. G. Ballard would have been disappointed.

What would have happened if Kelly had left Tom before the crash, as she so nearly did? Well, she might not have had the crash, for one thing. She also might have been happier, rather than resigned and thinking, 'Maybe this is as good as it gets.'

She might have discovered that she could live quite happily on her own, without the constant presence of an emotional airbag. Christ. We might even have been together now. Might have just drifted towards each other.

I didn't *want* her to leave him. I was happy – probably happier – just sleeping with another man's woman. But if she *had* left him, for her own sake, because it was the right thing to do, then I would have gone on seeing her. And who knows where that might have led? As it was, I was sad when she eventually decided to stay put, but not sad enough to do anything about it.

And that's when it dawned on me. For the first time in my life, I hadn't just bolted into the first available relationship with a woman prepared to be my lover, mother, brother, father, sister and third cousin twice removed. There was, I realized with creeping incredulity, a slim chance that, with just three weeks to go before my forty-ninth birthday, I had finally started to grow up. Or, at least, to realize that sex was one thing, and love quite another. Mostly.

After the Crash
Friday 30 January 2004

One of the saddest films I have seen is *The Others*, starring Nicole Kidman. Isolated in a lonely, mist-bound country house, she longs to be free of it and to step back into the light of the real world, but never finds the courage to defy what appear to be the ghosts who keep her prisoner.

Regular readers of this column (*Bonjour*, Doreen and Edgar Maldetete of Walton-on-the-Naze) will recall my torrid but brutally terminated fling with 'Kelly', which ended when I received a text message telling me that she had been in a car crash.

When we started seeing each other, she had explained her need to explore the wider world of passion outside her relationship with Tom, her live-in boyfriend, and her constant wrestling with the notion that she really had to move on and leave him, thus: 'I'm afraid that this is as good as it gets'.

And, quite clearly, it wasn't.

Then the crash. As she lies in a hospital bed, he, suspicious, digs my number out of her mobile phone. The upshot is that the distressed and post-operative Kelly agrees never to see me again.

But then, a couple of weeks ago, she calls. 'Hello, Mr G . . .' begins that familiar, slightly apologetic voice. She's at the station, heading down to work for the first time since the crash. By chance, I am in town and so I give her a lift.

As I drive, more slowly and safely than I have since I took my test, we talk. Tom, she says, had been nice to her while she was unwell. So what? Is she going to stay with him because he brought her a few grapes? Or leave him because it was, and still is, the right thing to do?

By the time we were inside the M25, she must have said, 'I don't know,' a hundred times.

A week later, we meet again. Sitting in a station café as she waits for the train back to her mist-bound country life, I feel depressingly like Trevor Howard in *Brief Encounter*.

All along, she has known that I, still crawling from the wreckage of my own relationship, have not been in the market for a new one. In fact, I haven't even been in the same county as the town where the market is held. But as we wait for the train, I have to say something, so I look her straight in the eye and say: 'If I told you I wanted to be with you in the full-on Christmas, birthdays, new year, weekends, holidays and mutual friends and family sense, would you leave him?'

She smiles and, without a moment's hesitation, says: 'Yes.'

'Then you really are a crash-test dummy,' I say, wishing I'd phrased it better, but meaning it. 'You shouldn't leave him for anyone but yourself.' Then, curiously, she bites me, hard, on my left cheek, bringing tears (well, more tears, actually) to my eyes.

Although only in her early thirties, she is afraid to take that running jump into the unknown. When we first met, I thought of her as someone slowly emerging into the light. Back then, she feared that her passion-lite life with Tom was as good as it got. And now, waiting for the train, post-trauma, I am horrified to hear her say that she is afraid to leave him – 'in case this *is* as good as it gets.'

When Kelly had her crash, I wondered for a while if the text messages I was receiving were from her or her boyfriend. At one point, I even seriously considered that she might have been killed. Now I fear that the crash, in halting her in her tracks, may have harmed Kelly more than either of us realized.

In *The Others* (and look away now if you haven't seen it: the ending is a throat-gripper), Kidman lives in fear of the ghosts who swirl around outside her walls. At the end of the film, she, and we, discover that it is she who is the ghost, and that what she has feared all along is the testing but ultimately fulfilling light of the real world and its living people.

Watching Kelly walk slowly away through the crowd towards her train is one of the saddest things I have ever seen.

17

How to Act Your Age

Dear Microwave Man

 Hi! My name is CHARLI and I'm assistant producer on this TV prog being put together for Channel 4 it's called Old Enough to Know Better it's really fun and it's like a reality show where they put four old guys like you together with four young dudes in this cool house and the game is to see which one of you gets the chick, who's like young enough to be your daughter!!! And I want YOU on the show because you are SO cool and I think dead funny. My mum likes you too. How about it? I'm twenty-three. Let's eat lunch!!

        Charli, Flickerin' Films, Teddington

Microwave Man writes: Thank you for your email. Microwave Man is unable to reply personally to all correspondents but thanks you for your kind comments. Just twenty-three? Really?

Be honest. If you had to pick one of the following to go up your bottom, which would it be? The lubricated fore and middle fingers of the largest (male) South African you have ever seen (on *or* off the rugby pitch)? Or the Aneros 'patented anal sphincter-driven, prostate-perineum massager . . . with proven efficacious hands-free self-pivoting mechanism' (which, in profile, resembles nothing so much as Charles de Gaulle's nose)?

 These, it seems, are the choices that a man faces as he enters the year of his fiftieth birthday.

 It comes as a surprise to learn not only that is there a male G-spot, but that there exists a device to help one play with it, should one be so inclined. My good friends at Love Honey – postal purveyors of plain-wrapped sex toys – sent me one just in time for it to qualify as 2004's Christmas Gift Most Likely to Remain in the Box.

According to the queasily graphic testimonials from the countless rectally relaxed fans of Aneros, this curiously shaped piece of plastic helps them to achieve orgasms even bigger, better and longer than those enjoyed by Barbarella trapped in the Orgasmatron during a power surge.

Oh, and there is, says Love Honey, a sound reason for shoving de Gaulle's *nez* up one's Channel tunnel (other than improving Anglo-French relations): such massage, it seems, 'improves prostate health'.

However, it was the intervention of a genuinely medical procedure that conclusively put me off the whole idea. Maybe Cornelia was right about anal, after all. Enter the South African (as it were), and enter Stirling Moss.

At about the same time as the Aneros was poking its nose through my letter box, I saw that Sir Stirling was in the news as the acceptable face of prostate cancer. He'd had it in 2001, he revealed, and now was fronting up the Prostate Cancer Support campaign to persuade the rest of us blokes over forty-five that it was nothing to be afraid of, and that we really ought to get ourselves along for a check-up.

Now, even though Mossie gave up driving racing cars in 1962 after an horrific crash at Goodwood, such was his fame in a nation generally starved of internationally recognized sports stars that, ten years later, when I was a newly fledged seventeen-year-old driver, tearing up the streets of South London in my souped-up Morris Oxford, policemen who stopped speeders were still in the habit of enquiring: 'All right, sir/sonny; who do you think are? Stirling Moss?'

As a deterrent, it sort of worked. They thought they were being droll; we were flattered by the implied comparison. Now the comparison is less flattering. Mossie has come over all soft on us, revealing that, as the years wore on, he found there were times when not only could he not get into top gear as fast as he used to, but sometimes he couldn't go at all. The worst side-effect of prostate treatment, as far as I can see, is erectile dysfunction. He'd had the one, apparently, and then the other. But then not much of *the* other. Now he's shouting the odds from the billboards. Well, it's all right for him. He's seventy-six. He shouldn't be doing anything with his penis except wetting the bed. It's disgusting, that's what it is.[95]

Sir Stirling (he was immediately knighted for his services to erections: 'Arise,' said the Queen and, rather embarrassingly, he did) bravely came out on behalf of GlaxoSmith Kline and Bayer HealthCare, the manufacturers of Levitra and supporters of the Prostate Campaign. Levitra, as far as I can tell, is a rival drug to Viagra, which, Sir Stirling confided to the nation and the Commonwealth, had failed to stiffen his sinews. Then he went on to scare the bejeebers out of every man in the country – but especially those approaching fifty – by announcing that 50 per cent of men who've knocked up a half-century can expect to suffer from erectile dysfunction.

Oh, great. So it's not just the increasingly lousy memory, then.

Don't worry, was the message from the former motor ace. You can always take a stiffy pill.

Oh, great. So it's not just the increasingly lousy memory, then.

If I had to rely on chemical scaffolding[96] every time I needed to raise my game, I think it might just be time to borrow Merv's hose, if you see what I mean. I'm surrounded by portents of impending impotence. My email inbox is stuffed with offers of Viagra, Shagara (which I suspect might be a fake) and Rhino Keep-It-Up Cream (which, incredibly, isn't). What the hell is going on? Who's been talking? How do these people know my age, let alone get hold of my email address? I can barely remember it myself sometimes.

Even my own son – as if his very existence isn't a living reminder of my own looming mortality – was tickled to mark

95 Check back with me for my view on this in twenty-five years.
96 I recently saw a scaffolding-company van in Ipswich with this slogan (which I thought at once boastful and yet modest): 'Erections all over East Anglia.' Mind you, it's a big region.

my forty-ninth birthday by breaking his greeting card duck with one featuring a drawing of a factory with the legend above the gates: 'Joe's Pipe and Tool Works'. Inside, it read, 'Hope yours does too, Dad!'

For this I had my testes tortured to bring him into the world?

But Mossie was right. At forty-nine it was time to do the sensible thing and take it like a man, and so I got myself down to my local branch of Bupa.[97] (If I was going to be anally invaded I was buggered if I was going to wait six months for an NHS appointment. Besides, I like those little boxes of breakfast cereal they give you in the waiting rooms at Bupa. Did you know you can help yourself, even if you've only popped in to make an appointment? To think I ever doubted that private medicine was the right prescription for the country.)

I had been banking on an encounter with the delicate, dark-haired female doctor I had seen on a previous visit (when, sadly, no internal had been required), but my balls scurried back up into their hidey-hole with adroit trepidation when I saw the burly prop-forward snapping on his surgicals. Moss had reassuringly said that, 'the first stage of a check-up is a simple blood test and doesn't always include a physical examination,' but either Bupa had missed that part of the commercial or this chap was just determined to go through the motions.

By forty-nine, one has endured enough at the hands of 'experts' to know that when a doctor says, 'Now, this might cause you some discomfort,' one's eyes are, at best, going to water. I was invited to assume a position not dissimilar to the serving suggestion I had seen on the back of the Aneros packaging ('Lie on your side. Keeping the lower leg straight, bring your top knee to your stomach . . .') and which had finally turned my stomach and put me off the whole idea.

And now here I was paying good money for it.

Now, I don't want to undo the good work done by Mossie. God knows, I don't want to put anyone off doing the sensible

97 Despite their current TV advertising campaign, with its slogan 'At Bupa, all we are about is making you better.' Really? Do the shareholders know this?

thing and having their prostate probed. I don't even want to put anyone off jamming de Gaulle's nose up their back passage (although do bear in mind what happened to poor old Ted Heath).

But, *Jesus Christ*, it hurts.

After that, any kind of association with the Aneros would be nothing more than a wilfully perverse trip up a painful memory lane. On the upside, I now have a piece of paper that assures me that, 'your rectal examination was good, with a normal-feeling prostate'. Well, Doc, what can I say? It was good for me, too, and I'll be back in two years for our second date.

If I can remember to go, of course.

It was only when I could shower, get dressed, read the papers and toast a muffin in the time it took for my computer to wake up, that I realized I really had to do something about my memory. The nice man from Dell suggested I needed some extra RIM (or ROM or DOM or ramadangadingdong or something), and three days and £100 later it arrived in the post.

I spent an enjoyable hour or so doing no writing (nothing new there, then) and instead undoing every single screw on the back of the laptop (losing two but still, oddly, having one left over after I'd finished), before discovering that there was a convenient little trapdoor giving easy access to the memory banks. Worth remembering, that.

If only it were that easy to upgrade human memory.

Just after I turned forty-nine, I learnt something from an old schoolmate that shook my entire grasp on reality (such as it was). I had discovered on a Woolverstone Hall old boys' site a photograph of myself and six others in rugby gear, posing cockily with a wooden trophy in what I recognized to be the garden of Woolverstone House, the Lutyens-designed former nunnery in the Suffolk countryside that served as my school house from 1966 to 1973. (How we eleven-year-olds had laughed to learn of one of Sir Edwin's other triumphs – Tikli Bottom, a bungalow near Delhi, India – now almost certainly a Dell call-centre.)

I was slightly concerned that I recognized only two of my

contemporaries in the photograph and was able to name only one (Tony 'Thunder thighs' Silver, since you ask), but I put the visual clues together with what memory I could summon from 1973 (scant) and concluded that this was the triumphant Corners House rugby sevens team, led by me, that had yet again knocked off the school's Bombay trophy (awarded these days for Best Call-Centre Operative of the Month).

But not so, according to Shane Marshall, who was (apparently) in the year above and wrote to tell me that Corners had won the cup the year *before*. This photograph, he claimed, had been taken shortly before the dunderheads in the picture had thrown it away ignominiously. Most of the first-team players, it seems, had been sick.

Pardon? I thought I *was* a first-team player?

The correspondence escalated, and it got worse. Another old boy seems to be enjoying what I thought were my memories of playing in a (very rubbish) three-piece band at school. Worse, he also seems to have hijacked my recollections of a school governor's daughter but, as my memories are of a series of inept fumblings, he is welcome to them. (Besides, neither of us, shamefully, can recall her name.)

Frankly, it's all getting a bit Stephen King. Maybe all my recollections are false, or at least corrupted. Perhaps I'm remembering somebody else's life because it was better than mine – Nietzsche, after all, believed we all rewrite our personal history to a degree, because, as he put it, 'memory yields to pride'.

Brain doctors (forgotten the word – brainiacs?) say that all the details from a single event – the smells, sounds, sights, facts and tastes of, say, a dinner party – are stored in separate shoeboxes in the brain and reassembled on demand as a single episode by the hippocampus, that bit of the brain shaped like a seahorse. The problems start when the seahorse gets bored and, just for fun, starts calling up and assembling unrelated memories – confusing what one did, perhaps, with something one has read – as a related episode (hence all those Napoleons? Learn French, read the biography, buy the hat – *et voilà*?).

So perhaps I wasn't, after all, head boy. And did I really steal the show as Pisarro in the school production of *The Royal Hunt of the Sun*, or did I merely slap gold paint over hundreds of egg boxes? (And did Peter Shaffer really pen the alarmingly demanding stage direction, 'They cross the Andes'?)

At forty-nine, of course, it doesn't help that the old hard disk is clogged with undeletable rubbish. Nothing (as someone whose name I now forget may once have said) fixes a thing so intensely in the mind as the determination to forget it. The result? Less and less space for short-term memory. The downside of this is mislaying keys, forgetting to buy toilet paper and walking around with one's flies undone (he told magistrates). The upside . . . well, actually, there is no bloody upside.

But the thing that really pisses me off about teetering on the brink of fifty is the whole midlife crisis thing. I just don't get it. According to just about every source, I should daily be asking myself, 'What's it all about?', looking for the answer behind the wheel of a bright red sports car or in the arms of a pretty young blonde (or both) and, upon discovering that it's all pretty much about nothing at all, seeking comfort/oblivion courtesy of Prozac or an overdose of carbon monoxide.

Well, OK, guilty to the blonde, but I know what *that's* about – that Dove 'Real beauty' campaign was fooling nobody, least of all me. Yeuch! But *crisis*? What crisis?

My two remaining male friends – one slightly older than me, one slightly younger – have lived pretty conventional lives: successful careers, lovely wives, blood-sucking children, complete collapse of self-esteem and, thanks to GPs more than happy to let a wonder drug pick up the pieces while they pick up the pay cheque, instant and unquestioning elevation to the serotonin-ocracy – popping Prozac and listening to Jazz FM.

Personally, if I were a GP, I wouldn't issue Prozac to guys like Merv and Simon. Instead, I'd advise them to 1. Stop listening to jazz and 2. Invest in the stock of Eli Lilly and Company, makers of Prozac. And to cut me in for a share of the profits. That should cheer us *all* up.

And the good news for Eli Lilly investors is that life in the UK now is a hell of a lot more depressing than it was in 1995. According to Mind, NHS spending on anti-depressant drugs during the nineties rose from £15 million (barely enough to make a small town in Wales smile for a weekend) to an astonishing £395 million by the decade's end.

Now *that* is a lot of drugs. In England alone, according to the Prescription Pricing Authority, the number of prescriptions for the newer, SSRI-type drugs (among which Prozac is king) rose by a mind-numbing 732 per cent in just five years.

How the hell did we all manage before?

There is nothing new about the notion of the male midlife crisis: no doubt even pea-brained cavemen sussed out that life was, on the whole, pretty pointless – hunt, gather, breed, get clubbed to death/stomped by a mastadon. Moody middle-aged men were at it even in the Middle Ages: 'Midway this way of life we're bound upon,' droned Dante in *Divine Comedy*, 'I woke to find myself in a dark wood, where the right road was wholly lost and gone.'

Yeah, yeah. And Carl Jung was no youngster when he defined his five phases of midlife, which included 'separation' – rejecting the accommodated self – and 'liminality' – that period when life seems directionless.

Carl, meet Merv and Simon.

The difference is that now – now that we have conquered space, unravelled the knitted-scarf complexity of DNA and finally edged all those pesky, depressing undertakers off the high street – we think we should be doing something about the pointlessness of it all, rather than simply accepting our lot and cramming in as much fun as we can before the dribbling starts. I guess that's why the mad self-deceptions of religion have stuck around for so long (much easier to deal with one's short, nasty, brutal existence if one can see it as a mere anteroom to an altogether jollier hereafter, preferably with hot- and cold-running virgins on tap).

The problem *now* is that most of us are too smart (or too

dumb; just covering my options there) to put our faith in a divine being. Instead, we put our faith in our *own* divine beings: in our heart of hearts we know there is nothing beyond this life, but we can't bring ourselves to believe that, one day (and one day not too far off, if you're around fifty), these pampered, gym-pumped, seaweed-wrapped, chakra-chanting, acupunctured bodies of ours will be nothing more than worm feed.

Result? Midlife crisis.

Of course, not that many years ago, a chap would have dealt with this situation stoically: shrug, have another pie and a pint, get back down the mine, take a pew on Sundays and brace to meet his maker. Today, we waste our lives wriggling like surplus tomcats in a canal-bound sack. There must, surely, be a way out of this? 'This can't be happening to me! I'm special, for God's sake! I'm an individual! My life coach said so . . .'

Splash.

Self-obsession is a luxury for first-worlders: subsistence farmers are far too busy surviving to lean on their hoes and ask, 'So, what's it all about, then?' We spend so much time examining our own navels that, naturally, we find all that fluff in there, and this, inevitably, leads to all the big questions: What is life for? Is this all there is? And where does all that fluff come from? (Wool jumpers, since you ask. The *real* mystery is how it gets through the T-shirt.)

Nobody loves a cliché more than Hollywood and the media, of course, and, in the absence of more positive role models for middle-aged men, pretty soon the myth becomes something to which we all feel we have to conform. And while women in crisis is, naturally, treated as a serious *isshoo*, men are simply ridiculed. Indeed, sometimes we are made to feel not only entirely surplus to requirements, but a bit of a bloody nuisance, frankly, to boot.

Take this piece, which I read in a newspaper:

An independent think tank has calculated that men in Britain will be living, on average, eight years longer in 2020 than they did fifty years before. This will cost the Government an estimated extra £6 billion in pension costs alone, while the extra burden on the health service is likely to add further billions to the bill.

Oh, well, excuse me. Sorry for the inconvenience and expense.

Well, of course, I was thrilled. I immediately hit on a brilliant plan both to line my pockets, ensuring my last years were spent in relative comfort (rather than the currently anticipated penury), save the Government millions and rid the planet of the burden of a load of seemingly useless old gits. Patriotic, socially responsible *and* self-serving. Just like the East India Company. Brilliant.

Plus, I had some time to kill.

'Look at it this way,' I found myself enthusing to an official at the Department of Health who had had the misfortune to have my call put through to him (finally) by a cheesed-off switchboard operator.[98] 'Say there are – oh, I don't know – an extra 10,000 blokes like me around right now, pushing on fifty, who are going to wind up snuffing it at, say, eighty-five instead of seventy-seven.'

'If you say so . . .'

'Well, here's the deal: suppose each man is going to cost you an extra – what? £1 million over those extra years?'

'Yes, just suppose . . .'

'Well, why not – and here's the clever part, and it will probably win you votes as well – why not offer them *half* the money, up front, if they agree *not* to live for the extra eight years and instead to snuff it after four? You'd save millions, man! I'd do it, for one. Like a shot.'

A taut pause, then, 'Well, thank you very much for your interesting suggestion, which I shall put before the minister concerned at the earliest opportunity.'

---

98 The answer, whenever confronted with annoying telephone keypad options, is always to repeatedly push the number nine, which puts callers through to a room full of reluctant, idle operators sitting around, smoking, drinking coffee, playing cards and watching TV. In Wales.

'Earliest opportunity? When's that likely to be, then?'

'Oh, I don't know, let me consult the diary. Hmm, let me see
. . . yes, it shouldn't be much after, oh, something like 2080, I
should think.'

'Very funny. I'll be dead by then.'

'Oh, dear.'

'You think I'm mad, don't you?'

'I wouldn't put it like that, sir. More . . . *independently minded*,
shall we say?'

'Visionaries are always mistaken for nutters. They thought
John Maynard Keynes was mad.'

'No they didn't, sir. I am a Cambridge economics graduate
and I can assure you that they did not.'

'Well, be fair: he couldn't even remember his own telephone
number and got the worst mark in his Civil Service exam for
economics, for God's sake. That's why he ended up in the India
department instead of the Treasury. I mean, take all that stuff about
counter-cyclical demand management policies. Plainly bonkers.'

'It was not "bonkers", sir, whereas your plan, however,
evidently is. Look: if your willing co-suicides live for four years
instead of eight, in exchange for receiving half the sum the state
would have had to find to sustain them had they lived for eight
years, then quite plainly they would still be costing the state for
those four years, thus consuming half the predicted sum in the
normal fashion – heart bypasses, incontinence operations, Viagra
tablets and the like – while having received the other half up-
front. Net gain for state: zero.'

'So you saw through to the fatal flaw in the plan, then?'

'Well, I did mention, sir, that I was a Cambridge economics
graduate. For the state to gain, clearly the recipients would have
to die the instant they received the 50 per cent sum up front:
before embarking on even a day of the predicted eight years of
additional life they can now expect to enjoy. Hardly worth the
bother for all concerned, I'd say – wouldn't you?'

'You callous bastard. I could have a field day with this. In fact,
I think I'm going to call the newspapers. I can see the headline

now: "Government economist proposes euthanasia to save pension millions." Hello? Hello?'[99]

I never was much good at maths. Maybe that's why I can't see anything wrong in the equation 'Older man plus younger woman equals happiness': from where I'm lying, forty-nine into twenty-seven *does* go. Frequently.

And crisis? What crisis? Maybe the fifty-year-old guy who rides a Harley Davidson with a young chick's arms wrapped around his substantial belly isn't the sad loser society makes him out to be. After all, he's doing what we all wanted to do when we were too young to afford it (or too klutzy to pull): now he *can* afford it and he's got everything *and* the girl.

On the other hand, what do I know? Maybe I *am* in crisis and I just don't know it. Now, that *would* be depressing. Luckily, those nice people at Eli Lilly are there for confused guys like me and Merv. Visit the company's website (that's right, Prozac.com) and take its simple – *very* simple – twenty-question self-assessment test.

'If you score fifty or higher,' it says, 'consider printing the results to show to your doctor.'

I score forty-six. Depressingly borderline. Just like my blood pressure and my cholesterol.

And it seems it doesn't matter what I do: no matter how much I go to the gym, run, swim, heft weights around. I'm running a losing race. I know this is obvious to you, and that it should be to me, but it hasn't sunk in. Or rather, it hadn't, until the day my son comes to stay for a few days and we go for a run together. Like we used to. Nothing competitive, just a gentle trot to mitigate against the beer and pizza we will almost certainly be consuming that evening. We are out for an hour. At the beginning of the hour, I am going to live for ever. By the end, I am very obviously not.

Once or twice Adam turns round to say, 'Come on, Dad,' in the way that I used to turn round to say, 'Come on, Ad,' when

99 This conversation actually happened. I made a recording for training purposes.

he was training to join the Royal Marines and I led him out on runs up and down the banks of the River Orwell. And Dad tries to come on, but there is nothing left – empty fuel tank, straining pump sucking up only vapours and those mysterious rusty bits at the bottom.

In the days when I used to run marathons for fun (for fun!), I kept the agonies in check by imagining the bridge of some kind of ship where my head actually was. When things started to get tough, an immaculately white-suited first officer would run checks over the various systems displaying warning lights – aching feet, sore legs, cramping stomach, straining lungs – and one by one despatch damage-control parties to get things under control. One by one the warning lights would go out and, by the time the whole procedure had been run through, I was a couple of miles further down the road and still in the race.

When things got really, *really* bad – somewhere in the vicinity of nineteen miles, usually – the first officer would buzz for the skipper, a white-bearded manifestation of professional competence, who would appear on the bridge, study the readouts, ease back slightly on the engines and steady the helm, and return to his bunk with a quiet imprecation to, 'Call me if anything changes.' The first officer, sinews stiffened, would glance back with admiration at the skipper as he left the bridge, and return to the job at hand with fresh resolve.

But right here, right now, with me blowing gaskets and blowing off steam in the wake of Adam's unstoppable dreadnought, the old boy's nowhere in sight. In fact, while the officers are panicking on the bridge, screaming, 'Abandon ship!', fighting over the lifejackets and threatening one another with six-shot revolvers, unbeknownst to them, the old boy – pausing only to cosh the purser, open his safe and bundle its contents into a waterproof sack – has changed into a boilersuit, lowered one of the ship's boats and rowed away into the night for all he is worth. Which, considering the amount of jewellery stowed in the safe by the ship's first-class passengers, is now rather a lot.

That's what happens when the brain doesn't get enough

oxygen. It hallucinates. What might not be an hallucination is the sight of Adam ahead of me, running effortlessly, his heels flicking up, arms pumping, casually looking around him, enjoying the view and sometimes glancing back and saying, 'You OK, Dad?' and me saying, 'Sure,' as calmly as I can and then paying for the rash consumption of sorely needed oxygen for the next twenty breaths with searing, red-hot-pokered lungs.

Ahead of me. My son is ahead of me, and that, I suddenly realize, is where he is going to stay from now on. It's only then that it dawns on me just how much of my life is behind me. I even turn to glance over my shoulder, although it makes me shudder to think what I might see back there, hard on my heels.

Luckily, we are running in London. If we had been crossing the Orwell Bridge at that moment, I think I might have thrown myself off.

Later, over pizza, we catch up with each other's lives. Sometimes I forget he's my son and talk to him like he's a friend. Sometimes, this is fine. Other times, I can see him shifting uncomfortably and realize I've gone too far, said too much. This is my loss, and his. I need a friend, but he needs a father.

After I finish telling him about Kelly and Alice and so on, I realize he is giving me what I can describe only as an old-fashioned look.

'What?' I say, putting down knife and fork and spreading my hands. He looks left, then right, and down at his half-finished pizza, and takes another swig of his Peroni.

'Nothing, nothing.'

'No, come on; what is it? Do I embarrass you? Is that it?'

I pull a face, rolling my eyeballs. I'm smiling, but I want him to say no, of course not, I admire you and wish I was the kind of man you are. But instead he says . . .

'Well, since you ask, yes, sometimes you do.'

Oh. He seems so puritanical. We're both from broken homes. Funny how differently we've reacted to it. I keep breaking them and he, faithful to one woman at twenty-two, seems to want nothing more than to make a home of his own.

'I mean, come on, Dad: are you genetically unable to sleep with anyone over thirty?'

'Anyone other than Raquel Welch.'

'Who?'

'Never mind. No, it's just that, it's just that . . .'

What? What is it – just – exactly? Is it because women of my age are few and far between? Is it because I like younger, firmer bodies, because they are easier to caress? Or younger, softer minds, because they are easier to impress? Or is it because I gave up a long time ago on successfully executing Plan A (finding and falling in love with my perfect lifemate and staying with her until death or, at least, unpleasant involuntary seepage, do us part) and have settled instead for sex and beauty and flattery and closed my mind to a future now not that distant when I shall be obliged to choose between Merv's hosepipe and sitting alone and quite possibly soiled in a strange armchair in front of an unfamiliar fireplace that fails to dance with stars of memories because dirty old coal has long since gone the way of all good things and no one – not even somebody who hates or pities or feels nothing for me – will be there to bring me my last meal or to feel their heart pound when they realize that I haven't touched it and oh, boy, what the hell is that foul smell . . . ?

Or maybe it's because, after a lifetime of living as though to be forever young is merely a question of exercise, and an exercise of will and attitude, to wake up every day staring at someone of my age alongside me would be like waking up every day to face my own inevitable mortality?

Yes, I think I'll go with that.

'It's just, I think, that maybe it's because to wake up staring at someone of my age lying alongside me every day would be like . . .' I'm waving my fork, looking around the room for the right words and inadvertently catching the eye of the waitress, who really is rather pretty '. . . would be like waking up every day face to face with my own mortality . . .'

I can see he isn't buying it.

The waitress is at my side. 'Yes, sir, what would you like?' Really very pretty and French to boot. I bet she's a drama student, or maybe studying film.

'Oh, you know,' I say, smiling my best, cool older man smile, working to squeeze out that whiff of tortured, existential despair that seems to attract so many young women and hoping she identifies with Maria Schneider in *Last Tango in Paris*, to whom, God help me, she does bear more than a passing, pouting resemblance, 'the usual things: a nice house, comfortable pension, easily parked car, beautiful wife, endurable children . . .'

She smiles thinly, as though she might have heard this, or something rather like it, one or two times before.

'Are you a student?' I say. I notice Adam shaking his head and smiling.

'Yes.'

'Let me guess: drama, right?'

'Wrong. Business studies.'

Bloody hell. But she isn't looking at me, or even really listening. She's gazing at Adam over the top of her order pad, tapping her pencil against her fingernails. First the run, and now this. This evening couldn't get much worse.

But then it does.

Valhalla, I am Coming
Friday 6 February 2004

Go on, be honest. It's January, 1971, and who would you rather be? The admittedly camp but libidinously heterosexual Robert Plant, tight-trousered frontman of the Valhalla-bound Led Zeppelin, soaring vocal foil to the screaming demons of Jimmy Page's Gibson Les Paul and official wielder of the hammer of the gods? Or Clive Dunn, one moment mincing around Walmington-on-Sea as annoying Lance Corporal Jones in the BBC shitcom *Dad's Army* and the next, astoundingly, seizing the No. 1 spot in the British charts for three weeks with 'Grandad', the most sickening, saccharine, suicide-inducing song known to man?

While Zep were marauding across America in their private

jet (Plant's fondest memory of the Starship was 'oral sex, in turbulence'), laying waste to a nation's groupies and destroying concert attendance records and hotel suites (nay, entire floors) in equal number, the dismal Dunn was surrounded by a group of equally dire, estuary-accented schoolchildren droning on about the dubious merits of grandfathers.

I was only fifteen and the proud owner of Zep's first two albums, played to destruction in the school boot-room on a tiny, tinny plastic mono record player, when 'Grandad' plopped on to *Top of the Pops*. I distinctly remember the stunned silence in the common room, where we gathered every week to peer through the black-and-white snowstorm at *Top of the Pops*, as Dunn wheezed his way through what appeared to be a selection of verses written for a range of Hallmark cards pitched at people celebrating the first anniversary of their arrival in the hospice. And the uniformed urchins we grew to loathe (the vile song infested the charts for a dispiriting twenty-seven weeks) mewed, with plodding meter, about how lovely they thought the old sod was.

Well, it wasn't quite what the bad boys at my school thought of him. We thought he was a disgusting old git with an unhealthy interest in schoolgirls who very probably smelt of urine.

We were altogether more keen on the antics of Zep drummer John Bonham (RIP. Valhalla, he really was coming, as it turned out) and the legendary Zep roadies (who almost certainly did, from time to inebriated time, smell of urine, but in a good way). Our clear and away favourite Led legend was the infamous incident involving a red-headed groupie and a freshly hooked and similarly hued red snapper. (Let us just say that, while Dunn's pre-PC 'fuzzy wuzzies' might not have 'liked it up 'em', Zeppelin's adoring female fans clearly had no such reservations.)[100]

Then last weekend, in my forty-eighth year and with record player long ditched for an iPod upon which the Zep canon lives

---

100 Besides, which girl could possibly have resisted the unattributed invitation, 'Let's see if your red snapper likes our red snapper'? Now *that's* what you *call* seduction.

on (although funny how it doesn't sound quite so good in stereo, and stripped of all that scratchy white noise), I learn something that brings the horror of the whole 'Grandad' grotesquerie back to life. My twenty-two-year-old Royal Marine son, just back from the land of the ice and snow after three months spent living in Norwegian igloos and leaping into frigid fjords, has clearly, upon his return to balmier climes, had a rush of blood to the heart.

He is, he announces breezily (and clearly undeterred by his old man's similarly tender-aged but ultimately doomed venture into spliced monogamy), getting married next year.

To a woman three years his senior and, he calculates (faintly disapprovingly, I can't help feeling), only two or so years younger than the one I am seeing.

I bite my lip, shake his hand and say, 'Congratulations.'

At least, I mean to, but actually I say: 'Christ, she's not pregnant, is she?', which sort of spoils the moment. On the plus side, at least they are getting married in Vegas (very Zep), and not Bletchley (which is probably where I took a wrong turn: should have stayed on the M1 and kept on driving).

Not that I am worried for him, or her. He's old enough to shoot people, after all, and she, a midwife, brings replacements into the world faster than he can despatch them. No. Being entirely self-centred, what struck me was that I had just moved a big step closer to the moment when I become Clive Dunn, who, fantastically, *was just forty-eight when he recorded* 'Grandad'.

Virtually my age, in case you haven't been paying attention.

And if that isn't a good cause for panic, Captain Mainwaring, I don't know what is.

18
How to Get the Picture

Dear Mr Macrowave

A copy of your article, 'Cold Turkey', dated 12 December 2003, has just been passed to my department and, given references in previous of your columns to Walton-on-the-Naze, I fear that the gas company to which you are alluding may be the one for which I act as public relations manager. It disturbed me to see that a responsible journalist such as yourself would treat the extremely serious matter of deaths from carbon monoxide, linked to gas-boiler installations, so light-heartedly. I can assure you that we do everything in our power to avoid such unfortunate accidents. Certainly, despite your supposedly comic suggestion to the opposite, our Christmas card portraying a traditional robin was nothing more than a seasonal greeting to our valued customers and in no way intended to serve as some kind of threat that, unless you had your boiler serviced by us, then you had 'better prepare to be gassed to death' in your sleep. This type of coercive marketing would be a clear breach of our industry's code of conduct, which we take extremely seriously. May I take this opportunity of wishing you and Mrs Macrowave a happy, safe, Christmas.

Mr Stephen Pennefather, PR Manager, Eastern Gas and Water

Microwave Man writes: Are you serious? Happy? It was hell. And I could have been gassed by now for all you care! As it is, I'm heartbroken, older and none the wiser. Does this mean you'll service my boiler for nothing? How's the robin?

If the Greeks have a case for taking back their marbles (and it would have to be a large one, obviously, perhaps lined with straw), surely we can play the same game and request the repatriation of selected British art from around the world?

Well, you would think so, wouldn't you? But when I went to Boston the guards at the Museum of Fine Art almost lost *their* marbles when I stopped off on my way to the airport and asked them to give me a hand to the cab with Frederic Leighton's *The Painter's Honeymoon*. I said they could keep their sole Constable (yet another dreary view of the Stour Valley) and their only Turner (*The Slave Ship*, a searing work of proto-photojournalism horrifically relevant to the New World), but they were having none of it.

My motives for attempting to save this great painting for the nation weren't entirely selfless, I must admit. For me, as for the East India Company, a trip to Boston is rarely a tea party, serving as it does as an opportunity to skewer myself with remorse on a pilgrimage to what I have always assumed to be Leighton's celebration of marital bliss – rendered poignant by the fact that the artist never married.

A beautifully framed, life-size copy of Leighton's touching painting hung for years over the bed I shared with Laura (with whom I might still be now, I have always told myself, had we both not been quite so keen on sharing beds with other people). She first saw the painting while visiting her brother in New England (at least, she *said* it was her brother she was visiting) and soon, courtesy of Athena, Freddy's fop-haired artist and besotted young wife were at it in duplicate in our bedroom.

But then, in Boston this time, a shock revelation. As I stood in front of *The Painter's Honeymoon*, pointlessly spinning the wheels of my regret, I noticed something about the painting which, incredibly, had eluded me until now. Perhaps Leighton wasn't, after all, pining for the lifelong companionship he never found. Maybe he was cynically recording his relief at having been spared the necessity of trusting another human being. Blimey.

As one of Queen Victoria's favoured artists (although she was not, I believe, a muse), he would have avoided naked references to anything so lewd or antifamilial as infidelity (although the latent sexuality fair bulges out of most of his work: *Actaea, the Nymph of the Shore* is awash on a sea of pheromones, while *Girl with a Basket of Fruit* is clearly good for rather more than just your five daily portions).

But there, behind the bride and lurking in the shadows with all the inevitability of a faithless future, framed by the window through which spills the light caught so brilliantly in the folds of her emerald dress, is a small tree, bending under the weight of ripe fruit – the neoclassical artist's shorthand for temptation.

How could I have missed it (although, and thankfully for Leighton's later ennobling as Baron Leighton of Stretton, Her Majesty did as well)? Well, in the same way that I missed for so long all the clues that the love of my life had a parallel love life, I suppose. We never see what's right under our noses (why else would men wear those ridiculous moustaches?).

On reflection, writing the column about sleeping with Laura *was* a mistake, but sleeping with her had not been. Wanting to sleep with her had been a vestigial itch that had irritated me for seven years, and finally scratching had exorcized it like an operation removes an inflamed appendix. I'm not sure what drove her to it. Maybe it was the same for her. I'd ask her, but we're not talking now. There had been plenty of times over the years when she could have slipped back into intimacy with me, but she lacked the urgency, perhaps because she knew that I would always be there for her, waiting. Like she would always be there for me. Like a certainty, a redoubt, a resort, a guarantee.

Like a parachute.

The night it happened just happened to be a night when both of us had nothing to lose. We were both between relationships and, for once, she was the needy one. Over the years it had always been me, trying it on, urging her into bed, seeking and hunting a resolution, a final act that would tip the scales in my favour, leave me feeling that justice, in some obscure, carnal way, had been done. She had always parried my advances, often with humour. 'Blimey,' she once said, feeling my ardour against her. 'You could have somebody's eye out with that.' The rejection –

so casual, so unfeeling at a time when she knew I was lying hurt and deeply wounded – had rung on in my mind for years, echoing louder and louder until only a response of Shakespearean proportions could answer it.

And tonight – finally, wearily, unexpectedly – was the night.

I knew she was between relationships. Maybe she was just feeling down, sentimental and vulnerable. She took for granted that I would take advantage of that, and I didn't let her down. Yes, my dear, this is a dagger you see before you, and it could, indeed, have somebody's eye out.

I couldn't help myself. For one thing I still found her attractive. For another, it was the second shoe that I had been waiting to fall for eight years, and this time I didn't even have to weigh the pros and cons of betraying somebody else. For the first time in eight years it was just me and her and a bed.

I don't know if I expected to feel anything, but I was surprised when I didn't. For seven years I had wondered and worried that, through my own blind and insatiable search for something special and irreplaceable, I had let go the one thing that was truly special and irreplaceable. But that night, when my unexpected chance finally came to conduct one last search for love among the ruins, I found only ruins, handfuls of shrapnel and freedom from a myth.

What astonishes me now isn't so much that I wasted seven years of my life in mourning, but that I spent eight years with a woman whose nipples were off-limits. And now I realize that the nipple thing was symbolic of the central flaw in our relationship. To her, love and sex were two separate things. To me, they were the same thing.

'There's more to love than just sex,' she would say. She would say this a lot. What she meant was, 'Your sex drive is too high for me' (or, possibly, given events that later emerged, 'I have had too much sex already this week with other men and I am sore,' but who knows?).

'I know that,' I would say. 'But when I make love with you I'm showing you *how much* I love you. It's a physical expression of how I feel.'

'Bollocks. You just want a shag.'

She was right. I did want a shag. But not *just* a shag. And I suppose she had no idea how resentful I felt when she treated me like this. Unluckily for her, some of our female friends were more understanding.

Hey, perhaps that could be my excuse! What do you think? Actually, I don't need an excuse now, and I didn't feel like I had to have one then. Just an opportunity. I was never in the grip of philosophy, or morality. Just geography and chance. And so she and I would, once again, lie there, rigidly side by side, and I would forget the lovers' contract under the bed, forget my granny's advice never to let the sun go down on a disagreement, and backs would be turned and another long, speechless, sleepless night would be added to our Antarctic winter of long, frosty nights.

Yes, writing that column may have been a mistake, but sleeping with her had not been. Although it nearly was. A huge mistake.

As we lay there, the first time since the last time, eight years before, it all came back to me. The good stuff at the beginning, the mediocre stuff in the middle, and the bad stuff at the end. All those years I'd spent mourning her loss – our loss – and it was only now I realized that what I'd mounted and framed and hung in the hallway of my heart wasn't a true picture of how we had been but an idealized representation of how it might have looked – how I wanted it to have looked. My Baron Leighton had fooled my Queen Victoria.

Christ. The time I'd wasted dusting that picture.

And then, lying in the dark, fingers touching flesh but barely recognizing what had become the unfamiliar landscape of her body, mouths and hands trying just too urgently to knead something warm and mutual from the cold, hard dough of our estrangement, I discovered that I wasn't the only one who'd been marking time, tricked by an inaccurate vision of the past into embracing only sceptically and half-heartedly the possibility of another life.

She whispered it so quietly at first that I wasn't sure I'd heard right above the squeak of the bed. I didn't break my rhythm but I whispered back, into her ear: *What did you say?*

Despite the tone of affection I had deliberately injected into my voice, I felt her body tense slightly. I guess she knew already that she had miscalculated, that she had lost the gamble. Now she was committed to the consequences. Her fingers dug sharply into the small of my back. I had no recollection of her doing that when we used to make love. But then, there was almost nothing about this body and the way it worked that I recognized. She was twenty-four when I first slept with her. She was thirty-nine now. God knows how many different hands had . . .

I said, she whispered, still rising to meet my slow thrusts, *'that I'm not on the Pill.'*

Holy Moses! She was thirty-nine now. And running out of time to have the child she had once said she could have only with me. I wonder if she'd mentioned that to the idiot for whom she'd left me?

I pulled out faster than the British from Suez. I wanted to say, *Christ! What the hell do you think you're doing? Are you insane? Is it my fault you never had children with anyone else? That you talked yourself into believing that you should only – could only – have children with me? Jesus, it was you who left me, remember? I'm screwing you now only because I can, because for me it ends a chapter, closes a circle, completes a cycle – because you bloody well had it coming! It doesn't matter to me that you are no longer with the man you left me for, it still works for me as revenge and what was mine is mine again, however briefly, and under my terms and you have to be insane if you think I would ever have you back . . .*

I *wanted* to say all that, but instead all I said was, 'Christ! Are you insane?'

And I could see that that was enough, that she was hurt, that she was bewildered, that she probably hadn't planned this, that maybe her madness had taken her by surprise as much as it had me and that she was trying just for once not to think too much and just to act and maybe – just maybe – find a way back to a golden age that actually, at its very best, as we both quite instantly and finally realized there and then, was almost certainly made only of tin.

She didn't stay the night, or even the rest of that hour. After she'd gone I lay there staring at *The Painter's Honeymoon* in its gilt frame, the couple frozen in that moment of supposed supreme affection. Whoever they'd been, I thought, they'd been dead for years.

In the morning I got up, took the picture down off the wall and carried it to an empty skip at the end of the street. I tossed it in, and the glass smashed as the frame hit the bottom. Over the next days and weeks it would be buried under rubble – half-bricks, concrete, smashed wooden windowframes, doors, empty Coke cans and crisp packets and all the crap and detritus of passing humanity. So much evidence buried under so much sediment at its moment in time. How long before it found its place in a landfill pit, and how long after that before it would simply disappear – or be exhumed and misinterpreted by some future archaeologist or palaeontologist who adds it to the fossil record because he thinks he knows it all but actually has absolutely no sodding idea?

Until the day before, that thought would have brought tears to my eyes. Now I'm just slightly miffed because I have to take sugar soap to the stain on the wall where the picture hung.

I heard from Laura just once more. Just before the column came out, I read it again and thought it did sound a bit harsh and, judging by the text message she sent me the day it appeared, so did she. It just said, 'Cunt', which, from a woman who, as far as I knew, had never used the word in her well-brought-up life, was saying something. I dug out the column and read it again. Somehow, it looked worse in print:

Revenge was about to be handed to me on a plate. Great. Only, I suddenly realized, I didn't want it any more . . . It was OK. Not unlike, I imagine, it would have been if we had stayed together for all those years.

Hmm. Yes, I suppose not great to have your bedside manner critically appraised in print. I read on:

It was curiously sad, yet settling, to discover that the flame of which I had been the keeper for so long had guttered out, unnoticed. Later, as I lay there staring at the ceiling, I deleted one more name from the list in my head headed, 'Is she the one?'

I thought about it for a bit and then hit on a brilliant, one-word reply: 'What?' Which, on further reflection, probably wasn't that brilliant after all. Beep beep, went the mobile a few minutes later. She had elaborated.

You complete and utter fucking disgusting selfish obnoxious self-centred heartless fucking cunt.

And that was the last time I heard from her. I guess she didn't get pregnant, and I guess she's pleased about that, but who knows?

It wasn't the only response that column provoked, but among them was one I really hadn't been expecting. It was an email from the Boer. I'd heard nothing from her since Christmas, hadn't expected to and, now that I had, thought it was, frankly, a bit rich.

'I cannot believe you slept with her, of all people,' she wrote.

I couldn't believe she really thought it was any of her business. So I replied: 'I cannot believe you think it is any of your business. How's Ben?'

Three days later, she called me. 'I need your advice,' she said. 'I found out something about Ben. You're a serial adulterer: I thought you might be able to advise me.'

Quite breathtaking. Lovers one minute, confidants the next? Sometimes I worried for this woman's soul. I should have told her to bugger off, but I was intrigued. Besides, I liked looking at her. And double besides, I was on a roll. Maybe I could exorcize two ghosts in the same week.

Only, I didn't like what I found myself looking at when we met an hour later in a Starbucks on the South Bank. Typically, it would be me who was early for an appointment, but she had beaten me to it and was slumped, head on hand, in one of the worn armchairs. She looked even more ropey than it did. She was in her traditional uniform: a grubby pair of old green combat trousers, T-shirt and pale blue surfer-brand fleece. Normally, she'd light up any old crap, but today she looked washed up, a long way from the surf of South Africa, or even Cornwall. Her hair was lank, untidy, her face blotchy. She looked like she might have been crying, or as if she'd stayed up all night. I hoped that it was crying. I looked around for it but, to my surprise, nowhere could I find even a twinge of a need to reach out and protect her. Outstanding.

'Hi, how's it going?' she said, trying hard to sound like her usual breezy, confident, indifferent self.

I sat down opposite her. Yes, she had definitely been crying. Blimey. Don't remember much of that when she was with me. As she spoke, a feeling of indignation started to build inside me. I listened, but I couldn't believe what I was hearing. She had been at Ben's house while he was out and had gone upstairs to use his computer and send some emails. She found that he'd left the computer on and, stupidly, had also left his email account open. Next, she found herself reading a series of exchanges with a woman whose name she had never heard him mention. To me, it was pretty obvious what was going on.

To her, too, I think, only she was trying not to believe it.

And only a fool wouldn't have seen the truth.

Sorry, babe, can't meet Saturday after all, K's now not working. Aagh! Maybe next weekend? I'll text you as soon as I know her movements. God! Can't wait to see you.

Aagh? She'd printed it out and brought it along for me to see. Me. You know – the guy she'd dumped to be with this jerk. Truly outstanding.

They had fought, obviously. He had denied hanky-panky (as one does in these situations), but she had stormed out and gone back to her own place. And now she was here. Talking to me. About her problems with the man she had left me to be with. I looked at her hard, trying to see in through her flickering eyes.

'What do you want me to say?'

She shrugged.

'I don't know; whatever you think. Am I overreacting?'

I stared at her. I told her what I thought. 'Of course he's screwing her. You'd be an idiot to stay with him, but I guess I would say that. Do you love him?'

The question seemed to take her by surprise. It kind of took me by surprise, too, and I regretted asking it in case she answered it. Then she started to cry and just nodded. Oh.

'Did you love me?' *Why are you asking all these stupid, redundant questions, you stupid, redundant old sod?*

She carried on crying and carried on nodding.

'Oh, really? That's nice to know. Until when, exactly? I mean, at what point did you stop loving me? The same time you started loving him? Or just before? Shortly afterwards? Was the baby thing ever really an issue, or just an excuse, a way off the hook?'

She looked bewildered and carried on crying. I didn't care. Weep away, I thought. Once, I would have melted: poor little thing, so far from home, so vulnerable behind her iron mask of fierce self-reliance. Once. But now I thought, sod that, and sod her. I'm finally out of the old protection racket.

'You want to know what I think?' I said. 'I think you have a hell of a nerve to ask me to come here and talk about this. I can't believe that anyone could be that insensitive. I loved you. In fact, since we're talking timings, I loved you until approximately thirty seconds ago.'

And, actually, maybe not even then.

And, come to that, I suddenly thought, maybe never, and maybe nobody.

The funny thing about excavating past relationships is that you come to realize how, over time, they become confused with each other; how the sediment of experiences we are laying down all the time crushes on itself, compresses months, years, lifetimes into a thin band of time called 'Then'. And this makes reminiscing fraught, and accurate archaeology and fossil interpretation impossible.

Do you remember that night we flew to Vegas on the spur of the moment, arrived in time for a slap-up brekkie at the Grand, drank martinis by the pool and gambled the afternoon away until we had spent £2,000 in slot machines and then checked into the bridal suite, drank two bottles of Dom Perignon and made passionate love in the spa before catching the plane home by the skin of our teeth? And you were sick on the plane as it touched down at Heathrow, two hours before you had to be at work?

'No. It must have been someone else.'

Yes. It must have been someone else. Who was this somebody else that it nearly always turns out to have been? I'd love to meet her one day. We seemed to have had so much fun. Then.

I got up and left her there and walked along the river. I really like the Thames. It's a constant. It runs through my London, it runs through my past and gives it a sense of time and place. It doesn't matter that there are too many tourists. It doesn't matter that the warehouses have all been replaced with luxury apartments topped by penthouses with rooflines as absurdly flicked up as the hair of the absurdly overpaid twenty-seven-year-old Porsche-driving ex-girlfriend-of-mine shagging bankers or derivative dealers or privet-hedge-fund managers, whatever the sodding hell that is. None of that matters. It is mine, and it can't be tarnished by the transient nobodies who pass through my city and my life. It is comforting to know that there, under the mud, are eighteenth-century pipe stems and Roman swords and Bronze Age bones. And, in all probability, old Kinks records. I know exactly what the great Ray Davies was on about when he wrote 'Waterloo Sunset'.

The air felt fresh and I felt free. In just one week I'd managed to jettison two pieces of baggage, years after they'd jettisoned me. As I walked, I rang Merv.

'Hello,' he said. 'I was wondering where you'd got to. Thought you might have topped yourself.'

He always says this if we haven't spoken for a couple of weeks.

It should be me saying it, of course, but that's part of the game.

'How's the asylum?'

'It's a madhouse. Very busy. Just spent a week in Germany, actually, recruiting trick cyclists.'

'Where?'

'Dresden.'

'Blimey. You must have gone down well, with a name like Harris.'

'I told them I was from the tweed branch of the family, rather than the carpet-bombing arm. Of course, Uncle Arthur was a bit of a godsend to all those post-war German town-planners. They'd have been eating turnips until 1965 if it hadn't been for him. Or nail soup.'

'Besides, they started it. They had it coming.'

'Well, yes, I think they probably did, but I didn't say as much. I was trying to win them over, you see.'

I had once worked on a local paper in Bedford with a sub-editor called Reg, who had flown in Lancasters as a bomb-aimer with RAF Bomber Command during the war. Once, a group of German publishers had toured the plant and, at one point, thanks to an oversight by the managing editor, they found themselves grouped around Reg as he marked up that week's WI reports ('the quiz was won by Mrs Drudge, Mrs Smith thanked Professor Gormley for his fascinating, thought-provoking and often humorous three-hour talk on variable-wave magnetron oscilloscope tracking, and the single entry for the cake-baking competition was Ms Pile's unusual life-size representation of a male organ in sponge and marzipan, which was enjoyed later by many ladies along with a cup of tea, made this week by Mrs Dole . . .').

'These chaps are from Germany, Reg,' said the managing editor, in the falsely intimate and patronizing tones of a normally unpleasant care-home owner showing around inspectors from the Department of Health. ('And remember: don't mention the cold baths, or it'll be the worse for you, you old bastard!') 'They're here to see how we do things.' Reg barely glanced up before returning to the business of subbing the WI reports. One of the men leant forward to see what Reg was doing, and Reg instinctively covered his papers with his corduroy-sleeved arm.

'*Ja*,' said the man, slightly embarrassed and straightening up again. 'We are from Dresden, actually.'

Reg pushed his reading glasses back up his beaky nose and grunted.

'Ah!' said the visitor, brightening visibly. 'You know Dresden?'

Reg turned to peer up at him and for a moment seemed to be scrutinizing his face as though he hoped to recognize the man. After a slightly strained silence, he said, 'Only from the air,' and returned to his work. The Germans moved on to Sport and, no doubt, some ribbing about 1966.

'And did you win them over?' I asked Merv.

'Yes. I told them Jung was all the rage now in the NHS, and they were ecstatic. And then I told them I was Jewish.'

'You are.'

'Yes, I know that, thanks. Play the guilt card. Works every time. Especially with Austrians.'

'I didn't realize Austria had been annexed again.'

'It has for psychiatrists. Anyway, I had to fight them off in the end. Bristol will be the new Vienna by the end of the year and the kids can have the latest pointless electronic toys for Christmas – huge bonus in it for me.'

'And for British psychiatry, too.'

'Well, I suppose so.'

I told Merv what had happened with the Boer, and he was off on his favourite subject. Well, *one* of his favourite subjects, with the loose heading, 'What is This Thing Called Love?' Or, as he prefers to place the emphasis, 'What is *this* thing called, love?'

'Believing in love is like believing in God. It's absolutely necessary in order to justify our otherwise unjustifiable existence. It's impossible to dispute because it is impossible to prove.'

'So *you* say.'

'Exactly. We have to believe it because without that belief we are left with nothing but to see ourselves exactly as we really are

– totally and absolutely alone and living lives of complete and utter pointlessness. Even frogs need other frogs around to make them feel part of a bigger, a bigger . . .'

'Frogdom?'

'Frogdom, yes. Exactly. We simply pick on the first person who drifts past in whom we can find some traits we find pleasing – a love of literature, a passion for horses, large breasts – and then spend the rest of our time with them deluding ourselves into believing they are The One and doing our level best to change everything about them that doesn't chime with the ideal we've carried around unwittingly since our love radar was hard-wired to a character we once met in a book, or a film or a painting. That's the entire and unspoken point of art. Art is the hope of love, and therefore art is a deceit.'

'Or a jar of pickles.'

'What?'

'You know. A character you meet: like Mrs Elswood on the pickle jars.'

'Oh, yes, I know who you mean. You too, eh? She is rather lovely.'

'Well, she's mine, so you can forget that. I saw her first. Besides, you have Helen. Your wife and the mother of your children. How are they, by the way?'

'I don't know.'

'What do you mean, you don't know? Well, are they alive, for a start?'

'After a fashion, yes. The male has lost the will to communicate, and the female has found the power of cosmetics.'

'Really? At twelve?'

'They grow up fast these days. I blame the parents.'

'Me too. So what about the love thing? Why are you with them if there is no such thing as love? Why aren't you living alone and drinking too much?'

'I *am* living alone and drinking too much.'

'I don't mean in the existential sense, dullard. By the way, did you know that "dullard" is one of only seven words of English to have passed unchanged into Inuit? So if you fall through the ice while trying to cut a fishing hole in the Arctic, any passing Eskimo is as likely to call out, "Dullard" as he is to use one of his own language's 800 words for "idiot".'

'I think it's 800 words for "snow", not "idiot". What are the other six?'

'Lemon, corduroy, flan, bitumen, Leonardcohen and septic,' I said.

'Surely Leonard Cohen is two words?'

'Not in Inuit. And you'll note that love isn't one of the words that survives translation to the frozen north. So if you don't believe in love, what do you say instead of "I love you" when the occasion arises?'

'I say "I love you" of course, because I do. I love my wife and I love my children.'

I stop by the Oxo Tower, gazing up. I'm not sure why, but God, that building annoys me. I frown up at it as though doing so might bring it tumbling down. I've noticed that, as I get older, I seem to be pulling faces on my own in public and even muttering out loud. How long, I wonder, before I start licking windows?

'But you just said . . .'

'Yes, but I'm only human.'

'What about the hose in the car?'

'That's in case I ever wise up. Got to dash. Ward rounds.'

I keep forgetting to ask Merv if he is still taking the Prozac.

By the time I reach the Festival Hall, I have devised another metaphor for love and life. Each relationship is like a glass slide, or a transparency, bearing the details of all that has passed between you. By the time you reach my age – provided you have been as indecently active as I have – there are so many slides, each stacked on top of the next, that, seen from the present – gazing down, as it were – there is such a profusion of overlaid colours and shapes that it is impossible to tell one memory, or even one relationship, from another.

Life is, eventually, all one big mud pie, so many colours and textures blended by time and perspective that they combine to form the single colour of the past: a dull brown not unlike the low-tide sludge that conceals the secrets of the Thames. I am so pleased with this that I record it on my iPod, there and then. That's how bloody modern I am, I tell myself.

As it turned out, that wasn't the last time I saw the Boer. I wasn't sure why, but we kept in touch, patching up the row first by email, and then over dinner. The next time we met she had her brave face back on, but I found that all her attractiveness had somehow drained away. Not that I wouldn't have shagged her had the opportunity arisen, of course, but it would have been out of plain spite. I certainly wasn't going to go out of my way to pull it off.

Sitting in Pizza Express, she admitted she had decided to give Ben a second chance. I laughed.

'Good,' I said. 'You deserve each other.'

I decided that this was to be our last supper, with absolutely no prospect of resurrection. I had my usual: Veneziana, with added pepperoni. I've been eating this for almost twenty years – ever since, come to think of it, Laura took me to my first branch because Pizza Express was the only company that gave money to the Liberal Democrats. She disliked pizza, and I couldn't stomach the Lib Dems, but we compromised. Now she has gone but the Veneziana remains, a constant in my life that has superseded its origins. As far as I know, Venice is still there. No matter which branch I am in, the Veneziana has never – not once – tasted the slightest bit different or ever let me down. And that's worth a lot. What's more, twenty-five pence from every one I eat goes to save Venice from sinking, and sometimes I think the fact that Venice is still there is down solely to me. I'm certainly responsible for at least a large chunk of St Mark's Square keeping its head above water. (I'm probably also to blame for half the candidates fielded by the Lib Dems at the last three General Elections, but I prefer not to think about that.)

I have never been to Venice, partly because if I keep eating the pizzas, surely it won't be going anywhere, and so there's no rush, and partly because it can't possibly be as lovely as the Canaletto paintings and is almost certainly a lot smellier. Some realities are best kept at a distance.

The Boer had a salad, with dough balls. We talked about her filthy book, which had so far failed to find a publisher, which was fine by me, as I wasn't too wild about all those fragments of me and her being detonated and flung out into the world. As usual, we tried to score points off each other. We never really did have conversations so much as verbal sparring matches in which neither of us ever had the last word. As she forked her dough balls I teased her about her fantasy of owning a small farm in Africa where she would keep dogs and raise chickens.

'You'll probably end up dying alone, or beaten to death by your fat, drunken Boer of a husband. Or pecked to death by your chickens.'

I asked her questions about Ben, so I could show her how much I didn't care, and told her in detail about the night Laura and I had spent together, so I could see how much she did. And then I told her I was thinking of having a vasectomy, and suddenly her face was a picture, and that's how I will remember her, until the memory slips beneath the surface of the brown mud along with all the others.

For a moment, just a brief moment, she looked almost angry, as though I had spoiled a plan which, although I wasn't a party to, she felt I must surely have known about instinctively. She looked hurt, cheated. I wondered briefly whether she might have been regretting our ending and had been struggling to find a way past her destructive stubbornness. A few weeks before, I might have said something to help her – given her a face-saving way out, a way of telling me she still loved me, wanted me back. But now . . .

A brief moment, a flash of faded feelings, an unbidden sound-track, courtesy of that old depressive Don Henley. For some reason best known to itself, 'The Boys of Summer' is the pitiful 'I'll win you back' anthem the in-brain iPod has selected for this particular failed romance. The sad boy pining for the surfer chick who's always peeking out from behind her Wayfarers for the next best thing . . .

But no buts, Don. Now I just didn't care.

But I did like the look on her face. It lasted only a second, but I knew her well enough to know that she had been taken utterly by surprise. Almost instantaneously it had gone, and now she was angry with herself for having given it away, but given it away she had.

Ha.

I win, I thought. And then I said it out loud: 'I win. Ha. Chocolate fudge cake? Or are you on a diet?'

Under the table, she kicked me on the shin with one of her big, ugly clogs. Three years. All the stuff we did, all the things we went through; in the mud, and sinking fast. Already I couldn't remember the last time we made love. And you know what? Even the memory of the first time was slipping away. And I didn't care one bit.

At least I got a final column out of her. And you'd be surprised how difficult it can be sometimes to find those 750 words every week. Sometimes.

Save a Drop for Me
Friday 13 February 2004

I was searching the internet this week, looking for information about vasectomies and sperm banks, and, having no immediate joy, wandered slightly off course, as you do. I'll get back to the banking thing in a second, but I just wanted to share with you a Google moment that brought to mind Shaw's observation that Britain and America were two nations divided by a common language.

Stumbling on to the website of Colorado's *Windsor Tribune*, I was delighted to read the headline, 'Woman celebrates ninetieth with spunk'. 'More than fifty people,' reports the *Trib* (slogan: 'We've got you covered'), 'came to celebrate her birthday.'

What an unusual tradition. Google the phrase 'Bette Keefer giggled' and enjoy this fine, Keilloresque newspaper.

OK, back to the chase: to snip, or not to snip?

I shan't try you with the details of the incident that threw into sharp focus the possible implications of accidentally impregnating the wrong woman (or, indeed, the right woman, whatever that is). Suffice to say that, having only two weeks ago suffered the body blow of learning that my son was getting married next year (and that grandfatherhood was tottering towards me, a Zimmer-mounted outrider to Death himself), I found myself facing the prospect of hanging around playgrounds at the age of sixty-five ('Officer, I assure you . . .').

Now it just so happened that our old friend the Mucky, Plucky Boer and I (lovers, regular readers will recall, reinvented briefly and precariously as friends in the wake of her ditching me for expressing a keen lack of interest in breeding) were bandying badinage over pizzas about our respective current belles and beaus when the sight of her slicing open a dough ball prompted me to mention that I was considering a vasectomy.

Blimey. Her normal poker face dropped like pork-belly prices on news of a porcine population explosion. 'Talk to me before you do,' she blurted out.

Why? Did she want to do it herself, perhaps with a rusty razor? Or . . . no, surely she wasn't harbouring the idea that, after a few years of playing the field, she could come back to me for a dose of the white stuff?

Sick, and wrong. I mean, what am I? A prize Charolais bull? (And where's the money in that? The going rate among the British Charolais Society for a dose from a bull on something called, wonderfully, the Semen Royalty Scheme, seems to be around £12, plus VAT: about the going rate for an upmarket margarita, although while the genetic cocktail seems to come with – or indeed *in* – a straw, there is no mention of a little paper umbrella. And I won't get into bed for less than £20.)

I didn't know whether to be angry or flattered, and I settled for smugly indignant, but it got me thinking: how many of the women I have been with would have been less interested in me, albeit in a subconscious way, had they thought that I was firing blanks?

The upside of a vasectomy is obvious, which is why one in five blokes has one. These days it's a walk-in (although possibly crawl-out) op that costs less than a 40gb iPod and much, much less than university fees. On the other hand, my friend Simon had one and ended up with a sac the size of an extremely tender grapefruit (which ruled out visits to New Covent Garden for a while).

Marie Stopes, which annually disconnects an impressive 180,000 testicles, says that severing the old *vas deferens* can make a vast and positive difference to a chap's love life.

On the other hand, what's all this about pain and ice packs? Experience tells one that when medics use the word 'pain', as opposed to 'discomfort', we are talking sheer bloody agony. And, I read, on occasion 'post-operative pain can be experienced for a long time, sometimes up to two years'. *Two years?* Christ. Almost as long as a degree course.

Meanwhile, if anyone's interested, my genes are yours. A snip at a tenner a straw. I might even toss in an umbrella.

19
How to Boil an Egg

Dear Microwave Man

I have just started reading your column regularly. I've known it was there for some time – I'm a big fan of the Times *cook, on the opposite page to you – but I never really got into it because I didn't think I could cope with two cooking columns in one day! Now, imagine my embarrassment as I finally realize that Microwave Man is not about preparing quick, nutritious meals for busy, professional people but about something entirely different. I get the joke now, but why the title? How was I supposed to know you were writing about relationships?*

Mrs C. Wildbore-Smyth, Woburn, Beds.

Microwave Man writes: I'm sorry, but I think you may be mistaken. It's never been about relationships; it's always been about knocking up a tasty hot dish or two in as short a time as possible. Now please ask the nurse to come to the phone.

Most things begin by mistake, and the microwave oven was no exception. It is not widely known outside MI5, MI6 – and, indeed, the M25 – that radar evolved as a by-product of a British attempt to develop a war-winning 'Death Ray' that would fry German airmen and reduce their aircraft to cinders as they crossed the Channel. This is true.

That proved a little ambitious and, as the project descended through disappointment to debacle, the mission objective was gradually downgraded from 'Death Ray', through 'Harmful Ray', to 'Quite Annoying Ray', who turned out to be an irritating little bloke who worked in the stores at Biggin Hill. This, if all went well, would overcook the onboard meals of the crews of German bombers as they flew on missions to deliver long-term employment prospects to London's town-planners and perhaps depress them a bit, leaving them feeling extremely peckish and temperamental by the time they got back to Germany.

Even this, however, proved beyond the scope of Britain's scientists, although several chickens near by did lay a few batches of hard-boiled eggs, and some German aircrew reported that chocolate bars in their pockets had mysteriously melted before they could eat them. Even this – had the phenomenon been recognized and properly developed – could have delivered a serious blow to Luftwaffe morale,[101] now known to have been heavily dependent on sugar highs.

One unfortunate side-effect, from the British perspective, was that the coffee in the airmen's flasks was often found to be still piping hot upon return to the Fatherland, which was especially odd as it had been no better than tepid at the time of departure (the Germans – putting all their energies into developing the jet engine, heavy water and intercontinental ballistic missiles – had failed to invent an equivalent to the British NAAFI: this simple mistake could well have cost them the war).

In 1942, the Germans retaliated with a 'Dairy Ray', operated from the bomb bay of a modified Junkers 88, which they hoped would curdle milk in the udders of cows grazing on the South Downs. Ironically, its only effect was to ruin the milky tea in the urns on a handful of radar stations along the south coast[102] (where morale nevertheless remained strong) and to provoke one small herd of heifers near Dungeness to produce what was then called 'The Devil's Wee', widely available today as 'skimmed milk' (which, in 1942 – when less was still most definitely a great deal less than more – was of no interest to anybody, let alone

---

101 Indeed, recent research has revealed that many German scientists were switched from vital rocket-production tasks late in 1943 to search for an ultimately elusive radar-resistant 'super chocolate' at the Hachez factory in Bremen.

102 Some sources argue that this was coincidence and that the milk used there may simply have been off.

worth an extra three pence a pint). The herd was machine-gunned by MI5 operatives disguised as dairy maids and then, for good measure, blown up and buried in quicklime. Churchill had it put about that the cows had been destroyed in a methane explosion and that, until the records were sensationally opened to the public in 1972, was an end to the matter.[103]

None of which is entirely true. What *is* true is that the microwave oven was developed as a by-product of radar, and purely by accident. After the war, scientists sat around trying to find other uses for things which, because they had invented them in a bit of a hurry while under fire, they didn't fully understand. One of these things was the magnetron, the device at the heart of radar that generated the radio waves that bounced off incoming enemy bombers and showed them up as blips on screens. This enabled the RAF to scramble fighter aircraft (had they known what we now know, it could also have enabled them to scramble eggs) and to win the war (a decision later revoked by Hollywood in favour of America).

Fast-forward, in fact, to war-winning America, 1946: Dr Percy Spencer, a self-taught engineer with the Raytheon corporation, is fiddling around with a radar tube, pondering to what use it might be put now there are no more enemy bombers to detect (at this stage the Iron Curtain was still under construction, or possibly had not yet come back from the cleaners). Umbrella stand, paper weight, doorstop? He ponders. Then he suddenly notices that the chocolate bar in the top pocket of his lab coat, which he had been planning to eat on his break, has melted.

Boy, is he pissed off. First impotence, and now this.

Never mind. At least he has invented the microwave oven. He

103 A special American force was sent to seize the German scientists responsible before they fell into Russian hands but was beaten to the prize by a fast-travelling lightweight unit of commandos from the British Milk Marketing Board, which raced ahead of the main body of Allied troops on specially converted experimental electric floats (later to be seen in peacetime service on the streets of many of Britain's towns). The Americans and Russians were left with nothing but a few rocket scientists, and Britain went on to lead the world in the production of semi-skimmed milk – a lead lost only when Margaret Thatcher banned school milk in 1970.

calls over his assistant and places an egg within range of the microwaves.

'Watch this, Eddie,' he says, chuckling to himself. 'No. Here; lean in: watch closer.'

Eddie leans forward, intrigued to see the egg wobbling and shaking by itself on the lab bench, and when it suddenly explodes he becomes the first microwave man to get egg on his face. But not, alas, the last.

Are we buying *this*? I hope so, because this bit really is true. Spencer and the rest of the lab gang had a lot of fun that week, driving popcorn crazy, bursting dozens of eggs and making the mistake (not for the last time in the otherwise distinguished history of the microwave oven) of trying to dry the wet fur of the lab's cat on full power for four minutes. All of which explains why the first microwave oven was called the Radar Range (and not, as Spencer had at first proposed, the Pussy Broiler: he was also a self-taught marketing man) and why, on early models, suburban cooks who lived near airports could often see inbound flights coming a long time before they heard them.

'And that,' I say, noticing that Cornelia's attention has already started to drift – she seems to be counting the bricks in the wall behind me – 'is why you should use me for other things: science, arts, interviews . . . I can turn my hand to writing about anything. Not just stuff about men and their midlife crises. It's shrivelling my brain. Not to mention my penis.'

A wince of distaste at the 'P' word. At least it gets her attention back from studying the fruits of the London Brick Company and on to what I was saying. Cunningly, I have followed her out of the office and on to the smoking deck, where she often retreats to read proofs and have a crafty fag.

'Oh, for God's sake, stop moaning,' she says. 'What's the matter with you? You're working, aren't you? You're having to fend off the attentions of deranged women readers, aren't you? Christ, never mind *pay*! I should be charging *you* a commission! Besides, who else have I got who would be prepared to expose the inner workings of his sick, tortured mind and reveal for the vicarious pleasure of our smugly settled readers the ins and outs – as 'twere – of his life?'

'So-*called* life, I think you mean.'

'Quite. Come on: look on the bright side. You're almost fifty you can retire in a couple of years.'

Yeah, right. To the Dun Bullshittin' Home for Distressed Old Hacks. Nice.

Cornelia takes a deep drag on her cigarette and peers at me through eyes half shut against the wreathing smoke. 'Tell you what. Do this thing for me tomorrow and I'll think about what you've said.'

What, like a last job, a final heist; the big one that'll set me up for life? I've seen that film. It always ends in a hail of bullets and a pool of blood. *No: I told you, Buggsie, I'm going straight. I can't do no more time.*

'Go on. I'm listening.'

Who's the wheelman?

'There's this new Jack Nicholson film out soon . . .'

Oh God. I can see what's coming. That hail of bullets.

'. . . which is supposed to be very good. It's called *Something's Gotta Give*. It's all about . . .'

. . . a dirty old goat who chases young skirt until he finally meets his match in a beautiful woman his own age and, thanks to her inner beauty and wisdom, realizes the error of his ways . . .

'. . . And I'd like you to go to a press screening in Soho tomorrow and then write me a piece for Thursday's paper about why men like you find younger women so appealing.'

Men like me? Heterosexual men, you mean? 'Can't I just write a list? The Editor likes lists.'

'No. Fifteen hundred words. Oh, and there's an added incentive, in addition to the prospect of further full-time employment. I'd like you to watch it in the company of a beautiful, younger woman.'

'Somebody of my own choosing, or do you have someone in mind?'

She smiles. 'Oh, yes. Yes, I do. But it's a surprise. She'll meet you at the screening. Oh, by the way: liked your piece about vasectomies. Had it done yet?'

'Er, no, since you ask.'

'Good. I should hold fire if I were you.'

Actually, I think I saw it coming, but I said nothing. We all like surprises. I certainly saw *her* coming the following evening, scraped-back blonde hair bobbing as she strutted down the west side of Soho Square, haughtily indifferent to the heads she was turning. The gorgeous, but definitely not pouting, Amelia. This must, I thought, be Cornelia's idea of a joke. Amelia and I have not so much as had eye contact in the three months since I realized that she'd been sitting virtually opposite me – in my case because I'd be buggered if I was going to give her the satisfaction of thinking I was like all the other blokes in the office, tripping over their tongues every time she walked past – and in hers because she had long ago learnt either to step over those tongues without even registering the faces of their owners or to pin them to the carpet with her heels.

And now here she was, shimmying towards me and our rendezvous with Jack. Nice. Oh, well. How hard would it be to maintain a façade of professional indifference for an hour and a half? In the dark? I rummaged around in my box of tricks for the mask labelled 'Professional indifference'. Come on, it had to be in there somewhere . . .

Besides, this was a good test of my fresh resolve, my decision to pick on women only of my own age. Well, give or take a decade or two. How old was Amelia? Maybe twenty-six. Possibly even twenty-five. Not good. Definitely not good.

She's reached the entrance and seems not to have seen me, sliding right past and through the door. It gives me a chance to look her up and down, from the tip of her thrown-back head, down the curvy lines of the soft, short, clinging dress, to the toes of her high-heeled shoes. *Oh, God, almost certainly wearing stockings*, groans a voice that I immediately suppress.

I follow her through the doors and say, 'Amelia?' She turns

and smiles and, I am certain, *pretends* not to recognize me. 'It's Jonathan,' I am obliged to add.

She looks at me for a moment and then, almost royally, extends one pale, freckled hand, and it's quite a fight not to kiss it, or maybe to bow, or curtsy. Instead I reach out to take it, but it is gone almost before my fingers have closed, sliding silkily out of my grip.

'Oh, yes, hello,' she says. 'I hope I'm not too late. I had an interview to do on the other side of town and the traffic was dreadful.'

She is late, but not too late.

'That's OK,' I say, 'it starts in a couple of minutes. I have our tickets . . .' But, as I head towards the stairs that lead down to the screening room, she moves across the foyer towards the bar. I stop and dumbly follow, and I can't help noticing the way that dress ebbs and flows around her bottom as she walks. It's helping to loosen my grip on my anxiety about missing the start of the film.

'I think I would like a vodka and tonic,' she says, not really to the barman and not really to me. 'With no ice.'

'Make that two,' I say to the guy, who's staring at Amelia. He makes it two, almost without once taking his eyes off her and taking as long as he reasonably can, and eventually we walk into the cinema. The film is just starting and there is tut-tutting as we edge along the back row to our seats, but these are free-loading hacks, just like us, I think, and they can just bugger off.

Back row? Cornelia's joke is beginning to develop depth.

Amelia sits down but then makes a bit of a show of removing her coat – Jesus: is that *fur*? – and turning off her phone, although first she sends a text. I know full well that all this is designed solely to piss off the tutters some more. And it does.

Finally, she settles, but then leans into me and whispers close to my ear. So close, in fact, that, with every third word or so, her lips brush my skin. 'Cornelia did tell me about this, but quite frankly I was dashing out and didn't really take it in. Why are we here?'

Why indeed . . .

'Have you heard of Microwave Man?'

'Yes, of course. He's the old saddo who ruins the fashion spread once a week by droning on about all the gullible young chicks he's supposedly shagging. Why?'

Oh, great.

'No reason. We're here to watch this film and then write a piece pegged to it about how older men are drawn to younger women, and what we think about that.'

She gives a sort of delicate little snort and says, 'I think I already know what I think about that.'

I take a big swallow of vodka, drain the plastic cup and wish I'd bought two for myself. If I am going to be ritually humiliated, I might as well be insensitive. As if reading my mind, she reaches into her substantial and, certainly, must-have bag, pulls out a miniature bottle of champagne and thrusts it into my hand. She has another for herself and opens it with a few slashes of her nails and a couple of practised twists of the wrist.

And so here I am, forty-eight and sitting in the back row of a private cinema alongside a woman twenty-one years my junior, and there's old Jack, pretty pleased with himself, driving across the screen in his sports car as the opening titles roll, beautiful young girl at his side and that patented latter-day Smug Jack look on his face that promises the Schadenfreude-psyched audience: 'Lordy, I'm riding high right now, but there surely is a long-due fall a-coming.'

Oh-oh, I think, pausing bottle to lips and trying really very hard to keep my left leg from making contact with the woman at my side. I really am not going to like this very much. I pull out pencil and notepad and lean away towards the empty seat to my right, resting on the armrest and writing in my head as I make notes.

Something's Gotta Give, the eventual piece will say . . .

'. . . from the pen of the writer-director Nancy Meyers, and starring Diane Keaton as the older woman who finally teaches Jack Nicholson the wisdom of picking on partners his own age, is either a) a sophisticated romantic comedy – as it says here, or b) a Middle-American morality-tale touting the Puritan lie that anyone who takes pleasure from pure sex must somehow be living a meaningless life.'

You can see what's coming from that single opening scene, without a word being spoken. Everything's the same, these days, whether it's heading for print or screen: men are dumb, women are clever. It's Mother's Day *versus* Farter's Day and you can't trust anyone not to toe the party line. Not even old Jack. Christ, he surely doesn't need the money but here he is . . . 'selling out his gender, by portraying Everyman Over Fifty as an overweight, over-rich, Viagra-pumped, shallow pleasure-seeker who pursues women under thirty until, one judgemental day, his heart right-eously and symbolically fails him and he is reduced to dribbling and staggering indecorously around hospital corridors, his fat bum hanging out of a surgical gown in a literal representation of the arse he has made of himself'.

Oh, very good, yes. Rather pleased with that.

Amelia is draining her vodka. She bends forward to place the plastic cup on the floor and, as she leans down, her right knee pushes out against my leg and her hand brushes against my ankle. I jump and some of the champagne spurts out of the bottle, which I have wedged between my thighs, and on to my trousers.

She giggles and offers me a prettily embroidered handker-chief. I take it, smiling, and dab at the damp patch as she watches. As I hand it back, I swear she touches the now-wet handkerchief to her lips. Again she giggles and leans in to whisper, 'Waste not, want not . . .', and this time her lips brush my ear with every word.

Oh, surely not? Lights are going on all over my dashboard, and the engine starts to tick over.

I take a swig of my champagne but don't put the bottle back between my thighs. For one thing, there's not really the room down there any more. I force my attention back to the screen and my notebook.

'Jack saved,' I write, 'by angelic intervention of older woman;

comes to realize that, all along, he has been missing the marvel that is life and love in the arms of proper, grown-up, wise and wonderful woman his own age, blah blah,' and whose daughter (the seat cover in the sports car) sees the error of her father-figuring ways and rushes off to breed and live happily ever after with a boy her own age. After this improbable, preachy scene I write in large capital letters the single word, 'BOLLOCKS'.

The End. 'Cue theme song, roll credits, bitter women queue here to buy soundtrack, let that be a lesson to all you pervy old guys. Only, get lost. This film, and the notions it peddles, insults just about everybody concerned, scattering its criticisms and scaredy-cat hypocrisy around like so much poorly aimed bird-shot . . .'

It's true. In the attempt to bury men under a pile of self-righteous poo, even older women get spattered by the Meyers Patented Morality Muck-Spreader. Keaton's character, a success-ful, divorced playwright, is presented as a sad, lonely old bag who has written off all hope of ever finding true love and great sex again. In her *fifties*, for Christ's sake.

And yet, while slimy old Nicholson is ridiculed for his interest in younger women, when Keanu Reeves's smooth young doctor takes a shine to Keaton, not only is it OK for her to sample the goods, but the reality fabric of the film really begins to fray when she rejects him for Nicholson. As one of the women I overhear in the bar afterwards puts it: 'What woman faced with a choice of Nicholson or Reeves would choose Nicholson? That's a no-brainer.'

Oh, really? I think. Why is that? Because Reeves is so clever, or a dab-hand in the kitchen? Or is it because he is good-looking and has a rock-hard torso with arms to match – compared, say, with Nicholson's lardy paunch and independently oscillating jowls?

'In which case,' I'm saying to Amelia, 'I guess it's OK for me to say, "What man faced with a choice of, say, a firm twenty-seven-year-old and a slack forty-seven-year-old . . . ?"'

'Oh, what man indeed,' she says, laughing. 'So, what are we going to write?'

I'm helping her on with her coat and, as she slips her arms into the sleeves, my fingers brush against her soft, bare shoulders. I can see now that the coat is fur for sure and suddenly I couldn't care less.

'Are you hungry?' I ask, and she says, 'I'm always hungry,' and before I can think of a nearby alternative to the inevitable Pizza Express (which instinct tells me will simply not do on this occasion), she says, 'Sushi!', seizes me by the hand and marches off. Instead of 'Raw fish: ugh!', I say, 'Great,' and follow.

In the packed restaurant, where small, dead aliens glide past on a conveyor belt, I make no attempt to keep my leg from hers. She feeds me uncooked beef and fish, pops the occasional edamame bean into my mouth and tells me about her love for her job, pugs and baking. And about how much she looks forward to having babies.

This is my cue to exit stage left, and I have no understanding of the force that is not only keeping me pinned to my seat and chewing bitter seaweed but is running a mental slide show featuring the world's ugliest little dog sat at the feet of Amelia wearing nothing but a flour-spattered pinny to a folksy fireside-vase-and-flowers soundtrack courtesy of Crosby, Stills, Nash and . . .

God. What's happening to me? Pugs? Raw fish? Babies? I mean, it's not as if I don't know all about pugs.

One weekend I found myself baby-sitting one of the little bastards, and it did nothing for my self-image as a tough guy. The pug, as everyone knows, is the dog of choice for gay male-porn stars. To that narrow if finely buffed demographic, we may add faded French beauties, William the Silent (1533–84: dog got his tongue, presumably), assorted fashion designers, Andy Warhol and the Duchess of Windsor. (Funny. You'd have thought she'd have gone for a German shepherd. Or maybe the other way round.)

But not, in short, the type of dog with which your average, insecure heterosexual might care to be seen about town.

Nevertheless, Lulabelle, a one-year-old beige pug whose owner – a distressingly camp but otherwise delightful neighbour

– had to go away on business to a place where they don't take kindly to wheezy dogs in tartan jumpers (not Paris, San Francisco or Berchtesgaden, then), came to stay. Not thrilled. As an apartment-bound city dweller I would never own a dog on principle (the principle being that life is simply too short to waste time picking up turds from the pavement), but it wasn't until a day or two later that the true horror dawned on me. I would have to take the damned thing outside to do its business.

People choose their dogs to say something about themselves; what would walking Lulabelle say about me?

It would, of course, be equally unthinkable to be seen with a doberman, a rottweiler or, even, in these sensitive, anti-nationalist times, a British bulldog. Living as I do in multicultural but not always racially harmonious Tower Hamlets (within Molotov cocktail-tossing distance, as it happens, of the plaque commemorating the 1936 anti-fascist riot known as the Battle of Cable Street), I might just as well pull on a Union Jack T-shirt and have 'BNP' tattooed on my forehead.

Finally, dog day dawned. Lulabelle arrived, cute enough in a wheezy, snuffling, bug-eyed, interbred-face-bashed-flat-by-a-genetic-shovel kind of way, and lots of tears and licking were exchanged (between departing owner and dog. I kept out of it).

And then we were alone. I tried to concentrate on writing, doing my best to avoid the baleful eyes, the gentle wheezing and the rattle of scampering paws on wooden flooring, but after a while it became apparent that Lula just had to go.

I was ready for this moment. I hadn't shaved for two days and was now dressed as butchly as my limited wardrobe allowed: jeans, boots, check shirt, heavy donkey jacket. I checked the mirror. Good. Hetero through and through. I picked up Lulabelle and checked again. *Christ! Was there a dog-fancying lumberjack in the Village People?* There was now.

I strode down the car-jammed street as manfully as I could, a little too fast for Lulabelle, who half-scuttled, half-slid behind me at the end of her bright red, dainty lead. Avoiding eye contact with the smokers outside offices and bored white-van men trapped in the traffic, I marched in a manner which, I hoped, conveyed at once my disdain for the laughable lifeform to which I was reluctantly attached, and the fact that I was an extremely butch hetero who was walking this joke of a mutt reluctantly and purely as a favour to his *beautiful blonde model girlfriend, everybody.*

I almost got away with it. Just as I was about to turn into my street, I bumped into a young man I had often seen walking his three small furry dogs (one of those breeds where it isn't immediately clear which end does the eating). Self-confidently camp, he has never once so much as glanced in my direction, but now, right alongside a halted van full of builders, he stopped and greeted me like a long-lost friend.

'Ooh, hello,' he gushed, bending down to pet the pathetically grateful pug. 'And what's *your* name, precious?'

I felt three pairs of eyes boring into my back. It's at moments like this that it's important to stand up against stereotyping, prejudice and bigotry, to have faith in oneself; to be a real man. I bent down and tickled one of his dogs under what I hoped was its chin, and then ruffled Lulabelle's delicate little head perhaps just a *little* too energetically.

'Butch,' I said, in a loud, deep voice.

And I can just see Amelia with a string of the little tikes. Outside the restaurant, pug woman announces suddenly that she has a party to go to, but before my face can fully drop, she is kissing me goodbye more like she is kissing me hello. My hands fly magnetically to her waist and the touch of a half-inch of bare flesh on my fingertips curls my toes. For a moment she just stands there, smiling at me, and then leans forward again. But instead of kissing me again, she whispers into my ear, 'Goodnight . . . Microwave Man.'

So she did know. Bugger, bugger, bugger.

'So you knew?' Bugger, bugger, bugger.

'Of course,' she said brightly. 'How could I not? We *have* been sharing a spread for the past year.'

Crap, crap, crap. 'Do you ever read it?'

She is moving away now, towards the kerb, looking for a cab. 'Of course! I've read every one.'

Cobblers. That's me buggered, then. But suddenly, she comes back towards me, taking a scrap of paper out of her bag and pushing it into my hand. 'I almost forgot. Here are some thoughts I scribbled down in the film. Use them in the piece if you want to. Bye-bye, MM!'

A cab switches off its light and coasts across the road towards her, and she turns to face me, a golden angel framed against the brilliance of the headlights behind her, her blonde hair a halogen-lit halo. I've let enough of them pass me by to know exactly what this is. It's one of those now-or-never moments.

'So I suppose that means there's no chance of seeing you again?' I say.

'Professionally, you mean?'

'No. Unprofessionally. Frankly amateurishly, even . . .'

The cab comes to a halt. She turns away and leans through the open window to speak to the driver, and then turns round again. At least she's laughing, but then maybe the cabbie just said something funny. He's smiling as well, but probably just at the thought of having her in the back of his cab.

'No, sorry. No chance,' she says, but she is still smiling. And shouting. It's 11.30 p.m., and Soho is extremely noisy. 'Well, not until next Tuesday, anyway. I'm free then. Why not come round?'

I can think of several million reasons why I *should* come round, but not one why I shouldn't.

'I'll cook,' she says as she pulls open the door of the cab. 'I think it's about time you had something out of a conventional oven. It might take longer, but in the long run it's a lot better for you than all that microwaved crap.'

The cabbie ducks down to peer at me, beaming idiotically on the pavement as Amelia climbs in. 'Too right, mate,' he says as he punches his meter. 'Meat and two veg. Can't go wrong. Those microwave ovens will cook your nuts. There's two blokes who work in the caff I use in Smithfield, and they haven't got a pair between them.'

Then the cab is gone. I watch it until it turns the corner at the end of the street, and she doesn't turn round once to look back.

Back home, I open a beer, switch on the laptop, type out what I've written so far and finish the piece.

The centrepiece of the film, which sums up what director Meyers thinks of older guys who date younger women (er, been dumped for one recently, have we, Nancy?), comes early on, setting the tone. Keaton's sister, Frances McDormand's feminist lecturer, posits the theory that guys like old Jack date younger women because they can't handle the challenge of grown-up women who know their own minds.

Yup, that'll be it.

Now, who is insulted most by that pile of dog-do dogma? Men? Well, maybe, but we're used to it. Or how about younger women, who, Meyers implies, couldn't possibly possess any of the above qualities and are in thrall to the first male authority figure who breezes past twiddling his moustache and squeezing their pretty little knees?

I take a swig of beer and think of the piece of paper in my pocket bearing Amelia's handwriting, and think of her pretty little knee brushing against my leg in the cinema.

Today's twenty-seven-year-old woman knows all about sexual politics and the battles fought and won by generations of sisters, but isn't so bent on flagging up her psychosexual political correctness that she is prepared to miss out on having fun.

And this picture of weak men awed by strong women is self-deluding. One of Meyers's previous triumphs was the woeful *What Women Want*, starring Mel Gibson. Maybe this latest film should have been subtitled, *What Women Want to Believe*.

Amateur and ageing anthropologists such as Meyers see an older man with a younger woman and conclude, self-reassuringly, that the coupling is the product of the former's need to boost his ego with arm candy. Well, yes, beauty is attractive, skin-deep or otherwise. But you know what? I enjoy the company of younger women. They are smart, fun and open to new ideas (and some old ones they think are new); they introduce me to ideas and places I would otherwise never know, encourage me to rethink my entrenched views and generally bubble with a zest for life that has been boiled off from many older women by the blaze of bitter experience.

And it's a crass aphorism, but I'll share it with you anyway: women of my age are generally either married or mad. (Or both.) When people (older women, usually) ask me why I go out with younger women, I rarely bother to justify myself. But if I did I might recall that when I was thirty-nine, and the relationship that was supposed to be The Big One (with a thirty-one-year-old) went off the rails after nine years, I was left behind by my generational train. By the time I had dusted myself off, I was out of sync with my age group: my female peers were either married (or mad), and younger women were the only stock in store.

And then I made an interesting discovery. Not only are younger women fun to be with and blessed with all the shallow advantages of youth, but there is (whisper this) a special blend of danger and excitement about being with a woman in whom the potential for reproduction is so riotously, infectiously obvious . . .

There is? Am I serious? Am I slightly pissed? Do I mean this? Then I remember the piece of paper in my trouser pocket. As I lean back in my chair to reach down and take it out, I see the stain on my crotch. And the paper is damp and it smells of champagne, which is unfortunate, as stale champagne smells like nothing so much as wee. But I smile as I read what she has written in her tight, neat hand, and return to the laptop.

Take my young companion.

Indeed.

We adjourn to a sushi bar, and she sits there, a bright blend of professional élan and ripe femininity poised on four-inch heels, popping edamame beans and pulling off the trick of flirting and talking about babies in the same breath without triggering my flight instinct. Her allure has as much to do with her overwhelmingly blatant fecundity as her soft skin, intellectual fruitfulness and beautiful shapes . . .

I read it back. Now I'm scaring myself. On the other hand, surely it has to be safe? I mean, she's read all the columns, she knows as much as anyone could know about me who hasn't actually met me: my form, my fears, my foibles, my failings (well, as much about me as anyone could know beginning with an F, anyway). If any woman had ever walked into a relationship with her eyes open, it would be her. So why would she? What's in it for her? I look at her note again, and write . . .

So what's in it for the younger woman who goes with an older man? I ask her, and this is what she says:

'The general presumption is that he gets more out of it than you do, and that perhaps you haven't quite realized that yet. This comes from men and women, but more often older women. It's depressingly cynical. It's as if you couldn't possibly be together just because you rather liked or loved one another – that you are together because of the age difference rather than despite it.

Within the relationship, the age difference creates an interesting dynamic. Most of the time it doesn't matter and you're careering along and it's all divine, and then suddenly a gap will open up in conversation and the age difference will be very apparent – which can be good or can be bad.

One of the most appealing things about being with an older man is that, frequently, things are more resolved, more steady. They know what they want and are less flighty. But sometimes, of course, they are not much different at all to men half their age.'

So there you have it, out of the mouth of a babe (sorry: just responding to stereotype. Someone has to now that Jack's gone bad). I think that's what they call a solicited testimonial.

Eat your stupid hat, Radish! And then I notice that on the back of the note she has written her address, her phone number and the words, 'Tuesday, 8 p.m.: please bring an appetite. Warning: conventional oven, so time won't vary.'

The next day, I catch Cornelia in her office after conference and hand her my piece, which she reads quietly. As usual, I wait for the occasional snort of laughter. As usual, there is none. I wish I could be sure that she was laughing inside. Then she lays it down on the desk in front of her and says, 'This isn't a feature, it's a bloody love letter. Are you sure about this?'

That evening I get home, slap a Marks & Spencer cannelloni into the Panasonic and call Merv.

'Merv, you remember I told you I'm moving into a new flat soon?'

'Sorry, mate, would love to help, but it's my back, you see . . .'

'I don't want you to carry anything, you lazy bastard, I want your advice. I have a major purchase to make and I think you're the man to set me straight.'

'What is it? A piano? Accordion? Hosepipe, perhaps?'

'Hey, if I ever need a hosepipe, I'll just borrow yours. And if I ever feel the need for an accordion, I think I'll have long taken advantage of the hosepipe first. No, it's your years of experience of slaving over a hot stove I'm interested in. I want one of those things they talk about on the back of these packages . . .' I grab the cannelloni and notice it's past its use-by date. Never mind. Only by a couple of days.

'Here it is: "For best results use conventional oven." That's it. One of them there Conventional Ovens.'

As Merv starts laughing, I push the start button and pick absently at what appears to be a small piece of fossilized baked cheese on the Panasonic's glass door. Merv is still going strong when *Ding!* goes the bell and, in three and a half minutes flat, both microwave and Microwave Man are out of the game.

But it was fun while it lasted.

A New Dawn
Friday 9 April 2004

I woke up the other morning in my new bed, in my new flat, very happy to find myself lying alongside a new woman. The most beautiful woman, in fact – the sort with whom the old me, after just a few such mornings, would have fallen hopelessly in love.

Nuzzling her soft neck, I opened my mouth instinctively to whisper, 'I love you,' but, to my surprise, out came the Googled translation: 'I adore you.'

Eh?

Falling in love is as easy as falling off a bicycle and, usually, just as painful (unless a lorry is involved, in which case I concede that the comparison does start to wobble). Or, at least, it used to be. I got married (at twenty-one) because, during my impressionable teens, I had fallen in love with an unseen and, for all I knew, entirely imaginary woman, suggested by no more than a few words and notes in a Paul Simon song. She haunted me through my teens and, when I actually met a woman called Kathy, it was all over bar booking the register office (Bletchley: as grim as it sounds).

And if you think *that's* bonkers, you'll be locking me up and melting down the key for bullets when I tell you that I once fell in love with a jar of pickles. Well, the painting of a woman on the jar, purporting to be one Mrs Elswood, supposedly responsible for a range of pickles and whose big, flaming hair, prim pinny and matronly sexuality, for some murky reason, jarred my preserves.

But at some point in the past few months, I think I finally fell out of love with falling in love – grew up and out of falling in love with ideas rather than people.

And curiously liberating it is, too, to be cured of a clearly bonkers strain of optimism that not only places an unfulfillable burden of expectation on the duly empedestalled one (and if that isn't a word it should be), who ends up crushed beneath it, but is doomed to end in disappointment.

Naturally, I blame my mother: no father, no siblings, no breast-feeding – no wonder I'm needy. We emotional orphans can go one of two ways (three, but utterly normal is both boring and deeply unfashionable): bitterly expecting nothing from anybody, or selfishly demanding everything from everyone. More than one partner has complained that becoming my lover also entailed accepting the satellite roles of mother, sister, brother, father and (in rare circumstances) third cousin twice removed.

I have always recognized that there is no one person who can give you everything you need, all of the time, but that hasn't stopped me looking. This, I guess, is your typical triumph of hope over experience.

The cure, it seems, has been living alone for months. It's a lot tougher to be needy when there is nobody at hand to pander to one's every need.

Increasingly (and rather like a member of those Amish communities where everyone turns out on a Saturday afternoon to build a neighbour a barn), I find I am valuing friends for the individual components they bring to my party: the nails, the bolts and (ahem) the screws.

One female friend (Ms K) laughs at my weak jokes; Miss T keeps an eye on my dress sense (such as it is) and Mrs H scans my prose for garbage (and, depressingly, recycles rather a lot). Now, OK: they *are* all women, true. But not only have I not slept with any of them, but now I probably never would (even if they'd let me, which I doubt), for fear of losing all the other goodies they bring to my party. I'm told this is called being grown up, but it's all new to me, and I like it.

And, back in my new bed, I play with my new friend and my new word. We talk easily of adoration, but not of love. She knows I love to be with her, but that I am happy when we are apart. She, in turn, is relieved of the burden of becoming a one-person extended family. Free at last, perhaps, of that tyrant Love.

Having said that, if you are reading this, Mrs Elswood, the door to my heart is still ajar. (That one's for you, Ms K.)

Epilogue

Merv returned to university to retrain as a psychiatrist but was struck off and briefly jailed after being found guilty of impersonating a psychiatric recruitment consultant at a NHS jobs fair. He is now a successful leading top psychologist who appears regularly on afternoon TV and has a string of books to his name, including *There's No Such Word as Kant!*, *Never Turn Your Back on a Friend's Bicycle* and *Get That Hose out of the Trunk and Start Watering your Garden*.

The Boer finished her novel, which was number one on the bestseller lists of both the *Sub-Saharan Informer* and the *Port Elizabeth Express Review of Books* for eighteen straight months. After Ben died alone in a mysterious fruit-and-lingerie accident (open verdict) during a business trip to Belgium, the Boer returned to South Africa, where she bought a farm, married an alcoholic hog-breeder and proceeded to raise large numbers of children and chickens. Tragically, she was abandoned by her husband and, during a nationwide cornfeed shortage, was pecked to death by her birds. She was found dead the day before her second book, *The Woman Who Didn't Know What Was Good For Her*, hit the shelves to critical acclaim. 'The Great South African Novel,' pondered the *Informer*. 'Is this it?'

Percy Lebaron Spencer, inventor of the microwave oven, was inducted posthumously into the National Inventors Hall of Fame of America in 1999 in tribute to patent number 2,408,235 – the blueprint for the high-efficiency magnetron that became the microwave oven. He died in 1970, aged seventy-six, filthy rich, and had a building at Raytheon's headquarters in Boston named after him. So microwaves certainly didn't do *him* much harm.

Microwave Man was, as he had hoped, made expensively redundant and invested the money in a new iPod, an old Triumph TR4A (with sound chassis), a small yacht and a large number of Premium Bonds (guaranteeing a lifetime income of £50 a month). He went to dinner that Tuesday with Amelia and discovered, to his joy, that her appetite was as large as his. Strolling home along the Thames early the following morning, he paused to watch the sun come up over Tower Bridge as the words of 'Mr Blue Sky' rang out – for once, not poignantly – from his iPod. At that very sublime moment he felt the mobile, tucked into the pocket over his heart, start to vibrate, but before he could read the message he somehow let the Nokia slip into the fast-flowing river below. Where, joining the pipe stems, Coke cans and Bronze Age bones, it sank slowly, deeper and deeper into the dull brown sediment that blends and conceals all the secrets of the river's past.

Now, *surely*, we are buying this?